CRAM DOWN

A
3J LEGAL
THRILLER

MARK
SHAIKEN

Cram Down
Mark Shaiken

Published by 1609 Press LLC
Denver, Colorado

ISBN (print) 978-1-7345571-9-0
ISBN (ebook) 978-1-7345571-8-3
LCNN: 2023909204

Cover Design and Interior Layout by *Damonza.com*
Editing by Melanie Mulhall, Dragonheart, www.thedragonheart.com

First Edition
Printed in the United States of America

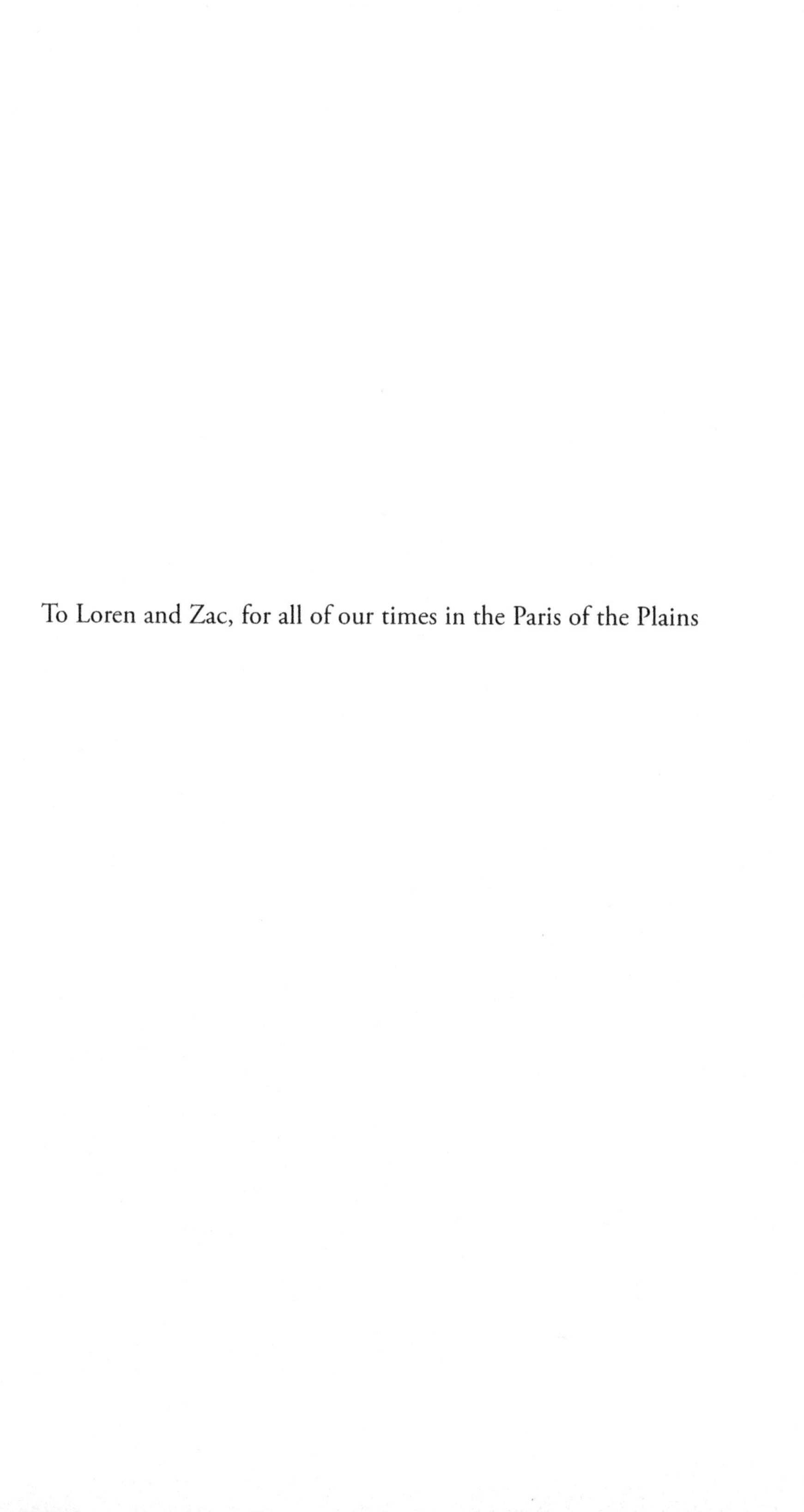

To Loren and Zac, for all of our times in the Paris of the Plains

Prologue

Wednesday, November 20, 2024

THE TWO BROTHERS sat in the bank's executive conference room. Archival black-and-white photos adorned the walls, each in an unpretentious brushed nickel frame and mounted with a simple off-white mat. They captured scenes of 1930s Kansas City and famous Black owned businesses of the time.

The Commonwealth Savings and Loan Bank was now at the intersection of East Armour Road and Cherry Street in Kansas City, Missouri, and the room where they sat was home to a large, oval, mahogany conference room table and eight chairs with embroidered seat cushions, three on each side and one at each end of the long table. Since 1901, the table had been a part of the bank. Back then, the bank sign read The Commonwealth Colored Penny Savings and Loan Bank.

It was the same table where the bank's founders, the brothers' great-great-grandparents, had discussed and approved loans for small, Kansas City, Black owned businesses and homeowners in the post Civil War era. It was the same table where their ancestors had fended off threats of assaults, lynchings, and hangings and strategized ways to advance the plight of Black families. Not every Kansas Citian believed the city needed a Black owned bank. Not back then and not in the present either. In the late 1970s, their parents had sat there and discussed expanding the bank's lending reach to all minority customers throughout the metropolitan area.

Thanksgiving was approaching, but they were not there to give thanks.

Rather than sitting across from each other at the middle of the table, they sat at opposite ends, as far from each other as the table and room permitted. Amadi Washington Browne had been born moments before his fraternal twin, Jordan Lincoln Browne. They didn't look like each other and they didn't think alike. Their only commonality was the womb they had shared and the house in which their parents raised them. Nothing else bound them together. Nothing else about them was similar.

Five years earlier, they had inherited the bank from their parents, although in unequal shares. Under the will, Amadi was the majority owner. But this meeting would be different from past meetings. Things had changed.

The meeting's agenda item was a single loan their parents had made to Abode LLC decades ago. Over the decades, the revolving line of credit had grown to a loan with a preset borrowing limit of twelve million dollars. Abode could tap in to the loan and draw money out as needed up to the limit. As Abode repaid, the loan balance went down and the amount Abode could tap in to went up. Abode had historically used the loan to buy land and pay contractors to build houses on the land.

They sat but made no eye contact. Amadi surveyed the photos on the walls while Jordan stared at his clasped hands. It was yet another in a long string of uncomfortable moments the pair had shared.

Recently, things had changed at the bank. While Amadi kept the title of bank president, he had recently sold a portion of his bank shares to his brother. Jordan was now the controlling, majority shareholder, which meant that the bank was now Jordan's. And with that change, Amadi felt a new era of Commonwealth banking on the horizon. He didn't like the feeling. He saw significant changes coming, and he didn't like what he saw. New wasn't always bad, but this new was no improvement—not for the bank customers, not for the community, not for the city, and not for Amadi. While Jordan called it state-of-the-art banking, Amadi called it a disaster waiting to happen.

The conference table was big enough for the ghosts of their ancestors to attend the meeting in spirit and occupy the empty chairs between the brothers. Perhaps the spirits could provide a measure of control from the great beyond. In the meeting, Amadi would learn if anyone, dead or living, could rein in Jordan.

The Abode line of credit had matured each December 4 over the years, and on each maturity anniversary, the bank had renewed it without fanfare and with minimal discussion. There would be three hundred sixty-five more days of Abode's bank funded eleemosynary work. But if Jordan got his way, this time, the loan committee would have a different tone: One of nonrenewal. A tone of "Find another bank." A tone of "We don't want your business anymore."

Amadi had prepared the usual loan renewal form for Jordan's review. The form made the case for loan renewal and continued support for Abode. Jordan had the form, but he hadn't read it. He didn't need to. He knew his brother, he knew Abode, he knew what the form said, and he already knew what he wanted to do with the loan.

Amadi had just reminded Jordan of the bank's simple obligation to the community and to Abode and its founders, Bella and James Franklin: to continue to fund Abode's operations. "Bella and James are good folk. The best," Amadi said. "We've gone to church with them, prayed with them, and gone to schools with their kids. We've mourned with them and we've marched with them."

But his audience of one wasn't hearing him.

"It's just good business to put minorities in their first home," Amadi argued, touching on Abode's business model of building homes for lower middle-class families to provide access to the American dream—home ownership—for members of omitted groups that all shared the dubious honor of being on America's historically long list of the shamefully treated. They were the invisibles, those left behind and marginalized in America. It was Abode's vision to build homes in transitional neighborhoods and provide stability, not only to the families who bought the homes but to the neighborhoods as well. With Commonwealth's help, Abode offered a piece of the American dream.

"Amadi, just this once, don't lecture me. Listen to me. I don't give two shits about dreams. People who dream have nightmares. I have no nightmares. I have data. I have a sense of where this bank is going now that I'm finally at the helm. *I* am a twenty-first century banker." As he spoke, he unclasped his hands on the conference room table and, palms down, appeared to push as if he were attempting to lower the table and reduce its historical influence on the discussion.

"I give a shit about what I would do with the Abode collateral if I had to foreclose. The data is this: I can't off-load the collateral. None of our banking partners have showed an interest in sharing the Abode loan. They won't buy a participation in the loan. They won't join in a lending syndicate. Why? They don't want the collateral. They don't want the prospect of foreclosing on collateral and owning houses in *these* kinds of neighborhoods with *these* kinds of proximate neighbors. And guess what? Neither do I."

"We've never had a participant in the Abode loan before," Amadi said. "We don't need one now. Abode is a good loan. It's good for Abode, it's good for the bank, and it's good for the community. A win-win-win. It's a solid borrower. They've never missed a payment. Nothing has changed. Not Abode, not the Franklins, not their mission, not the collateral. Nothing. Same data it's always been. And to handle things differently for 'these kinds of neighbors' and 'these kinds of neighborhoods' is wrong thinking. Not to mention illegal."

"Right now, I don't give a shit about the law. And you're wrong," Jordan yelled back decisively. "Everything has changed. Maybe you've forgotten. I control the bank now. I'm in charge, and I want out of the inner city. I want the bank to be everywhere. I want out of the Abode loan so I can use the capital to make more profitable loans. Profit is colorblind. Profit is not in it for social change. Profit is not part of a decades-long movement. Profit doesn't march in the streets demanding its rights. It doesn't care about any of that damn stuff. It's just data: numbers; bottom line dollars and cents." Jordan paused, slapped the conference room table with both hands, making a noise like a gunshot, and added forcefully, "Or s-e-n-s-e in your case."

They had never been close. As adults, the two brothers had grown further apart, and they could no longer even agree to disagree. Such an agreement would be one too many accords in their lives of constant disunity. Amadi surveyed the chairs around the table. Empty they were; empty they remained. Apart from Amadi and Jordan, the room was silent. He looked for help from his ancestors but received none. He made his case to his brother alone.

Jordan had always been the emotional one and Amadi had been the calm, reasonable one. But now, Amadi couldn't speak unemotionally. Not with Jordan yelling at him. Not about the direction Jordan wanted to take the bank and not about Abode.

Amadi countered his brother's voice by raising the volume of his own. "I'll tell you what's wrong, Jordan. You can't change the DNA of this bank any more than you can change our family's history or the color of your skin. No matter what we do, we're still Black and always will be. That means we have an obligation to reach out and help our community. The community made this bank what it is. The Browne family builds hope one community member at a time. Abode builds hope one family, one nail, one board, and one house at a time. Building hope. Abode's always done it. Commonwealth has always done it. I've always done it. And goddamn you, Jordan, this family has always done it. It's our unique commodity."

Amadi paused just long enough to see that Jordan wasn't hearing him. "I'll tell you what makes no sense: suddenly changing the relationship this bank has had with Abode for more profit. You don't need more money, but this city needs Abode to fulfill its mission, and Abode needs this bank to partner with it to do so." Amadi stopped. He had lost his cool. Sometimes pushback helped. Sometimes it made him feel better. Not this time.

"I don't give a damn about Abode's mission. I don't give a damn about what you say this city needs. And most importantly, I don't really give a damn what you, with your minority ownership interest in this bank, think. You hear this loud and clear: You will not be the minority shareholder of this bank with ninety-five percent of its mouth. Not out there and not in here at this table! Our commodity will now be crypto! Here's the deal. you are either with me on my vision for the bank's future or the future will get crammed down your throat. Either way, it's happening."

If Amadi was waiting for the ghosts of his parents to take charge and scream, "Enough, Jordan!" from the afterlife, he waited in vain. They didn't and wouldn't.

Jordan brought Amadi's thoughts back to the living. "This bank has been taking care of the community for more than a hundred and thirty years. I don't see the progress. I don't see the profit. It's time for this bank to take care of itself . . . and the Brownes. The hell with community commitments! I hate those words you throw around."

"Not my words, Jordan. The words you so disdain are from our grandparents, uttered when they took over the bank, and they invoked those words every day thereafter. Our parents as well."

"More irrelevant pearls of wisdom from a long gone past. Only you quote them. Only you remember them. Jesus, Amadi," Jordan said shaking his head disapprovingly as he scanned the photos on the walls with a look of contempt. "Sometimes I think you've got so much of the past roiling around in your brain that you don't have enough gray matter left to appreciate the present and future sitting there right before your eyes. With all the history shit you spout, I worry you consult with the dead to make your decisions for the living. Well, not anymore. This bank, under *my* leadership, will no longer be captive to your version of history. It's going to *make* history, and to do so, it must and will distance itself from its past."

Jordan looked away and said nothing. He didn't need to. Amadi had lost the bank to his brother, and he knew it. He had lost the debate, if it ever even was a fair exchange of ideas by advocates of different positions. And Amadi was about to lose Abode as a bank customer.

The history of the bank, once made sitting around this table, was slipping away. The table was no longer a symbol under Jordan's reign. Now it was nothing more than wood, screws, glue, brass, and glass.

"Maybe so, Jordan. Maybe so," Amadi said softly as he slowly shook his head in defeat.

Jordan's face slowly curved into a victory smile. He had won. "Good. Then it's settled. The loan committee hereby denies the renewal request. It's your customer. Tell the Franklins to move the loan out of this bank. I'll give them thirty days from maturity to do so."

"And then?"

"And then this bank will do what a bank does when it wants its money back and a borrower doesn't pay. I trust you know how that goes."

1

Amadi Browne remembers Wednesday, November 20, 2024

ANOTHER MEETING WITH my only flesh and blood in the record books. We sat there and argued under the photos, all of them a slice of African American history depicting our ancestors' struggles to find prosperity in a society that tried mightily to prevent, and then contain, our people's advancement.

The photos always reminded me of our ancestors. I remembered well the tales my parents told me of my great-great-grandparents. Both were born into slavery. As the Civil War began, a White plantation owner in Arkansas sold my great-great-grandfather, not even ten years old, to a slave owner in Missouri. Once in Missouri, the slave owner's lender recorded notice to the world that my young ancestor served as collateral for the slave owner's loans. Later in life, my great-great grandfather would chuckle and describe the collateral filing as the first time his name appeared in a public document.

I once asked my parents, "How could he laugh at something like that?"

They replied, "His alternative was to cry, which he would not do."

Then the South lost the Civil War. News travelled slowly, but eventually, each of my great-great-grandparents learned they were free. Single then, they both gravitated toward Kansas with a caravan of other freed slaves. They were part of the Exodusters, post Civil War African Americans who trekked to Kansas, home of the Free Staters, seeking to own land under the Federal Homesteaders Act of 1862. He traveled with a couple who said they were his aunt and uncle. She traveled with a woman who said she was a cousin. Family lore maintained that they both fell just short in the quest to reach Kansas and instead settled in Kansas City on the Missouri side, the city so central to the South's Civil War loss. In their new home, they began the long journey of learning to live in a racially divided city where it was unclear if General Grant's memo about the outcome of the Civil War ever reached many of Kansas City's White residents.

They grew into adulthood, met, fell in love, married, and somehow forged a life on the east side of the city, first working jobs requiring few skills, then selling clothing to other Blacks from a storefront near Sixteenth and Vine. And later, after the Panic of 1873, they had the audacious notion to form a Black-owned and Black-run bank whose mission was to better the Black community. It would be in the heart of the Black community and be part of the collective heart that beat in the Black community.

On June 17, 1892, against all odds, the Missouri legislature granted my great-great-grandparents a banking charter, and The Commonwealth Colored Penny Savings and Loan Bank was born. They chose the name "Commonwealth" because it meant a body politic founded on law for the common good. It would be the bank where Black people could safely deposit their savings and turn to for a loan, the bank that supported the Black community. Its commitment to better the Black community would be as solid and reliable as the granite forming its first building's keystone. It was a bank for the common good.

Imagine. They opened the bank doors for all to enter in 1892 at a time when they couldn't even open the door to a White-only diner and enter. And to their surprise and joy, deposits grew to over five hundred thousand dollars, and not only deposits from Blacks but from White patrons as well.

Over ninety percent of the Black depositors had never established an account at any banking institution before. But as my grandfather liked to explain, the goal wasn't to gain deposits, it was to serve the people who made the deposits. Good people. Hardworking people. People who desperately wanted to bank with an organization completely dedicated to their welfare. Instead of lining their pockets, they used the deposits to lend money to businesses and individuals in the community.

My great-great-grandparents weren't showy people. The fanciest things they wore were a black top hat for him and pearls for her. They were small in stature, larger than life, and known far and wide.

My great-great-grandparents were the first of five generations of Brownes. When my parents, Andrew and Tali, took over Commonwealth's operations, they stayed the course, always hoping to make their ancestors proud and always remembering why the bank existed. I joined the bank after college and trained under them. Ten years ago, the time was right, and I took over the operations from my parents. Five years later, they died within months of each other.

Commonwealth and the Brownes survived through everything: the panic of 1893–1895 when over five hundred banks failed; the recession of 1895–1897; the Great Depression; two world wars; more recessions; the explosion of the dot.com bubble; the failure of Lehman Brothers and the resulting financial recession of 2008; the pandemic; and the tech bank collapses of 2023.

When my parents took over the bank, they had a dream to expand the bank's reach to all members of marginalized communities and find someone in Kansas City who would provide affordable housing to those communities with Commonwealth financing. They were looking for someone who would buy land, divide it into small lots, build homes, and sell the homes to those people for a small down payment and favorable repayment terms. If my parents' dream of Commonwealth financed home ownership could get off the ground, the homes owned by members of marginalized communities would serve as collateral. Quite an advance from the days when human slaves, like my great-great-grandfather, served as human collateral. My parents hoped home ownership would kindle a small glimmer of hope that people America had always left behind could finally have their share of the American dream. They just needed to find that partner who shared their vision and passion.

The dream remained unfulfilled for years as my parents searched for the right partner. Then along came Abode LLC, a nonprofit founded and run by Bella and James Franklin. Abode's mission was to build homes for members of all minority communities. The bank and Abode partnered, and the aspiration of homeownership in Kansas City slowly became a reality.

So why have I told you all this? Martin Luther King said that we don't make history, we're made by history. I tell you this because *my* history makes *me*. I'm made by my ancestors' dream of a Black owned bank as the vehicle to afford members of all marginalized communities a home to live in.

Was Abode deserving of the loan from Commonwealth? Only if we are made by history, and we are. Was Abode's homeownership mission important enough to warrant the support of Commonwealth? Only if we are made by history, and we are. Was the loan to Abode the right thing to do? Of course. History tells us so if we would just listen.

But not according to Jordan. According to him, there was nothing to listen to. When I controlled the bank, Jordan pointed out, "Abode is a goddamn nonprofit," as he jabbed his finger in the air at me. "Damn it, Amadi. This bank is a for-profit institution, and we want to lend to for-profit companies. For-profit companies know how to make money. Nonprofits are mission driven. Who in this bank, besides you, gives a shit about missions?"

Back then, he was wrong, shortsighted, and money-in-his-own-pocket driven. After the Abode meeting with him, it was clear he was now even more so. Back then, I ran the bank and could ignore him, so I did. I came to learn my parents did as well. But my brother was now in charge of the bank, the result of my unfortunate need for cash and my sale to him of Commonwealth stock, leaving him in control. I had become nothing more than a powerless figurehead with no seat at the table and no place on the bank board. I only had a voice in the loan committee that no one respected.

Despite their headstone inscriptions, my ancestors couldn't possibly be resting in peace with Jordan running the bank. They must have been spinning in their graves. To Jordan, history was of no moment. "We are where we are, and I don't give a shit where we've been or how we got here," he liked to say to cut off any ties to the past and any obligation to continue to fulfill Commonwealth's mission. "All I care about is where we're going and how quickly we can get there," he would explain, trying to justify his rejection of history. He may have been the only Black person I'd met who had no interest in how we got to where we were.

I was confident that to get to his version of "there," he would make changes, painful changes, starting with Abode. Unworthy of Commonwealth's support, said Jordan. Hurting Commonwealth's bottom line, argued Jordan. The plight of the modern minority family is not his problem, explained Jordan. He would make his own history, he declared, by being the most profitable bank, not just a profitable Black owned bank, in Kansas and Missouri.

How could he fail to understand that he couldn't *make* history? My lord, how did he and I both come from the same lineage?

My brother's plan was a complete betrayal of my family, our community, our city, and the bank's mission—my mission. Sometimes I just wanted him to disappear—from the bank, from Kansas City, and if need be, from the planet. Forever. I wasn't proud of my thoughts, but I didn't run from them either. I had to stop him. It was my duty.

2

Friday, November 22, 2024

"Kansas City. Y'know, it's not a place where change comes quickly, or dramatically, or sometimes ever," James Franklin said with a tinge of bitterness he didn't hide. "It's a place you can leave for a while. And when you return, the same old friends'll greet you and the same old enemies'll confront you." He looked over to his wife, Bella, as he spoke.

She smiled, but it wasn't a happy smile. Smiles could silently convey so much: joy, humor, reassurance . . . and pain. Bella's smile was one that told you she was in pain. It was one of those smiles that silently said she was fine when everyone in the room knew she wasn't and wouldn't be.

James continued. "This ain't an easy place to be Black, that's for damn sure. Least not for my family and me."

They sat at a conference table in Room 28A at the Greene Madison law offices, high atop downtown Kansas City, Missouri, overlooking the Power and Light District. The firm's lawyers called it the conference room for prospective clients and deals. Around the table sat Bella, James, and Josephina Jillian Jones, 3J to her friends, the first Black female partner in the law firm, but no longer the only one. She was a New Orleans kid with bright, hazel eyes who made it out of the Big Easy and into a successful law career. A bankruptcy lawyer by trade.

The late afternoon sun streamed in through the conference room picture windows, diffused only slightly by sheer curtains as it shone light on the table. Sometimes it was the light of illumination and sometimes the light of hope. It was the perfect conference room to meet with potential bankruptcy clients and offer them illumination and hope.

Bella and James Franklin, now in their sixties, were long-standing corporate clients of the firm. 3J had met them in passing at several client appreciation cocktail parties the firm sponsored. Three days earlier, Jason Arledge, the corporate lawyer now responsible for the Franklins' account, talked with 3J to let her know the Franklins and their company, Abode LLC, might need bankruptcy protection. If they did, he would help her navigate the process.

The meeting began with an overview of Abode's business. The Franklins explained they were in the real estate development business and had been for decades, but their business model was unlike most traditional developers. They weren't in it for profit. They were in it to help build houses for those left behind, thanks to decades of prejudice. Abode, they explained, was a nonprofit.

Abode's mission was simple: acquire land, build affordable single-family homes, vet potential worthy homeowners, and sell the homes to members of racial, ethnic, religious, gender diverse, or disabled minority groups for below market prices and with below market financing terms. It was their formula for affordable housing. Upon occupancy, the homeowner signed a mortgage and promissory note in favor of Abode. Each month, Abode collected the mortgage payments. The rate at which their homeowners defaulted on the mortgage payments, they explained, was extremely low. They considered the homeowners part of the Abode family.

"Family members rarely default on money they owe to other family members," James explained.

"We're here to help and offer a way to fix broken people. To offer them the dream society has denied them," Bella added. "Hope. We like to think we don't really develop homes and peddle real estate. We trade in hope."

They explained that to make the business model work, Abode had a substantial line of credit with a local Black owned bank, Commonwealth Savings and Loan Bank. Abode used the mortgage payments it received to service the Commonwealth line of credit debt. As Abode built the home, it pledged the home and land to the bank to secure the line of credit. After Abode sold the home, the bank released the home and land as collateral and substituted the homeowners' mortgages and promissory notes to secure the line. Either way, if Abode ever defaulted under the line of credit, the bank's collateral was the home, the land it sat on, and all the other land Abode owned but had yet to develop.

James looked down at his hands clasped on the conference room table. "Decades ago, back when we started Abode, we went with Commonwealth as our bank. It had a great reputation. We knew the owners, Andrew and Tali Browne, and it was as solid as a lender could be: a four-generation community bank with a mission to help members of all minority communities. Eventually, Andrew and Tali passed control of the Bank to their son, Amadi Browne, and we continued to do business with him.

"We've now learned there are two brothers, Amadi and his twin, Jordan, and they're very different souls. We call them heart and heartless, although late at night, we've called the heartless one much worse. Amadi is the one with the decent heart. He's all-in on Abode's mission and willing to sacrifice some of his bank's bottom line for the good cause of putting families in homes. Doing business with Amadi was wonderful—an extension of the great relationship we had with his parents."

He shook his head in apparent disgust. "But Jordan . . . y'all gotta watch out for that one very carefully. He does bad things because it's just the way he is. He has no commitment to his community or the people in it. Just cares about himself and the mighty dollar signs sittin' on his bottom line. Bank profit is greatness for him, and it's what he aspires to. I'm not sure he even knows that the word *commonwealth* means 'for the greater good.' He's his own greater good. Hell, in *his* world, he's the only greater good."

"I've had no experience with Commonwealth. Do both brothers run the bank?" 3J asked.

"I'll take that one, James," Bella said. "Until recently, Amadi owned fifty-two percent of the bank and was on the bank's board. He dictated the bank's business plan and ran the day-to-day operations, including Abode's loan. There was no change in our relationship with the bank when Amadi took over from his parents. He made all the decisions and supported Abode's mission. He came to our fundraisers and cut our ribbons on new homes. We never even saw or heard about Jordan. Heck, I'm not sure Jordan was even in KC at the time.

"But six months ago, Amadi visited us unannounced. He shared with us that he'd sold enough bank stock to Jordan to raise two million dollars because he'd gotten overextended in his personal life and needed to raise money quickly. So while he retained his title of bank president, he wasn't the majority owner any longer and no longer sat on the board. We quickly realized the sad reality that he can't so much as scratch an itch on his elbow without Jordan's approval.

"And then we met Jordan. We've always found it interesting that the parents left one brother fifty-two percent of the bank and the other forty-eight percent. They surely must've known something was up with Jordan. We're also sure Jordan has a substantial chip on his shoulder because of it. Or maybe he always had one. Now that he's in charge, the chip seems to drive him to prove he can take Commonwealth in a different direction."

"What happened between you and Commonwealth?" 3J prodded.

"Really nothing," James replied. "We've never missed a payment. We've not changed our business or mission. The bank has the same collateral it's always had. Despite that, our loan came up for renewal this week and Commonwealth declined to extend it. As simple as that. Amadi told us the bank no longer wants minority owned homes as collateral. Of course, he didn't come right out and say that. He said the collateral's value wasn't sufficiently stable or attractive for his brother's taste. But we knew what he meant by the way he said it, and he looked pained about it. We knew that wasn't what he believed. He was just the unfortunate bearer of bad news." James shook his head and continued. "Imagine . . . a Black owned bank redlining."

"I see," 3J said as she took notes. "Talk to me about the redlining."

"Redlining in this town goes way back," James explained. "It refers to a bank's practice of literally drawing a red line on a map around a neighborhood within which people of color couldn't own a home. It goes all the way back to the days of Kansas City's most famous developer, J.C. Nichols. As old J.C. developed upper- and middle-class neighborhoods, he used restrictive covenants. When he sold a home to a White family, the deed included a covenant banning Blacks and others from buying a home.

"He formed homeowners' associations to enforce the covenants. He charged the associations with making sure none of the banned people lived in a Nichols neighborhood. J.C. was quite systematic in his approach. It kept White neighborhoods White and Christian neighborhoods Christian. He was one of the redlining innovators in the US, if you could call the use of widespread contractual racism an innovation. J.C. kept banned groups out of his neighborhoods with covenants, and banks jumped on that bandwagon. In hush-hush, smoked-filled rooms, they declined to loan money to the banned group members who then couldn't buy a home anywhere. It was systematic exclusion based on race, ethnicity, religion, sexual preference, and disabilities. J.C.'s dream—the *other* American dream, as we came to call it."

James stood up to pour himself a coffee refill. As he returned to his seat, he continued. "These were pretty prevalent practices here and elsewhere from the twenties to the early seventies."

James paused to sip his coffee and Bella picked up the story. "*They* wouldn't take you in *their* neighborhood. *They* wouldn't lend you *their* money to buy a home anywhere. Redlining. Simple, effective, and illegal. It's not something that just went away after the dawn of the Civil Rights Movement. It continued on, and it still exists. Banks and developers are just cagier about it, but every once in a while, a redlining bank gets nabbed."

3J looked up from her notepad. "But your line of credit is with a Black owned bank. Even with what you've told me about Jordan, it's hard to fathom a Black bank owner refusing collateral owned by people of color. His own people. Jordan's greed aside, are you saying a Black owned bank is redlining?"

"Yes, under Jordan's rein," Bella replied emphatically. "That's exactly what we're saying. With Jordan on the throne, we're guessing that for the bank to even consider keeping the Abode loan, it wants other banking partners to participate. And we're speculating the market for participants is pretty lean when the underlying collateral is so many homes owned by members of marginalized groups in neighborhoods where they predominate. Without participants, the bank now wants out of our long-standing relationship."

"Did Commonwealth have Abode loan participants before?"

"No. Never," Bella confirmed.

3J furrowed her brow as she considered Commonwealth's new edict that Abode should no longer be a bank customer. "But Abode has never defaulted. Is this new policy good for the bank's business reputation?"

"Turns out, Jordan thinks it's very good for the reputation he's trying to forge," James explained. "He's told us the things about our loan he doesn't like: The bank lends us money at a favorable interest rate, and the collateral is lower income housing in neighborhoods where Whites are in the minority. We've tied up a bunch of money he otherwise could deploy at higher rates, making more profitable loans. We've heard him say he wants Commonwealth to be the banking partner to those who know how to make lots of money, and we've heard him talk about crypto as the wave of the banking future."

The three sat silently as 3J absorbed the fact that a Black banker was continuing the White banker tradition of redlining for profit. "About how much does Abode owe on the line?" she finally asked.

"It's a twelve million dollar line. Right now, Abode owes around nine million, give or take," James replied.

"And the value of the collateral?"

"Maybe eight million right now based on the current housing market," James explained.

"How would the bank likely fare in a bankruptcy case?" Bella asked.

"In bankruptcy, based on your guess of collateral value, the bank would have a secured claim of roughly eight million dollars and an unsecured claim for the balance," 3J replied. "Abode would have the power to pay the bank over time on the secured part of the debt, and because Abode is a nonprofit with no owners, it might get away with little to no payments on the unsecured portion."

"So we'd pay the bank less than it's owed over time?"

"Correct. Potentially over a long time."

"And if the bank objects?" Bella asked.

"Abode would have the power to force the plan on the bank, called 'cram down' in bankruptcy."

"Cram down sounds like a court fight," Bella said.

"Oh, yes," 3J replied, nodding her head. "Maybe the biggest, highest stakes fight in bankruptcy. Most secured creditors don't take cram down lightly, and most don't suffer a cram down without a big fight. But the bankruptcy code permits it. The judges are used to seeing it and approving it where the debtor meets the bankruptcy code requirements."

"What are the bankruptcy downsides?" James asked.

"I see the biggest downside of a bankruptcy case is that Abode couldn't force the bank to loan any further money. Abode would be in a state of suspended borrowing for a while during which it would be my hope you'd be able to secure a line of credit from a new lender. But that's really the same place Abode is in right now. It's about to lose the line to maturity, and you're going to have to find a replacement lender. In bankruptcy, we'd have to come up with a viable strategy for this part of the equation. If we proceed, I'd need to give this some more thought and come up with a plan and recommendations for you."

"Abode is Commonwealth's largest borrower and Commonwealth's not a big bank," Bella said slowly. "If we strip off a percentage of the debt in bankruptcy, it would really hurt this bank, and since Jordan now owns the majority of it, it would really hurt him. I don't know, but the bank might even fail."

"All the more reason to expect a huge fight with the bank and Jordan to the bitter end if we try to cram down the bank," James added.

"If there's going to be a big fight, better to have it in bankruptcy," 3J said. "Bankruptcy levels the playing field to have a fair fight."

James took a deep breath, exhaled slowly, and shook his head. "Bella and I need to talk about this, and we'll be back to you in the morning."

With a smile of reassurance, 3J pushed her legal pad aside and said simply, "I understand. I think we can help. But you have decisions to make. Let me know if you have questions."

Over and over, she'd seen the stress a bankruptcy case could have on its owners. She wondered what that stress would do on the Franklins if they decided to file bankruptcy.

3

AFTER THE MEETING with the Franklins, 3J sat at her desk, disquieted. The Franklins had given her lots to consider. Abode's whole story led her to recall her own upbringing in New Orleans' segregated Lower Ninth Ward, growing up in a small home located on a spit of land three feet higher than other places in the Lower Ninth, sitting precariously between the Mississippi River and Lake Pontchartrain. Two angry bodies of water rising up from time to time and spilling onto the land seemingly trying to reclaim from Black families what each waterway thought was rightfully theirs.

They had lived just blocks from Fats Domino's Lower Ninth home. While he was alive, Fats could have left the neighborhood any time he wanted, but despite the floods, he stayed where he'd grown up and lived most of his life. Others, like her parents, weren't famous rock and rollers and stayed because they had to.

Their Lower Ninth house was a small, wood clapboard, single story home with two bedrooms, a small kitchen, a dining and living area, and an unfinished attic. As was the New Orleans custom, a hatchet was stored near the attic access, at the ready to punch a hole in the roof if there was a flood so the occupants could escape through the attic and wait on the roof for a National Guard helicopter or boat to rescue them. During Katrina, a country unfamiliar with that exit plan had seen horrific scenes of people who had escaped floodwaters this way frantically waving for help from their roofs. Abandoned houses in the Lower Ninth still had the Katrina hole punched through the roof.

The small home provided just the amount of stability needed for 3J and her sister to get an education and a chance to escape the poverty surrounding them. As an adult, she had heard it said that if you wanted to solve drug problems, solve the housing problem. If you wanted to solve gang problems, solve the housing problem. And if you wanted to solve education problems, solve the housing problem. Drugs, gangs, and education were inner city's holy trinity of challenges. They were poor and Black in a city still famous for its Confederate sympathies, but for her small family, the home had managed to help keep the sisters in school, out of gangs, and off drugs. For them housing had worked.

Then she thought of the Franklins. Abode gave families hope and a chance for the same outcome: keeping kids in school, out of gangs, and off drugs. It was a noble cause Abode pursued against long odds, and it was one near and dear to 3J's heart. But Abode was able to fulfill the mission one family and one home at a time only with the support of Commonwealth's line of credit. Considering Abode had never missed a payment to Commonwealth, she wondered how Jordan Browne and Commonwealth could ever abandon Abode and the mission.

As she pondered Abode, Commonwealth, the Franklins, and the Brownes, she looked up from her desk to see William Pascale hovering in her doorway. Pascale was her sixty-eight-year-old law partner, mentor, and friend who had hired her out of law school. He'd recently done an about-face on the decision to retire. After deciding to retire from the law practice, he'd reconsidered that decision and reached a one-year agreement with the firm to consult.

No one really knew what "consult" meant since the firm had

never before offered a consulting agreement to a senior partner. The extra year would give him more time to plot what came after his law career. 3J hoped it would also give him more time to bring some measure of order to his legendarily disorganized office. They both quickly realized that consulting was not all that different than practicing law full-time, so Pascale was able to transition from practicing law to consulting without breaking stride.

Chuckling, he'd said to 3J, "This consulting thing is interesting. I feel like I'm doing the same work at the same firm with the same people. I'm just getting paid less. But I still think it's a good thing for me. It's a good first step to whatever comes next when I hang up my wingtips."

She was relieved it had thus far been a positive experience.

"Did you meet with the Franklins yet, 3J?" Pascale asked from the doorway.

"Just finished up with them. Interesting couple. Admirable work they do here in Kansas City. Do you know them?"

"Indeed I do. I used to volunteer to help paint the houses Abode built. That was a few years ago when getting up on a ladder with a bucket and a paintbrush didn't seem as risky as it might be for me today. Now I just help out with contract work and free legal advice. And I go to their breakfasts and the annual gala."

3J explained the meeting with the Franklins. "Ever had a case against Commonwealth Savings and Loan Bank?"

"Can't say I have. Other than knowing it's run by Amadi Browne, I don't know much about it. I've met him around town from time to time. He's impressive—passionate and eloquent. Commands a crowd. He's a perfect match for Abode."

"Correction," 3J said. "Used to be run by Amadi Browne. Now it's run by his brother, Jordan Browne. It's now on a fast track to be a very different bank, one that'll have no interest in helping members of this country's left-behind groups. To that end, Jordan no longer wants Abode as a bank customer."

"Really? Hmm. Don't think I've ever met the brother, and I don't know anything about him. Come to think of it, I'm not sure I knew Amadi even had a brother, let alone one in banking. Sounds like a big fight between Abode and Commonwealth on the horizon."

"I need to understand more about the Brownes," 3J said.

"I wonder if anyone in the firm knows any more about Commonwealth and the Brownes."

"I was curious about the same thing. I think I'll send out an email for information and see who knows what."

"Good idea. Somebody here will know. I just stopped by to see if you wanted to take a walk and talk break."

"What did you have in mind?"

"Maybe head over to Sculpture Park by the art museum?"

"Sure. It might be nice to get out of downtown for an hour, commune with nature and the art, and collect my thoughts about this whole Abode thing. Just let me get this email out."

ঌ

Sculpture Park was a prominent part of the Kansas City scene, consisting of dozens of sculptures: bronze works by Henry Moore; a stainless steel tree by Roxy Paine; whimsical, oversized, badminton shuttlecocks by Claes Oldenburg; and works by others. It was all displayed on the front lawn of the Nelson-Atkins Museum of Art, itself the culmination of a dream come true to bring world-class art to Kansas City.

The unlikely duo of William Rockhill Nelson, founder of the *Kansas City Star*, and Mary Atkins, a retired schoolteacher and the reclusive widow of a local real estate developer, shared the dream and collaborated to make it a reality. The park created a sublime contrast to the opulent, neoclassical museum design just to the north of the park, the façade of which was supported by multistory grand Greek columns.

Like so many other Kansas City landmarks and institutions they frequented, she and Pascale used a hike around the museum grounds to organize their thoughts and sort out a strategy for whatever case they were working on. It was a place of solitude. The desk phone didn't ring there, and it was one of her locales of choice when a new bankruptcy case was on the horizon.

When they arrived, they picked up the path near their parking space on Oak Street, just north of the University of Missouri-Kansas City's campus. It was a typical Indian summer late fall day, pleasant and breezy as colorful leaves first swayed and then parted from their host tree as they began the short journey to the ground below. As they strolled, 3J gave Pascale the more detailed download on the Abode situation, Commonwealth, and Jordan Browne.

"Bankers will be bankers," Pascale observed.

"Meaning what, Bill?"

"Meaning nothing in particular. Whoever this Jordan guy is, he sounds like he oozes banker DNA and rhetoric. It's as if he went to a class at banking school to learn how to talk the stock banker talk. You know, stuff like 'move the loan,' 'no longer appropriate for our portfolio,' 'suspect collateral,' 'no interested participants,' and 'Regulators criticized your loan and want to classify it a problem loan.' The usual stuff you tend to hear even after a loan has been with a bank for decades, the collateral hasn't changed, and the borrower hasn't defaulted but the bank has a change in control. This one seems to check all the boxes."

3J said nothing for several minutes. "This one is different, Pascale," she finally said. "This one comes with history, and I don't mean lending history." She paused and looked off into the distance. "Banks have obligations to the community. Look at the 1977 Federal Community Reinvestment Act, the CRA. The law requires banks to meet the credit needs of the communities where they're chartered, including low- and moderate-income neighborhoods. Missouri chartered Commonwealth as its first Black owned, Black run bank. It did business on the east side of town where Blacks had to live because J.C. Nichols, a lack of education, their skin color, and exclusion from the mainstream economy colluded to make it impossible for them to live anywhere else. CRA is an important anti-redlining law."

She paused, stopped, and faced Pascale. "Now this Jordan dude is in charge, and he thinks he can snap his fingers and the bank will be out of the Abode loan completely. I'm not so sure he can do that. I wonder if the bankruptcy code can help adjust his mindset. From the little the Franklins have told me about Jordan Browne, he sounds like a guy who believes he was put on this earth to get his way. Maybe not this time. Maybe not in bankruptcy court."

Pascale nodded as they started back to the car. 3J was always quick to take up a new client's cause, and Pascale admired her for it. "We've got some legwork to do on this one, 3J, and for once, we have a little more time than usual since Jordan gave the Franklins thirty days to move the loan. Let's head back and figure out what we need to do. Oh, by the way, have Abode and the Franklins formally hired us yet?"

They stopped walking again. "Not yet," she said slowly. "Important detail. I got a little ahead of myself. Do you think we should wait to do any work?"

"Not necessarily. It's your call, but I'm game to jump in. Better to be ready to roll when they hire the firm."

"You mean *if* they hire us."

"No. I think I said it right. When we get back, maybe I'll stroll around and see Arledge, whose client this is, and see if he can reach out to the Franklins and help them make their hiring decision."

When they returned to the office, Pascale headed for Jason Arledge's office and 3J began reading the email responses to her request for information about Commonwealth, the Brownes, Abode, and the Franklins. She had dozens of emails offering information and assistance. She wasn't surprised at the level of detail her colleagues could share with her. The firm was connected and in the know about all things Kansas City.

Within short order, she was up to speed on Amadi Washington Browne and Jordan Lincoln Browne and their family's banking history. For every fact she learned and admired about Amadi, she learned three about Jordan that set off her alarm bells. Lawyer after lawyer told her Amadi was the salt of the earth and the few who knew Jordan all told her he was the definition of an undesirable. Another described him as noxious. One offered that Jordan knew nothing about banking and if he was now running Commonwealth, he was in way over his head.

As she organized the notes she took about the brothers, Pascale returned from his meeting with Arledge and said, "Game on." The Franklins had signed the engagement letter and hired the firm to represent Abode and them personally against the bank.

"I think we should set up a meeting with the brothers and try to find some middle ground that works for Abode and the bank," she said. "Frankly, I'm more than a little worried here. Without Commonwealth, Abode will need a new line of credit from another lender, and that's going to be a tall order to fill. They need twelve million dollars, and that doesn't grow on trees for a nonprofit. A successful cram down fight with the bank might be quite satisfying, but without the new line, it could very well be a hollow victory. What do you think, Pascale?"

"I totally agree. Abode can inflict a lot of damage on Commonwealth in a bankruptcy case, but without a new line of credit to replace Commonwealth or Jordan Browne coming to his senses and renewing the existing loan, Abode's business model just doesn't work. It could spell the abrupt end to the whole process of building homes for lower income members of marginalized communities. We have things to trade with the lender if Commonwealth will be interested in trading. Among them, less bankruptcy pain in exchange for the continued line. But maybe Jordan's strategy will be no trades. Instead, he'll wait until Abode fails to find a new line and goes out of business."

"Yes, maybe," 3J acknowledged worriedly. "I have some ideas for how Abode might use its current business model to generate new money to pay down the loan. Let's see how the bank reacts to a proposal to pay down the loan but not close down the line of credit. I guess what I'm saying is, let's see if there is any flex in the bank's view of the world."

4

AFTER HOURS, JORDAN sat in his bank office, the corner one he took from Amadi when he bought the stock and took control of the bank. It was his now, just like the bank.

He was certain he could get the Franklins and Abode under control. He had the position of power and they had nothing. But he didn't have his brother under control, and he knew he had to corral Amadi. Jordan was worried about what Amadi might do if permitted to roam free in Kansas City. The passion with which Amadi spoke at the loan committee meeting made it clear to Jordan that while Amadi lost the Abode battle, he wouldn't give up. He would find some way to impede Jordan's plans for the bank.

When Jordan bought Amadi's stock, they signed a stock purchase agreement. While not his usual custom, Jordan had read the agreement, or at least enough of it to see the repurchase option clause. It said Amadi had the option to buy the stock back from Jordan for the original purchase price until the right expired at 11:59 p.m. on December 13, 2024. Were there enough days left for Amadi to send a written notice of repurchase with a certified check for two million dollars? Jordan feared that Amadi had enough time to pull it off, and he had to assume Amadi would somehow figure out a way to come up with the money—even that much.

So Jordan had to figure out what to do with Amadi. If he couldn't convince Amadi to see the bank's true future, could he pay Amadi for his silence? Could he pay Amadi to go away? Could he prevent Amadi from meeting with all his contacts looking for a two million dollar loan? Sitting there, he even allowed himself to wonder if he could hire someone to kill Amadi.

He needed to understand his options. He needed to meet with his friend, Robbie, and get advice. He and Robbie went way back. Robbie dealt with things like this all the time. Robbie would know what to do.

Interlude

Thursday, April 8 to Saturday, April 10, 1993

"Look, May, I don't see how I can take 3J to live here while things keep changing for me," he said into the phone. "Yes, I completely understand it's not fair for you to have both girls all the time. I get that. I really do. But I wanted you to have the house, and now you have it. It's stable there. That's important to me."

May worked at a church in the Lower Ninth, and on her days off, she cleaned houses for well-heeled White folks who lived in Upperline or the French Quarter or the Garden District. She was always tired. Two jobs, two growing girls, one old house, and now a divorce and a lonely bed, and always one storm away from being washed into the Pontchartrain. When she asked him to move out, he took serial temporary residences in neighborhoods close to the Lower Ninth, renting from landlords willing to rent to a single Black man in the Deep South.

He too now had a lonely bed. Part of the divorce gig. He wanted the benefit of full joint custody promised in the divorce papers. But he believed in his heart it was safer for the girls to stay with May while he tried to forge a new life, keep his job at the factory, and find permanent living accommodations close by. Only then could he relieve his wife of the day-to-day responsibilities.

It was his primary job to keep the girls safe, and the only way for him to do that was to have them with May, at least for now.

"Look, May, this weekend I'll take Jo. I don't have much room right now, but she's young and she can sleep on the couch. Or if not, I'll sleep there and she can have my bed."

He listened as May spoke. When she finished, he replied, "You're welcome. I know you're worried. Hear me. Just because we didn't make a go of it doesn't mean I'm going to be an absentee father. Never gonna happen."

❧

Saturday morning, bright and early, May drove Jo—Josephina Jillian Jones—to her father's temporary living quarters. Jo had a backpack stuffed with books, pens, a pad, and clothing. As the car pulled in front of the small rental, her father came out and waved for her to come quickly.

"Hi, Papa. What's up?"

"I got a lead on a house. We need to go see it right now."

"Where at?"

"Tremé."

"Ooh. Sounds like an adventure. And with you, Papa." Jo quickly moved to his old, rusting Dodge. "Let's go!"

He put the radio on and tuned to WWNO, public radio in New Orleans and home to weekend jazz and New Orleans blues. Music was his passion. With a little Snooks Eaglin begging his baby to come home, some Johnny Adams telling you about his room with a view of the blues, and Louis Armstrong singing about a wonderful world, they had the beginnings of a music roux, browning over a slow rhythmic heat as it developed complexity. Stir in some Marsalis brothers and they were cooking in New Orleans music gumbo as they pulled up to the address.

As they parked, they saw a small, neatly kept house with three front steps, two supporting columns, and a tiny front lawn and garden. He smiled. He hoped this house would be the one.

Jo smiled. If her father was happy, she was happy.

They went in and surveyed the surrounds. It was the size of a postage stamp but homey. A typical New Orleans shotgun style house, it was long and narrow with the rooms all lined up in a row. The porch was unusual for Tremé. This would be home for him. It was a relatively safe and stable neighborhood, and he was happy.

After they toured the home, he suggested they head to City Park and the Morning Call restaurant in the park. It was Jo's favorite. Beignets with a mountainous side of powdered sugar. Orange juice for her; chicory coffee and steamed milk for him. The first bite of the beignet she had dipped into the sugar covered her entire mouth with white, sweet powder, and a breeze blew some of the sugar onto his shirt. They laughed. Heaven. The park was close to Tremé, and the park's Morning Call was the beignet outpost where the natives went for the famous coffee and fare to avoid the tourists who flocked to the famous Café Du Monde restaurant in the French Market at the edge of the French Quarter, just steps from the Mississippi River. After the beignets, they strolled the quiet park grounds, heading to the area near the lagoon where they could linger and talk under the canopies of the live oaks, residents of the parkland for over five hundred years. It was a favorite place for them to do what he called their walks and talks.

Then they headed back to the car and an afternoon of hanging out together followed by some of his famous shrimp creole, Louisiana popcorn rice, and Crystal Hot Sauce. With New Orleans jazz on the stereo while they ate, life was good.

They talked over dinner. He told her it was hard to find an affordable house in the city. She listened as he shared some of what was on his mind. She loved it when he treated her as an adult and shared what was on his mind.

He shook a few more drops of hot sauce on his shrimp. "Someone here needs to figure out a way to get people into homes of their own. It's almost impossible without a helping hand. But I think the tide may be turning. I knew my gris-gris would come through. I think I can swing that house in Tremé, and then there'll be a place for you, your sister, and me to be together. *Chez moi.* Then we'll have to concentrate on your studies, your soccer, and track. How about we go back to the park on Sunday and kick the ball around a little?"

"Can't wait, Papa."

"That foot of yours is your ticket out of this swamp, sha. Drive your shots. Bend 'em. It's a big world. I want you to see it all."

She smiled and shook her head. "Not me. I'm never leaving New Orleans, Papa."

"Well, for heavens' sake, why not?" he asked, surprised by her comment.

"'Cause then I'd be leaving you and Momma."

"Nah. There ain't no place on this planet you could go where we wouldn't be with you. You know that."

"Even if you're not with each other, Papa?"

"Yeah. That's right. Even if we're not with each other, we're both with you and your sister. Everywhere, all the time, for always."

"Okay, Papa. Then maybe I'll try to see the world. For you. Maybe I can even be one of those helping hands and find homes for people, like you were saying."

Her father smiled. "I have no doubt. You'd be good at it." That was his Jo.

5

Saturday, November 23, 2024

3J and Pascale sat at the Ibis Bakery counter in the Crossroads District, a ten-minute walk from the Greene Madison offices. From their vantage point, they could sip a morning beverage—Messenger coffee for Pascale and crème Earl Grey tea for 3J—as they watched the bakers expertly fold, knead, and mold yeasted dough, then dust it with flour for one more rise before heading to the million-dollar ovens and the creation of artisan breads like no other in the city. Bakers, like lawyers, worked on Saturday. And Sunday.

3J had invited Jordan and Amadi Browne to a meeting at the firm on Monday to discuss Abode. Jordan replied he would attend. She had heard nothing from Amadi.

"3J, before the meeting, I wonder if we should talk to one of our banking regulatory lawyers at the firm. You know, get some intel like the lowdown on Commonwealth and what will happen to the bank if its largest loan matures and the borrower is protected in bankruptcy. Is the bank adequately capitalized? Would the regulators require the bank to set up additional cash reserves to protect against any loss it would suffer because of Abode's nonpayment?

Would the owners have to put in more money to shore up the bank if Abode's loan matures but doesn't pay off?"

"Sounds like a plan."

When they got to the firm, they found Tiên Luong, a Greene Madison banking regulatory partner, at her desk on Saturday. She said she could take some time out to talk, and a few hours later, 3J and Pascale met with her. With some quick research, Tiên Luong was able to develop an impressive dossier of information to share with them. They learned Commonwealth was a medium-sized community bank with assets of roughly six hundred million dollars, determined from public financial information. She explained that the bank's loans had ratings ranging from "satisfactory"—those with good collateral where the borrower was paying on time—all the way down to "nonpayment"—those in default. She explained Commonwealth reported capital of approximately 9 percent of its assets, fifty-four million dollars.

"Tiên, what happens to all these calculations if a large loan—like the Abode loan—moved from satisfactory to nonpayment and bankruptcy status?" Pascale asked.

"There are lots of factors at play, Bill, especially for a bank of Commonwealth's size. Would the bad loan have to be revalued at less than its face amount to account for the risk of continued nonpayment? If it did, what's the resulting value of the bank assets? What's the treatment of the Abode loan in bankruptcy? In other words, how bad is the Abode loan? But suffice it to say, the regulators could require the bank to raise more capital. To do so, typically, a bank would make a cash call on its existing owners, and if that didn't work, it might have to issue more stock and offer to sell it to new investors."

As Luong spoke, 3J realized that any capital call on existing ownership would hit Jordan Browne hard now that he owned a majority of the bank. 3J and Pascale gave Luong the basic facts as they knew them, and Luong offered them her back-of-the-envelope estimate. If Abode's loan was in trouble, a capital call on Jordan Browne could be for more than a million dollars.

They wondered about his capacity to raise that kind of money quickly, especially after having spent millions to buy controlling shares from Amadi. And what would Amadi say about cooperating?

6

Monday, November 25, 2024

After 3J had extended an email invitation to Jordan and Amadi Browne for a Monday meeting, Jordan quickly made it clear to his brother in a terse email that only he would be attending the meeting. The meeting began with Jordan Browne, the Franklins, 3J, and Pascale around a Greene Madison conference room table. Jordan attended without a bank attorney. "Thank you for setting this up, Ms. Jones," he said to open the meeting. "I've been to many such meetings in my years with the bank."

In fact, he had not. Before he took control of the bank, he had told Amadi that meetings with troubled borrowers was dirty business and he was uninterested in such matters. But now he ran the bank. "Each of these troubled loan situations has its own challenges for success, Ms. Jones. What do you have in mind for today's agenda?"

3J led the discussion. "Mr. Browne, we disagree there's anything 'troubled' about the Abode loan, but you've given Abode thirty days from loan maturity to move the loan to a new lender. That makes the loan D-Day January 3. We'd like to discuss alternatives to moving the line of credit."

"As I expected. What do you have in mind?"

"There are some legal matters to discuss and some business issues to address. I had hoped you would come to the meeting with a bank lawyer so we could make progress on the legal matters, assuming we can find common ground on the business issues."

"I deemed engagement of counsel an unnecessary expense at this point. But I think I'm familiar enough with Abode's legal options to have the discussion." In fact, Jordan had no understanding of Abode's legal options because he'd sought no lawyer's input and advice before attending the meeting. But since he had no intention of making business progress, he was right. He needed no lawyer.

3J presented a proposal for the line to remain open and to adjust the interest rate upward by fifty basis points offered as a bone she and the Franklins had decided to throw the bank's way.

With the Franklins' approval, she proposed that Abode would attempt to sell or securitize the existing mortgages in the secondary mortgage market and use the proceeds of the sale or securitization to pay down the line. When she had discussed the option with her clients, she explained that hundreds of homeowners paid Abode every month, and like any other lender, Abode had a mortgage on each home to secure the payments. She told them there was a marketplace where investors and lenders, private and public, purchased mortgages and promissory notes like Abode's for cash. Mortgage sales. Sometimes the mortgage buyer bought at a discount. Sometimes the buyer bought at par or even paid a premium.

"Why would a buyer pay a premium?" Bella had asked.

"Lenders are required to invest in assets, mortgages in this case, in lower income minority neighborhoods under the Federal Community Reinvestment Act, CRA for short. There are penalties for banks who fail to do so," 3J had explained. "If a bank finds itself in need of more minority neighborhood mortgages in its portfolio, to act quickly, some banks will pay a premium to buy such a mortgage rather than pay the penalty to the feds and suffer the resulting bad press."

"What about securitizations?" James had asked. 3J explained that sometimes, investment banks packaged loans together into a security and then sold interests in the security to investors. "It's another way to monetize in the present mortgages paying out over a long period."

She explained all this to Jordan and said that both cases presented a way for Commonwealth to receive a lump sum of cash to pay down the line in the present rather than pay the line down over a much longer time with the monthly payments Abode collected from homeowners. She told him Abode would need at least twelve months to go through the process. In exchange, Abode was asking Commonwealth to keep the line available for new borrowings so Abode could continue to acquire land and build homes.

Jordan listened respectfully but asked no questions about the sale or securitization of the mortgages. When 3J finished, he thanked her for the proposal and slowly rubbed his chin. "Things at the bank have changed since I've taken control. Our mission and business model are changing. Think of it as a modernization refresh. While I can support the notion of mortgage sales or securitization of the existing mortgages, or both, I can't support continued borrowing. If the plan is to pay down the debt through whatever means, I applaud the proposal and would say, 'Let's all roll up our sleeves and get to work.'

"However, if you're conditioning the proposal on more line of credit lending and a continued relationship between Commonwealth and Abode, I'm afraid we're at an impasse. Continued lending, even with a half a point higher interest rate, is not on the table, nor will it ever be. You offered mortgage sales or a securitization as an alternative to the bank being paid out over a long period of time. The bank isn't going to get paid out over a long time period. The loan will mature and Abode will either pay the bank or the bank will do what banks do when borrowers owe lots of money."

As Jordan responded to the offer, James began to shake his head in disgust and became visibly upset. He spoke up when Jordan finished. "Look, Jordan, you're telling us we can't. But we can. Not only that, we have to. We're an organization with a mission to put marginalized members of the community in affordable housing. It's not only important work, it's long overdue in this town. And it's exactly the same foundation on which your ancestors built Commonwealth."

"Such passion, Mr. Franklin. Admirable. I'm impressed. But I'm not saying you *can't* do anything. You can do whatever you can do . . . as long as it's designed to pay off the bank. That's your takeaway from this meeting because Commonwealth is now a 'can't and won't fund it' bank. If you can figure out another way to continue Abode's mission, more power to you. But you need to figure out a way to do it without Commonwealth's money. That is your new mission. Only by paying off Commonwealth will Abode be able to be on its way."

James glared at Jordan and looked away. "Your bank is not just any institution that lends money. The bank has history. Your family's history. This community's history. Our people's history. The bank has an obligation to the community. It's always had a similar mission as Abode's." James paused for a moment and looked up at Jordan. "That's why we banked with Commonwealth in the first place. It has a moral—"

Before James could finish, Jordan raised his hand like a traffic cop stopping traffic. James abruptly stopped in mid-sentence. "I don't need a lecture about my bank. I don't need your views on the community, the history, the moral obligations, or my ancestors. I'm far from a history buff, Mr. Franklin. I find history an annoyance. As I said, the bank is under new control—mine. There's a new business plan—mine. Abode is not part of that plan. So move the loan. Pay it off. Securitize the mortgages. Sell the mortgages. Hell, buy a lottery ticket or go to Vegas and hope for the big payday at the craps table. I don't really care and I really don't need to know how you'll do it. Caring and knowing are not part of my job. All I need is the check or a wire for the balance owing."

While his tone had been low in volume, while still condescending, Jordan now raised his voice. "Just don't ask me for more money because the answer is a hard no! No today. No tomorrow." Jordan paused and stood. "I gave you thirty days from maturity. That's Friday, January 3 at quitting time. Very generous of me. Ticktock, everyone. You have work to do and not much time. Good day."

He offered to shake no one's hand and quickly left the conference room. No one around the table said anything as they absorbed the crystal clear message delivered by Commonwealth's new majority owner.

Bella spoke first. "What a total waste and what a pathetic man. I knew this meeting would fail as soon as Jordan came through that door alone. Amadi is still the bank president. He's our bank contact. He should have been here. Jordan's not hard to read. Amadi's absence was a not-so-subtle forewarning of how the meeting would go."

James nodded his agreement and slowly shook his head in disgust.

"Folks, sometimes when a bank says no it really means maybe," 3J said, trying to find a silver lining for the Franklins. But she didn't believe Jordan Browne was saying maybe. And based on their faces, she could tell that the Franklins didn't believe that's what he meant either. Jordan Browne had dashed any hope for a straightforward, golden nugget solution to their problem.

"3J, we have another problem," James replied. "If word gets out we're broke, have no line of credit, and have to cease building homes, we'll lose our ability to fundraise. Many will stop donating. Abode gets a significant amount of its needed capital from the Commonwealth line, but it also relies on donations to cover construction costs. If we lose the line and fundraising dries up as a result, we'll be dead in the water even quicker."

Bella nodded and appeared to be fighting tears. They looked like a couple on the verge of an insoluble disaster. "Look, we've been on the case only a few days," Pascale said. "We need to get up to speed quickly and completely and then make a recommendation to you on how to proceed. Give us a few days to get our legs under us and then let's reconvene."

~

3J and Pascale debriefed after the Franklins departed.

"Bill, I'm looking for a reason to explain why Jordan Browne is acting this way."

"Yeah. He's definitely a piece of work. But there isn't always a good reason to explain how people act. People are people and do inexplicable, indefensible, bad things for idiotic reasons or no reasons at all."

She shrugged and thought about the bankruptcy case they had just completed and the difference between it and this situation. "When Woody Clarke tried to kill Jacob Steinert, the Melanshins, and me, at least I understood his reasons—sick, warped, and hateful as they may have been. White Nationalist. Bad man. Bad reasons. Bad beliefs. Completely abhorrent. While I could never fully understand why anyone would have that much hate, once I understood what he was, I had discovered the reasons for what he would try to do."

"Well, not everyone is as transparent as Woody Clarke," Pascale replied.

She sighed. "I think the idea of mortgage sales or securitizations to raise money is the way to go whether or not there's bank agreement. I've also been thinking that Abode should draw down on the rest of the line of credit before maturity—three million dollars—

just before we put Abode into Chapter 11. That will give Abode a war chest to use to buy more land and build more houses . . . and fight Commonwealth, at least for a while. If we go that route, we'll need to understand from the Franklins how Abode's draw requests have worked in the past and if they can generate legitimate uses for more money so quickly."

"I like those ideas. Especially the draw. No need to leave money in the bank's coffers. Better to use it to fund Abode's war chest. Let's put some meat on the bones and present those ideas to the Franklins."

The two sat in silence. Then Pascale rose, shuffled to the window, and gazed out over downtown. "3J, I've been wondering if we could possibly turn one brother against the other?"

"How so?"

Pascale turned to look at her. "Amadi is still the bank president. He must know what Jordan is doing. He can't possibly be okay with it. Maybe we could talk to him, or if need be, depose him right after the Chapter 11 filing and see what his views are about the loan, the Franklins, and this new business plan Jordan referenced." He shook his head and looked away. "Modernization refresh. What a bunch of shit. Maybe we can use Amadi to present to the judge a conflicted bank that recently abandoned the 'do the right thing' business model."

"Setting brother against brother? Hmm. Boy, that sounds very messy."

"Sometimes the messy way is the only way out. But if it leads to evidence Jordan's new business plan is based on redlining, it could very well give Abode quite an advantage in a bankruptcy case."

"Well, maybe we should test the waters by having a meeting with Amadi. Y'know, if he'll agree to sit down, we may have something to pursue. If he won't, that probably tells us he's not willing to help Abode."

"Sounds like a plan. Do you want me there with you?"

"I'm thinking for the first meeting, maybe it would be better for just me to go," 3J explained, hoping it wouldn't offend Pascale if she excluded him.

"I agree. Makes good sense. I think that's a better approach than both of us going. He might feel more comfortable talking if there was only one lawyer sitting at the table."

"You're not offended?"

"Not in the least. One lawyer is a friendly meeting. Two could be threatening. Too much firepower."

"Look, I need to gather my thoughts and get all of this down on paper. I think that'll help me go back to being the lawyer as opposed to a social commentator and therapist analyzing Jordan Browne. I'll have plenty of time to issue my Jordan Browne scathing final report and diagnosis later after we save Abode." She paused. "I'll include the Amadi idea in my outline," she added. "It's a good one."

❧

Jordan returned to the bank satisfied with himself. He had delivered his message and gave himself an A for the performance. The Franklins had come to the meeting with do-gooding on their minds. They had left knowing their only option was to pay the bank off. And quickly.

On the way to his office, Amadi intercepted him. "How did it go?"

Jordan ignored the question as he sidestepped Amadi and entered his corner office, and when Jordan tried to close the door behind him, Amadi followed him, caught the door before it closed, and entered. Jordan looked at his brother as if he were a trespasser. It had been Amadi's office for many years, but it no longer was, and Amadi had no right to enter without permission. When they faced each other, Jordan gave Amadi a disapproving look for good measure and then looked away.

"I said, how did it go with the Franklins and their lawyers?" Amadi repeated.

Jordan hung his coat and aggressively wheeled to face Amadi. "The loan will mature. They mentioned something about mortgage sales and securitizations. They'll never get that done, though. Look, just leave the big issues to me, Amadi. I'll take care of the bank's pivot to its new business model and the direction this bank will head in. All you need to do is just keep running the bank on a day-to-day basis."

Without waiting for a response, Jordan sat in his high-back leather executive chair, grabbed his phone off the receiver, dialed a phone number, spun the chair so his back faced Amadi, and ignored his brother. Amadi had been dismissed, directed to leave by Jordan's body language like a common transgressor.

Jordan had Amadi right where he wanted him and the bank right where he wanted it.

7

LATER THAT NIGHT, 3J left her office for the short walk on Walnut Street to the glistening, modern glass and steel building housing her corner condo. On the south edge of downtown, her condo overlooked the Power and Light District. After the quick elevator ride, she entered, kicked off her shoes, and stood quietly taking in her usual nightly view of the Kansas City skyline to the north. The skyline lights were Kansas City's take on a family of metropolis high-rises that seemed to shimmer in close proximity to the twinkling stars above.

As she gazed over the city, her city, Ronnie Steele—her foil, security detail, boyfriend, armchair psychologist, occasional investigator, voice of reason, and lover—came out of the kitchen, hugged her from behind, and placed his chin on her shoulder. They both watched in silence as the skyline came to life, first against the backdrop of the dusky blue and then the darkening navy blue evening sky.

A month ago, Steele had moved in with 3J to try out how it would be to live together. Steele broke the embrace and teed up several versions of the song "Can't Take My Eyes Off You," the first version famously performed by Frankie Valli, and then two lesser known covers by Lauryn Hill and Gloria Gaynor.

As the music started, he resumed his hug from behind 3J, resting his hand on her shoulder. She closed her eyes and placed her hand on his. They pressed close against each other, slowly moving their hips from side to side in time with the music, swaying and savoring the song and the message. Steele's hands slowly glided down her body from her shoulders to her hips as she continued to sensuously roll them up and down, side to side. It wasn't jazz, but she adored the message in the iconic song and considered it one of the greatest sensual anthems of all time. There was nothing better for a couple newly taking up residency with each other—and perhaps even in love.

As Lauryn Hill finished her cover and Gloria Gaynor began hers, 3J turned slowly around to face Steele. "Why, Mr. Steele, are you trying to send me some not so subliminal lyrical message across the airwaves?" He nodded and slowly grinned.

Shortly afterward, they sat quietly and ate dinner at 3J's kitchen island. He'd whipped up lamb hunter's stew after getting off his shift at O'Brien's, the local bar he managed in the Westport District. As always, his take on one stew dish or another was filling and memorable. Steele always amazed 3J with what he could do with potatoes, carrots, onions, garlic, celery, broth, wine, a little flour, and a protein.

She was miles away, twirling her empty fork in her left hand.

"A nickel for your thoughts?" Steele asked.

The question transported her back to the kitchen. "A nickel? Whatever happened to a penny?"

"Costs a nickel now. Like everything else, inflation has kicked in. Don't you watch the news? The smart folks at the Fed are still fighting the inflation disease." Steele reached into his pocket and placed a nickel on the granite between them.

3J looked at the nickel, nodded, and pocketed the coin. "Got it."

She explained the new representation of Abode and the Franklins and asked if he knew them.

"I do. Quite well. I sat on the Abode board for a number of years, starting after I finished my tours of duty on the vice squad. I can't say enough good things about them and what they do for this city."

"Oh, wow. I didn't realize that. Good to know. What about Commonwealth Savings and Loan? Ever hear of that bank?"

"Only in the sense that Commonwealth has been Abode's lender since forever."

"Well, despite what James Bond may have said about forever, nothing's forever, diamonds and banks included, and it looks like Abode's time with Commonwealth may be coming to a sudden and an unfortunate end."

Steele looked surprised, and his expression quickly morphed to one of concern.

"Ronnie, ever run into Amadi and Jordan Browne? They own the bank."

"Only in passing. Amadi occasionally came to Abode board meetings to give us a pep talk about how important Abode's work is in Kansas City and how honored he was for the bank to be part of the mission. I never really spoke with him outside board meetings, and I've never met Jordan. As I understood it, Jordan is the minority investor in Commonwealth and never gets too involved in the bank's day-to-day business."

"Again, nothing's forever. Not too long ago, he bought a portion of Amadi's shares and became the majority shareholder. As a result, he now controls and runs Commonwealth. I'm not sure why Amadi sold out so much of his interest. As Jordan explained to us today in no uncertain terms, change isn't a-comin' under his leadership. It's already here. The biggest change for Abode, if Jordan gets his way, is the impending end of its line of credit."

Steele whistled softly. "Jesus."

"He seems to have little interest in fulfilling the traditional role of this Black owned bank. He has no interest in continuing the bank's partnership with the community, unlike every single one of his forefathers. And his brother."

"Why doesn't he want to continue to bank Abode?"

"My impression is that he has much grander plans for the bank."

"Such as?"

"Such as ditching the inner city for greener pastures, where he probably thinks all the green money grows. Sounds like he thinks he's on a train to greater prosperity."

"Can he do that?"

"Maybe. Some of my partners have met him and think he's bad news. But he's shrewd, and he's driving the bank train right now. In this case, I think it's going to be my job to derail his locomotive."

"You mean like a superhero?"

3J smiled and nodded. "Yep. Sometimes that's the job description. Don the costume and the mask, swoop in, defeat the bad guys, and save the day."

Steele grabbed the plates and moved them to the sink. "Well, for now, how does the superhero feel about moving out of the kitchen? The dishes can wait."

"To where?"

Steele raised his eyebrows as he nodded toward the bedroom. As he did, he turned to face 3J. Her sexy smile said it all. Words weren't necessary. They were two adults and knew the lay of the land. Instead of speaking, she slowly peeled off her white dress shirt and unhooked her bra. Then she began drifting backward to the bedroom, never breaking eye contact with Steele, her hazel eyes twinkling, mischievous, and coaxing him to follow her.

Looking as if he were in a hypnotic state, Steele followed her with a look of anticipation on his face and showing no resistance to the spell she had cast. His look was one that suggested a developing conflict between a body that was beginning to say hurry up and a brain that was trying to take control and take it slow. Just the look she was hoping for. She had the power. Her spell was working.

Later, they lay silently in bed watching the overhead ceiling fan gently spin clockwise. "Mesmerizing."

"What is?" 3J asked.

"Y'know. The circling of the fan blades. Mesmerizing."

She joined him in staring at the fan and smiled. "Oh. I thought you meant me."

"You mean the superhero? Mesmerizing, maybe. But I was thinking the superhero was more like alluring, hypnotic, seductive, and beautiful. So beautiful."

"Mmm. I'll take that," she said as she rolled over onto his shoulder and looked at him from point-blank range, letting the sheet fall off her shoulder. His gaze moved from her eyes and smile to her shoulder and naked breasts.

"And sex with a superhero? Stupendous."

"Why, Mr. Steele, I think this moving in together thing is off to a brilliant start."

"Brilliant, eh? I'll take that," he said as he pulled her naked body close to his.

8

Tuesday, November 26, 2024

JORDAN BROWNE SAT at a dark wooden table in the rear of a dark, wood paneled bar under a dim weathered brass light fixture and waited for his guest to arrive. His guest was a high school friend from way back he'd met when they both attended Pembroke Day School. Pembroke was the elite private college preparatory school on the Kansas City, Missouri, side of State Line Avenue, the street straddling the border between Missouri and Kansas. The two had stayed in touch, as much as anyone conducting a mainstream business could with someone who operated in the shadows, often well outside the bounds of the law. Despite his friend's line of work, Jordan admired him.

The bar was in the Kansas City Bottoms, the area of the city where, among other things, the late nineteenth and early twentieth century cattle drives from Western Kansas, Nebraska, Oklahoma, Texas, and Colorado ended and immigrant stockyard workers then herded the cattle onto trains headed for Chicago's slaughterhouses or to more local final resting places. The nation's insatiable insistence on more beef for dinner was big business in Kansas City at about the same time Commonwealth opened its doors. Commonwealth had survived. The stockyards hadn't.

The bar's blue and yellow neon sign flashed "The Bottoms Bar" on and off.

Moments later, Robert McFadden came into the bar and strode to Jordan's table with his two bodyguards a step behind him. He was a trim, well coifed, clean-shaven, fifty-something who was a touch over six feet. That day, he sported a dark-brown suit, pressed and starched white shirt with mother-of-pearl cuff links, and a pastel-yellow paisley tie, wound in a perfect half Windsor knot. With his athletic build, clothes looked good on him. He looked good in a suit in a smoke-free empty bar. He looked good in a leather jacket with a turned up collar in a smokey pool hall. He could have been a model, a red-haired, steel-blue-eyed, freckled model of Irish descent. People looked at him when he entered any room. He knew it; he liked it; he expected them to stare.

McFadden's father had run numbers for the Kansas City Italian mob back in the day. He wanted his only child, Robert, to avoid that life. The University of Pennsylvania accepted Robert McFadden, and his father, bursting with pride, managed to scrape together the money to send his son to the Ivy League school. While he was there, McFadden's father died in what people believed was a mob dispute that ended badly.

When McFadden graduated with a business degree, he returned to Kansas City and tried to make a go of it in the legitimate business world. But it bored him, and gradually, he drifted into the same industry as his old man: crime. He was good at it. And different. He was the educated and refined mobster. He swore less, often sounding like the Ivy Leaguer he was, and he could speak softly while still sounding menacing. Despite his college degree, he talked like a stereotypical mob boss at appropriate times. He liked the way he sounded when he spoke that way, and it could come in handy. After all, he employed and dealt with mobsters. People hired McFadden expecting him to sound like them. It was good for business. With his bodyguards, he could sound like one of them, joking and swearing. There was an upside to telling people what to do or not do in a way they wouldn't forget. Mobster-speak had its place.

Jordan stood to greet his guest and shake his hand. The two sat, and each ordered a vodka on the rocks.

McFadden's version of a mobster was new for Kansas City. He wasn't a member of a secret national organization with connections in gambling, drugs, and the underworld. Not a member of a Cosa Nostra Kansas City crime family from the north end of town. Not affiliated with East Coast mobster families. But a powerbroker nonetheless. Not the power wielded by Tom Pendergast, the Irish boss who had owned a concrete company and run Kansas City behind the scenes from his Main Street headquarters for decades. McFadden wasn't a member of the mob factions who went to war in the River Quay, blowing up buildings and killing each other.

He was definitely a different sort of mob man. No capo and no made men in his organization, just "associates" who worked for him. Irish roots instead of Sicilian ones, he came with his signature swagger and good looks and quickly rose to prominence with his organization. He held court in one bar or another and said to skeptics, "Hey, Kansas City was an Italian mob town back in the day. Civella, Lazia, Bonadonna, Cammisano, Farina, and others. Founding fathers, if you will. Thanks to them, this town is wide open now. No reason the Italians should continue having all the fun . . . and money."

Unlike organizations of old, he didn't compete with other families for a piece of one illicit trade or another. He sat on no committee of mob family bosses and attended no summits to divide territories. His organization had no layers of hierarchy. Its structure was born from a Wharton Business School education, run by a lone man of Irish descent with a nose for the business world—his business world, run his way. Some of that was learned at Penn, but some had been learned from his pops and some he'd learned on the streets. He managed his affairs underground, far out of the limelight.

McFadden portrayed his business enterprises as legitimate, of course. He would explain that he was just another businessman, but he wasn't. He had drugs, hookers, firearms, and numbers. He was a loan shark and a bookie. And he had police and politicians on his payroll to do his bidding. Lots of them. Often, the biddings were "projects" third parties hired and paid him to handle. It was the results for hire division of his empire.

His view was that mobsters of old hadn't been careful enough. He'd studied the implosion of the Kansas City mob families culminating in the seventies, and he'd learned from the history. His studies led him to be careful and to insist on discretion in all his ventures and have structure in all his organizational divisions. He was more careful than the powerbrokers who came before him and for whom the power ultimately went to their heads, bringing them down.

McFadden was grounded, tuned-in, well-informed, powerful but not drunk on power, and measured in his business dealings. In other words, he was a modern-day, CEO style mob boss. So not only did he look good in a suit, he looked good giving the kill order and he looked good running his version of a corporate conglomerate.

"Jordie, I'm not familiar with this bar," he admitted. "Good ambience. Good location. Good find. I like it. I'm going to have to meet the proprietor and add it to my short list of places, you know, to conduct business." He smiled, but as always, his smile was ambiguous. It could have been a smile of friendship. It could have been a smile of warmth. Or it could be the smile before he ordered someone's throat slit. He never tried to clarify his smile. Ambiguity was valuable in his line of work.

Jordan nodded as the vodkas arrived at the table, and they clinked glasses.

"Most people think of the Bottoms as a cattle drive destination," McFadden added. "But it's way more. For instance, did you know there was a tent village down here along the Kaw River called Juniper where your people lived after migrating from the South? It's true. They lived there at about the same time your great-great-grandparents somehow convinced Missouri's Jim Crow legislature to grant them a bank charter. Can you imagine what those legislative crackers must've thought when your ancestors showed up and told them they wanted to open a bank? I don't know how they did it, Jordie. You relatives had some kinda moxie. I could sure use some folks like that today in my organization.

"Anyway, the Juniper folks in the Bottoms were on the verge of starvation, and the city fathers tried to make 'em vacate. To where? I have no idea and neither did the city fathers. But the city fathers backed off and let the Juniper folks stay after a former slave, Covine Patterson, lobbied for them. Imagine, a former slave saving former slaves. Only fitting. Yeah, history tells us nobody treated your people very well back in the day. Maybe still don't. It's a damn shame." McFadden sipped his vodka. "So much history in this city. Hope it never gets lost."

"I didn't know you were such a history buff."

McFadden chuckled. "Yeah. I kind of slept through history class at Pembroke, right? Maybe more than just the history class. But this history thing kinda grows on you. I started to figure I oughta know a little bit about this place where I live and conduct my business. A little bit turned into an obsession, I guess. Guilty as charged. I usually sprinkle my business dealings with something from KC's past. My clients seem to like it."

Jordan didn't like it at all, but he wouldn't share his dislike with McFadden. "It's interesting, Robbie."

"Another quick Bottoms tale. This is where Tom Pendergast's brother, Jim, flush with his winnings from betting on a horse named Climax, bought a combination bar and hotel and named it Climax as well. The Hotel Climax. At the time, Kansas City had a population of fifty-six thousand. Less than thirty years later, its population swelled to two hundred fifty thousand. It grew on the back of booze, broads, and bad guys. Branding is everything, right?"

"Interesting. Some other time, maybe I could hear more."

"Don't get me started. Someday, after we've knocked back a few more, I'll tell you the real history of this town's crime organizations."

"Did you hear I'm running the bank now?" Jordan asked trying to move the conversation away from small talk and history lessons.

"I caught a drift of that recently. Are congrats in order?"

"Not quite yet. That's what I wanted to talk to you about and get your thoughts."

"I'm listening."

Jordan explained he needed his brother out of the way for a week or ten days. He didn't go into details or explain why.

"Sounds like a messy situation you have brewing, Jordie," McFadden replied. "Look, I don't need to know all the details at this point. But I can do this for you. I'm going to introduce you to a guy I know, Maximilian Cruz. Big man of Cuban descent. Looks White but isn't. He does odd jobs for the boys and me from time to time. Solid associate in the organization and trustworthy. For your purposes, he's good on a tail and good on a snatch. And he's even roughed up some folks for me in the past. You know, helped some guys who owe me money see the light."

"A snatch?"

"Some people call it kidnapping."

While Jordan had thought of ways to put his brother on ice until the repo deadline expired, hearing McFadden utter the word was jarring, and it surprised him. He could think of nothing to say in response.

"Kidnapping. Back in the day it was all the rage in Kansas City. A solid source of revenue for the mob."

"All the rage?"

"Yeah. Depression era stuff. Bad guys, I'd call them entrepreneurs, kidnapped thousands of people and held them for ransom around the country, including here in KC. Some famous. Some went free after someone paid the ransom and some never saw the light of day again.

"Take Mary McElroy. Ever heard of her? She was quite the looker. Two guys kidnapped her from her bathtub in KC. Right from her fuckin' bathtub. Can you imagine? They were gonna haul her ass out in her birthday suit and whisk her away but she insisted on getting dressed."

McFadden liked the McElroy story, and as he told it, he drifted into mob speak. It was the best way to tell her story. "That took some real balls, eh? Big brass ones: her and them. Not only that, she was the kid of Pendergast's handpicked city manager. So they took on one of the boss man's inner circle. Can you believe that? What balls!

"They took her to the basement of a bungalow in rural Wyandotte County, Kansas. Even gave her a radio and a fan. Kidnappers wanted sixty K, but her old man negotiated them down to thirty. She and her kidnappers bonded while they held her hostage. When the old man paid, the kidnappers released her with a bouquet of roses. When she heard they had released her for only thirty, she laughed with her captors that she was worth at least a hundred K. She had come to like them so much that she visited them in prison after the police caught them."

"No shit!"

"True as the sun rises. Another one? They kidnapped Nell Donnelly of Donnelly Garment empire fame from her front stoop. Big ransom. Snatch and pay was big business in the thirties."

"Robbie, why are you telling me all this?"

"Can't know where you're going, m'friend, unless you know where you've been. History matters."

Jordan said nothing. Suddenly, Robbie McFadden sounded a lot like Amadi Browne: too much history. Trying to move the conversation back to Maximilian Cruz, Jordan asked, "What would Max be able to do for me?"

"You said you wanted your brother out of the way for a while. You can talk with Max about it. He does that kind of thing for clients."

"But kidnapping?"

"What'd you expect? You have another way to make someone scarce for a while?"

"I suppose not," Jordan replied as he contemplated kidnapping Amadi.

"Look, Jordie, I'm gonna leave those details to you and Max. You talk and then you're the boss. If it's what you want, then great. But if you decide to use Max's services, you keep track of him and your bro. That's what being the boss means."

When Jordan said nothing, McFadden added, "Look, before you get started, my strong suggestion is this. Friend to friend. Figure out what you want, what you really want, come up with a plan, and don't start down any path until you know the endgame and have decided you're the man to make it happen. Endgames are tricky. There's no place for cold feet and indecision in the game you're about to play. Us businessmen, we've got to consider everything and weigh the consequences. And then we've got to be decisive. It's in the job description. Be the man with the plan."

Jordan nodded.

"You understand what I'm saying here, Jordie?"

Jordan nodded, but he wasn't clear he did.

"You've got to have a good plan. You've got to keep tabs on your mark and your snatcher. Strange shit can happen, and strange shit is not good for the project or the plan. You know what I mean?"

"Maybe. I think so."

"Good. Last order of business. You pay me, right?"

"Yes."

"That gets you my services: advice, oversight, and access to my crew. You pay Max. That gets you his services. Understood?"

"Yes."

As he stood to leave, McFadden nodded and said, "And once you decide and implement, if you need an investor to help move your bank to the world of crypto, you know where to find me. Would be fun to be in a crypto business venture with an old high school buddy like you. I'm always lookin' for someplace to park some of my money, if you know what I mean."

9

THE FRANKLINS, 3J, and Pascale sat around the small table in conference room 27B, an interior space where 3J and Pascale often developed the strategy for an upcoming bankruptcy case. It was their war room. The Franklins had provided the lawyers with Abode's relevant financial and historical information, which gave 3J and Pascale a chance to shore up their thinking on the strategy they'd recommend.

The second hand on Jordan's payment clock was ticking away relentlessly, first toward the maturity date and then the thirty-day countdown to move the loan or face the inevitable Abode financial meltdown. The Franklins and the lawyers could hear each tick.

"Thanks for coming in folks," 3J said. "Let's talk about how we might deal with Commonwealth in light of Jordan's view of the world. First up, if it's possible, we think Abode should draw down on the line for the remaining amount available. It looks like that would be about three million. The draw would require some planning, and we'll need to understand the past process you used to get money from the bank."

James explained the process in detail. To buy land, Commonwealth typically delivered funds into escrow at closing to enable Abode to close the purchase. To build homes on the land, in the early years, the bank required contractors to first perform the work and deliver an invoice to Abode and the bank. The bank would then send an engineer to the home to inspect the work and ensure Commonwealth's contractors had performed everything in a workmanlike manner. Only then would it fund the payment of the invoice from the loan.

But as the years went by and the relationship and level of trust grew, the bank dispensed with the inspection requirement. Instead, the bank relied on Abode to assure proper construction. Abode would present a home building budget for all the homes in a project it would build. Then the bank would review it and deliver the entire budgeted funds to Abode to use as contractors performed work and built homes. The extra interest Abode paid because it borrowed all the budgeted construction costs at once was worth it in the Franklins' estimation to enable them to control the funds and better manage the project. Construction was more seamless, and homes got built quicker if they didn't repeatedly have to pause construction while they waited for an engineer to arrive, inspect, and write a report. In addition, they no longer had to draft multiple draw requests and wait for funding.

"Do you have any land acquisitions in the works?" Pascale asked.

"In fact we do," Bella said. "The purchase price is one and a half million. We've done all our due diligence and we're ready to close on the land. Closing was set for later this month, but we have the contractual right to accelerate that date, and the bank has already approved the acquisition. So we could close in the next day or two and request that the bank fund the purchase price."

"Do you have a budget prepared for the construction of homes on the land?"

"Again, yes. The bank has reviewed and approved it. So in conjunction with closing, we could request that the bank fund the budgeted construction amount of approximately a million and a quarter," Bella explained. "That should yield six completed homes, and we could help six more families while we try to sort all this out."

"That doesn't get us quite to the full three million, but if we could buy the land and get those funds to build, then at least for a while, even without the bank line, Abode would still be in business. To the outside world it would look like business as usual, and we could also continue to fundraise," James added.

"Good. Very good," 3J said, nodding slowly.

"Why would Commonwealth let Abode draw more money under the line?" Bella asked.

"It's not entirely clear Commonwealth will," Pascale explained. "But from what we've learned about the transition in power, maybe the small group at the bank charged with reviewing and approving line of credit borrowings still reports on a day-to-day basis to Amadi, not Jordan. Jordan seems like a big picture guy and may not have gotten his arms completely around the bank's day-to-day operations. And maybe he doesn't want to. He seems like someone who wants to be a mover and shaker, not a ledger reviewer or desk jockey bean counter."

The Franklins seemed to be listening intently.

"You have your relationship with Amadi," 3J continued. "You have your contacts in the group that's approved Abode's borrowings in the past. If we can get a little lucky here, the bank will fund your request before Jordan sees the borrowing recap reports the next day."

"But once he does figure it all out, won't he move the money out of Abode's bank account at Commonwealth and back into the bank's own coffers?" Bella asked.

"We think not. As soon as Abode has the building funds in hand, you'll transfer them to an account we want you to open at a new banking institution," Pascale explained.

"You've told us that Kansas City Bank and Trust handles your cash management needs, correct?" 3J asked.

"Yes," James said. "Some years ago, we needed a bank to handle the many payments Abode receives, and Commonwealth didn't offer that service. So we signed on for cash management services at KCBT. Our homeowners make payment to a KCBT post office box or their bank automatically pays each month. The PO box is an account at KCBT, which opens the mail, sends us a report of who paid, how much, and on what day and then wires the money to the Abode account at Commonwealth.

"Good. What we want you to do is open a new bank account at KCBT into which you'll transfer everything in the Commonwealth account, which will include the new loan amounts, and then also direct KCBT to send the cash management funds to the new account," 3J advised. "If this works, all the money will be at KCBT in a matter of moments and the Commonwealth account will have a zero balance."

Bella and James glanced at each other briefly with growing distressed looks on their faces.

"Ordinarily, a bank's loan documents require the borrower to bank only at the lender. Here, the documents are silent on that point," 3J said, trying to set them more at ease.

After a few moments, James frowned, shook his head, and said softly, "Jeee-sus. And I was worried the other day about a big fight in bankruptcy if we went the cram down route. I mean, having another two plus million would be terrific. But from what I'm hearing, the cram down fight might pale compared to the animosity we'll spawn after Jordan figures out what we've done to him and his bank if we pursue this strategy."

"I tend to agree," Bella said. "We're going to need to think about this, folks. We've never done anything to hurt Commonwealth, or any bank for that matter. We've done nothing underhanded." She paused and added, "You know, the sand always has a line in it. Some people step over it easily. But not everyone. One side of it's in the light of day. It's the honorable and trustworthy side of the line. The other side is in the shadows. It's the dark and sinister side of the line. Are you asking us to step over to the dark side?"

3J and Pascale understood Bella's concern. They had recently completed several cases where they had to decide if the ends would justify the means of stepping over to the dark side of the line. They had talked after each case ended, and neither liked the moral dilemma posed by the line. But they didn't think the ends *never* justified the means. In moments of quiet reflection, 3J liked to remember something Leon Trotsky had said. "The end may justify the means as long as there is something that justifies the end." She and Pascale had learned that sometimes the end was so important, like saving a life, that they were willing to employ a means only found on the other side of the line.

Here, however, she didn't think they were asking the Franklins to step over, or even get close, to the line. She believed there was nothing to justify. Abode had rights and what she and Pascale proposed was proper. All they were asking the Franklins to do was use Abode's rights and fight back.

"For what it's worth," 3J said, "what we're proposing is proper under the law. We don't think borrowing more money from the bank before maturity is wrong or even immoral. The bank promised to lend you up to twelve million. The bank approved the upcoming land acquisition and the construction budget. You're merely taking the bank up on its promises while they're still on the table before maturity, after which we are certain the promises and the right to borrow will vanish into the ether."

The meeting ended without 3J and Pascale sharing the other steps in the plan: meeting with Amadi to test his appetite to help Abode and triggering potential capital calls at the bank, based on the status of the Abode loan. It was better to ease the Franklins into the plan in small sound bites. If the Franklins approved phase one, 3J felt strongly they would be more amenable to phase two.

The line in the sand always influenced decisions, and 3J knew that. She respected the Franklins' decision to further discuss the line. She knew everyone's tolerance for stepping over the line was different. And different circumstances could lead to different decisions about how far a person was willing to go. When she learned Woody Clarke was out to kill her and others and she approved a computer hack to prevent it, she knew she and Pascale had stepped over the line. But she also knew the hack justified the end—the safety of all involved. In the Clarke matter, she had learned something about herself: She would do almost anything to combat a killer. The Franklins would have to decide if they were being asked to step over their line and if so, if they would do it to save Abode.

With more of Commonwealth's money in hand, the Franklins could build six more houses and start six more families on the road to the American dream and economic stability. It was like her papa had said to her many years earlier: "Sure is hard to find an affordable house in this damn city."

She respected the Franklins' concern for the line in the sand. But once you're in, you have to be all in. She wondered if the Franklins were ready to be all-in. Certainly, Abode's survival depended on it.

10

Tuesday, November 26 through Friday, November 29, 2024

The Franklins included Amadi's mobile number in the background information they had provided to the lawyers. The best course of action was to cold-call him, but 3J felt it best to await the Franklins' decision on the draw on the line of credit and the new bank account before reaching out to Amadi.

Later in the day, Bella called 3J and said, after considerable consternation, they had decided they should decline to follow advice of counsel only in rare situations. She and James understood it would be a struggle to save Abode, and they were willing to set up a new bank account, draw on the line, and move the construction money as soon as Commonwealth funded the draw. They were prepared to fight, but she made it clear they had a line they weren't willing to cross.

"Bella, please rest assured we will do everything in our power to refrain from presenting you with line crossing options."

Even though it was right before the Thanksgiving holiday, the Franklins were able to set up an account at KCBT. Once they did, they formally submitted the borrowing requests to Commonwealth and moved closing up on the sale of the real estate to the end of the day on Wednesday. Neither Amadi nor Jordan had informed the small Commonwealth team reviewing draw requests of the impending maturity of Abode's line. The Franklins had been careful to say nothing false in the request, and the bank was aware of Abode's construction plans. The team reviewing the request saw it as nothing more than ordinary in Abode's relationship with the bank and set up the transfers for the draw without questions.

To their surprise and relief, the bank said nothing to the Franklins, funded the land acquisition, and deposited the money in the Abode account. The sale closed promptly at five that afternoon.

3J began her quiet Thanksgiving holiday alone with Steele, football on the television, and a small turkey dinner in the oven with the first part of her plan completed.

Early on Friday morning, the Franklins directed a different team at the bank to wire all the funds in the Commonwealth account to their new bank account at KCBT. By ten that morning, the funds moved out of Commonwealth and into their deposit account in the new institution. They also instructed KCBT to deposit all future cash management funds into the new KCBT bank account.

Late that morning, it was business as usual at Commonwealth when Jordan stormed out of his office, heading toward his brother. "What the fuck just happened, Amadi?" Jordan boomed to his brother, who was sitting at his desk on the floor. Dozens of people were within earshot.

Jordan had a printout of loans funded Wednesday rolled up in his fist as he yelled. Amadi looked up as Jordan quickly bridged the distance between them. Amadi knew which report Jordan clutched because he had seen the same report earlier that morning. He said nothing and looked back down to the papers on his desk. Bank employees, customers, and security guards all turned to see what the ruckus was about.

"Amadi, goddamn it! Look at me. What did you just do?"

"Jordan, maybe we should take this discussion into your office."

"Answer my question!" Jordan boomed again, content to yell in the bank lobby as virtually everyone in the bank stopped their business to watch the brewing dispute.

In a soft tone, Amadi said, "I did nothing this week. Previously, this bank approved Abode's request for the bank to fund its acquisition of the land in question, and apparently, Wednesday afternoon was the closing." Amadi looked up but couldn't tell if his brother was comprehending. "Previously, this bank approved Abode's construction budget to build houses on the newly acquired land. Again, I did nothing because there was nothing to do. You told me to take care of the ordinary course of business matters here. This is nothing more than ordinary course of business. I didn't need to take care of it because it took care of itself. That's how we conduct business with good customers like Abode and the Franklins. The matter, therefore, is complete."

"Complete my ass! Did you know that early this morning, I tried to move the building funds out of Abode's account and back into the bank's general funds only to discover these Franklin fuckers had already moved the money to a different bank. Not only the building funds, but all funds in the account!"

Amadi was not aware, but he smiled. "Do you blame them after the meeting you had with them a few days ago?"

"You're goddamn right I blame them. But more than that, I blame you!"

"Me?"

"What the hell were you thinking?"

"There was nothing for me to think about. The loan documents we've used for the Abode loan for years don't require them to bank here."

"Not that *we've* used here. That *you've* used! They're your docs, and if they're deficient, it's your deficiency."

Amadi shrugged his shoulders. "They're not deficient, Jordan.

They've always worked fine. Anyway, it's your bank now. You've told me you're the new thinker on the block. So put your thinking cap on and put that brain of yours to use. I'm sure you'll figure something out."

Amadi looked away from Jordan again. It was now his turn to end the discussion through his body language. He picked up his phone, swiveled his chair away from Jordan, and began a conversation when the person he'd called answered the phone.

Amadi had to repress a smile. He had brushed off Jordan just as Jordan had brushed him off. Jordan fumed. It's what Jordan did. He had been like that since he popped out of the womb moments after his older brother. With his first breaths, Amadi looked around the hospital room quietly. Moments later, Jordan came out and began screaming, and he'd been screaming ever since. The best way to handle Jordan was to simply ignore him.

As he completed his call, Amadi looked up to find Jordan standing there at his desk again. Amadi looked away again. "Look at me, damn it! I'm not through with you," the frustrated Jordan screamed, saying each word slowly, loudly, and emphatically. When Amadi declined to look at him, Jordan turned and padded quickly to the bank's front entrance and left the building. There was no door to slam behind him for emphasis, just the whoosh of the revolving door. It was another Jordan temper tantrum.

Amadi took a deep breath, held it, and exhaled. As he did, one of the security guards approached him. "Is everything all right over here, Mr. Browne?"

"Thanks, Bill," Amadi said as he smiled at the guard. "Oh, sure. It is for now. Don't know how I'll answer that same question in the morning if you ask me again but for now, no problems."

~

That afternoon, 3J and Pascale were on a conference call with the Franklins. "Now that you've deposited the building funds in KCBT, we think we should reach out to Amadi, without Jordan present," 3J explained.

"For what purpose?" James asked.

3J explained the plan of trying to turn one brother against the other. When she finished, there was nothing on the phone line except resounding silence. Then she and Pascale heard Bella take a deep breath. Moments later, she said, "Commonwealth's done good work in this community for over a hundred and thirty years. We would hope that it would continue to do so for another hundred years or more. We've talked. We have serious doubts there will be another bank where we can move the Abode line, at least not quickly and easily. And maybe never. Not in this town because there isn't another bank like Commonwealth—or at least the Commonwealth we knew and partnered with before Amadi ceded control.

"As I told you yesterday, we have a line we won't cross, and we certainly aren't people who break the law. But from time to time, we've had to protect what's ours and stand up for our rights. What Black business couple hasn't? We're now prepared to take steps with Commonwealth to protect Abode's interests and the community it serves. We're prepared to push back and do it by any *legal* means necessary, and we want to emphasize that it must never become an ends justify the *illegal* means mission. Do we have agreement?"

Lawyers identify options. Clients dictate strategy. 3J and Pascale looked at each other and nodded. Together, the lawyers responded, "Agreed."

⁂

Amadi said nothing for a few seconds when 3J called him, identified herself and her clients, and asked if there was a time when she could meet with him to talk. "What would be the purpose of our meeting, Ms. Jones, if I might inquire?" he finally asked.

"You're the banker responsible for the relationship between

Commonwealth and Abode. After our meeting with your brother Jordan, it seems clear to us things are heading for a direct conflict. It may be quite contentious for all involved. I was hoping to meet with you and open a dialogue. In my experience, talking usually helps these types of situations."

"I'm sure the Franklins have told you I'm no longer the relationship manager for their account at the bank. That responsibility has passed to my brother, Jordan, who I think told you that at the meeting you had with him recently."

"Yes, but I'd like to meet you regardless of your current role, or lack of any role, in the Abode line of credit."

"Hmm," he said. "Well, I can't see any particular downside in a meeting between us. But not at the bank or your offices. Are you familiar with Kauffman Gardens? It's off Emanuel Cleaver II Boulevard, easy to get to from downtown and the bank's offices in Midtown. There's a bench in the gardens near where Muriel and Ewing Kauffman are buried. Do you know the spot?"

"I'll find it."

"Good. Say, Saturday afternoon at two?"

"See you then."

11

Saturday, November 30, 2024

As she drove to Kauffman Gardens, 3J considered the location Amadi had chosen to meet—near the grave of Ewing Kauffman and his wife, Muriel. In his early adult days, Ewing was a lowly pharmaceuticals salesman for Lincoln Laboratories and turned a five-thousand-dollar investment into Marion Laboratories, worth billions of dollars. Later, by merger, it became the even larger Marion Merrell Dow.

He was also the founding owner of the Kansas City Royals and one of Kansas City's true hometown benefactors. Kansas Citians knew him as one of their most famous rags to riches stories. She hoped her meeting with Amadi would be as successful as Kauffman's career had been. Kauffman's life oozed positivity and a can-do attitude. She hoped some of that would rub off when she and Amadi met.

When she arrived and made her way to the meeting place, she saw Amadi Browne sitting. He wore a dark gray, tropical wool suit, a solid red tie, and black wing tip shoes. Bankers and lawyers shared similar attire habits—a shared uniform. He could have passed for a senior partner at Greene Madison.

3J sat down and the two shook hands. "Are you up to speed on the Abode loan situation?"

"Well, I certainly know the loan terms. But as to recent events, I know only the very basics, I'm afraid. Jordan doesn't share much with me. When he does share with me, I don't always listen. Better for my health."

He smiled, but it was a look of pain.

"What I do know, Ms. Jones, is this: The loan matures on December fourth as it has each December for decades. We've renewed it each year. My parents renewed it and later, I renewed it. But this year, I'm told the bank won't renew it. My brother's decision. Abode drew on the line earlier this week and bought land with the funds. It also drew on the line to fund the construction budget. I think Abode may have also moved the construction funds out of Commonwealth."

He smiled again, but this time, the look was more one of satisfaction and approval. He pursed his lips and added, "The draws made Jordan upset. Moving the money *really* pissed him off. To be honest, it launched him into the stratosphere."

"Can you explain why the bank won't renew the loan, Mr. Browne?"

"Some questions are better posed to my brother, Ms. Jones. That's definitely one of them. I no longer dictate matters such as loan renewals. Suffice it to say I went to bat for Abode, but I had no chance."

"I see. Well, perhaps this conversation will progress more easily if I tell you how I see this going."

"Please do."

3J explained that circumstances would force Abode to file a bankruptcy petition, and it would use the cash drawn from the line to build homes. In the meantime, she explained, when the Abode loan matured, the regulators would make the bank reclassify it as a bad loan. Nonperforming. Perhaps even insufficient collateral.

In a bank the size of Commonwealth, that would trigger a need for more capital. She expected the regulators to require a capital call on ownership. Maybe millions of dollars. All of that could be avoided by renewing the loan.

"Do you and your brother understand all that, Mr. Browne?"

Amadi nodded slowly. "I certainly do, Ms. Jones, but I can't speak to Jordan's level of comprehension or even his interest in knowing."

3J explained they knew Jordan had purchased a portion of Amadi's shares in the bank and in doing so, became the majority owner of the bank's stock. "Our research suggests he may not have the financial capacity to come up with required millions of dollars quickly to capitalize the bank."

"Another matter better discussed with Jordan," Amadi replied. "I'm not privy to his personal wealth or lack thereof."

It seemed Amadi was willing to provide some insight into his brother's difficult personality but not into his brother's personal financial situation.

The two had been talking while looking out at the gardens in front of them. Like CIA agents trading information, neither had looked at the other. But now Amadi turned to face 3J for the first time. "Does your research reveal why I sold the stock to Jordan, Ms. Jones?"

3J turned to Amadi before speaking. She could see the pain in his eyes, and it was deep personal pain, not financial pain. "We have not uncovered the reason to date."

"My wife passed away a couple of years ago. We had one daughter. Overnight, I became a single parent running a bank and raising a young girl alone. After my wife's death, my daughter got terribly ill with Gaucher disease. Fatty substances built up to toxic levels in her spleen, liver, lungs, bone marrow, and eventually, her brain. Children's Mercy Hospital said there was nothing they could do.

"Before she died, I learned of an experimental treatment doctors were developing in Sweden. Of course, it wasn't covered by insurance. But a parent will do almost anything to save a sick child. The treatment, the trips to Sweden, the hospital stays over there, the cost of the doctors—all of that would cost almost two million dollars. I didn't have that kind of ready cash. My brother did. I asked him to help his niece and me. But rather than loan or give me the money, he wanted something in return: a sale to him of my stock in the bank. He is a quid pro quo person. Always has been. If you haven't seen that yet in your discussions, you will shortly. He can't hide it. It's just the way he is.

"I should've just borrowed the money from a bank, pledged my stock as collateral, and kept control of Commonwealth. But I wasn't thinking clearly. A dying daughter can do that to a parent. In retrospect, I'm not sure how fast a bank would've loaned me the money, and I needed it quickly. So I sold him the stock, ignored that he would take control of the bank as a result, and shuttled my daughter back and forth between here and Sweden for months. Unfortunately, the treatment failed and she died a few months later. At that point, I had lost all of my family and control of the bank."

As Amadi explained the story, he looked down at his lap and fiddled with his gold wedding band, twirling it on his ring finger. "When I got back to Kansas City, I had to bury my daughter next to my wife, and then all I had was my work at the bank, its mission, and the legacy of my ancestors."

He closed his eyes for several seconds. "That legacy has always run like a long, majestic river runs, from my great-great-grandparents at the headwaters straight through to my parents and then to me at the river's mouth. They entrusted me with the power of the river to use it to serve the community—as we have for more than a century. Note, I didn't say to Jordan at the river's mouth, just to the community and me. Jordan doesn't believe in the river. Not a bit. He doesn't care where the river waters come from, and he certainly has no intent to use its power to help anyone."

Amadi sighed. "The bank's mission was simple but sustaining because the need for the mission continues. That mission has always been to use the bank to help our community. Without the bank, I fear the community will suffer a fate similar to my daughter's. Rather than prosper, it will regress and become terminally ill. I can't fathom being part of a community burial, like a grave worker lowering the casket containing the souls of all the members of left-behind groups into a hole in the ground. The hole my brother dug.

"After my daughter died, I thought I could throw myself into the bank work, redouble my efforts with Abode, and do everything in my power to ensure as many members of the left-behind communities as possible have a home they own. For them, having a home is a key element to independence, freedom, education, and family stability. It no longer can or should be ignored, and I'm proud of Commonwealth's role in helping to solve the marginalized communities' housing problems in Kansas City. Every city needs an Abode."

Amadi paused as if exhausted by his explanation.

"Well, what happened?" 3J asked.

"Jordan happened. He has a different . . . I'll call it a notion, because it's certainly not a well-considered and planned business proposition. When I sold him my stock, I didn't want to consider that he'd decommission my role at the bank and take a different path. I couldn't. All I could think about was my daughter. I needed the money. Period. But what's happening now isn't surprising. He's all about maximizing profit, even if it means abandoning the mission. He likes to tell me the bank is not a nonprofit organization. He says it should do business with for-profit borrowers and therefore, not Abode."

3J sat quietly.

He added, "My ancestors lived by the Maya Angelou idea of giving if you get. I try to as well. Not Jordan. If he gets, he wants more. He counts it carefully, and then he keeps it."

"Amadi, how did your brother make his millions?"

"Some in the old-fashioned way and some in the new-fashioned way, I'd say. He made some money at the bank and invested in crypto. As I understand the story, he parlayed his bank money into crypto winnings. I don't think it's dirty money, if that's what you're getting at."

Amadi had opened up during the conversation, and 3J could tell he was probably now more willing to talk about Jordan's personal financial situation. "Do you agree he couldn't meet a capital call of millions at this time?"

"Of course, I don't know for sure. But my sense is that buying the stock from me coupled with the volatility in the crypto market—and at the moment it's way down—would make it damn near impossible for him to put millions into the bank. He'd have to turn to other sources for his funding needs."

"Such as?"

"I'm not sure, and a lot of the time, I don't want to know for sure. What I do know is that Jordan has friends in all kinds of other industries. Many of them are in lines of work that, if they owned an interest in the bank, would not make bank regulators happy. Indeed, if they had their tentacles in the majority owner of a bank and threatened his ability to make independent decisions, there would be even more regulatory unhappiness. Jordan knows all of that but mostly ignores it. I'm sure he thinks some of his friends would stake him the money he'd need if he had to capitalize the bank. And I'm sure he figures he can manage the regulators like he figures he can manage anyone and any situation."

"What do you think?"

"He and I have always travelled in different circles, and I have only a passing knowledge of many of these so-called friends—Kansas City mob types. I have serious doubts they'd give him money merely to save the bank. They don't do things out of the goodness of their hearts. If they wanted to spend millions to own a piece of the only

Black owned bank in Kansas City with a mission to help the inner-city communities, it would be for an ulterior motive. Cleaning up dirty money comes to mind." As Amadi said this, he smiled wistfully and shook his head. "I also know the regulators. Jordan's relationships would spell the end of the bank as we know it."

"What about you?"

"What *about* me?"

"Could you raise the money to buy back the bank?"

Amadi looked up at the cloudy sky. "Now that's a real interesting question, Ms. Jones. I'm pretty sure it's not for sale. If there was a capital call and Jordan had to issue new stock, I might be able to get a bank stock loan from a traditional lender. But Jordan would have to be of a mind to issue new shares to provide Commonwealth needed capital. No doubt, he'd try to do it in a way to assure he'd retain a majority of the stock. Maybe there are other options as well, but most options couldn't happen unless Jordan came to his senses."

"My firm has lots of bank clients. Between those clients and your banking connections, I bet we could find a financial institution to lend you the money to buy Commonwealth stock."

With her comment, 3J offered the possibility of a partnership between her side of the table and Amadi to help him retake control of the bank. When she made the comment, he was poker-faced. If he caught the subtlety, he didn't let on and he didn't respond. Instead, he stood.

"Let's walk through the gardens, Ms. Jones."

3J followed him, and they walked on the brick pathway in silence through the perennial beds, now dormant, past bronze sculptures, unique trees, and beds that would display ever-changing annual plants in the spring. But now they were home to cold tolerant plants, added for a splash of color as horticulturists awaited the frost and snow of the hard-core winter months. The garden looked different than it did other times of the year, but it was still serene.

Amadi stopped and faced 3J. "Ms. Jones, if you don't mind me asking, why exactly are we meeting?"

"Mr. Browne, tell me a little about the history of the bank." They began to walk again. It was clear to 3J that Amadi loved to talk about the bank's history, and he gave her a detailed tutorial of Kansas City's first, and now only, Black owned bank, his family tree, and the commitment to the improvement of marginalized communities in the inner city. He spoke eloquently, convincingly, and passionately with obvious pride and a deep knowledge of the plight of people still left behind in the twenty-first century. At times, he sounded like a combination of Martin Luther King, Malcolm X, and Booker T. Washington, drawing from the best of each in his discussion.

When he finished, the two paused before a long rectangular flower bed where, during the summer, roses and wildflowers thrived and bees and butterflies coexisted harmoniously as they shared a common goal: dancing from flower to flower, butterflies to gather nectar and bees to collect pollen. Stone walls framed the garden, and beyond the roses, fountains still gently delivered water to a contemplation pool. In a few more weeks, park managers would shut them off for the winter.

"Mr. Browne, your reverence for your bank's history and your commitment to the community are why we're meeting. This city needs Abode. This city needs Commonwealth. *Your* Commonwealth, not your brother's. Abode will have to commence a bankruptcy case. In it, your brother will not find the treatment of Commonwealth pleasant. Abode will have the right and the power to cram down a bankruptcy plan over Commonwealth's objection. It'll likely knock the size of Commonwealth's claim down. It'll pay that smaller claim over time—I'm guessing over a longer time than Jordan will be able to tolerate.

"On the other hand, back in our shop, we've been thinking that if we collaborated with you, we might somehow turn all this into your investment opportunity, the chance for Abode and the Franklins to cut a deal with the bank, and a return to community service, with you in command again. Then both Abode and Commonwealth can get back to the important business of building homes in the core."

"What would your cram down plan do to Jordan in the process, Ms. Jones?"

3J bit her upper lip. "In my line of work, we quickly learn there are often winners and losers in bankruptcy cases. On the loser side of the ledger, sometimes there are big losers. I've seen both sides of the ledger." She turned to face Amadi eye to eye and said firmly, "He will be a loser. Bankruptcy cram down will not be kind to him."

He raised his eyebrows in surprise and nodded. "Much to think about, Ms. Jones. Much to think about. I'm glad you reached out. I'll find you to talk some more in a few days."

❧

As Amadi returned to his car, a large man wearing a fashionable hat sat in a late-model, black Ford sedan shrouded by tinted windows. He watched Amadi say goodbye to 3J, start his car, and drive away. Then he slowly pulled out of the parking lot and began to follow Amadi, several car lengths behind.

He took out his mobile phone and made a call. "Cruz here. Yeah. He just finished a long meeting with that Jones lawyer. He's driving away and so am I."

He asked if he should keep following Amadi, nodded to himself when he got an affirmative, and listened for a while until he finally replied, "Right. I'll wait for your word. Just let me know when."

12

Amadi Browne recalls Saturday, November 30, 2024

I DIDN'T RETURN to the bank after the meeting with Ms. Jones. I needed to think, but not at the bank. Lately, when I was there, I could feel Jordan watching me and I could imagine him plotting, so it was no longer a place where I could gather my thoughts. Instead, I drove, meandering throughout the city as I tried to focus. Focusing proved to be no easy task. The car seemed to cruise the city streets as if it knew where to go and had a mind of its own. I was just along for the ride.

As it wandered through the city, so did my thoughts. No destination in mind for either. Just a tour through the city I loved in the hopes the drive would help me decide what to do. I drove on Rockhill Road to Emanuel Cleaver II Boulevard, then to Southmoreland Park, past the mansion that was the former Rockhill Tennis Club, past the art museum and the small neighborhood of old granite rock houses surrounding it, down the steep winding hill to Gillham Road, and across Gillham into Hyde Park and its stately turn of the century mansions. Then I drove back to Gillham, past more mansions in various states of repair mixed in with Depression era high-rises hoping for their turn at a renaissance now decades overdue.

Then past Hallmark and onto The Paseo, one of the longest and oldest boulevards in the city. It was one of my favorite places to drive and think. But like so much of historical Kansas City on the east side of town, the once grand houses that lined The Paseo had now fallen into disrepair. As I drove, I could still see the grandeur of times gone by, but I could also see that grandeur fading—faint glimmers of hope in the rearview mirror of time. In the moment, it was decay, and the moment was bleak. Once the grandeur vanished for good, the memories would be gone, and The Paseo would look like nothing more than a long-blighted road with an unkempt park in the middle. Jordan would look at The Paseo and see decay. I looked at The Paseo and saw what it was and what it could be again. History mattered.

I drove on The Paseo to 18th Street, then to Vine and the old neighborhood where the bank first opened its doors and where Jordan and I were born, just blocks away. I parked and hiked a few of the blocks that were once the hub of Black commercial activity in Kansas City, but now, after years of neglect, were close to deserted and in disrepair. Gone were the many Black owned barber shops, fruit and vegetable stores, clothing stores, tailor shops, catering businesses and restaurants, boarding houses, dry goods stores, the headquarters of the weekly African American newspaper, and the many Black shoppers who had once regularly frequented those establishments. That day, I encountered no shoppers out on the streets. Once a Black economy thriving separate from its White counterparts, it was now simply separate, no longer thriving, and no longer viable.

As I walked down one street with trash blowing near the curb, I saw a place where blight replaced hope and pride, and there I was, on my pilgrimage to the old neighborhood, hoping for inspiration and answers. With every step, I wondered if I could wrestle control of the bank from Jordan. If I did, could I save the bank from financial ruin occasioned by an improvident move to crypto banking? Was there a way to partner with Ms. Jones and her clients?

I grappled with my sale of the bank stock to Jordan. When we agreed on the price, my lawyer drew up a stock sale agreement. I was certain Jordan never read it word for word. That wasn't his custom. Jordan didn't engage a lawyer for the stock sale. He simply came to the office, signed the sale agreement, and delivered two million dollars to me. I remembered seeing in a draft of the agreement a repurchase option, a repo. Under the repo, I had a period of time to buy back the stock from Jordan at a set price. The choice was mine. Jordan could do nothing to stop me from exercising the repo.

I read an early draft and later sat in my lawyer's office as he pointed out the repo protection. I asked simply, "Why bother?" At the time, the Kansas City doctors had convinced me that my daughter had little chance of surviving. I had heard them, but I knew I still had to try to save her. I saw no chance that I would ever regain my stock and run the bank after she died. All I saw was the end. The end of my small family, the end of my bank, the end of my ancestors' long legacy, and the end of Commonwealth's role in the community. All I saw was the beginning of a new dawn for Jordan, a new dawn I had no part in. Contrary to my usual custom, I neither paid attention to the protection my lawyer built into the agreement nor to the final contract and its terms. I signed and Jordan delivered the money.

But now I realized I needed to know whether the repo provision survived the drafts, and if so, what the provision said in the final executed version. I returned to my car, and on my drive home, I called my lawyer. He confirmed that the repo survived in the final draft. He told me the right to repurchase the stock expired on December 13, 2024—Friday the thirteenth. When I got home to my empty house, I went to my study, retrieved the final executed sale agreement from my desk, and studied it. Indeed, as my lawyer confirmed, the right to repurchase the stock had a sunset provision that expired soon.

So it wasn't irrevocably Jordan's bank quite yet. And it wasn't quite the beginning of Jordan's new banking dawn either. I had a chance, and as a result, so did Abode. But I wasn't so sure there would be enough time to find my own financing to buy back my stock and take control of the bank.

I needed to talk with Ms. Jones again.

13

JORDAN SAT ALONE in his living room with a glass of bourbon. Two things were on his mind: Robbie McFadden and his brother, and they were no longer separate matters. They had merged in his thoughts and were now inseparable.

He had hired Maximilian Cruz to follow his brother. That was it, so far. But what was he willing to do? And how far was he willing to go? Kidnap his own brother? Did he have it in him to do that? Maybe. But it would be a step squarely into the darkness that was Robbie's world of shadows.

Such indecision. Words like "maybe" weren't in Robbie's vocabulary. Questioning how far he would go wasn't the McFadden way. Robbie had said there was no place for indecision in the business world. Maybe not in *his* business world, but Jordan saw his own business world as being full of indecision, and if he was going to follow Robbie's business model, he needed to figure out how to banish "maybe" from his deliberations. To do that, he needed to learn more about himself and figure out how far he would go.

He took a deep breath and exhaled slowly. He decided to drink his bourbon. Maybe it would help him reach a decision about his Amadi problem.

14

Sunday, December 1, 2024

3J SAT IN Pascale's office surveying the splendor that was his patented mess. Mess was an understatement. For several months Pascale had used Sundays to try to get the mess under control, and for the last month, 3J had been committed to helping him. Even though it was the Sunday after Thanksgiving, they both fulfilled their Sunday commitment to bringing order to Pascale's chaos.

She had hoped he would use his stint as a consultant to get things in his office under control. When she offered to come in on Sundays and help him get organized once and for all, he smiled and told her in all seriousness that over the past decade, he had already organized his papers. Every piece of paper in its place, he would say, but only he knew what those papers were, and presumably—the firm would say *hopefully*—he also knew where each was.

She countered by defining "organized" as every piece of paper in a file, files in drawers, and in the best of all worlds, files in alphabetical order. She called it a traditional law firm cataloging system. She knew if they ever got to the point of putting papers in actual labeled files, alphabetizing the files would likely be a bridge too far. But she kept the faith that together, they could organize his papers, if he only had the will.

"Bill, organized means nothing scattered on the floors, chairs, tables, and desk," she told him.

He said he understood and accepted her offer to help, but she knew he was only avoiding the problem. In the end, he was winning the organization battle, and soon she might abandon all efforts to help corral his mess. It was in his DNA and she wouldn't be able to alter it.

"Bill, I met with Amadi Browne yesterday and then he called me back later in the day. He wants to meet again, tomorrow."

"Sounds positive."

"I think it is. But he has an odd penchant for conducting business with me at outside locations. Yesterday it was Kauffman Gardens. Next time he wants to meet along Cliff Drive by the waterfall. Feels like spy versus spy stuff."

"Odd. But at least he has good taste in locations. Any idea what he'd like to discuss with cascading water as his backdrop?"

"He wants to show me the Commonwealth stock sale agreement he and Jordan signed and talk about it. He said Bryce Donaldson at Lockhill Johnson drew it up for him. He mentioned there were some provisions in the agreement to review about repurchasing the stock he sold to Jordan, but they'd soon sunset."

"It does all sound pretty cloak and dagger. Did he add to the drama by saying you had to come alone like in the old film noir detective movies?"

3J smiled at the reference. "He did not. So I'm thinking you should come this time."

"Will that scare him away?"

"I don't think so."

"Okay. I'm in. What time?"

"Three thirty. I'll swing by your office tomorrow at three and pick you up."

15

Monday, December 2, 2024

MONDAY, PROMPTLY AT 3:00 p.m., Amadi left his house, locked the front door behind him, and headed for the car parked in the driveway. The streets were empty. At the curb sat the man in a dark Ford. As Amadi began to back out of the driveway, the man slowly drove his car forward, blocking Amadi's exit. He got out of the car and approached Amadi, and Amadi got out of his car to see what the problem was. As he did, the man drew a gun lodged in the back of his trousers between his shirt and the beltline, ordered Amadi to turn around, duct taped his hands behind his back, and marched him to his car. The gun made Amadi go along quietly. The man opened the back door, ordered Amadi in, and once he was seated in the back seat, the man placed a dark hood over Amadi's head.

As the man drove off with his captive, he said, "They told me you're a banker. I guess you bankers usually have meetings all the time, right? Well, I'm afraid no meetings for you today, my friend."

ණ

At 3:00, 3J and Pascale headed to Cliff Drive and their meeting with Amadi Browne. Established in 1895, Cliff Drive was four and a half miles long, making it one of the shortest scenic byways in America. There were limestone bluffs, steep forested slopes of maple trees, natural springs, a waterfall, and panoramic overlooks high above the city. Old Kansas City neighborhoods flanked it. They arrived a little before 3:30, parked near the waterfall, and awaited Amadi's arrival.

"I used to ride bikes here with Jess before Nikki was born," Pascale said. "One of our weekend rituals. It's a beautiful park."

3J had long ago learned how to avoid welling up with tears when Pascale remembered his now deceased wife and daughter, both killed in a tragic car wreck at the hands of a drunk driver. This was one of those opportunities to employ her coping mechanisms and avoid crying. With her hazel eyes wide, she said softly, "You and Amadi have some similarities. He told me he lost his wife, became a single parent, and then lost his daughter to a terrible illness."

Pascale nodded knowingly.

By four, their banker still hadn't arrived. 3J had called and texted Amadi's mobile number several times, but each call went right to voice mail and she received no response to her texts. Her calls to his direct line office phone number went right to voice mail as well. "I don't know what's going on but I don't think he's coming, Pascale."

"Let me call the bank, 3J, and see if he's there or if they've seen him today."

The bank receptionist reported Amadi had not been to the bank that day, put him on hold, came back on the line, and told Pascale no one reported seeing him. She also volunteered that he kept his calendar in a small, bound diary he always carried with him, so there was no way for her to see if he had any appointments outside the bank.

The pair headed back to the office. Pascale texted Amadi several more times from the car, but he didn't respond. "Cold feet?" Pascale asked.

"He didn't seem like the cold feet type, Bill," she said after a moment. "At the gardens, he came across as thoughtful and analytical. And I assume, as a banker, he's decisive and not afraid to communicate he's called off a meeting. When he called to set up today's meeting, he sounded like he had made some decisions and had information he wanted to share. It didn't sound like he was on the fence at all."

"I hope he's okay. We should check with the authorities and make sure he didn't get into an accident today."

When they returned to the firm, they called Anthony Rosini, a former Jackson County Sheriff turned full-time process server and part-time investigator. They explained their planned meeting with Amadi Browne and asked if he could check and make sure nothing had happened to Amadi to prevent him from meeting them. Within a half hour, Rosini reported he found no police reports, and as far as he could determine, Amadi Browne was not in any of the area hospitals.

"What do you think, 3J?" Pascale asked.

"I don't know what to think. Do you know his lawyer, Bryce Donaldson?"

"Only in passing. He has a reputation as a good corporate lawyer. Years ago, I had a case against a bankruptcy lawyer at his firm, and they brought Bryce in to redraft agreements after the parties cut a deal. You want to call him and see if he knows what's up?"

"Couldn't hurt."

Pascale dialed up Donaldson, who answered on the first ring. Pascale explained the situation and asked if Donaldson knew Amadi's whereabouts.

"How odd. I talked with Amadi a few days ago. I think he was in his car. He asked some questions about a stock sale agreement I drew up for him not too long ago. He sold Commonwealth stock to his brother Jordan a little while back, and with it, he gave up control of the bank."

"Would you be able to share the agreement with us?"

"Don't see why not," Donaldson said after considering the request for a moment. "It's filed with the Missouri state bank regulators because it resulted in a change of control at the bank. So it's a public record. I'll dig out the executed copy and email it over to you."

Within minutes, Pascale and 3J had the agreement, and within several minutes thereafter, they had found and read the repo provision. They immediately saw that the repo provision expired in only eleven days. 3J shook her head slowly. "He said it would expire soon on the phone. I'm assuming he wanted to discuss how he could borrow enough money in time to buy the stock back, Bill. It has to be."

"Agreed."

3J looked past Pascale to the downtown skyline beyond. "Bill, I'm concerned that something bad has happened to Amadi. If he's out of the picture, I don't know how he'd exercise the right to repurchase the stock. He only has to be out of commission for eleven days for the right to expire. Then the bank is assuredly in Jordan's hands. I don't know enough about this Jordan character. When we met, Amadi mentioned his brother hung around with some unsavory types. Do you think Jordan would have it in him to partner up with some bad guys and cause harm to his own brother?"

"Totally unclear to me, 3J. People do all kinds of crazy stuff, including killing, in the name of money and greed. They can screw with anyone's moral gyroscope."

"Well, matters are definitely coming to a head. At this point, I don't see any way around the bankruptcy filings. The Franklins need time to find a new lender." She paused for a moment before continuing. "And we need time to find Amadi. I hope he's alive."

༄

At quitting time, 3J donned her workout gear and headed to her new thirty-minute core routine with trainer Megan Ricci. Megan's modest, one-on-one studio was on Broadway in Midtown. Megan was quickly becoming the city's trainer for the stars, but she was still a well-kept secret with open time slots to take on new clients like 3J.

3J had only been training with Megan for a month but looked forward to their sessions. They helped clear her mind and Megan had a way to make the pain seem worthwhile. At the beginning of her first session, Megan had asked why 3J had decided to start with a core trainer.

"In college, I had a six-pack. In law school, I had a four-pack. As an associate at Greene Madison, I had a two-pack. Now, as a partner, I have a no-pack. I want some pack back."

Megan took a step back, put her hands on her hips, and surveyed 3J.

"In the old days," 3J continued, "running and soccer were all I needed. Today, no more soccer for me. I still try to run. You can take the girl out of the track, but you can't take the track out of the girl, I guess. But running alone doesn't seem to counteract the legal profession's relentless quest to add chub around the middle."

As 3J talked, she noted that Megan continued to survey her.

"Well, pack or no pack," Megan said, "what I see is flat. And I see an athletic build. That's not what most of my lawyer clients show up with."

3J nodded.

"Other than abs, do you have other exercise goals?"

"I'd like to get stronger," 3J added.

3J knew a more accurate answer would have been that after her altercation with Woody Clarke's goon near O'Brien's, she decided to prepare herself for the next attack, if one ever came. That incident had left her feeling vulnerable. She needed a way to better defend herself. She considered carrying a gun, but she couldn't bear the thought. Instead, she concluded she wanted and needed to be stronger and faster. She knew that while she inflicted serious pain and injury on the man, she ended up underneath him rolling on the sidewalk as she tried to push him off. It was only a blackjack to the man's head administered by her process server Anthony Rosini that saved her life. She later learned the goon had a gun. It was a harrowing experience that still haunted her and would for some time to come, but she hadn't yet shared the experience with Megan. She figured she'd share the real reason for training soon enough.

In the meantime, they dove into the intensive thirty-minute exercise routine, working muscle groups in combination exercises conjured up by Megan as 3J's heart rate went up and stayed elevated. 3J looked at it as thirty minutes of hell, but good hell. She already felt stronger after only a month of the workouts, and she peeked at her belly in the mirror from time to time and hoped that outlines of the abs of old would reveal themselves soon. Her examinations revealed she had more work to do.

When they finished, Megan said, "See ya' in a few," as 3J gasped for air and could only wave goodbye. 3J left the studio for her condo, a quick shower, a change of clothes, and a quick meal, and more work after dinner at her kitchen counter hunched over her computer. As she worked, her thoughts returned to a common theme: the effect of the practice of law on life, and in this case, on a healthy body. She concluded it was no wonder she had a no-pack. Even as the practice of law hardened the mind, as a rule, it turned the body to mush. She committed herself to being an exception to the rule.

16

Amadi Browne recalls Monday, December 2, 2024

I sat in a chair with a dark hood over my head. I felt someone remove the duct tape from my wrists and then tape my wrists to the chair's arms. I smelled whiffs of a man wearing what might have been Old Spice cologne. Based on the strength of the fragrance, he was near me, but he said nothing. I wondered what in the hell was going on. I was a banker, not a criminal. I was a trusted member of the community, not a made man in some underworld family on the FBI's watchlist.

The cologne scent seemed to fade, and then it became stronger again. I heard shoes shuffling, and I had the sense he was circling me, moving away, and then moving closer again. I couldn't tell if he was assessing me, deciding what to do with me, or preparing to kill me. It was chilling.

Then I felt him suddenly grab the hood and lift it off my head. I looked around, absorbing as much information as I could: dimly lit room, no windows, concrete floor, an unfinished ceiling with joists revealed. Maybe an old locker room. My captor stared at me as I stared back at him. He was tall, light-skinned, and square-jawed with deep blue eyes. He had a handsome, rugged look about him, and he was wearing a black suit, tan banded fedora, and white shirt with a skinny black tie. I had no clue who he was.

"What's your name?" I demanded.

"Can't tell you that," he said with a very slight accent suggesting a Central or South American upbringing.

"What're you doing with me?"

"I'm just an observer. That's my job. I watch people. Like you."

My eyes got wide. "Watch me? Bullshit! You've done more than that. You've kidnapped me!" I yelled. "At gunpoint!"

"No. Please calm down, man. All I did was divert you to this room for a while."

"Divert? A while? Where the hell am I?"

"Can't tell you."

"Then who hired you?"

"Can't tell you that either."

"It's my brother, isn't it? Damn it, tell me! Who else would it be? He's a slumlord. This must be one of his buildings."

He said nothing.

"Do you know who I am?" I asked.

"Don't know. Don't need to know. Not necessary for me to do my job. Please don't talk. And don't move unless I tell you to."

"How would I move? You've got me tied up."

The man in the hat said nothing.

"So you expect me to sit here in silence?"

The man in the hat shook his head slowly. "Look, like I said, be calm. And please, be still. I need to go out. I'll be back soon."

He kept using the word "please" as if he was trying to be as nice as he could under the circumstances. My mind was racing, trying to think of everything and anything all at the same time. Then I remembered my new 5G iPhone. "Wait. Before you go, I need my phone near me."

"Please," he said again, this time with a gentle, pleading tone as he lifted his right hand, palm pointing upward. "You know I can't give you your phone."

"No, you don't understand. I need it *nearby* me."

"Why?"

"I have a pacemaker. It communicates data via bluetooth to the phone and then on to the doctors. They can monitor my heart remotely. If they don't get the data, they may think something's wrong with my heart and imprudently adjust the device remotely from the hospital."

The man in the hat looked around the room for a solution. "Look, it's powered on. I'm going to put it right over there in that locker. I've got a padlock here in my bag, so I'm going to padlock the locker. It's eight feet away from you. Close enough for your bluetooth to work, eh? But you won't be able to get to it. I'll come back with a charger cord so it can stay powered on."

The locker was old, but it was made of steel and appeared to be sturdy. And it was affixed to a concrete pillar in the room.

I couldn't believe what I was about to say to this kidnapping, blue-eyed hulk of a criminal. "Thank you."

"*De nada*—you're welcome."

As the man placed the phone in the locker, he asked me for my password. After a few minutes with it, he told me he'd put it in "do not disturb" mode and silenced it.

I couldn't believe it, but I said it again. "Thank you."

He nodded, said, "Of course," touched the brim of his hat as he departed, and left me alone to try to sort out what in heaven's name was happening to me. I heard the door lock behind him. Two tumblers. I was alone in a room, kidnapped by someone in a tan hat right out of a forties movie. I was being held somewhere against my will for some unknown purpose and for some unknown period, all at the direction of some unknown person. I knew much too little. Still, I knew just enough to conclude this was all Jordan. It had to be. It was shocking how far he would go to further whatever plan he had in mind.

17

JORDAN SAT AT his desk at the bank, opened his personal laptop, and closed the door as it booted up. He logged on to a tiny remote wide-angle camera he had set up in the room where Cruz had taken Amadi. He wanted a way to monitor the situation and observe the unfolding success of the captivity part of his plan. With some minor adjustments, the picture came into focus. A click or two and he would also hear what was transpiring in the room. At first, he saw his brother, hood over his head, hands tied to a chair, with Maximilian Cruz circling him, not threateningly, but more in what appeared to be curiosity.

He then saw Cruz remove the hood. He listened to Amadi question Cruz, and he was pleased Cruz followed instructions precisely: Do not engage, do not converse, and do not answer questions. He turned away from the live feed before Cruz and Amadi discussed the pacemaker and the phone, distracted by someone on the street passing by his office window. Several moments later, he turned back to the video and watched Cruz depart, leaving only his brother in the chair looking unnerved and then slowly, anxious.

So far, Jordan's plan, at least the part he had finalized in his mind, was working to perfection. All he needed now was to decide how this all ended and then how he would make the ending happen.

18

Wednesday, December 4, 2024

Days passed. 3J still had heard nothing from Amadi. She'd made more texts and calls with no response. He was missing, vanished into the Great Plains wind or wherever Kansas City bankers went when they disappeared off the grid. Bella and James reported they'd driven by Amadi's house in Fairway, a Kansas border town a short distance from downtown Kansas City, Missouri, but the house was dark. They saw Amadi's car at the end of the driveway, almost as if he'd started to leave but never did. The garage was empty, and several days of mail was stacking up in the mailbox by his front door.

The Abode loan matured at the close of business later in the day. Jordan's ticktock countdown for loan enforcement had thirty days left.

Early in the morning, Commonwealth served the Franklins and Abode with a lawsuit it had filed alleging the bank had made the most recent line of credit advances erroneously and bank employees without proper authority implemented the improvident advances. The suit sought return of the money and alleged Abode breached the lending agreement by moving the funds to a different bank. In the papers, the bank also reserved the right to sue Amadi

Browne for breach of his fiduciary duty to the bank, both by honoring Abode's last draw requests and failing to block the transfer of Abode's money. Hannah Carson had signed the complaint. She was a young litigator who had made the "Forty Under Forty" list in the *Kansas City Business Journal* honoring up-and-comers in the business community.

Hours later, the Franklins were on the phone with 3J and Pascale. "No authority my ass," James said bitterly. "Like we told you before, we follow the law, and we certainly don't breach our contracts. Jesus! Everything done was completely proper!"

"The lawsuit is a real Hail Mary," 3J explained. "The bank had approved the land purchase advance and the construction budget advance weeks ago. The bank rescinded none of the approvals and the loan documents don't require Abode to bank at Commonwealth. But the lawsuit certainly gives us a sense of what Commonwealth and Jordan have in store.

"Commonwealth won't be sitting around waiting for your next move. The bank is telling us it will be proactive, and likely, by tomorrow or the next day, it will sue Abode and you both for the amount owing under the line—almost twelve million plus interest and attorneys fees. Consistent with an aggressive approach, we'd expect the bank to try to foreclose on its collateral and take over receipt of cash from homeowners under the mortgages."

"3J, Bill, how do we stop the bank?" Bella asked.

"While you could fight the lawsuit in court," 3J admitted, "that would be expensive, and it wouldn't fix the problem of the Abode loan maturing later today or the fact that there won't be a renewal. We expect the bank will next write every homeowner and tell them to start paying the monthly mortgage payments to Commonwealth and not to Abode. It'll be chaos when that happens. Some will pay Commonwealth. Many won't pay anyone. Either way, Abode's stream of money will dry up instantly."

Pascale picked up the thread. "Folks, we think the only viable option is to put Abode into Chapter 11 and do the same for the two of you to protect you from enforcement of the guaranties.

"Us too? Why us?" James asked.

"The bankruptcies will stop the lawsuit from proceeding and keep the money flowing to Abode," 3J said. "It will also give us all time to try to find a take-out lender to replace Commonwealth. And it may give us a friendly forum for Amadi to take on his brother if we can find him. We've simply got to find him."

"How quickly can we file these bankruptcy cases?" Bella asked.

"We're ready to go," 3J replied. "Come in and sign, and we can file today and stop this lawsuit."

"We're game," James said. "We're on our way in to sign."

When the call ended, Pascale looked at 3J and shook his head. "Shit. This got real ugly real fast. No Amadi, no replacement lender, a big lawsuit, and the need for quick-filed bankruptcy cases."

"I can see if Ronnie has any time to dust off his old vice squad clothing and look for Amadi. Maybe he can file a missing person report with the police as well."

"It would be great if he could jump in. He had decades of experience in this town finding drug dealers, gunrunners, and pimps who didn't want to be found. I'm not sure any of his targets were bankers, but he certainly knows this town and every nook where a kidnapper might stash someone. Still, we don't have much for him to go on."

As 3J reached for her phone to dial Ronnie Steele, Pascale asked, "What about Aaronson and Rome?"

Aaronson was Moses Aaronson, the New York City private investigator who had helped 3J and Pascale in two prior bankruptcy cases. Rome was Aaronson's technology sleuth. "Maybe they could help develop some background information and a profile of Jordan Browne and see if there is any online information hinting where Amadi might be."

"Good idea," 3J said. "While I reach out to Ronnie, why don't you see if you can set something up with Moses and Rome for this afternoon."

"Maybe we should have the Franklins on both calls. They'll have a much more complete dossier of background information for Ronnie and the investigators than us."

3J dialed Ronnie and put him on speakerphone. She explained the need to get the Franklins on the line as well, and while she put Ronnie on hold, she connected with the Franklins and explained the purpose of the call. The press of a button joined everyone on the line.

Ronnie explained he had a few days off coming to him and would be happy to help. The Franklins then provided Ronnie with a detailed overview of the Browne family's history, the bank, and what they knew about Amadi.

"What about Jordan? What do you know about him?" Ronnie asked.

"Much less than we know about Amadi," James said. "Why do you ask?"

"Truth is, if you want to find the kidnapper—and you should view this as a kidnapping—find the person with the most to gain. Relatives or someone familiar often commission the abduction. Here I'm thinking Jordan. From what you've told me, he seems to have the most to gain with Amadi out of the picture. Power and money could motivate him to take action."

"Unfortunately, until the very recent unpleasantries with Jordan, we really had no contact at all with him. Amadi was our sole point of contact at the bank," Bella explained.

"Understood," Ronnie said. "Let's see what I can dig up on both of them. 3J, Bill, are you going to enlist anyone else to help?"

"Bella and James have approved getting Moses Aaronson and Rome on it as well." Steele had worked with Aaronson and Rome on the Woody Clarke case, so he didn't need any further explanation.

"That would help immensely," Ronnie said. "Any information

and leads will be greatly appreciated. I'll drop off now, finish up here at the bar, and then get started."

3J said she had collected some information about Jordan and would text a summary to Ronnie. After the call ended, Pascale reached out to Moses Aaronson to set up a conference call.

"Do you need any help with the bankruptcy papers, 3J?"

"Thanks, no. They're mostly ready to go. The Franklins are amazingly organized and responsive. I wish all my debtor clients were like that."

By late morning, the Franklins had signed the bankruptcy papers, and 3J's team filed them over the lunch hour. Initially, the clerks assigned the cases to Judge Felicia Harrison. 3J called Judge Harrison's chambers to ask for a hearing the next day to consider the usual preliminary matters. But Judge Harrison's law clerk told her the judge would not preside over the cases. Judge Harrison had grown up in one of the Abode houses, and she was concerned about the appearance of impropriety and whether she could be impartial deciding Abode and Franklin legal issues. So she recused herself.

That meant the cases would have to be reassigned to a different judge. Later in the day, 3J learned the chief judge reassigned the cases to Judge Daniel Robertson. She called his chambers to obtain a hearing date and time and learned he had set the matters for Friday at 1:30.

Under the bankruptcy code, debtors couldn't compel a lender to loan more money, so there would be no further borrowing from Commonwealth, and anyway, the line had matured. The flow of money from Commonwealth had dried up. Whatever amount Abode had not borrowed under the line was no longer available. But the bankruptcy cases had neutralized Jordan's countdown. While his countdown would eventually expire, the bankruptcy law prevented the bank from enforcing the loans, contacting homeowners, or taking back collateral. It created a temporary standoff.

But 3J and the Franklins also had only nine days left to find

Amadi and somehow have him exercise the repurchase option to buy back the bank stock. 3J worried there wasn't enough time. Therefore, the bankruptcy cases would not provide the needed relief and solution. "And there's not a damn thing I can do about it," she whispered to herself.

Pascale returned to 3J's office and learned of the bankruptcy filings. "For now, Abode keeps building homes," he said. "Six more first-time homeowners get their piece of the American dream. Easy peasy, right?"

"The first days in bankruptcy are supposed to be the hard parts, but in this case, they look easy compared to our need to find Amadi, and soon," she replied. "Then if we find him, we have to hope he wants to buy his stock back and has the ability to do so."

Two hours later, 3J, Pascale, and the Franklins were on a call with Moses Aaronson and his tech guru Belita Davies, nicknamed Rome. Aaronson was an investigator of some repute, although he had disdain for the title "private investigator." Thought of as an investigator's investigator, he had an impeccable reputation for solving mysteries. He lived in New York City near the Flatiron Building and Madison Square Park, off Broadway, but he had quickly learned in the digital age, his team's services were useful, and he could provide them to clients all over the world.

Rome, who lived in London, was Moses' high tech guru and a graduate of Bryn Mawr College. She was a wallflower in real life, but she flourished in the online cyber world of the internet and beyond. Her digital investigatory skills were legendary.

3J and Pascale had worked with them on two prior matters, most recently when Moses and Rome cracked a Civil War era cypher just in time to save 3J's life and the lives of others.

"Good afternoon, my favorite Kansas City legal team," Moses said warmly. "I hope you are both well and back to your daily grinds after our last adventure together. What brings you to my virtual office?"

3J explained the Franklins' loan situation and the troubling disappearance of Amadi Browne. The Franklins provided the same background they'd given Ronnie Steele. They shared Steele's comment that Amadi's disappearance should be viewed as an abduction, and as a result, in their view, Jordan Browne was a prime suspect.

"Is it possible Amadi Browne is somewhere and does not wish to be found?" Moses asked.

"Yes, but we think that's less and less likely," 3J said. She explained her meeting with Amadi, his return call, and his desire to meet again.

"Very well," Moses said. "Rome, what are your thoughts?"

"I think the best place to start here is to sleuth on the internet to develop information. Active websites, news outlets, journals, educational background, business ventures, archived information, and a quick look on the dark web would be in order. Considering Ronnie Steele's observation, we should include both brothers in the deep dive."

"I agree," Moses said. "While Rome does her deep dive, I can reach out to my real estate contacts and see about Jordan Browne's holdings and other companies he is involved in or owns an interest in. While mere speculation at this point, if it turns out he abducted his own brother, he must have his brother hidden away somewhere. That will likely be someplace familiar to him and perhaps in a nondescript structure he owns an interest in. Someplace he is comfortable with and to which he has ready access. Perhaps in an out-of-the-way neighborhood in your metropolitan area."

"Anything you can come up with, folks, would be a tremendous help," 3J said. "Feed us what you find as information develops."

"Of course," Moses replied. "Of concern, most abductions have a simple path: payment of ransom in exchange for release of the abductee. There have been no ransom demands?"

"None, Moses," 3J confirmed.

"A gap in the analysis. Hmm. Then why abduct Amadi?"

3J explained the stock repurchase deadline.

"Fascinating," Rome said.

"Right now, we are completely in the dark," Moses said, "but with some targeted sleuthing and inquiries, we should start to shine a light, and in doing so, we can unravel this mystery. That is, of course, what we do on the Moses Team. We shine the light of discovery on the dark alley of deceit."

When the call with Moses and Rome ended, 3J and Pascale stayed on the line with the Franklins.

"Those two folks seem a bit quirky," Bella said. "But you've worked with them before?"

"More like a little eccentric," 3J admitted. "But I'm here talking with you for no reason other than they are the best at what they do, and they literally saved my life."

"Well, if they're *that* good, I'm glad they're going to be involved," James said. "We need all the help we can get . . . and quickly."

19

After the call ended, Rome sat on her bed with her back resting on the wall and MacBook in her lap. She developed a list of searches, first for Amadi Browne and then for Jordan Browne, and began with some preliminary information inquiries, quickly learning Amadi Browne was hardly a private person. His years as the head of the bank required him to be a public figure in the Kansas City community. Based on the staggering number of search hits, she concluded he relished the role. He was everywhere: charity events, groundbreakings, political gatherings, membership lists in numerous Chambers of Commerce on both sides of the state line, church fundraisers, guest appearances at sporting events, and on and on. It appeared Amadi Browne never slept.

She found his LinkedIn profile and discovered thousands of connections. Almost nothing seemed to escape his attention and almost everything worthy of a benefactor drew his support. Parsing the vast amount of information about him would be challenging, especially since it was difficult, if not impossible, to determine what might and might not be relevant.

She learned he graduated from Colorado College in Colorado Springs with a dual degree in American history and American literature. Afterward, he immediately returned to Kansas City and worked at Commonwealth, training under the close eyes of his parents. He had a college era Colorado criminal record of trespassing and disorderly conduct, apparently related to a campus sit-in to protest the school's alleged lack of commitment to minority communities, including those with students at the college.

He drove an electric Nissan Leaf and had lived in his Fairway house for decades. After the death of his wife and daughter, he stayed in the house and appeared to live alone. If anything, the volume of Good Samaritan articles and information about him increased after their deaths. Amadi must have been filling the gaping hole left by their deaths with even more community service.

Her searches of Jordan revealed a much different story. After he graduated from Washington University in St. Louis with a BA in economics, Jordan returned to Kansas City and seemed to drift. For many years, he didn't work at the bank. Rome couldn't tell if that was his choice or his parents'choice. She wondered if he had forged his own path or if his family had ostracized him.

She found small bits and pieces of information showing he worked in real estate, first selling commercial properties and then working for a title company, closing large commercial transactions. Eventually, he'd worked for different Kansas City agencies promoting inner-city real estate development to combat urban blight. In the last job, he didn't last long. Perhaps he was fired or resigned because he was uninterested in the work he was doing. At some point, he left Kansas City and moved to Chicago, where he worked for a financial tech start-up specializing in the crypto wallet industry, a place where investors could store, buy, sell, and spend their cryptocurrency.

For a long while, he appeared to have nothing to do with Commonwealth. His parents ran Commonwealth and then passed the management torch to Amadi, making him bank president. Shortly before they died, Jordan returned to Kansas City and began to work for the bank . . . and his brother. Unlike his brother, he didn't seem to use the bank platform to be out in the community. He appeared to be a private person and not an ambassador for any causes.

After his parents died, he came out of his shell and gave interviews to the local business journal. He explained his focus was on bringing the modern world of lending and crypto to Commonwealth. He wanted to open the bank up to new, cutting-edge business territories. In one interview, he told the reporter that expanding the bank's reach would mean moving away from its model of community service to the inner city. Rome noted several letters to the editor challenging that idea. She also found a number of Twitter posts in which it was apparent Jordan's view of the bank's future was unpopular, at least among active Twitter account holders.

Rome located another business journal article published several weeks later in which the same reporter tracked down Amadi for comments. It was not a long piece, nor were Amadi's reported comments extensive. At that point, he seemed to be mostly avoiding a public argument with his brother. The paper quoted him as saying, "My brother and I are different people with different ideas for the future and different commitments to the community. Suffice it to say that under my guidance, Commonwealth will stay the course. My parents and my ancestors would expect nothing less."

She found it interesting, perhaps Freudian, that Amadi referred to his parents and ancestors as "my," not "our." The brothers were quite different and the follow-up interview provided some small insight into what might be brotherly discord.

She noted their parents' wills had been probated in Jackson County, Missouri, state court. From the probate filings, she confirmed their parents had left the principal asset—ownership of Commonwealth—to Amadi and Jordan, with Amadi holding the majority share. She assumed the unequal division of ownership was meant to assure that Amadi would continue to run the bank, and she wondered if the disparate treatment fueled an already simmering resentment deep inside Jordan. She had to assume it did.

Rome searched on several background information websites and found Jordan had no criminal record, no record of any marriages, an expired Missouri commercial real estate license, an expired Kansas real estate appraisal license, and an active Kansas driver's license. She found a real estate record revealing a house he owned and where he presumably lived off High Drive in an old section of Leawood, Kansas, an affluent, close-in suburb of Kansas City. He drove an Audi and was a member in good standing at the Kansas City Country Club in Mission Hills, Kansas.

She pivoted to researching the club, and to her surprise, she discovered it had an infamous past. In 1990, Donald Hall, chairman of Hallmark Cards, nominated Henry Bloch, founder of H&R Block, as a new member of the club. The club declined to admit Bloch, a billionaire and Jewish Kansas City entrepreneur. When one of Kansas City's own, legendary professional golfer Tom Watson, whose family was Jewish, learned of the snub, he publicly resigned from the club as a matter of conscience. Based on this history, she found the admission of Jordan Browne as a club member in 2019 curious. She wondered if it was progress or tokenism that led the club to admit a Black businessman.

She found the *Kansas City Star* and *Kansas City Business Journal* articles briefly confirming the stock sale from Amadi to Jordan, but with no details. Last, she found guest contributor articles Jordan wrote about the future of FinTech, short for financial technology, in banking, and in particular, cryptocurrency. He wrote that in 2021, US Bank launched a bitcoin custody service for institutional investment managers, and in 2022, Wells Fargo offered crypto funds to wealthier customers. Other banks soon followed suit, and FinTech had quickly become the darling of many banking industry institutions. He described the move to FinTech as the future of banking, lauding the eventual move away from a centralized banking system to a decentralized crypto system where no one person or institution would hold all the data or power. He dubbed it "power to the people banking."

To her surprise, she found a follow-up article written by Amadi challenging the notion of power to the people banking and arguing there would always be a place in the world for community banks, where the power to help others was centralized in the bank and the American banking system. He suggested that without centralized power in community banks, the "people" could never make a collective decision and urban cores would suffer. By the time of Amadi's response, he had obviously decided to go public, revealing his substantial disagreements with Jordan's view of banking.

How fascinating, she thought. Two brothers arguing out their visions for the future of banking in public journals.

She drafted a memo for Moses outlining the information about Jordan she had collected so far and emailed it to him, letting him know she would call to discuss a strategy to develop background information on Amadi.

While Rome developed background information about the brothers, Moses learned from his real estate contacts of a number of limited liability companies in which Jordan owned an interest, some of which owned real estate. Moses' contacts informed him the properties were all in rundown parts of Kansas City, and they questioned if Jordan was a slumlord.

He passed the information to Rome.

20

Amadi Browne recalls Wednesday, December 4, 2024

My days running from meeting to meeting until all hours of the day and night had abruptly ended. I wondered if it was temporary or a permanent condition. Sitting had replaced the running. I was alone in that room down two flights of stairs. I recalled that the last staircase had fifteen stairsteps. I didn't know why I counted the steps as we walked and why I still remembered that fact. Maybe it was the banker in me. I seemed to always remember a mass of numbers from any financial statement I reviewed. It was both a blessing and a curse, I guess.

I exercised my powers of observation. The room—my room—was a rectangle, maybe ten by fifteen. There was a fridge, a sink, a connecting bathroom, a table, and one solitary locker now padlocked and firmly attached to a concrete pillar, within which lay my silenced mobile phone. I saw a steel door to the outside world with two locks, a cot, a small, empty bookshelf, a concrete floor, and walls painted gray. No windows, no television, no connection to the outside world. Nothing to do and no food to eat. There seemed to be electricity and enough heat that I wasn't cold but not enough to make it comfortable.

I pondered my new home. That led to a series of questions I

couldn't answer and wasn't sure I could ever answer: Why? Why me and why now? Where was I? For how long? Who was this hat man working for?

I pondered why the door to the room locked from the outside. It was almost as if someone designed the door to hold a person captive. I'd seen my share of Hollywood portrayals of gangsters. They always seemed to be guys who restrained their captives in a chair in an out-of-the-way location and beat the captive from time to time, demanding information. "Tell me what I need to know!" The captive would decline or knew nothing, and someone would slap the captive across the face. In the movies, you never learned much about the room. Only enough to know it was out-of-the-way, and of course, that it locked from the outside, like this one.

I wondered if my room in the basement was a place where some mob boss brought his prey to beat him senseless and then kill him. Was my captor—I had begun to call him the hat man—going to take care of me until it came time to kill me and then discharge his duty? He didn't seem like a cold-blooded killer type, but then again, I didn't really know what a cold-blooded killer type looked or sounded like. I was just a banker.

My mind raced with more questions and no answers. Would anyone ever be able to find me, dead or alive? How could they? Was anyone even looking for me? I had lots of things to say to my brother. How would I ever communicate with him? I wondered what the lawyer for Abode, Ms. Jones, must have thought when I never showed for our Cliff Drive meeting.

That I had more and more questions wasn't surprising actually. Sitting there, all I had were those four walls and my thoughts. I could list all the questions my brain could think of, but what I needed was answers. Information. That was a banker's approach to solving the problem. Facts and data. I needed more of both from the hat man. Lots more.

21

Thursday, December 5, 2024

THURSDAY MORNING, RIGHT after midnight, London time, Rome called Moses, wanting to brainstorm a strategy. She explained her successful searches of Jordan and Amadi, explained the breadth of information available about Amadi, and told him she wasn't sure what she was looking for. Unless she could narrow her search to defined topics, she could not use a search app to find hits.

"My dear Rome," Moses replied when she was done, "it appears relatively easy to build a profile of Jordan Browne because there is only a modest amount of information available. A self-proclaimed FinTech man of the future. A bit in your area of concentration. But Amadi is a different matter. Based on what the Franklins and you have told me, we know he is a passionate community activist, leading to internet information overload. Hmm. But I do not think we are looking for a true profile of Amadi."

"Then what are we looking for, Moses?"

"It seems to me there are two directions to follow here. He might have intentionally gone off the grid because he had second thoughts about proceeding forward with Ms. Jones. In that case, nothing nefarious happened. He simply changed his mind, and to implement his change in heart, he went somewhere he thinks no one can find him, perhaps because he could not face Ms. Jones and the Franklins, given his decision not to help. Meaning, in this scenario, he is safe somewhere he believes no one can find him and, importantly, he does not wish to be found."

"Do you think we should pursue this scenario?"

Moses paused to sip his pu-erh tea. "A bank president would have no problem directly telling Ms. Jones, 'No, I cannot help you.' *This* bank president speaks all the time and tells people what is on his mind. So, in order to triage here, I think the answer to your question is no. I find this scenario highly improbable and one to set aside rather than pursue."

Moses looked over to his mixed breed, rat terrier, rescue canine companion, Emily, resting on his bed. She was mostly white with a brown muzzle that was graying as the years rolled on and had an off-center brown spot near her tail. Emily had rules. Whenever he spoke, she watched him. Studying Moses was her purpose in life, her job.

Always at the ready and often watching over him from her perch on the bed, she had assessed the current situation and had satisfied herself that for the moment, all was safe and sound in his world and therefore in hers. Later, they'd go for their walk to Madison Square Park, where she'd hold court as passersby kneeled to rub her ears. In her own way, she was a big personality sent to Moses in a small package. But for now, she rolled over on her side, exposing more of her white, silky fur to the sun streaming in his windows, and sighed.

"The second scenario seems much more likely to me," he continued. "In this potential explanation, something terrible has happened to him. Here we can indulge some educated speculation and let our imaginations wander a bit. Who would benefit from harm to Amadi? Certainly, Jordan, but to be fair, perhaps others as well. A disgruntled borrower perhaps? Someone to whom the bank denied a loan? A homeowner whose house went into foreclosure? Someone unrelated to the bank to whom Amadi owes money? There are many possibilities, although in my gut, I think we should focus on Jordan. What is your gut telling you, my dear Rome?"

"My gut tells me that the world is driven by money, power, and greed. Jordan's vision is to march a bank he controls into what he sees as the crypto future. In doing so, he will generate fame and fortune, largely for himself as the primary bank owner. Amadi stands in his way. Amadi can take back control of the bank. Ergo, Jordan resolves he must manage Amadi."

"Splendid. I completely agree. We must now set out to marry fact with educated guesses and determine how Jordan would 'manage' Amadi. Simply holding him captive for a limited period might be some form of a plan, but it would be far from a well-thought-out plan because it offers no endgame at all. Most kidnapping has an endgame of a ransom payment in exchange for the release of the captive. This would not seem to be the endgame here. Also, and quite fundamentally, if Jordan abducted Amadi, we must try to deduce where he would stash his brother in the short-term."

"I am still confused, Moses. What am I looking for?"

"We have made some assumptions about the 'what'—kidnapping—and the 'why'—the usual human trifecta of money, greed, and power. Let's accept those assumptions as fact and start with the 'where,' Rome. I sent you information about real estate holdings. Start there but keep reading as well. Something may spark a glimmer of daylight on the horizon to replace this sea of darkness that engulfs us for now."

~

Pascale and 3J sat in the back of O'Brien's bar at their usual weathered oak booth waiting for their lunch. The Thursday lunch crowd was slow in arriving and quiet by O'Brien's standards. They sat in silence, both thinking about the Abode case and the missing bank president. As their food arrived, they ate in silence. Near the end of the meal, the conversation picked up.

"You know, 3J, I've been thinking. If someone kidnapped Amadi in the hopes the deadline to exercise the repo would pass, it might work unless it was Jordan behind all this."

"How so?"

"If it was Jordan, he would be interfering with Amadi's performance of their contract. You can't sign a contract and then do something, like kidnapping, to make the other side's performance impossible."

"That would mean the kidnapping would be ineffective if someone could prove Jordan was behind it," 3J said, picking up on Pascale's comments.

"Exactly. The expiration of the repo would be null and void and the law would permit Amadi to buy the stock back even after December thirteen. But without the proof Jordan was behind it all, it just might work."

"This is scary stuff. If it's Jordan, it might also mean his best play isn't to merely kidnap Amadi. With Amadi alive, it would be easier to prove Jordan was behind the kidnapping. To really make this work, he'd have to kill Amadi and then get rid of the body and hope no one could tie him to his missing brother."

Pascale nodded.

"Lots and lots of doom in this case," 3J said with concern. "I'm fearful for Amadi's life, and I'm fearful for Abode's ability to survive without the Commonwealth line of credit. This one really worries me, Pascale."

"We keep pressing forward, 3J. Not only is that all we can do, it usually leads to something positive. In other words, we don't give up hope."

She nodded. She knew he was right. He usually was. But this time, she felt much more concerned than she did in her usual

Chapter 11 cases. She had bought into the Abode and Commonwealth mission and now felt personally responsible. If the mission failed, she would share in the failure. Somehow, she had to find a way for the mission to continue under her watch.

Rome turned to the list of properties Moses sent her. It was a welcomed diversion from the mountain of information about Amadi she had begun to read. She quickly located the properties on MapQuest, confirmed street addresses, found the street views, looked at the properties and the neighborhoods, and found basic information about the age, size, and condition of the properties. She also located tax records to determine if the LLCs were delinquent in the payment of real estate taxes.

There were nine properties in total. She learned all the properties were located in blighted areas in the city. Rome researched the buildings' occupancy rates and discovered four were empty and in significant disrepair. From all appearances, they were abandoned. Of those, three were over a year delinquent on real estate tax payments and one more had many outstanding city safety citations. The remaining five had tenants but were not in much better shape. She paused to research Jackson County, Missouri, tax records and discovered that while Jordan Browne's properties typically were behind in payment of real estate taxes, none had gone into tax foreclosure, so she concluded paying taxes as late as possible was a strategy, not happenstance.

She also considered that in addition to owning Commonwealth, Jordan had a side gig as a slumlord. Because there were so many properties in his portfolio, using an internet search to identify one where Jordan might have stashed Amadi would be hard, if not impossible. Amadi could be somewhere in any of the buildings, whether or not abandoned, or in none of them. 3J's team would have to go to all nine properties and investigate.

She wondered where she would stash someone she abducted. She concluded it would have to be someplace where no one would hear the person screaming for help. That could be in a basement or an abandoned building. She was able to access building records for the nine buildings, and all had basements, but one also had a subbasement—a basement area one floor below the regular basement, deep underground.

At noon, Kansas City time, she passed along all the locations and information to 3J and suggested that her team have someone drive by each of them and walk around and through as many of the locations as possible. She pointed out that the building with a subbasement might be promising. Maybe 3J's team would get lucky and hear someone screaming for help behind closed doors.

Since Moses sent her no information about properties Amadi owned, she searched and determined he owned no companies outside his interest in Commonwealth and appeared to lack any business side gigs outside of the bank. He was solely a banker and community activist and therefore an interesting contrast to his brother.

Having come up with some preliminary leads on where Amadi might be, she then moved her research station from her bed back to her small kitchen table and stared at the Google home page on her computer screen. No additional searches came to mind and no areas of inquiry presented themselves. She was a complete blank. She looked around her small flat for inspiration but found nothing.

She needed a walk. What else could she do but use the exercise time to try to reboot her brain? She figured she must be missing something. Maybe London's gray December sky and cold mist would shock her system into a revelation hiding in plain sight but lurking just beyond her grasp.

She threw on her coat and went down three flights of stairs to the street level and a short jaunt to the Chelsea Farmers Market, where she liked to go for investigation inspiration from a cup of fresh roasted African coffee and a French pastry that was mostly butter and sugar, the two major food groups in her life. She ambled around the market and watched the merchants at work and the patrons shopping as they ignored the weather. She well knew that if you wanted to enjoy living in London, you had to ignore the weather a good deal of the year.

This time, the walk yielded nothing specific, just as so many of her searches had revealed nothing specific so far. Sometimes *nothing* was the answer she was looking for, but not this time. Nothing was nothing, and it was unacceptable. Riding a modest sugar and caffeine high, she dejectedly headed back to her flat hoping she could somehow turn nothing into something. Like the alchemists of old, she had done it before. The laptop was her wand, and she simply needed to summon the magic.

Late in the afternoon, Maximilian Cruz, the man in the hat to Amadi, stood in Jordan Browne's bank office. At six foot four, he towered over Jordan when they both stood. While Jordan sat, Cruz appeared to be a skyscraper soaring into the clouds seventy stories above an adjacent three-story building. He took off his treasured fedora hat and cradled it in the crook of his left arm, held in place against his chest with his left hand.

"Status, please," Jordan demanded. Jordan had not told Cruz about the hidden camera he installed in the room to monitor the situation in real time.

Cruz looked up from his hat to Jordan and said, "Subject is restrained in the subbasement of the building you told me to stash him in. Right now, he's tied up in a chair, although the restraint is unnecessary because he can't leave the room. It's double locked from the outside. With your approval, I propose to let him roam free in the room. It's an old workers' locker room. There's a bathroom, shower, cot, and fridge, and I can bring him three squares a day."

Jordan contemplated the proposal for a moment and said simply, "Approved."

"Then there's the matter of his desire to talk with me. He's gabby, but so far, I've not engaged. He's only looking for comfort and information."

"Exactly. Excellent. He needs no comfort at the moment, and for him, chatter is comfort. He's been a talker from the moment he sat up in his crib. Been driving me crazy ever since. Let him talk to himself if he needs the company."

"Finally, he needs his mobile phone nearby."

"Yeah, right. I bet he does," Jordan said sarcastically. He looked down to papers on his desk reinforcing the summary dismissal of the request.

"No, no, Mr. Browne. You don't understand. I think he really does need it nearby. He says the phone receives information from his pacemaker and passes it along to his docs, who can monitor and adjust the device remotely if necessary."

Jordan slowly looked up at the man as he considered the pacemaker development. After a couple of moments, he frowned and shook his head with a look of disgust. "I see. The banker with a heart is now the banker with a bum heart." He continued to shake his head slowly. "Yeah, his wife and kid died and the next thing you know, he crumples in a heap, laying face down on the Folly Theater's tiled floor during an intermission for a Pat Metheny concert to raise money for underprivileged kids. Pat grew up here but doesn't play much in KC. My brother, activist to the stars, somehow convinced him to play for charity. Another one of Amadi's causes.

"Except this time, *he* was the cause célèbre. Patrons gathered 'round him as he lay on the Folly floor out cold. They called 911. The emergency medical techs carted him off to St. Luke's, and the docs inserted a pacemaker. The head doc said he was lucky he got to the hospital so quickly. Said the EMT's saved his life. Told me he could've died." Jordan shook his head. "Shit. What am I going to do with you, Amadi?"

As Jordan pondered, Cruz raised his eyebrows, as if asking for Jordan's decision.

"Not ready to decide on my endgame quite yet. I have some options. For the time being, is there a way to have the phone near him but somewhere he can't reach it?"

"There's an old locker in the room with an iron mesh door. It's attached to concrete and can't be moved. I've determined that the phone can be put in there and plugged into the wall so it doesn't run out of juice. A padlock on the locker would do the trick to keep him from accessing it."

"Does he have coverage down there?"

"Affirmative. A couple of bars."

"Yeah, okay. Let's do that. Let his docs monitor him remotely. Not too much longer before his right to buy back the bank stock expires, so this is all temporary. Anything else?"

"Not yet."

"Good work. Keep me apprised." Jordan reached into his desk drawer and removed an envelope. "Oh, one more thing. Give this to Amadi."

"What is it?"

"It's a lawsuit the bank filed that mentions him. My lawyer says you should serve him with the papers even though we haven't sued him just yet."

Cruz nodded with an anything-you-say look, put the envelope in his lapel pocket, and with the hat placed back on his head, ran his left pointer and thumb along the brim, adjusted it, turned, and exited. Jordan watched him leave. Cruz seemed a little too dramatic for Jordan's taste, but McFadden had told him Cruz did good work and would get the job done. For now, that was all he needed. That and a decision on what the endgame of the job would be.

22

After Cruz left, Jordan stepped out from behind his desk, closed his door, and sat down in one of the faded brown club chairs in his office and looked out his window to Cherry Street. The sun had set. Darkness bathed Cherry Street except for an occasional flickering light coming from a nearby streetlamp as it came to life for the evening. What would he do about the endgame? He had presented his crypto ideas to Amadi many times with excitement and passion, but his brother was always dismissive, as if he considered them not just lacking in soundness or creativity, but downright banal.

Jordan would explain that during Amadi's tenure as bank president, the bank's return on equity was abysmal—one of the lowest among Midwest community banks. He complained the dividends paid to the two owners would barely put a meal on the table. Jordan liked to quip at cocktail parties, "What's the difference between ownership in Commonwealth and a pizza?" His answer was, "Only one of them feeds a family of four, and it's not the bank." He often saved his biting joke for moments when Amadi was within earshot. He couldn't change the return on equity so he at least could use it to take shots at his brother.

When Amadi was at the helm of the bank, there had been a

constant clash between Amadi's desire to support the community and the prudent ways Jordan advocated to run a bank to maximize profitability. Their arguments turned into regular brotherly skirmishes without any hint of brotherly love. Jordan would point out that Commonwealth was a community bank and say, "Emphasis on *bank*." He would make his case over and over: The good Lord put banks on this planet to make money for shareholders.

Amadi would counter that there were plenty of banks in the world, but only one Black owned, Black run community bank in Kansas City and say, "Emphasis on *community*."

To Jordan's frustration, every time the brothers engaged in the argument, it ended in a stalemate, except that Amadi had the final say. He wondered regularly how any businessman could be so blind to progress and so indifferent to profit.

Now things had changed. As he sat in the chair in what had formerly been his brother's office, he said to himself softly, "Now it's my turn." Jordan was in charge now, and his goal was for Commonwealth to quickly become the most profitable bank in Kansas City. As he had told Amadi countless times, cryptocurrency was the salvation. Huge banks had begun to invest in crypto. He would bring crypto to Kansas City community banking, and in doing so, he would lift Commonwealth out of the community gutter and into the twenty-first century glitter of highly profitable banking. He would be on the front page of the *Kansas City Business Journal*, the business section in the *Star*, and someday, *Forbes*, the *New York Times*, and the *Wall Street Journal*. His pitch in Kansas City: Your local bank is now the place for your old-school greenbacks *and* your new age tokens.

By changing Commonwealth's model, the bank—*his* bank—would be at the cutting edge of financial institutions offering crypto products to customers. He hoped US Bank or Wells Fargo or Morgan Stanley would buy him out and he would make his mega fortune. He fantasized that maybe Commonwealth could grow large enough to acquire other banks.

Lord knows, he had tried to educate, convince, beg, berate, and threaten Amadi. In the past, he even considered suing Amadi, and now he was close to doing so. Nothing worked. Amadi was president of a twenty-first century bank conducting business the same way their ancestors had done in the nineteenth century. That was, until Amadi's daughter got sick and he needed cash and lots of it to try to save her. His niece. "Who would have thought a four-year-old's fatal ailment was the beginning of my ticket to crypto wealth?" he said to himself.

He cleared his mind of the history lesson. He hated history. He hated it when Amadi invoked it. He hated having to listen to Robbie McFadden recount it. He lived in the moment, and in this moment, he couldn't let Amadi buy back the stock and take control of the bank again. Fortunately, the repurchase option would be off the table soon.

He had told Cruz he had options once Amadi's right to buy the stock back expired. He liked the way it sounded when he said it, but the options were his endgame and he hadn't decided how to end the kidnapping game he had started. He also still held out the hope he could somehow finally convince Amadi to follow his crypto plan, and together, they would lead the caravan on the journey to the promised land.

He would give it one more try, but it wouldn't work. Amadi was, after all, Amadi. Someone else might use the incarceration time to see the error of his ways and join his brother on the path to riches. But not Amadi. No. History clouded his judgment and led him astray. Like history, Amadi would never change. So while he would have the talk with his brother one last time, he didn't consider it a real endgame option.

Soon enough, he would have to figure out what to do with his brother, and he might need further guidance from Robbie McFadden.

ꟹ

After the meeting with Jordan, Cruz headed to the building where he had stashed Amadi. It was a two-story, abandoned, nondescript building with a brick façade that had been built in the early 1940s just before the United States entered World War II. He wasn't sure who owned the building, but he assumed it must be Jordan. It still had running water and electricity, but Cruz wasn't sure for how much longer, especially since he wasn't certain anyone was actually paying the utility bills. The elevator didn't work, and he had no interest in riding it to the basement even if it had. He was confident no city engineer had inspected it in the recent past. His inclination was to hate all government regulations, but with elevators, he was more than fine reading a comforting certificate on the elevator wall saying it had passed inspection, a certificate he felt certain no city agent had posted on this building's elevator wall in some time.

He descended the flight of steps to the subbasement with its small labyrinth of hallways, some lit by the occasional naked bulb dangling from a socket hanging from wires and some in the dark. Fading, flaking gray paint covered all the hallway walls. At the end of one of the passages was a metal door with two locks on it to keep whatever was inside the room from getting out. What the hell was in the room years ago that needed locks to prevent someone or something from getting out? Why would anyone need a prison-like room all the way down there? He finished opening the two locks with keys Jordan had given him, swung the creaky door open, and slowly entered the room.

"I'm back to check in on you," he told Amadi. He walked over to Amadi, leaned over, and cut the restraints off Amadi's wrists with a switchblade. "And I have some good news. This room is yours. Bathroom, bed over there, shower, fridge, and three squares a day from me. I'll bring you some toiletries and a change of clothes as well. It ain't the Ritz, right? But it's better than a prison cell, and we can make the best of it."

"You say that as if you have some personal experience with the difference between a cell, these accommodations, and the Ritz, Mr. Hatman." Cruz didn't respond. "I guess I should be thankful for small favors."

"I got you and your phone covered too. Got a long charging cord, and we'll continue to keep the phone in that locker over there. Padlocked, but turned on so you and the phone are connected and your docs can attend to your bum ticker if need be."

"Thanks," Amadi replied. "Any chance I can have a radio or TV?"

"Negative, at least for the time being. But let me think about that some more."

"It sounds like the plan isn't to starve me to death? I'm hungry."

"I was about to head out for some chow for you and me. Any dietary restrictions?"

"None. What're you going to get?"

"It'll be a surprise. Can't tell you the cook or the restaurant 'cause then you might figure out where you are. But not to worry. You'll love the chow."

Cruz reached into his lapel and felt the envelope Jordan wanted him to give to Amadi. He considered delivering it to Amadi but decided against it. If he handed over the envelope, it would be patently obvious where he got the envelope and therefore, for whom he was working. He wasn't ready quite yet to share that information with Amadi. He'd have to raise the issue with Jordan at the next meeting.

"I'll be back in a flash," Cruz said as he left.

Within forty minutes, he returned with two bags of prepared food.

Amadi tore into one, and he began to eat enthusiastically, savoring the fare. "What kind of food is this, Mr. Hatman?"

"Cuban. Like *mi abuela* made me when I was a kid. Black beans and rice with mango—*frijoles negros y arroz con mango*. Side of the best fried plantains. My cousin cooks it up every day, but like I said, I can't tell you where, so don't ask me."

As Amadi ate, he surveyed his surrounds. "So this is where I'm gonna die, I guess?"

"Jesus, who said anything about dying?" Cruz replied, blinking and then frowning at Amadi.

"There's no other possible endgame here, right? I've seen you. I can identify you. Once I do that, you'll have to give up whoever hired you to keep me here."

"I don't know the endgame, but I ain't heard nothing about nobody dying. Certainly not down here. And I don't give up nobody. I ain't a snitch. Not good for business."

Amadi continued to eat. "So what's your story, Mr. Hatman?" he finally asked.

Cruz said nothing for a few moments. "Not supposed to be talking to you."

"Who told you that? How can it hurt? I'm certainly not going anywhere, so I won't be telling anybody what we talked about."

"Suppose not," Cruz said, considering Amadi's point and nodding his head. "I'm of Cuban descent. Both sets of my grandparents fled Castro and Cuba and moved to Miami and then somehow ended up here. They were schoolteachers in Cuba before the revolution. In Miami and then Kansas City, they were whatever they needed to be to put food on the table and keep the family together."

"Other than your command of Spanish, I'd never guess you were Cuban," Amadi said.

Cruz munched on a fried plantain and continued. "Yeah, I get that a lot. Parents were brown-skinned. I showed up light-skinned. I've always been able to pass in a crowd for White if no one looks too closely. But as soon as the crowd learns I'm Cuban, things change. Passing works only as long as the crowd you're standing in is ignorant. Once they know, some of them can turn on you in a split second. I started calling it 'passing until' a couple of years ago."

"I get that. I don't get to pass with this skin, but I sure know about those kinds of crowds. Where'd you grow up in KC?"

"Because both of my parents were brown-skinned kids of Cuban immigrants, it meant they couldn't seem to own a home in Kansas City. Too many obstacles. They couldn't buy a house in a White neighborhood and they couldn't get a loan to buy a house in *any* neighborhood."

"Redlining. Nasty business," Amadi said somberly.

Cruz nodded. "Redlining is definitely a nasty fuckin' business in this town and has been for decades. My parents moved around a lot because of redlining. They were everywhere in the city, but they really didn't live anywhere. They couldn't. Not a lot of neighborhoods wanted Latin-American folks living next door. Them red lines kept 'em out. So like so many other minorities—racial, ethnic, religious, sexual preference, disabled, you name it—we were invisible urban nomads, always moving. No friends. Different schools every six months. And I got pulled into the gang life. It became my new family, a place where I could belong, and I scared my parents. They probably didn't sleep for months. Eventually though, my folks found a house, and lo and behold, they managed to buy it. Lord, did that make them happy and proud. Changed everything for us."

"A house, huh? Where at?"

"A diverse neighborhood pretty near downtown off Charlotte—a melting pot neighborhood. Even some poor White folks. A little bit of everything. A run-down, seedy area of town: drugs, prostitutes, illegal guns. And lots of gangs hung out there. Gang disputes meant more dead people in the streets each morning than residents living in what was a miserable excuse for a neighborhood. The only people who lived there were people who had to 'cause they had no place else to be—no place else they *could* be.

"Then this outfit in town bought some neighborhood lots dirt cheap, cleaned them up, built some small houses, and sold them for a song to folks like *mis padres*—my parents. The outfit financed their purchase price to make it all happen. My parents didn't have lots of money, but it didn't matter. They still got the financing. Families moved in. Drugs, prostitutes, guns, and gangs left. That was the plan, I guess. And for *mis padres*, it was a piece of the American fuckin' dream, right? To replace the life their parents lost to Castro. More than twenty families from all kinds of places lived there. It was our own little United Nations, except the neighborhood actually seemed to work. Go figure."

"An outfit, huh? What was it called?"

"Hmm. I'm trying to remember. Something like Adobe, I think."

"Adobe? Nah. That's a software company, Mr. Hatman. I bet you mean Abode. Is that it?"

"Yeah, yeah, that's it. Abode. You know about it?"

Amadi explained his bank's financial relationship to Abode and his family's and Commonwealth's history.

Cruz listened closely. "So, what you're saying is, you're the reason *mis padres* got their house?"

"You might say I probably had a tiny part in it," Amadi replied with a weak smile.

"Well, I'll be damned. It's a small fuckin' world, ain't it?"

"Small fuckin' world indeed. And what's with the hat?"

Cruz smiled. "You like?"

"It's very becoming. Reminds me of leading men in old black-and-white movies. You know, Humphrey Bogart in *The Maltese Falcon*, that kind of thing."

"It's definitely a throwback. In those old movies, the hat man, as you like to call me, had a code of ethics. He always seemed to be respected. It ain't easy to get respect. You gotta work at it all the time. That's what I'm after. It's all about commanding the respect I'm entitled to."

Amadi nodded. They continued to eat in silence. Cruz looked up at Amadi for a few moments and then said softly, "Mr. Banker, ain't no one killing no one."

"Words to live by. A sobering thought, Mr. Hatman. Let's hope not."

❧

Jordan watched the beginning of Cruz's interaction with Amadi on his spy cam. All good. There were only a few days left until he was free of the repo. He continued to watch and listen in until Cruz left to get food. The conversation was less than riveting. Somewhere between minimal small talk and no talk. Certainly no communications that would give Jordan any concern, and more importantly, nothing to give Amadi any hope. Hope was the last thing Jordan wanted Amadi to have. Jordan didn't think his brother deserved it.

Jordan logged off and didn't log back on when Cruz returned with the food.

23

Friday, December 6, 2024

"PASCALE, I KNOW this will sound crazy, but I think we need to try to line up a loan for Amadi at the same time we're trying to find him." 3J had cleared papers off one of Pascale's worn club chairs in his office. She sat in it talking as she sipped her Earl Grey tea, her hazel eyes peering at Pascale over the edge of the cup she held in both hands.

"Geez, 3J. How exactly would we go about doing that?" Pascale asked as he rubbed his hand through his thinning silver and white hair. "He's not our client. He's not available to meet with any banks. It scares me to say this, but I'm worried he may not even be alive."

"I hear you. I'm worried too. But I think we have to grease some lending wheels so we can march him into a bank where he can sign the preapproved papers if we find him. And then he can buy back the stock. If we wait for all that until we find him, there might not be enough time left."

Pascale raised his eyebrows. "I've never heard of anything like that before."

"We know lots of banks around town. Tiên Luong and the other bank lawyers in the firm know even more. Add in Bryce Donaldson and there's even more we know. I bet we could make a short list of lenders who would listen to us. Maybe two that have some emotional investment in Abode and the Franklins."

"Emotional investment aside, what would be the pitch? 'Mr. Banker, if Amadi is still alive, and if we find him in time, and if he's willing to borrow, would you please loan him two million quickly?'"

3J closed her eyes. "Pascale, I know it sounds crazy. I know I sound crazy as well. But it's all I can think of, and we have to try."

Pascale frowned. Then he slowly smiled. "Well, it wouldn't be the wackiest thing I've ever been involved in. Close, but not the top of the list. Maybe we can call it more of a creative idea than a crazy one. Look, if you're in, I'm in, 3J. But it's going to take a very special banker to listen to us, let alone entertain any of this."

"The judge set the motions for this afternoon at one thirty. I'll do the legwork on this banker idea when I get back from court. As I think about this possible stock loan, maybe the best play we have here is to talk to the Franklins first. I'm going to find out from them what banks have supported Abode's projects in the past and in particular, which bankers. Who knows? Maybe we get lucky and there's a banker benefactor waiting to jump in and help.

"I also got information from Rome about buildings where Amadi might be. Nine of them. All properties in which Jordan owns an interest. I need to get the list to Ronnie. Amadi has got to be in one of those, right?"

"All rise. The Honorable Daniel Robertson presiding." Judge Robertson entered his courtroom with his law clerk, Jennifer Cuello, and took his seat on the bench several steps above the floor. His courtroom deputy clerk watched him get seated and announced, "You may be seated."

"Good afternoon, Ms. Jones. What brings us together today?" the judge asked cordially.

3J sat at one of the two large tables behind the podium from which she would address the court. The Franklins sat with her. Pascale remained at the office working on the stock loan issues. She rose, approached the podium, and said, "Thank you, Your Honor. Yesterday, my firm filed Chapter 11 cases for Abode LLC and its two owners, Bella and James Franklin. They have been involved in what have now become failed discussions with their lender to extend a twelve-million-dollar line of credit. The line matured two days ago, and the bank has made it clear it will shortly start to enforce its loan documents. Abode is the borrower and the Franklins guarantee the loan so we have filed bankruptcy cases for all three."

As 3J spoke, she watched only the judge. "Your Honor, this case is a bit different from other business bankruptcy cases we have filed in the past." The judge raised his eyebrows to show she had his attention. "Abode is a nonprofit company. As with most nonprofits, it is management organized and run. It has no owners. There are no equity holders."

The judge nodded. She then explained Abode's business and its mission in Kansas City. "For years, its trusted lender and partner in the fulfillment of the mission has been Commonwealth Savings and Loan Bank in Kansas City. Each December for over thirty years, the bank has renewed the line of credit. But over this past summer, the bank had a change in control and the new majority owner has decided not to renew the loan. Hence the need for bankruptcy protection to assure Abode can continue its important work in the city."

The judge seemed to mull the bankruptcy consequences of no owners. "Judge, we have some standard motions to present to you this afternoon for consideration."

"Thank you, Ms. Jones. Before we get to those, does anyone else wish to enter an appearance and be heard?"

A woman sitting in the row of seats immediately behind the

lawyers' tables rose. "Hannah Carson, Your Honor. Representing Commonwealth Savings and Loan Bank." Carson appeared to be in her thirties and had platinum blonde, shoulder length, straight hair.

"Welcome to my court, Ms. Carson," the judge said as he invited her to the podium with a hand gesture. "Do you have anything you would like to put on the record before we get to Ms. Jones' motions today?"

3J ceded the podium to Carson and returned to her chair at her table.

"Yes, Your Honor. My client is the largest creditor in these cases. We want to go on record and make it clear that the debtors will not use the bankruptcy code to institute further draws on Abode LLC's line of credit." Carson spoke rapidly. She sounded nervous, as if she wanted to finish her comments as quickly as possible and sit back down. "The bank will vigorously fight any such efforts."

Carson was not a regular in the bankruptcy court. As 3J listened, she wasn't sure she'd ever seen Carson appear for a client in any of the Kansas City bankruptcy courts. 3J wondered why the bank had hired counsel who did not specialize in bankruptcy for the Abode cases. While knowledge of bankruptcy law was not a prerequisite for appearing in bankruptcy court, 3J often mused that maybe it should be. She had seen other lawyers who were not experts in bankruptcy law appear from time to time, and many of them were without even a fundamental knowledge of bankruptcy procedure or law. When they addressed the court, they often unwittingly revealed they were in over their heads early in a case. Hannah Carson had just done the same. 3J saw Judge Robertson pick up on Carson's faux pas. She also saw the judge's law clerk raise her eyebrows in anticipation of the judge's response.

"Ms. Carson, I don't believe I've seen you in my court before," Judge Robertson said with an all-business look on his face. "Rest assured, Abode will not be forcing the bank to lend it more money under the line of credit, whether matured or not. Because, while bankruptcy law can do many wondrous things, one thing it does not permit is a debtor to force the lender to loan more money."

As he spoke, the judge's look morphed into the beginnings of annoyance. The cases had begun with a need for him to provide continuing legal education credits to an uninformed lawyer. And 3J knew this was not his favorite use of time.

Carson appeared to have picked up that the judge was lecturing her on a part of the bankruptcy code with which she was not, but should have been, familiar. "Very well, Your Honor. Thank you."

The judge nodded to Carson, indicating she could step away from the podium, and turned his attention to 3J. "Ms. Jones. Let's take up your motions."

3J presented the usual motions for the judge to approve: a motion to employ her firm to represent the debtors, a motion to allow Abode to operate in the ordinary course of business, and a cash motion asking the court to permit Abode to continue to use the funds deposited at Kansas City Bank and Trust. Attached to the cash motion was a budget setting out how Abode proposed to spend the money in the first ninety days of the cases.

3J explained that the cash would be used to build homes and that the homes became more valuable as Abode built and completed them. Therefore, she explained, use of the cash would increase the value of the bank's collateral, and the completed homes would be worth more than the cash it took to build them. She pointed out that the bank retained its lien on both the land and the homes and therefore continued to be protected. The cash motion did not offer to pay the bank any of the mortgage payments Abode received each month from homeowners. The unstated strategy was to allow the debtors to use the mortgage payments to increase their war chest to temporarily replace the draws under the lost line of credit.

The judge nodded, and for each motion, he asked for comments or objections. He looked over to Carson, inviting a comment or objection, especially on the cash motion, but she offered none. The judge forced a smile and approved each motion and asked 3J to submit an order to him to sign reflecting his approval. It surprised 3J that Carson allowed the judge to approve the motion to use the cash without objection. It was the rare cash motion that didn't draw some comment, requested tweak, or full-on objection from the secured creditor seeking post-bankruptcy payments. Carson's silence confirmed 3J's impression that she was definitely not a regular in bankruptcy court.

When the hearings concluded, 3J retrieved a business card from her briefcase and turned to introduce herself to Hannah Carson, but Carson had already stood and was near the door at the back of the courtroom. She was as fast on her feet exiting the courtroom as she had been speaking from the podium. 3J smiled to herself, wondering what Carson would be like as her adversary.

On the walk back to the Greene Madison offices with the Franklins, 3J explained her idea of finding a banker ready, willing, and able to lend money to Amadi Browne to buy back his stock as soon as anyone could locate him. She acknowledged how unusual it would be to make such a request of any banker and told them she hoped to identify someone so familiar with Abode and the mission that they would want to help in any way possible.

They approached the high-rise at the corner of Twelfth and Walnut, passed the stainless steel sign listing the building's occupants, featuring Greene Madison as the marquee tenant, and entered the elegant, granite-lined lobby. James stopped and said, "3J, I think we know just the banker to seek out. His name is Altair Galanos. He's an executive vice president at Bank of the Heartland, and he's been a tireless supporter of Abode over the years.

"On many Saturdays, he's shown up at work sites with a dozen bank employees to paint homes, nail boards, and raise the frames. Time and again, he's found contractors for us willing to donate their time. You name it. He's been there to pitch in. He's raised money for us. I even think he's been behind the scenes helping potential Abode homeowners with their finances, including offering them personalized financial education classes.

"His parents immigrated from Greece to Kansas City, and early on, they were one of our homeowners. When he helps, he tells us he's paying off a long-standing debt he owes to Abode. When he says 'debt,' we're pretty sure he means his life. He was a gang guy before his family got their home."

"Does he know Amadi Browne?"

"I'm not sure, but even if he doesn't, I feel certain he'll be willing to listen and help in any way he can."

During the discussion, Bella was quiet. When James finished, she said slowly, "I agree he'll help in any way he can. I simply don't know what those ways might be."

"All we can do is try, folks," 3J said. "Unless there's a reason not to, let's set up a meeting with Mr. Galanos, either at his bank or at our offices, as soon as possible."

The Franklins agreed and headed for their car in the adjacent garage as 3J made her way to the elevator ride up to her office.

Later that afternoon, 3J received an emergency motion to dismiss the bankruptcy cases, filed by Hannah Carson. She alleged that they were filed in bad faith and argued that without a line of credit, Abode would fail and the court shouldn't allow it to use up the balance of what it had borrowed from the bank right before the bankruptcies. Instead, she argued, the court should dismiss the cases and order Abode to return the money to the bank.

As 3J read the motion, she shook her head. Nothing was ever simple in the bankruptcy world. Then she sent the motion on to the Franklins, who were on a call with her almost instantly.

"Should we be worried?" James asked.

"Motions to dismiss are serious, but I think we'll be okay on this one. Normally, the judge focuses more on what you're doing during the bankruptcy case than what happened before the filing.

Here, what happened was the bank honored the request to borrow more money. Once he hears that, my guess is he'll side with the debtors and deny the motion."

"Should we plan on being at the hearing?"

"Please."

❧

After court, Judge Robertson and Jennifer Cuello returned to his office, and as he hung his robe and turned back toward his desk he said, "With no owners, Jennifer, Abode is going to have an easier time than many debtors proposing a plan."

"How so, Judge?"

"The absolute priority rule. We've had little controversy over that rule in our Chapter 11 cases so far, but I predict we may in these cases. It's an old rule, now codified. Under it, the plan can't allow owners to keep their stock or get paid anything unless the debtor pays all unsecured creditors fully plus interest.

"The rule came out of the huge public company bankruptcy cases in the forties and fifties. Because of it, either unsecured creditors got paid in full or stockholders lost their interest in a reorganized debtor. It's usually a real impediment to debtors paying less than one hundred percent to unsecureds since the people who run the debtor—usually the stockholders—want to keep owning and running the debtor.

"Here, since Abode has no owners—no stockholders—there won't be any impediment to unsecured creditors getting less than full payment because there's no one keeping any stock."

"Would those unsecured creditors include Commonwealth if its collateral is worth less than its debt?" Jennifer asked.

"You bet, Jennifer. I do wonder, however, if attorney Carson has any idea about that. She didn't even object to the cash motion. That's highly unusual. Based on her only comment in court today, she's obviously a little lacking in the broader bankruptcy picture, let alone the fine points."

"Do you need any preliminary research from me?"

"Why don't you find the nonprofit Chapter 11 cases from around the country and pull them? Review them and then summarize them for us."

"Absolutely, Judge."

"Also, if you can find any analogous situations that have popped up in Chapter 11, that would be icing on the cake."

When Jennifer left to start her new project, the judge sat at his desk and surveyed his daily papers to review. Instead of diving into the pile, he opened his laptop and did a Friday afternoon Google search on Hannah Carson. "Let's see who you are," he whispered to himself.

Later, shortly before they left the courthouse for the weekend, Judge Robertson read the motion to dismiss and discussed it with Jennifer. "Carson wants an emergency hearing. Let's give her one. Please set the motion to be heard on Tuesday and notify the parties."

"Will do, Judge."

Judge Robertson smiled at her. "No need for research on this one. Enjoy your weekend."

❧

That afternoon, 3J delivered the list of properties in which Jordan Browne's LLCs had an interest to Ronnie Steele and asked him to check out each one. She also asked him to make a missing person filing with the police. She told him time was of the essence, which, of course, he already knew. He decided to enlist assistance to surveil the properties from his former vice squad partner, Monica Sterling—Moe to her friends and colleagues. Like Steele, after a multi-decade career in vice, she departed for the private sector and began her new work in security. From time to time, she and Ronnie did one-off investigations for friends.

The two met before the end of the workday and developed a checklist of things to look for at each property. When Ronnie said they might get lucky and hear someone screaming in one of the buildings, she shook her head and replied, "Honey, where these buildings are located, I'd be shocked if we hear anything *but* screaming . . . and moaning and who knows what else. Walls are thin in those places. Doors even thinner. My guess is we're gonna find all kinds of folks living in the abandoned properties: squatters, folks with needles in their arms, pill poppers, and folks who don't know nuthin' about nuthin'."

Ronnie agreed but said simply, "We've gotta try."

24

Saturday, December 7, 2024

IT WAS JUST after midnight, London time. The feeling of being overwhelmed by a large volume of data didn't happen to Rome often. But this time, the data didn't just overwhelm her, it inundated her. While she found the information interesting, it added nothing within the context of the project. Her discussion with Moses didn't shine a light on any research strategies she could employ to help get her arms around the mass of information on Amadi Browne to which she now had access.

Her takeaway from the call with Moses was that he wanted everything because somewhere in the pile of everything was the nugget that would reveal where Amadi Browne was and why he was there. He was upbeat when he assigned the project. She was *not* upbeat after she had seen the volume of information. She feared she was looking for a needle in a haystack in an endless field full of haystacks without knowing which haystack to look in and with no sense of whether there was even a needle in any of them.

Moses seemed to think there would be something in the data linking Amadi and Jordan Browne in an unexpected way, an intersection between the two besides the bank and their familial ties. But now that she had parsed through a large volume of the Jordan

Browne information, she had found nothing connecting Jordan to Amadi in a suspicious, concerning, or nefarious way. They were brothers and they didn't get along, but there was nothing out of the ordinary.

Rome simply needed to find something in the Amadi information. She figured it would have to be something she'd find where she'd least expect it or of a nature that she'd never have guessed . . . or both. Something mundane that wouldn't jump out at her when she saw it. And to find it, she now resigned herself to the task she was hoping to avoid—a deep dive review of all articles written about Amadi Browne over the last several years. There were no apps she could use and no search terms she could employ. All she could do was an old-school manual review of everything. She knew most of what she was about to read would be useless. She only hoped she would find a nugget of information that would unlock the mystery.

For this part of the project, she needed help, and she reached out to a London friend and colleague on the Moses Team who had worked on other projects with Moses and Rome. There were few techies in the Western world who could count themselves as Rome's equal. Her friend, Byron Jackson, however, was one of those few. The project interested Byron and the challenge appealed to his desire to deliver results where none seemed possible. They talked and came up with a plan to divide and conquer the information. Her discussion with Byron gave her some much needed hope.

She poured a coffee, sat at her kitchen table hunched over her reading materials, and hunkered down to look at everything available about Amadi Browne. Across town in his small flat in London's Grove Park, her colleague Byron was doing the same at his desk. They had agreed to read for a few hours and then talk to describe what they had found and see if it triggered any leads for the other.

They talked four times, but nothing either of them had found set off any bells. They had plowed through information about Amadi's Colorado College education, his on-campus activism, numerous interviews about Commonwealth, and countless fund-raising events he'd attended. They found the obituaries describing his wife's death to cancer and his daughter's death to Gaucher disease. But they had read nothing providing any insight to his whereabouts.

Four hours later, Rome and Byron were on the phone again. By this point, when each described what they had read, it was with an air of resignation that nothing they had found was enlightening and a feeling of defeat that nothing they would find in the future would lead them into the light of discovery. They were in the dark, and it was an unyielding lack of illumination.

Rome reported she had found an article about the Folly Theater fundraiser during which Amadi collapsed and the EMTs rushed him off in an ambulance to a local hospital for stabilization, observation, and a procedure. Byron reported a similar article he read in a different news report. The one he read quoted Amadi's attending physician who said the procedure was the successful implantation of a pacemaker and described it as a small electronic device usually placed in the chest below the collarbone to help regulate a heart's electrical problems. The article explained Amadi's cardiologist recommended the pacemaker to ensure that Amadi's heartbeat didn't slow to a dangerously low rate.

They both knew very little about the pacemaker procedure, but neither looked at the nugget of information as vital in the search for Amadi. A health issue seemed to have no relation to his disappearance. The team in Kansas City had checked. He wasn't in the hospital. So they moved on to complete the reporting session and get back to the task of reading.

Rome recalled college friends who wrote her extolling how exciting a private investigator's life must be. If they only knew it was often hours and days of monotony as she tried to achieve the one fleeting moment of revelation.

She stood, stretched, and realized she needed to step away

from her laptop. She donned her trench coat and made her way downstairs again into the misty day. This time, she decided not to head to the Chelsea Farmers Market for a coffee, her usual routine. Instead, she used her twenty minutes—the maximum time she had learned she could be apart from her laptop—simply to walk the local streets past street vendors and performers, eclectic one-of-a-kind shops, and commuters who used bicycles as their primary form of transportation, oblivious to the rain as they darted between cars, taxis, and buses.

On the way back to her flat, she looked in the window of an electronics shop touting the latest stereo music device that extended the range of bluetooth connectivity. She ruminated about the pacemaker articles she and Byron had found, initially presumed to be irrelevant, and focused on the word "device." In her world, a device often meant connectivity she could exploit, but she knew little about modern pacemakers. What kind of device was it?

Once back home, she found several pacemaker manufacturers' websites explaining the latest technology. She moved her laptop to her bed, sat against the wall, and with the laptop in her lap, resumed the reading process, this time focusing on pacemakers. She quickly learned several things. First, the Food and Drug Administration required medical device manufacturers to develop a system by which they could track each device if its failure would cause serious harm to the patient. She continued to read and learned these devices had begun to use geolocation technology. The device implanted in a patient's body could now connect to the internet and allow an authorized person to locate it easily.

She also learned that health care providers and sometimes even concerned family members could remotely monitor a pacemaker. The manufacturers designed the pacemakers to transmit data—the regularity of the heartbeat, beats per minute, and location of the device. And of late, a medical team could adjust it remotely to correct irregularities. In other words, they could make remote tweaks to adjust the functionality of the heart. If this wasn't remarkable enough, in an unexpected twist, she even found a criminal case in which the prosecutor used the pacemaker data against the accused to prove both his location at crucial moments during the commission of the crime and heart rate to show physical exertion and anxiety levels.

It was a device, after all—another internet of things, IoT, connected to the worldwide grid like a smart appliance. So she wondered if she could hack into Amadi's device remotely and learn his specific location. Of course, the articles she and Byron found about Amadi mentioned nothing about the brand of his pacemaker. She would need more information about the device to even begin to consider such a hack, and she was concerned it wouldn't be one of her normal hacks, to the extent any hack could be called normal. Here she wouldn't be hacking into an IoT smart home device. This time, the hack would be of a medical device inside a human keeping the human's heart beating regularly and as a result, keeping the human alive. In effect, she would be hacking into a human, and that was the thing of science fiction novels.

It would be a risky proposition. Highly risky. Even if she could do it, one slipup and Amadi could die. As she thought about it, she concluded the prospect of rooting around inside a human was too risky, even for her prodigious technology skills, and she decided to eliminate it even as a possibility . . . for now. There were too many ethical issues presented by such a hack for even Rome to consider.

She returned to reading about pacemakers and learned one more thing. Like so many smart devices, the pacemaker could pair via bluetooth to the patient's mobile phone, which would then send the data to the patient's medical team even when there was no internet connection—bluetooth connectivity followed by 5G transmission.

Rome pushed her laptop to her bed, closed her eyes, and tried to concentrate. If hacking into the device was off the table, could she instead find Amadi because his medical team was likely using mobile phone bluetooth technology? Possibly. At least this idea presented no health risk.

She suddenly opened her eyes, sprang from her bed, realizing she had the beginnings of a way to find Amadi. She needed to run it by Byron.

"Byron, I am proposing to send a spoof text message to Amadi's phone," she said when they connected to discuss the case for the sixth time that day and she explained her idea. They were both familiar with the use of text messages to locate a mobile phone. In her plan, she would send a text to Amadi's mobile phone. It would be a spoof text to look like one sent from his cardiology team. The doctor who gave the interview in the article Byron had read would do. His name was Frey. At Amadi's end, the text would show it was from the doctor, not Rome.

The text would ask Amadi to click on a link in the text to confirm the pacemaker was causing him no problems and he was feeling good. It would describe the process as a new routine check to confirm all was medically sound from Amadi's end. When Amadi clicked on the link, Rome could use one of many online websites to geolocate where the phone was and get Amadi's location. The geolocation might not provide the precise location, but with any luck, it would tell everyone where he was within a several block radius.

They both estimated that the plan had no better than a fifty-fifty chance of success. There was a slew of variables they couldn't control. If it worked, it would be the most valuable piece of information gathered so far. But it was a complicated idea. They needed to make sure they had considered all angles and refined their idea before they presented the SMS spoofing plan to 3J, Pascale, Moses, and the Franklins.

"Are there other options?" Byron asked.

"We could try to use a cell site simulator like StingRay to determine the location of the phone as well, but I see problems and delays if we go down that path," Rome explained.

"Such as?"

"The StingRay device simulates a cell phone tower. In effect, it places itself between the phone in question and a cell phone tower and intercepts information about the phone—the IMSI, the international mobile subscriber identity. If the interception works, it could tell us the cell phone tower the phone is using. So like the SMS spoof, it wouldn't give us a precise location. But there is another problem. The IMSI information from a 5G phone is now encrypted. When law enforcement uses the StingRay interception, it gets the mobile phone carrier to decrypt the information for it. We wouldn't have that option, so we would have to decrypt it ourselves. No small task. I am sure I could decrypt it, but it would take time. So I have viewed the IMSI interception as a second choice to pursue if the SMS spoof fails. Do you agree?"

"Yes," Byron replied after a brief pause.

"Okay. So let's figure out what could go wrong with the SMS spoof."

"First, the obvious," Byron replied. "Amadi Browne's phone needs to be turned on."

"Correct. My thinking is that it may very well be on to enable it to continue to send information from the pacemaker to his doctor's team."

"That would mean the kidnapper was aware of the pacemaker issue, agreed the phone could remain on, and wasn't trying to kill Amadi, at least not yet," Byron mused. "So what do we think? The kidnapper left the phone plugged in but inaccessible to Amadi, and as long as the phone was on, it would generate no medical alert to the cardiology team to any medical problems? Seems plausible. It might also mean Amadi asked the kidnapper to help him out and the kidnapper complied."

"Correct. Amadi may already be dead for all we know. But we have to count on the kidnapper *holding* him for the time being instead of killing him. Maybe he is alive because the kidnapper needs him alive for some reason. Maybe he is alive because the kidnapper is his brother, Jordan, as I strongly suspect. I have to hope that since Jordan is likely new to the killing game, he may not have gotten up the nerve to kill his own brother. He may get there but has not yet. There are lots of variables and possibilities here. We do not know. But it all starts with the assumption that the phone is on for whatever reason."

"Okay. Next, if I were the kidnapper and left the phone on, I'd want it set to 'do not disturb' mode and silenced," Byron said. "Otherwise, the phone will ring for every call and ding for every text Amadi received over a period of many days. Amadi is the president of a bank and a public figure in the community. He must get hundreds of calls and texts each day. Unless the phone is in do not disturb mode and silenced, the phone will ring and ding away incessantly."

"Correct again. Do not disturb is a common feature, and it is my feeling that it is in widespread use. My hope is that Amadi and his medical team would have discussed setting up his phone to override or bypass it and the silencing so no matter what, the medical team could get through to him. If that is the case, when I send the spoof text, the phone will still ding, indicating it is a text from the medical team, no matter the do not disturb and silencing settings."

"Anything else you can identify that could go wrong?" Byron asked.

"Importantly, for this to work, Amadi or his captor will have to click on the link."

"Yes. Quite a weak link in our plan," Byron acknowledged. "The spoof text geolocation only works if someone clicks on the link sent to Amadi's phone. It is the only way."

The two were quiet as they considered how many things had to fall in place for Rome's plan to work.

"I think we have identified plenty of things that could go

wrong," Rome said. "So much has to come together for this to work. Too much. But there is no downside in the plan, and after all the data absorption of the last couple of days with nothing to show for our time and efforts, it is really all we have. I cannot believe continued data analysis will lead us to a better result.

"It is most definitely a long shot, but if it works, it will provide 3J and her team valuable information. It might be the breakthrough they need to find and save Mr. Browne. I will tell Moses what we have come up with and set up a conference call with everyone. You should be on the call, Byron."

When she hung up, Rome wondered what they would do next if this plan did not work. And she wondered if Amadi Browne would still be alive when they figured it out.

25

3J SAT IN her office on Saturday morning developing strategies for the bankruptcy cases. She wanted to examine Jordan Browne under oath and called Hannah Carson to agree on a date and time. Carson answered on the second ring. She was also working on a Saturday. 3J explained what she wanted and Carson said nothing in response.

"Hannah, are you there?"

"Yes and no."

"Yes and no what?"

"I'm here and the answer is no. An examination? If that's the same as a deposition, then I'm not going to agree to it. You've filed no lawsuit. You have no right to depose him, and I won't agree. No one worth their salt in court would. I've done my due diligence on you. It's an outrageous request."

Not the usual response from one bankruptcy lawyer to another 3J expected among the Kansas City bankruptcy bar. The bankruptcy bar was a small group and mostly congenial to each other. They knew when to agree and when to fight. A simple request to examine a witness was one of those times to agree. 3J wondered what due diligence Carson had done.

"Look, Hannah. That's not right. Please go look up Rule 2004.

I have the right to examine Mr. Browne under oath. A filed lawsuit isn't a predicate. You have the same right to examine the Franklins. In these parts, bankruptcy lawyers get together and agree on dates and times for these 2004 exams. They don't bother the court with a baseless opposition."

"I don't need to look up Rule 2004 or any other rule for that matter. The answer is no. If you want a favor, go ask the judge. I'll object and we'll see what he says. And anyway, I've filed my motion to dismiss the cases, and my guess is the judge will dismiss them summarily, so you won't need a bankruptcy examination of Jordan Browne or anyone else."

Trying to appease Carson, 3J continued down the path of what was quickly becoming a dead end. "Hannah. I have the right to examine the man. Your motion to dismiss has nothing to do with my right to examine him. He's the majority owner of the largest creditor. The judge already was a little cheesed off in court when he had to explain to you about the lending issue you raised. If you say no to me and I have to file something to get his permission, I'll have to say in the motion that I asked you to agree to dates and times but you wouldn't, further pissing him off."

"Not worried and I don't need you to tell me what makes the judge mad. And . . . I'm not going to talk about this topic anymore. Besides this ridiculous request, do you have anything else you want to discuss with me?"

"No. This discussion has been quite instructive. I think that's all I have for now. Good day."

After the call ended, 3J sat at her desk, flabbergasted. Now she'd have to file a request for an order to examine Browne. When she did, she'd have to explain in the request that she asked Carson to agree and Carson said no. Flat out no. Well, it's her funeral, 3J thought.

She opened her laptop and started typing. "Fuck," she said under her breath. Later in the morning, she filed her request and wished she could be a fly on the wall when Judge Robertson read it.

ණ

Cruz entered Amadi's room carrying Saturday morning breakfast for two. Meshuggah Bagels, the city's best take on New York bagels. "Meshuggah Bagels?" Amadi asked, staring at the bag. "You're feeding me better than I feed myself at home, Mr. Hatman."

Cruz smiled.

"Meshuggah's on Thirty-ninth Street. Am I near the Thirty-ninth Street corridor?" The corridor was a shopping area similar to the Crossroads District. It offered a colorful collage of culture and cuisine and was near the University of Kansas Medical Center campus.

"Good try. Not a chance, my friend. Meshuggah has more than one location. These bagels tell you nothing about where you are. You should assume that from now on, the location of the food and the location of this room have no connection."

"Can't fault a guy for channeling his inner Sherlock Holmes."

"I don't fault you. I don't want to encourage you either. You're just way off base."

Amadi sighed. "You know my name and I don't know yours. I find myself thinking of you as the hat man, and all I can call you is Mr. Hatman. Maybe a first name for me to address you by? After all, I won't know if it's a made-up name or a real one."

After a few moments of reflection, the man in the hat said, "What could it hurt, right? Max. Short for Maximilian. *Mi madre* told me it means 'the greatest.'"

"Well, Maximilian, thanks for the bagels."

"You're welcome. And it's real."

"Huh?"

"The name. It's not made up. It's real."

The two ate bagels and cream cheese in silence.

"What was it like growing up in an Abode home, Max?"

Max explained what home ownership meant to his mother and

father and how it got him out of the gangs and ended up keeping him in school through high school graduation.

"So how did you get into your current line of work?"

Cruz sighed. "I was the usual teenager—no longer in a gang but still the usual. I knew everything. I didn't need anyone telling me how to live or what to do with my life. Every seventeen-year-old knows better, right?"

Amadi nodded. Max's comments had him thinking of how different Jordan and he were as teenagers. Amadi had been the compliant, dutiful son doing what his parents wanted and following the life path his parents had charted for him. Jordan had been the rebellious, disagreeable son. The only thing Jordan managed to do that met with his parents' approval was attend college at a school of their choice. Never grateful for the Washington University education, he was always quick to point out that his parents selected the college. Besides the college, Jordan rejected any path his parents identified. If his parents wanted him to do something, the answer was no. Every time.

"My folks wanted me in school," Max continued. "I gave them that through the end of high school. A real school, learning from real teachers and then graduating, not the street school of hard knocks, learning from gang members and drug dealers and then dying. After all that, I figured I knew what I needed to know and found this line of work. Pays well, I'm good at it, my boss seems to appreciate me, I feel like I belong, and I try not to think too much about the consequences."

After a few moments, Amadi changed the subject. "I assume you know why I'm down here?"

"Do not. Need to know basis. Didn't ask."

"I've supported Abode and organizations like it both personally and through my bank." He paused and added, "Well, what *was* my bank. Abode builds the homes. I'd like to think we helped make it happen in our small way."

"It's good work, amigo. Honorable. Kinda like your own code of ethics without a fancy hat."

Amadi smiled. "Yes. No hat and no Ingrid Bergman." He bit into his bagel and shook his head. "It was good work, and now it's over."

Cruz raised his eyebrows, surprised by the comment.

"I'm down here because the new person running the bank wants to move in a different direction. He wants no part of the community. As step one in his plan to abandon everyone who needs help, he pulled the loan from Abode. Without the loan, there will be no more houses. Probably, no more Abode either. That simple."

"No more homes?" Cruz asked.

"No more homes."

"And all of that couldn't happen with you on the scene?"

"No, it could not."

"All by yourself you could stop the new head of the bank?"

"I'm not sure, but I'm here, right? So I guess he believed I could. That's why he had you kidnap me." Cruz didn't contest Amadi's statement, providing silent confirmation that Jordan was behind the kidnapping.

"Why do *you* think you're down here?" Cruz asked.

"I have the right to take back control of the bank, but that right goes away very shortly."

"Ahh. You think you're on ice to prevent that."

"That's my assumption. Then, no more Abode. No more houses. And the next teenage Max who comes along ends up joining the gangs instead of going to school."

"So you're not here while someone negotiates a ransom payment?"

"I kinda doubt it."

"Hmm. What do you think happens when the deadline passes?"

Amadi bit his lower lip. He had been watching Cruz as they talked. But now he looked away and said, "I have no idea, Max."

Max said nothing. He wiped some excess cream cheese from

his mouth, slowly filled the Meshuggah bag with the waste, stood, and said, "I gotta run some errands. Take a shower. Chill out. You want anything to read?"

"Maybe a James Baldwin book. Any of his will be fine."

"I'm a big fan of Baldwin. I'll bring you one of mine. Maybe some others too." He ran his fingers across the brim of his hat and then was out the door, locking both deadbolts behind him.

Jordan was at his desk on a Saturday when Cruz appeared at his office door. No longer were banking hours limited to Monday through Friday. He looked up, motioned for Cruz to sit, and asked, "Report?"

Cruz provided his update on Amadi's captivity much the way a police detective would tell his captain the status of an investigation: monotone, efficient, emotionless, and nothing but the facts. Jordan listened carefully, and when Cruz completed the report said, "Well done. Only six days left."

"Six days? And then what?"

"Like I said before, I have my options. Before the six days expire, one of those options will become my plan to implement."

"What I mean is, how does this all end?" Cruz asked. "What happens to your brother, bro?"

It surprised Jordan that Cruz pressed the issue and sounded insistent. Cruz seemed to take control of the conversation. Jordan needed to be in control, so he stared angrily at Cruz for a moment and then pushed back. "You're my observer, you're my snatcher, and you're my watcher. I don't expect you to be my endgamer, so not to worry. You take care of Amadi as you have been. Your gig'll be over shortly."

Then, without waiting for any further inquiries, Jordan lifted his phone off the receiver, swiveled his chair away from Cruz, and began to dial a number. And because he was facing away from Cruz, he did not see it when Cruz took a round metal device the size of a dime from his pocket and attached it to the bottom of Jordan's desk. Nor did he see Cruz turn, smile, and leave.

Nevertheless, after Cruz left, Jordan was concerned. He had not been regularly logging in to observe and listen to Cruz's interactions with Amadi. Things had been going well, and he was busy planning the bank's pivot to its future self. Jordan had not set up the hidden camera to dump video and audio footage into a cloud storage, so he had no way of going back in time and reviewing older footage. In a matter of fifteen minutes, he did so. He needed to keep a more watchful eye on his snatcher.

26

Moe and Steele got an early start on their investigation. By eleven in the morning, they had made a missing person report and had been to all the properties except a rundown, two-story building near the intersection of Seventeenth and Brooklyn, blocks from the Eighteenth and Vine District. Decades before, the Vine District and the surrounding blocks were home to jazz clubs doing business side by side with businesses offering entertainment options like female impersonators, drag shows, live sex shows, burlesque, and scarlet houses staffed with ladies of the evening. The aim of the local establishments had been to meet all of the patrons' needs. Now, like so much of Kansas City, the District had mellowed and was home to the American Jazz and Negro Leagues Baseball museums and the Gem Theatre. All were historical, all were important, and all were worth saving to preserve the District's story.

Unlike the Vine District, the nearby Seventeenth and Brooklyn area no longer offered anything historical, important, or worth saving. Just old empty buildings whose stories were never that interesting and now were lost, buried in the ever-shifting sands of history. Brooklyn was a north-south thoroughfare intersected between Nineteenth and Twentieth Streets by railway lines. More rail tonnage passed through Kansas City than any other city in the United States, even though it was only the country's thirty-sixth most populous city. So there were railway lines everywhere. Proximate and noisy rail traffic was nothing unusual in Kansas City.

As Moe got out of her car and joined up with Steele, she said over the roar of a passing freight train, "This is the one with the subbasement, right?"

Ronnie looked at 3J's notes and nodded.

"Well, this corner has certainly seen better days."

"You sure about that, Moe? I think this little area was born rundown, seedy, and dangerous."

"You might be right, Ronnie," Moe yelled. "Someone built these buildings with that vintage Kansas City decaying look from the git-go."

They approached the front of the building and went in through a large entryway with two doors, only one of which seemed to work. The working door wasn't locked. Once inside, they heard nothing except people groaning in the hallways and behind closed doors. "Like I said before, groaning now and screams coming any second. Kind of reminds me of the good old vice days," Moe said.

"Yeah. Jesus. Stakeouts in dank buildings like this one where all you could hear were the groans of junkies and hookers and who knows what else," Ronnie replied. "Do you miss those days?"

"Not me, partner."

"Me neither."

"Look at this place. What a dump," Moe said. "This guy Jordan is a real slumlord banker." Thin walls muffled but didn't silence faint moaning sounds that passed into empty hallways devoid of anyone to hear. "Doesn't sound like a banker calling out for help. That's for damn sure. Sounds more like people on a heroin high as they settle in for another duji flight through time and space . . . if they live through the takeoff."

Steele nodded.

They opened each door on the main floor and either found an

empty storage closet, someone on a mattress looking blankly off into the distance, or an empty room, except for the scurrying rats.

As they made their way down the hallway, Steele said, "Look. There's an elevator. Whataya think, Moe?"

Once at the elevator, Moe pushed the button to summon it, but there was no response and the elevator never came.

"Just as well," he said. "We can walk. It'd be safer."

Steps beyond the elevator they saw a steel door above which was a broken sign that at some time in the past illuminated the word "Staircase."

"All right. Here we go," Moe said. They walked down the unlit stairs to the basement. Neither was sure where the power came from, but the basement hallway had several naked bulbs that still worked, providing enough light for them to see several more doors. They opened four unlocked doors and found nothing except stale air and more rats. One remaining basement door was locked. Ronnie removed his small lock-picking cases and set out to gain access. Darkness bathed the door and he had to balance his small penlight in his mouth while he bent over and tried to pick the lock. After a few minutes, he stood straight and conceded defeat.

"Moe, I can't get this one open. See if you can give it a try."

"Like old times, Steele," Moe said as she moved toward Steele and the recalcitrant door lock. "Sometimes you have to know your limits and call in the professional cavalry."

"Yeah, yeah. Here's a light for you. Just give it a try, will ya'."

After several minutes, she opened it. Beyond the door was another staircase to a subbasement level. They stood there trying to listen for any sounds from below but heard nothing.

"I got a feeling about this one. Be alert," Ronnie said, and the two began the descent to the next level.

At the bottom of the stairs was one more door, this one unlocked. No sounds came from behind it. Moe turned the doorknob, opened the door, and they entered. This had to be the room.

They shone their phone lights on the room and stood there. It was empty. It had been empty for a very long time. It contained nothing to suggest humans had occupied it in the recent past. All they saw were rat and roach droppings.

"Shit," Ronnie said dejectedly.

They went back upstairs, searched the upper floor, found nothing, and went back to the car. On the drive back, Ronnie called 3J to give her the bad news: a complete bust; nothing. There was no kidnapper and no Amadi.

With a healthy dose of the Franklins' prodding, an executive at Bank of the Heartland agreed to meet the Franklins, 3J, and Pascale later in the day on Saturday. The three met outside and the guard let them into the bank lobby for their hastily called meeting with Altair Galanos.

Galanos wore many hats at the bank. While many in Kansas City knew him as the bank's executive vice president, he was much more than that. He was also the lending officer, head of the loan committee assigned to review and approve new loan applications, and in charge of bad loans. And he was a community leader. He knew and admired the Franklins and Amadi Browne, with whom he had cochaired many fundraising campaigns for inner-city causes over the years.

While many bankers had moved to business casual dress, foregoing suits and ties, especially on weekends, Galanos wore a white long sleeved shirt and a smart, striped tie. The Franklins had told 3J a few things about Galanos that the general public might not know, among them that he was a kid from the hood who now ran a good-sized bank in Kansas City. When he extended his hand to shake 3J's, the shirt sleeve pulled up on his arm slightly, and she saw part of a snake tattoo, perhaps a viper, poke out from under the sleeve. The ink was elaborate, and she wondered if his upbringing included any gang stints, and if so, whether she'd just gotten a peek at a gang tat from a prior version of Galanos' life. She also wondered if the sleeves hid more ink on his arms.

He led them to a conference room, and once they'd settled into their seats, 3J thanked him for making time on his Saturday and immediately moved into the reason for their visit. After explaining the Commonwealth stock sale and repurchase option, she asked if he knew Amadi's brother, Jordan.

"Can't say that I do, Ms. Jones."

"Please call me 3J."

"Very well. Thank you. I don't know Jordan Browne. I do know Amadi Browne well and think the world of him. I count him as a friend and a banking colleague. We've cochaired a number of fundraising events together. What is it that brings you here today, 3J? How can I help?"

"We have a very unusual request to make. Given the very short deadline before Amadi's stock repurchase right expires, we're hoping to find a bank that could loan him the necessary funds to buy the stock before the deadline passes."

"If I might, why isn't Amadi here asking me for the loan himself?" Galanos asked, looking reflective.

3J explained what she suspected and what she feared. As she spoke, Galanos' face changed from surprised to disturbed and then to concerned.

"Altair, we have numerous resources out looking for Amadi," Bella explained. "Private eyes. Former cops. People scouring the internet. We hope to find him before December thirteen when the repurchase option expires. If we're successful, he'll have the right to exercise the repo, and we expect he'll need a loan to do so. We know there will be precious little time left to go through the lending process. We're hoping you and your bank can do the necessary legwork to be ready to make that loan to Amadi on very short notice."

"If he's alive," Galanos added in a hoarse whisper, shaking his head. "Let's say you find him before the thirteenth and he's unharmed. If we make him the loan, what happens next?"

"Everything happens," James explained. "Amadi takes control of Commonwealth again. Under his direction, the bank will no longer ask Abode to move the loan. We expect it will reinstate and renew the loan, and that will be our ticket out of bankruptcy. We'll stay in business and continue Abode's mission."

"We expect the bank will then abandon its plan to leave the inner city and will instead continue its long-standing commitment to the many minority communities," Bella added.

Galanos clasped his hands together in front of his mouth with his elbows on the conference room table. His eyes darted around over his hands, but he made no eye contact. Finally, he lowered his clasped hands and smiled. "We can do due diligence on Commonwealth before December thirteen and assure ourselves the value of the stock exceeds the two million dollars Amadi would apparently seek to borrow. That would normally be the most time-consuming part of this type of loan underwriting process anyway. We can glean much of the bank information from public filings.

"Then, when you find Amadi, assuming you're correct and he wants to pursue this loan, we'd need financial information from him. With that, I figure we'd still need twenty-four hours to present this to the full loan committee for approval. So that means you've got to find Amadi and have him ready to go with us by early on Thursday the twelfth, at the very latest, if there's any chance to fund the loan by Friday the thirteenth."

For a moment, no one said anything. "So you're not saying no, Altair?" Bella asked, gushing with anticipation.

"I'm not saying no, Bella. But you have to slow down because I'm not able to say yes either. I can't make a loan to someone who's missing. I know it doesn't exactly say that in our loan committee manual, but it's one of those 'goes without saying' requirements.

Just a stark reality. I need a flesh and blood borrower with a beating heart, completing our forms and giving us financial information, and then with pen in hand, signing loan documents. So while we have some work in front of us here at Heartland, it's nothing like the work you have in front of you to find him . . . and quickly."

27

Sunday, December 8, 2024

CRUZ DELIVERED BREAKFAST as usual to Amadi. That morning, it was takeout from Homegrown Kansas City in Brookside. They ate largely in silence but eventually began to talk about Abode.

After Max left Amadi, he drove his Ford toward downtown, parked in the Crossroads District at Nineteenth and Wyandotte Streets, and hopped into Mildred's for a cup of his favorite coffee and a table where he could think in solitude. He didn't believe Jordan had identified his options. Not at all. Everything about Jordan oozed a guy who had grown up in privilege and now was out of his element. To Max, he was the worst kind of man. Max was worried that people of privilege like Jordan eventually felt cornered and took rash actions. He believed that people of privilege were no different from anyone else, regardless of whether they were White or a member of a marginalized group. Money and the privilege that came with money forever altered them. As he finished his cup of joe, Max wished he could confront Jordan and put an end to all this.

He had left the bug under Jordan's desk because he didn't trust him. Everything Cruz observed about Jordan screamed he was in way over his head and not to be believed or trusted. The bug was Cruz's insurance policy against Jordan Goddamn Browne.

He wished he could do more, like tell Jordan, "Here is what your damn endgame is going to be dude: Either spring Amadi from captivity or I'll do it myself." He now knew that Amadi didn't deserve to be held captive. He wanted to say, "Let your brother go, bro, or I will." But that wasn't in Cruz's job description. Instead, he would continue to be the watcher, and now the listener as well. He needed to make sure he knew what Jordan Browne would do next.

While Amadi and Max ate, Jordan observed the captivity ritual on his laptop as he attended to bank business. But at some point, he realized Amadi and Cruz were discussing Abode, and their conversation suggested it was not the first time they had talked about it. Jordan instantly became concerned and then angry. "What in the hell is going on here?" he wondered out loud. To him, Cruz was nothing more than an idiot in a hat who was now not only engaging with his brother but openly talking about the root of all the current problems: Abode.

He continued to watch and listen, and to his shock, he heard Cruz talk about his family and the Abode home they lived in. Jordan slammed the lid of his computer shut forcefully. "What a fuckin' shitstorm," he whispered to himself.

Jordan remained sitting at his desk after watching Max on the video, and his paranoid nature took over. Max was flipping. He was an Amadi sympathizer. He sat there unmoving—not even blinking. Anyone looking into his office would have concluded he was paralyzed with most of his systems offline and would have called 911 concerned Jordan had just suffered a stroke.

But he hadn't. All his energy was directed at trying to gather his thoughts. His mind was racing to the exclusion of all other bodily functions except his heart pumping and his lungs breathing the occasional breath. For the moment, he couldn't move his arms, hands, or legs, which were frozen by the immensity of the fresh problem that was now his to solve.

No longer was his only concern Amadi and the ultimate sentence he was yet to hand down. That was his problem number one. Now his own snatcher was turning against him. That was his problem number two, and it had dropped in his lap before he had even completed solving problem number one. He realized he had no choice but to accelerate his thinking and decision-making process because he needed to solve problem number one immediately so he could figure out what to do about problem number two.

He had to reach out to Robbie McFadden again. He needed to hire someone new who would first take out Max and then deal with his brother. Max worked for McFadden, who described him as "my guy." Since Max came to Jordan through a McFadden referral, he wasn't sure how McFadden would react to the news that Max had to be eliminated.

When his body came back online, he called McFadden and explained that they needed to talk as soon as possible. McFadden groused but agreed to the meeting, and a short time later, he appeared at Jordan's table at The Bottoms Bar.

"This better be good, amigo. Sunday is my day for family and football," Robbie said as he stood over Jordan, who was already seated.

Jordan nodded but said nothing.

"Okay. So why am I here on a Sunday morning instead of telling the priest what a great sermon he gave to all the good Catholics sitting in the pews?"

Jordan continued to say nothing.

"We got problems, bro?" Robbie asked as a waiter delivered two vodkas on the rocks. "And by 'we' I mean you." He slowly sat down at the now familiar table across from Jordan as his two bodyguards lingered by the bar. They all waved off menus. The vodka was good. No one was sure about the food.

"Well, in a word, it's still Amadi. And now it's Max as well."

"Max? Jesus. What could Max have done? Last time I told you I didn't need to know the details, but now I'm thinking I do." McFadden sighed. "From the top, what's up now?"

Jordan explained the stock repurchase option now set to expire in five days.

"Ah, now I understand. Important fact indeed. We've identified a complication, and a significant one at that. Now all this reaching out to me makes more sense. Complications are there for us businessmen to solve. Right?"

"This time, Robbie, its layers of complications."

"Well, that's the business world. Us businessmen, we handle those complications, right?"

"I suppose so, although I'm not doing a very good job of it to the moment. To be honest, it's all so confusing."

"Jordie, we live in a confusing place, not to mention in confusing times. For example, here we are in the middle of the fuckin' country in the largest city in the state that doesn't even have a unique name. People think it's named after the state next door. How confusing is that? But it's really named after the Kansa Native American tribe that lived around here back in the day. I've heard that after the Civil War, the idiots on the Kansas side tried several times to get the legislature over there to annex KCMO. Can you imagine? But at least if they had, there would only be one Kansas City and it would be in Kansas. Would've made a whole lot more sense, right? Instead, now we have two Kansas Cities right next to each other in two different states in god knows how many different counties, separated by two goddamn rivers at that, one named the Kansas River and one named the Missouri River. Can you imagine? It's crazy. History is confusing as hell, ya' know?"

Jordan said nothing but wasn't sure how many more history lectures he could withstand.

McFadden grimaced slightly as he shook his head and said, "But enough of today's high school history lessons. You didn't come here for that and neither did I. Back to your problems. Anything else I should know?"

Jordan explained the new problem with Max. "And I've come to some decisions," Jordan said, trying to sound decisive but sounding tentative as he uttered the word "decisions."

McFadden studied Jordan. "Recent decisions, I take it. Max pushed you over the edge? Sounds like you didn't take my advice the last time, Jordie. Look, we go way back. I take time out in my busy day to meet you in this bar so I can give you the benefit of my experience and wisdom. Not worth the vodkas and the trips down memory lane if you file away what I tell you in your 'deal with it later' folder. I may've warned you about something like that before, eh?"

Jordan nodded his head in agreement with McFadden and then shook it slowly in disgust with himself.

McFadden continued. "So now, m'friend, you've got yourself some kind of serious problems, plural, not just a problem. You're telling me you think Cruz has flipped and now he's sympathetic to Amadi's plight. Kinda the reverse of Patty Hearst's Stockholm Syndrome deal. It happens. Not often in my line of work, but it does from time to time. Not unlike that Mary McElroy story I told you. So now you're telling me he's aligned with your brother instead of working for you. And you're telling me that if your bro is out and about, he can buy back the bank. At least for a while longer. At least while he's still breathing air on planet Earth."

Jordan said nothing.

"By the way, how the hell do you know all of this about Cruz?" Robbie asked.

"I've been watching and listening to them talk in the room. There's a hidden camera I installed."

McFadden whistled. "Nice. I'm impressed. What're you, like a Fed on a wiretap or something? Jeez. So you're saying you've heard and seen all this?"

"Yes."

"You got footage?"

Jordan took out his phone and showed McFadden the recording of Cruz and Amadi.

"Jesus, would you look at that? Motherfucker. You're not recording *me* are you, Jordie?"

"Jesus! Of course not."

"Good, good."

"And, Robbie," Jordan continued, "Cruz is now so bold that he's been in my office trying to discuss what I'm going to do with Amadi."

"Well, this is certainly messy." McFadden smiled and leaned back in his chair. "Yep. Pretty big fuckin' mess you've got going here, Jordie. Never woulda gotten this far if you'd taken some action right after Max snatched Amadi."

McFadden shook his head and sighed. "I guess it's like my pops used to say to me. 'Robert, we are where we are.' What are you looking for from me?"

"I need Max out of the picture and then I need Amadi out of the picture—immediately and permanently."

"Look, Jordie. I told you to figure out what you want. You're telling me you want Amadi out of the picture. I don't know what that means. What you really want is he should never sign a notice buying back the stock." McFadden narrowed his eyes and put both hands on the table. "Jordie, did you know you can't prevent a guy from performing his contract with you? It doesn't work that way."

"How do you know that?" Jordan asked, surprised.

"It shouldn't surprise you that I have a good stable of lawyers on my payroll. One of them's a corporate guy. Yale man. That's what he told me a while ago when I found myself in a, let's call it similar, situation. No interfering with a guy who wants to perform under a contract."

"What are you telling me, Robbie?"

"Really, the same thing as before. You need an endgame. The endgame has to make what you want to happen a reality. Now that I know what's going on here, snatching alone doesn't get you there."

"Well, I think I've come to some decisions that do get me there," Jordan said softly. "Amadi has to go away—permanently. Like in dead. And now, Max too."

McFadden tilted his head and said softly, "Decisions?" McFadden cleared his throat as he nodded slowly. "Well done, Jordie. Finally, I might add. Out of the picture? Yes indeed, m'friend. Yes, indeed." McFadden rubbed his upper lip slowly. "Yeah. Taking out your flesh and blood is serious stuff, but it just might do the trick. But that's a pretty big step for anyone, Jordie. Anyone considering it should be thinking long and hard about it."

"Look, Robbie. It has to be done. I need another referral. Someone to finish all of this off for me once and for all." Then in case McFadden didn't appreciate Jordan's decision, he added, "Amadi *and* Max."

"Yeah, I heard you. I gotta tell you, I'm none too happy that if I give you a referral, unfortunate harm may befall Mr. Maximilian Cruz, one of *my* guys. One of my guys who up until now has done good work for me. Real good work." He paused and added, "Don't know when or where he grew a conscience." McFadden shook his head. "You think you know a guy. Shit. You know, I don't really give a damn what happens to Mr. Amadi Browne, but I've got my guy and my business I need to look out for."

Jordan studied McFadden's face for any hint of what he would say next. McFadden was schooled in the art of giving away nothing. He milked the moment for more than a minute, and Jordan sweated out the wait. There was nothing else he could do. He hoped the sweat had not broken out visibly on his brow.

"I'm gonna have to think about the Max part of this. Meet me back here in an hour."

McFadden rose and strode quickly out of the bar, followed by his men, before Jordan could say anything.

An hour later, the two were back at the table in the bar facing each other. Without a history lesson this time to break the ice, McFadden came right to the point. "All right, this is what we're gonna do. You've already paid me the usual fee for Max's work, for which I thank you. But the fee for what I'm gonna call phase two of your operation is going to cost you. It's triple. You've got two problems and they're much bigger. Like we agreed, now it's very complicated. You're talking about a hit for hire here. Two of 'em. So you'll need to pony up more. Understood? And you'll have to work out whatever fee there is for this new guy. Heads up—he's not cheap."

"Understood. Not a problem," Jordan said without hesitation.

"Jordie, there are lots of smart guys coming up the ranks of my organization. Smart, ambitious, many even ruthless. So how do I survive? Am I smarter? They may think I am but I'm not. I know lots of things and I've got this Ivy League sheepskin, but I also know my limits. Ambitious? Sure, but less so today than years ago when I was making my moves and setting up the organization. These days, I'm satisfied with what I've got and where I sit in the scheme of things."

McFadden leaned in closer to Jordan. "But ruthless? You bet. On this one, I excel. Always have. Always will. Probably got it from my pops. I've gotta keep what's mine. Don't fuck with me is my motto, and everybody knows it. But even that's an understatement. I'll do what others won't. I'll do it when others can't. And I'll do it to anyone who doesn't toe the line. Anyone. I have no problem doing whatever it takes to protect what's mine. They all know it and whether or not they like it, they respect it." He paused and then finished his thought emphatically. "And they stay the fuck outta my way." McFadden stared at Jordan, opened his eyes wide for emphasis, and leaned back.

The way McFadden described himself and his business was the most chilling monologue Jordan had ever heard. Cold-blooded was not something he was accustomed to hearing, so he said nothing and just continued to listen. That was just as well because it seemed to be what McFadden expected.

"Now you're in that same boat. Doing what you need to so you can protect what's yours. I appreciate that. I respect it. Look, I sent Mr. Cruz out on a job. Now it seems he's unilaterally changing the terms of engagement. Not me. I didn't change things. All him. I can't have that kind of thing in the rank and file. Bad for business. I tell a guy to do something and he does it. Plain and simple. If not, well, then I don't have a satisfied customer. In this case, that's you. Can't have that either. Word might get out on the street that I don't keep my customers satisfied, and that's also not good for business. If you're not satisfied, then I didn't earn my fee. What did I just say? Not good for business. Mine's a people line of work and I'm a people kind of person. My future business endeavors depend on happy clientele in the present. First year college business stuff. Understood?"

McFadden paused. Jordan offered no response and showed no emotion on his face.

"Shit. Next, that crazy Cuban might even try to spring Amadi. I can't have that. So this is what we're gonna do here to rectify all of these fuckin' problems. Yours, and now mine as well. On my way out, one of the boys will give you a piece of paper with some contact information on it. Man's name is Bobby Ray. Be warned. Bobby Ray is no Maximilian Cruz. He's a little, shall we say, edgy and unrefined. Less cerebral than Cruz. Not as fancy a dresser as Cruz. But he does good work, he's fast, and he does what he's told. Period. You contact Mr. Ray. He'll know you'll be calling and you take it from there. You work out the fee and pay him. You wait for him to deliver on whatever you tell him to do."

McFadden narrowed his eyes as he finished explaining what would happen next, leaned closer to Jordan, breathed in through his nose and out through his mouth forcefully, and asked, "Understood?"

Jordan could feel McFadden's breath and recoiled from his face. This time, he wanted to say something, but as he listened to Robbie McFadden's instructions, he wasn't able to utter any words. The enormity of what was unfolding paralyzed him. He simply closed his eyes and nodded. When he opened them, there was a folded piece of paper on the table next to the bar tab and he looked up to see the door to the bar close behind Robbie McFadden and his two bodyguards.

Jordan was now on his own.

28

ROME SET UP a Sunday call with 3J, Pascale, the Franklins, Ronnie, Moe, Byron, and Moses for later in the morning, central standard time. 3J and Pascale each dialed in from home. Once everyone joined the call, Ronnie told the group that when he filed the missing person report, he'd talked to a detective he'd known for years and filled him in on Amadi's family situation, pointing out that his brother was Amadi's sole remaining family. When the detective and his partner interviewed Jordan Browne, he told them that Amadi often left town with no warning since the deaths of his wife and daughter and that eventually, he would be back. As a courtesy, the detective reported back to Ronnie what Jordan had said and let him know that the police had back-burnered the missing person investigation.

Rome then outlined the plan she and Byron had fashioned. She explained the torturous process of wading through mountains of information that led nowhere. "Then we both found articles about Amadi's collapse at the Folly and his pacemaker. At first, we did not think much of it, but they are, after all, modern devices, and devices intrigue me. I was curious, so I did research. In the modern era, these tiny devices not only regulate the heart, they also offer a trove of information for doctors to help make it easier for the patient's heart to remain properly functional. We can use that to our advantage."

"You mean hack into the man's heart?" Pascale exclaimed. "My Lord!"

"No, no. Not that, Mr. Pascale. Much too risky, and as our thinking has developed, unnecessary."

"Then what, Rome?" 3J asked.

"We propose to employ an SMS—otherwise known as a text message—spoof," Rome said.

When she finished explaining the overview of the SMS spoof plan, there was silence on the line. 3J broke the silence and explained that Ronnie and Moe had visited all the properties on the list and Amadi was not being held captive in any of them. "We simply need to do something else to locate Amadi."

"We think the spoof is our best chance, given the timeline," Rome replied. "To be sure, the plan is not perfect. But if everything works out, we will know within a several block radius where Amadi is."

"Or at least where his mobile phone is," Bella corrected.

"This is correct, Ms. Franklin," Rome agreed. "We are hopeful he and his phone are together."

"This is an awful lot to process. I would find it helpful if you can take it from the top and give us the deep dive into what you're proposing," James said.

"Rome, it *is* an ingenious idea. Please give everyone the complete picture. Leave nothing out," Moses said. "They will have decisions to make, and we want to make sure they have the best information at their disposal when they decide."

"Of course, Moses. Mr. Franklin, when you receive an ordinary, run-of-the-mill text message on your mobile phone, you see the sender identified on your phone screen, either with his or her phone number, or if the sender is in your contacts, the sender's contact name appears. For this discussion, we'll set aside those texts you receive that say 'blocked' instead of a name or number.

"At its core, SMS spoofing, otherwise known as text spoofing, is an electronic impersonation. You may have received texts in the past where there is a link in the text. Maybe the text says your bank froze your account, and to unfreeze it, you must click on the link and follow the instructions. The text says the sender is your bank, but in reality, someone is impersonating your bank. The sender has changed its details, masked who he or she is, and sent you a text suggesting it is your bank writing you. Simply put, the spoof is the impersonation, so the sender appears to be someone or something else."

"You would steal the identity of one of Amadi's doctors?" James asked as he started to understand what Rome was proposing.

"No, Mr. Franklin. We are not proposing identity theft. In some circles, identity theft is called 'smishing.' We would not do that."

"A one-off impersonation?"

"Correct. My text would pretend to be Amadi's doctor. We know his name from an interview he gave after Amadi received the pacemaker. The information we are looking for here is Amadi's general location. To make that happen, the text would ask Amadi to confirm he feels all right. The text would represent that it is being sent as part of a new cardiology procedure to assure that the doctors do not need to make any remote adjustments to the pacemaker. There are several events that must come together for this to work. But importantly, no harm to Amadi's health can or will occur. All he or his captor needs to do is click on the link, and in a moment, we will then know his general location. Questions so far?"

No one had any.

"To implement the spoof, we will use a website called localize dot org. There are many such sites on the internet," Rome continued.

"Dark or clear?" 3J asked, referring to the clearnet and dark web.

"Clear," Rome replied. "With the words we wish to include in the text, Amadi's mobile number, and the name and number of the doctor we are impersonating, the website will generate the link we will need Amadi to click on. And if he does, the web page will quickly generate the approximate geolocation of his phone for us."

Bella had been quiet to this point. Sounding suspicious, she asked, "And the legality of all this?"

"Without doing any criminal law research, I suggest you assume a plan to impersonate a doctor using a mobile phone would skate the boundaries of legality if not step over them," Pascale offered.

Bella and James were sitting at a table in their home for the conference call, and as Pascale offered his sobering observation, they looked at each other.

"Everyone, we need to talk for a moment," Bella said. "We're going to put you on mute. We'll be back shortly."

Bella muted the conversation and looked at James, shaking her head slowly. Ignoring Bella's body language, James said, "I'm good with this. You, Bella?"

"I'm not so sure. What about the line? He called it a boundary."

"Fuck the line and fuck any boundaries. If we don't do this, we're gonna lose Amadi—if we haven't already lost him. This is one of those situations where crossing the line hurts no one. We're not spoofing here to gain illicit access to someone's passwords or accounts. We're not risking Amadi's health. We're not stealing anything. We're trying to save a friend's life and we're fighting back. That's all we're doing. Keeping Amadi alive and trying to keep what's ours and what we've worked our whole adult lives for. Fair and square."

When Bella said nothing, James continued. "Look, since Abode's inception, we've faced hurdles you and I couldn't have even imagined and a degree of racism not even we could have predicted. Through all of that, we've told everyone that we're not 'by any means necessary' folks, and we're not. But at this point, I'm more than willing to say we're also not 'turn the other cheek' folks. Not anymore. I for one don't want to be the person who swivels a cheek to avoid this fight because of a goddamn line. Certainly not if it means we're contributing to the death of a valued colleague and a trusted partner of many years. Like I said, fuck the line. Times change. The line moves all the time. This time, so should we."

James could tell that Bella was listening intently, but she continued to say nothing, so he kept talking.

"The damn line stopped no one from keeping Black and Brown and Asian and marginalized groups from living next door. We've made progress in erasing the red line of discrimination drawn around neighborhoods. If we need to impersonate a doctor this way to keep moving forward in the mission, then I say we do it. At least, that's my vote."

When Bella still said nothing, he asked, "Bella, what do you think Amadi would say?"

Bella sighed. "He'd tell us to do it, no question. Okay. I'm in too. I suppose we'll have to add this little incident to the items on our list to discuss with Saint Peter when we arrive at the pearly gates some day."

James smiled. "The line to talk with Saint Peter will stop moving for a while when I meet up with the good saint. My list will be long. I've done lots worse than this spoof thing. When we get to the front of the pearly gates line, let me do the talking. I'll charm the angel wings right off his back. Old Saint Pete won't have a chance."

Bella smiled, pressed the mute button, and rejoined the conference call. "Folks, we're back and we're in. Rome, do it."

❧

When the call ended, 3J immediately called Pascale back. He answered and chuckled. "What's so damn funny, Bill?"

"I suppose nothing Belita Davies comes up with should surprise me anymore. As I look back over the past few years, she's hacked into a financial advisor's computer to find evidence your client hid assets, hacked into Woody Clarke's computer and saved your life,

Jacob Steinert's life, and Donny and Lil Melanshins' lives, and now she wants to impersonate a doctor—a cardiologist at that. Compared to those other ops she ran, this one seems tame. Don't you agree? Or maybe I'm getting so used to her antics that nothing she suggests seems so bad. And knowing her, this impersonation gig could work."

"Hell, I don't know," 3J replied. "After talking to Rome, sometimes I feel like saying that I'm just a simple bankruptcy lawyer adjusting debt. All her high-tech stuff makes my head swim."

"I certainly know the feeling. But seriously, this seems less bad, doesn't it? No one gets hurt. At least not as far as we can see. And unlike the financial advisor and Clarke, if Amadi knew what she was up to, he certainly would approve."

"True enough."

The two paused in their discussion.

"I guess I'm glad she's on our side," 3J said. "Every time I talk to her I learn something I'm not sure I want to know. Not if I want to sleep soundly at night. Internet of things. Intercepting a financial advisor's computer communications to a public router. Pushing altered plugins to a bad guy's computer. Creating fake identities to watch what the bad guys are saying in chat rooms. And now we can add SMS spoofing. Is there nothing private anymore? I guess it's like our IT folks tell us all the time with wide eyes, 'Whatever you do, don't click on links.'"

"Well, no link clicking, except this one time by Amadi. And I'm quite certain nothing is private anymore unless you're completely off the grid living in a mountain cabin somewhere in northwest Montana."

"Bill, I've been worrying about this whole mess. There's no way that merely kidnapping Amadi will work for Jordan. He's going to have to kill Amadi. This has gotta work, Bill. Otherwise, Amadi is not long for this world and Abode will go down. Let's hope this spoof works and we can find him before it's too late."

Pascale was quiet for a moment before saying, "Yes, let's hope."

29

WITHIN AN HOUR, Rome set up the spoof SMS message: "Mr. Amadi Browne, This is Doctor Frey, one of your cardiology team members at St. Luke's you met while you were in the hospital. To further the efficacy of our remote pacemaker monitoring system, we are implementing periodic secure texts like this one between office visits to assure you are feeling in good health. To confirm that you are, all you need to do is click the following link. If you have questions or any problems with the link, please contact our office at 816-587-2200. James Frey"

A URL link created by Rome followed the spoof message from Dr. Frey. Rome hit send, and she and Byron waited to see if the spoof would work.

❧

Cruz unlocked the steel door leading to the subbasement and walked down fifteen concrete steps to the hallway and the door behind which Amadi now lived. It was dinnertime, and he had another food delivery with him.

It was also a chance for another discussion with Amadi. This time, maybe they'd talk about literature in more detail. Baldwin, Hughes, Ellison. He had left Amadi with his copies of books by each: Ellison's *The Invisible Man*; Baldwin's *Nobody Knows My Name*; Hughes' collection of poetry. There was much to talk about if Amadi was willing, and Cruz figured he would be. He was a smart guy. It was like a good college kid talking to a good high school grad, and Cruz thought he'd do anything to pass the time and take his mind off his situation.

Cruz unlocked the door and entered Amadi's room, put the food on the table, and moved to the locker where he had stored the phone. He checked, and it was on and still charged. As he had done all along, he removed the phone from the locker and deleted all the texts. No point keeping old texts on the phone and clogging it up. Amadi watched him perform the daily phone ritual in silence, and Cruz returned the phone to the locker and locked the padlock when he was done.

As Cruz turned away from the locker, the phone audibly dinged. A new text, but not silenced. A text had made it through his do not disturb and silence mode settings. He turned back to the locker.

"Amadi, did you set this thing with do not disturb overrides?" Cruz asked over his shoulder, surprised.

"Yes, I think so. Only one. The doctor's office gave me instructions of what to do to enable the emergency bypass option. I completely forgot about it."

"That must be why your phone dinged." Cruz opened the locker again, retrieved the phone, and read the text aloud. "Frey? Y'know him? Is that your doc?"

"Yes. Yes, that's him. He's the head cardiologist who attends to me. Max, you have to respond."

"Mmm. Don't know."

"Look, it's not even really a response to Dr. Frey. It's all automated. Just click on the link and Frey will know I'm okay. Otherwise, he'll tinker with the pacemaker adjustments and I might end up on your floor here writhing or passed out or worse. You don't want that, do you?"

Cruz wasn't sure what to do. Amadi was right. Cruz wanted none of those health events happening on his watch. He had no CPR training and wanted none in real time. And he certainly didn't want to figure out how to bring a passed out, kidnapped banker with a bad heart to an emergency room. On the other hand, he wanted Amadi to have no contact with the outside world, including his doctor.

While he pondered, the phone dinged again. "Jesus, how many more times is thing gonna ding at me," Cruz muttered.

"Please, Max."

"No contact with the outside world, Amadi. That's the rule. You know that."

"The rule wasn't designed for heart health, was it? If Dr. Frey calls, we won't answer. So it's just one click, just this once, Max. Please."

"No. We can't."

"But we already have contact with the outside world. The doctor's team gets updates from my phone. My heart to my phone to the team, right? This wouldn't be a new outside world contact. Just the same one."

Cruz said nothing and shook his head slowly as he tried to figure out what to do. He decided he didn't want Amadi dying on his watch any more than he wanted Jordan to kill Amadi on his watch.

"All right. All right. There, I clicked on the link. Frey will know you're fine, which you are. No adjustments. No writhing, please."

"Thank you."

Cruz put the phone back in the locker and spun the dial on the padlock, locking it again. Then he returned to the table and sat silently across from Amadi. "I had a heart-to-heart with your brother yesterday," he said after a while.

"My brother? Why would you have occasion to speak with him unless you can now confirm he's behind all this?"

Cruz smiled. "Not much gets by you, does it? Yeah. Anyway, he needed a talkin' to. He texted me later to tell me he should be by tonight to talk to you mano a mano. We'll see what comes of that assembly of brothers."

"He won't come. No way. Why would he suddenly come by?"

"He says he will." Cruz nodded slightly as he locked eyes with Amadi. "Here's the thing. Not really my issue, but if I was you, I'd be on my best behavior when he gets here."

"What the fuck, Max. He hired you to kidnap me and hold me in this godforsaken place. Now he's coming over to check on me, and I'm supposed to welcome him warmly into my new home? I can't believe this."

"Yeah, yeah. I get it. It's a lot to take in, and I'm not good at the mediator role. But I'm just sayin', think about it."

They ate in silence.

3J sent the information she received from Rome to Ronnie Steele as soon as she got it. The spoof had worked. The geolocation was a four-block area in Kansas City, bounded on the north by railroad tracks, on the east by Wabash Avenue, on the south by East Nineteenth Street, and on the west by Olive Street. Rome had reported that a MapQuest satellite view of that area showed many buildings of all shapes and sizes.

Ronnie picked up Moe, and they sped over to the new coordinates to see what they could see. While it was only several square blocks, it held a large number and variety of structures. They tried to enter several of the buildings but found, to their surprise, that they had robust electronic security locks or systems, making entry impossible. If they went from building to building pushing on one door after another to try to gain access, it would look suspicious to anyone in the neighborhood and even more concerning to any police patrolling the area. The last thing they needed was to get dragged away from the neighborhood in a patrol car and have to explain what they were doing. They continued their search on foot, observant of possible building entry points not easily seen from the street and trying doors as surreptitiously as possible.

As they lost the sunlight to dusk, they shifted their focus from buildings to cruising the neighborhood looking for anyone or anything suspicious. But they observed little activity. There were no hookers coming and going, no johns looking for a lady of the evening, and no pimps keeping watch. There were also no junkies shooting up on a street corner and no obvious pushers selling small baggies of smack. Then they observed a well-dressed, tall man in a tan fedora get into a black car near three buildings on the corner of East Eighteenth and Olive. It wasn't clear which building he'd come from or how far he had walked to get to his car.

"Could be a pimp," Moe said as they watched him.

"Yeah. Could be, but he's awfully well-dressed, and conservatively at that, to be in the short-term rental of concubines for hire, don't you think? That's really not a pimp's hat. It's a forties upscale haberdashery hat. And that Ford? Definitely not a pimpmobile. Besides, there are no visible working girls."

"I agree. Likely not a pimp."

"Think we need to follow this guy?" Ronnie asked.

"Do we have a choice? I think that's our new Plan A."

"A? We have a Plan B, Moe?"

"I don't know about you, but my Plan B is to confront this guy and hope for the best. B ain't much of a plan just yet."

They followed the car to the West Bottoms, where they watched the man exit his car and enter a bar. They were on a side street near where the interstate passed over the area. It was a few blocks from the Livestock Exchange Building and looked like it might be a local watering hole where residents and Bottoms workers could drink at the end of the day. The bar looked nondescript to them.

Typical Bottoms: a little seedy, featureless, and unmemorable but potentially historic.

"Ever been here before, Moe?"

"Not me. Thought I knew every dumpy joint down here in the Bottoms. Guess I was wrong."

"Yeah. Me too. Nothing fancy here at all. Just that neon sign on the wall flashing 'The Bottoms Bar.' I guess we sit and wait and see what we can see."

"Yep. It's what we do."

❧

Robbie McFadden had summoned Maximilian Cruz and knew he would show up pronto. That's what his people did when he snapped his fingers. McFadden sat at the back of the bar in a booth with his usual entourage, and when he saw Cruz enter, he motioned him over and one of the entourage stood, allowing Cruz to squeeze in to be sandwiched between McFadden's men on a bench too small for them, facing a somber looking mob boss.

McFadden had no drink and offered none to Cruz.

"Max, give me a little update on this Amadi Browne job I set you up with. Everything going okay?" McFadden asked in a controlled soft voice.

"All good, Mr. McFadden. No problems."

"None?"

"Yes. Like I said, all good."

"What's this Jordan Browne guy like to work with? Seems a little squirrelly to me. Kinda the jumpy sort."

"Also all good. He's fine. Unsure of himself, but that's not my concern."

"How is this Amadi guy taking his little stay in my building far below Kansas City?"

"As expected. He ain't happy, but on the other hand, there ain't much he can do about it. So I'd say he's got no complaints, except the usual you'd expect from someone I just snatched."

"How're you and him gettin' along?"

"I look in on him, feed him, give him a change of clothes, and leave. He showers, dresses, reads. Not sure what else he does to pass the time. He's got no TV. He asked for one but I said no. No contact to the outside world. That's Mr. Browne's instructions. That's about it."

"That's about it?"

Cruz nodded.

"You and he talk about stuff?"

"Not really."

"Nothing?"

"Like I said, not really."

"He ask you how long he's gonna be down there?"

"Once in a while is all."

"He ask you what's gonna happen to him?"

"Not really."

"You like this guy Amadi."

"Y'know. Not my business, but he seems all right."

McFadden scratched his earlobe. "You and he ain't bonded, have you?"

"Bonded?"

"Y'know, become good buddies?"

"Nope. Nothin' more than another snatch and watch job for me."

McFadden said nothing for several seconds to make Cruz uncomfortable. "Max, what do you know about this outfit named Abode?"

"Abode. Never heard of it."

There it was. The big lie. McFadden could have reacted but looked poker-faced and said nothing for several more seconds. Then he nodded. "All right. Good talk, Max. Always good to check in when there's a job in progress. I've gotta keep the clients happy, and you know you've gotta keep me happy. That's how it goes. Just good business. You call me if you have any issues or if anything changes. Understand?"

"Sure thing, Mr. McFadden."

One of McFadden's men stood to clear an exit path for Cruz. Cruz rose slowly and left the bar.

Robbie McFadden and his entourage left the bar shortly after Cruz, and as his SUV pulled away from the curb in front of the bar, McFadden said to one of his bodyguards, "Here's the thing. I needed to know firsthand if Cruz was shooting straight. That's why I called the meeting. I don't think he came clean at all. Jordie's right. The video doesn't lie. Cruz likes Amadi. He's flipped, goddamn it."

McFadden leaned forward to make sure the driver could hear him. "Motherfucker! That's one thing I can't have. If you work for me, you work for me. Period. If I give you an assignment, you do what I ask. We're an organization with rules. We can't have chaos breaking out by someone going rogue. No one goes rogue in my organization. It's bad for business and it's bad for my stress level."

He paused to catch his breath. "And if I ask you a question, you answer it and you answer it fully. And the answer better be goddamn straight."

"Exactly boss," the driver said.

"Yep. I'm afraid this *is* a job for Bobby Ray. If that idiot Jordan Browne gets cold feet and doesn't follow through, I may need to take matters into my own hands and deal with Mr. Cruz." McFadden sighed. "My Lord. What a fuckin' business."

30

RONNIE AND MOE had watched the man come out of the bar and get into his car. But as they were about to resume their tail, they saw Robbie McFadden come out of the bar too. One of his bodyguards opened the rear door of his black SUV, and he climbed in.

"Motherfucker. Would you look at that," Ronnie said. "It's Robbie fuckin' McFadden. In the flesh. Boss man of everything underground in KC. The Irish punk we spent years chasing. He was always one step ahead of us and everybody else in vice. Smarter and more careful than all the boss men who came before him. I used to hate seein' those eyes mocking me from his black-and-white eight by ten glossy mug shot on the bulletin board every damn morning. Seemed to say, 'Not today, Mr. Viceman. You ain't gonna get me today. You ain't smart enough, fast enough, or good enough.' Used to really piss me off."

Ronnie grimaced as he remembered McFadden from his days in vice. He knew Moe shared his feelings about McFadden because everyone on the vice squad did. "What in the hell have we stumbled onto here?"

"Coincidence?" she replied.

"Don't believe in them."

"Me neither. I have no feeling for what McFadden's doing here, Ronnie, but we can only tail one of them at a time. Which one?"

"That other guy looks like small potatoes. I say we stay with McFadden. Who knows who he'll meet up with next. Maybe the mayor or even the president."

They followed McFadden's SUV to Twelfth Street as it ascended from the Bottoms lowlands to the city above, but they stayed a healthy distance back. From Twelfth, McFadden's driver headed south past the Plaza to Ward Parkway. Once on the Parkway, McFadden's SUV headed to his home, one of the many mansions that lined the grand, winding boulevard. His was a Tudor on three quarters of an acre that had been built in the 1920s by another famous Kansas City mobster. It was surrounded by a tall wrought iron fence, and it was adorned with impeccable landscaping reminiscent of the gardens that had inspired Monet. He lived down the block from the Ward Parkway mansion built by the political boss who had ruled from the mid-twenties until the end of the thirties, Tom Pendergast. Pendergast had been the most famous and powerful boss of them all, and Irish to boot. And Steele knew that Irish roots mattered to McFadden.

McFadden joked about his house saying it wasn't the biggest mansion on the parkway, but it was the best, and he liked to tell people it was a smaller version of Bruce Wayne's lair. To anyone who would listen, he said he'd lived in a shed-sized house in his early days. Now he lived in a mansion like any successful businessman might. McFadden had purchased the mansion to lend support to his legitimate businessman persona. Most everyone believed that whoever lived on Ward Parkway was legitimate.

During one interrogation that went nowhere, Steele had asked McFadden about his house. McFadden had smiled and said, "It's where all the legitimate businessmen live, right, Ronnie?" McFadden seemed to enjoy pushing Steele's buttons. In one interview, McFadden had asked Steele, "Where do you and me live these days, Ronnie? You? Your shed. Me? My mansion. All the same thing, right? We both have a kitchen and a television and some bathrooms. A couch and a bed to sleep in. Just a matter of scale."

The gate in front of the McFadden mansion opened electronically, and the SUV pulled into the circular drive leading to the front door. McFadden exited the SUV and entered his house. It was Sunday. McFadden could be conducting more business, or he might be spending the day with his kids. There was nothing Moe and Steele had in their arsenal to connect Robbie McFadden to Amadi Browne.

"As I sit here and watch nothing going on, I can feel my blood pressure rising like the old vice days," Steele admitted. "I gotta move on from this scumbag someday. He's just not good for my health."

"I hear ya' partner."

"Look, we got nuthin' here, Moe. We got nothing at all. Shit, maybe he's just in there watching the Chiefs like everyone else in the city does on winter Sundays."

"You wanna stay here or leave, Ronnie?"

"We need to regroup. McFadden is not hard to find if we need to. Let's go."

He pulled away from the curb and headed to Moe's house near Seventy-Fifth and Wornall, where the regular people lived. While she lived in a nice house, McFadden would have described it as similar to the "shed" he had lived in years before his mansion. Moe's house was adequate for her needs. McFadden's met his needs as well. Just a matter of scale.

Steele dropped her off saying they could pick it up first thing in the morning and left. He was dejected, and from the way she'd looked when he dropped her off, she was too. They had spent a full day and had nothing to show for their efforts. The building with the subbasement on the first list seemed to be the place they would find Amadi. It had been promising and then in moments, it had proved to be a dead end. Dead ends were part of the investigation business, but they were painful nonetheless.

Now they had no more leads. They hadn't been able to access all of the buildings they'd tried, and there was no place left on the list they could search. Steele headed for 3J's condo and a much needed chance to get away from the search for Amadi Browne, if only for a short period.

Once there, 3J told him that her friend, the renowned chef Celina Tio, would cook dinner for them at her restaurant, The Belfry. Normally closed on Sunday, Tio opened it on occasion to cook a special meal for friends.

They walked the several blocks south on Grand to the restaurant, their favorite place to grab an evening meal during normal hours and a special treat when Tio offered to cook for them on her days off. It was an unassuming bar in a former industrial building off Grand Boulevard, and it was one of Kansas City's best-kept secrets. Those in the know would tell friends to go to the bar for the libations, of course, but also have a world class meal cooked by the chef who'd won a James Beard award.

Tio let them in and sat them at the only table set up for dinner, and they exchanged small talk. When they asked what was on the menu for the evening, Tio smiled, said they would know shortly, and headed off to the kitchen, leaving them alone to talk.

"3J, we looked everywhere," Steele said. "Run down building after building. Hookers, junkies, pushers, pimps, homeless—you name it, we saw it. Everything except Amadi Browne. Reminded me 'n Moe of the not so good old vice squad days. That's the thing about being a cop. Lots of legwork with nothing but the elimination of leads to show for it. This entire investigation has brought us back to our 'nothing to show' roots I'm afraid. We need to find Amadi, not eliminate buildings where he's not stashed. We're running out of time."

Tio brought them whiskey tumblers of bourbon, and they both aimlessly twirled their glasses, releasing the bourbon's caramel and vanilla aromas.

"Do you think it'll help to talk more about today, Ronnie, or do you think it would be better to set this on the back burner?" 3J asked. "Sometimes, stepping away from a problem brings clarity."

"Both. Neither. I don't know," Steele replied dejectedly. "I don't feel we have enough time to put any of this on the back burner."

"Well, for the moment, you've exhausted Rome's first list of potential buildings and done what you could with the Olive Street list. So whether or not this is on the back burner, other than beating yourself up, what else can you do?"

"I suppose nothing."

Tio appeared with three dinners. There was garganelli pasta for 3J and Tio: garlicky tomato sauce, smoked prosciutto, smoked portobello mushrooms and cream. Steele grinned as he saw the polenta ragu for him: crispy polenta under a tomato-mushroom ragu, sunny egg, gorgonzola cheese, and his add-on, crispy pork. He was hungry, and as he dove in, he asked, "How do you invent these dishes? Lordy! They're amazing."

"I guess that's why you're a James Beard chef, right?" 3J said.

Tio laughed and shrugged.

With Tio at the table, the conversation drifted away from Abode and Amadi Browne, and Steele found himself relieved to talk about anything else, relegating the search for Amadi to the back burner for the moment. After dinner, Tio brought over a bottle of her own Moon Age bourbon for the three to share, and they had a spirited discussion about how inventive her menu was.

As they strolled back to 3J's condo after dinner, Steele found himself hoping 3J was right about stepping away from the problem for a bit. Maybe if he stopped thinking about Amadi for a while, something would come clear. Something. Anything.

31

Later in the evening, Jordan Browne drove to the Olive Street Building alone and went down the steps to the basement and then to the door leading to the next set of steps and the subbasement. As he walked through the first basement hallway, he passed several junkies using the building for a free rent shelter and a place to get high and later come down . . . if they were still alive and breathing by then. He wondered if Robbie McFadden knew about his nonpaying tenants.

He unlocked the door to the subbasement staircase. When the subbasement door creaked open, it unleashed a stench familiar to Jordan from the decaying buildings he owned. Sure, there was the faint whiff of stale air, vomit, mold, and urine. Those were all to be expected. But the other smell was stronger and unforgettable: the lingering smell of hopelessness that hung in the air. No hope for the destitute junkies he passed. No hope for the many downtrodden he was sure came and went in Robbie McFadden's Olive Street building.

He tried to push the prevailing odor out of his mind as he paused at the precipice of his confrontation with Amadi. He took the first step down and began the descent, and as he reached the hallway at the bottom, maybe he was now fifteen steps closer to hell. Maybe he wasn't just closer, but in fact had just descended right into hell. Maybe that was the price for his growing association with Robbie McFadden. Maybe the subbasement staircase was his own River Styx, the poisonous, murky, river of hate in Greek mythology that formed the boundary between Earth and the underworld. Here, there was no boat to carry him across and no elevator to deliver him to the next level, only the dark, murky staircase down to Jordan's underworld meeting with his brother.

He walked to the door restricting Amadi's exit, unlocked it, and stepped in to find his brother lying on the cot reading the Langston Hughes poem "I, Too" aloud. As he stepped into the room, Jordan looked around and confirmed what he had seen on his camera feed: Cruz had taken good care of Amadi, all things considered.

"Well, if this don't beat all," Amadi said softly, sitting up. "The criminal son finally arrives here to the makeshift prison to meet the prodigal son." Now standing and raising his voice, he added, "Before I forget, I want to make sure I say this right to your face." His voice quavered, and it grew louder as he said each word slowly: "Fuck you! Fuck you, you son of a bitch, Jordan Browne!" "I oughta kill you right now with my bare hands! Then when I'm sentenced to time in Leavenworth, I can tell the judge that the world should thank me for ridding it of a demon like you!"

Jordan had not expected Amadi's explosion. Instantly, he was not in control. To assert himself, he fired back, "Don't you ever talk to me that way! Your days of disrespecting me are over, Amadi!"

"Disrespecting you? Is that why I'm down here, Jordan? What the hell are you talking about?"

Quickly, both brothers were howling at each other like wolves screaming at the full moon. But the moon never seemed to hear the wolves, and the brothers didn't hear each other. Nor could anyone on the street and in the building. No one anywhere heard them. And they sounded so much alike when they yelled, if anyone *had* been listening, they would not have been able to tell one brother from the other. Neither yielded an inch.

"Jordan, how long are we going to keep talking at each other instead of to each other?"

"We never talked to each other any more than Mom and Pop talked to us."

"Our parents? Jesus, Jordan. What do they have to do with this?"

"Yes, our parents," Jordan said with disdain. "Mom and Pop. Fuck them. Fuck 'em when they lived. Fuck 'em now that they're gone. They never loved me. Hell, they never loved *us*. You've always been too damn ignorant to know that. Too blind to see it. You've always mistaken the discharge of their parental obligations for love. It wasn't love. It was another goddamn transaction for them! They did deals. No love, just deals. With the community, with borrowers, and with us."

Amadi said nothing in response.

"The only thing they loved was their bank and the goddamn community they talked about incessantly."

"They certainly loved both, but they loved us as well," Amadi countered. "My god, Jordan. Mom always told us we were twins. How could that be? No one with Mom and Pop's DNA could ever act the way you act. Or hate the way you hate."

"Oh, I hate all right. I didn't come to work at the bank after college because by then, I hated the bank. I hated our parents. And when you came to the bank after college, I hated you. I couldn't compete with the bank for their love. I couldn't compete with you and I couldn't compete with the community. I wanted no part of it. You're right. You were the prodigal son. Not me."

"But Jordan, you *did* come back to the bank."

"I did, indeed. It's what they wanted, but they never said thanks. Instead, what did those two do to show their appreciation? They gave the bank to you. You, goddamn it! Not me. Yeah, I came back, I bided my time, and I figured it all out. Now the bank's mine, not yours, not theirs, and not any of those goddamn ancestors of ours you always talk about. The bank will be my vehicle to show them, wherever they are now, and you, wherever you'll end up, what this bank can be."

"Wherever I'll end up? What the hell does that mean?"

Jordan looked down and didn't respond.

"We can't live like this, Jordan," Amadi said.

"Not to worry. With that I agree. But soon enough . . ."

"Jordan, don't you see? In your blind zeal to prove some point you want to make, you're hurting innocents. You're going to start by trying to kill off Abode."

"Abode is hardly innocent. It's a shining example of an outfit that's too entitled. It thinks it has a right to money. The bank's money. My money. Abode thinks it has a right to loans in perpetuity. No one does. Certainly not the Franklins and their little nonprofit. Shit, Amadi, if it has to go, then it has to go. It's acceptable collateral damage for this bank to move into the modern era. Now Abode filed bankruptcy. Just a small temporary setback before its complete demise."

"Bankruptcy? Abode's in bankruptcy now? Then you can't do anything to it. Who did Abode hire as counsel? Josephina Jones and William Pascale? They're the best, and you have zero experience with bankruptcy matters. You have no understanding what's about to happen to the bank. It won't be pretty, and you won't like it. You and the bank will be big losers."

"I'm not worried. I know what'll happen. Sure I do. I've hired Hannah Carson to battle with Abode's lawyers."

"Hannah Carson? And who the hell is she?" Amadi asked. Jordan did not reply. "My god, Jordan. You didn't even hire a bankruptcy lawyer, did you? Jesus, she's gonna get her clock cleaned. Abode will file a plan and cram down the bank." Amadi shook his head in disgust. "You'll cost the bank millions, you fool."

"Those Franklin fuckers aren't going to cram the bank down!"

Jordan yelled back. "Not while I'm at the bank's helm. Let them send me their goddamn cram down plan. I'll take it, crumple it, and cram it *up* their ass! Carson's gonna get the cases dismissed. End of story." As he screamed, Jordan stamped his left foot in frustration, like an eight-year-old.

They each took a moment to catch their breath. It was yet another argument between them without a winner. But Jordan heard an imaginary bell ringing to announce the start of another round.

"What the hell were you reading when I came in the room, Amadi?"

"I've never been a religious man. Even less so after Meg and Alice died. Mr. Hatman brought me some books to read. Luckily, he didn't bring me the Bible. He brought me this," pointing to the Langston Hughes book of poems. "You should read it sometime. You've lost your way. It might give you some much needed guidance."

"I don't need guidance. Guidance is for people who are lost, and I'm not. I know exactly where I'm going."

There was a pause in the shouting match before Amadi said in a quieter voice, "Jordan, why the hell are you here?"

"Damn good question. I'm here because in the end, you're my brother, and that means I'm supposed to give you one more chance to join me and ride this bank out of the past and into the future. Crypto. We'll be rich."

"I don't live in the past, Jordan. I respect it. There's a difference between those two things. And I'm not riding anywhere with you. I do fine. I don't need to be rich. I need to help the community. Do you hear yourself? You're crazy. Certifiably crazy."

"You listen here. For more than a century, you and those ancestors of yours have tried to fight the crackers' prejudice by helping some Black folks here and there. Made you feel good every night, didn't it? But you didn't change a thing. Crackers still hate. Me, I got my solution. I'm dropping in on the crackers where they live.

I'm taking a page out of their handbook. I'm gonna do what they've always done: make money, see profit, and focus on the green. I generously figured I'd give you a chance to come along, but I guess I'm gonna be doing that alone."

He shook his head. "Shit," he whispered and then glared at Amadi. He'd come to say his piece. He'd come to give Amadi one last clear chance to avert what would now come next. It hadn't worked, but then, he hadn't expected it to. It never did.

He wheeled around, left the room, and locked the door behind him. There had been no meeting of the minds. Traveling back through his River Styx, he ascended to ground level. He expected it was the last time he would see his brother. Not a loss. Amadi was merely more acceptable collateral damage. He'd given Amadi a chance, and Amadi hadn't taken it.

Jordan drove back to the bank and punched in the code on the entry keypad to permit his entry into the bank after hours. Once inside, he walked passed the night guard without exchanging words, entered his office, and closed the door behind him. He phoned Robbie McFadden, and after several rings, McFadden answered.

"Kinda late, don't you think, Jordie?" McFadden said as he answered, sounding tired and exasperated. "Did ya' see the Chiefs today, Jordie? Mahomes isn't from this planet. Insane stuff he does on the field. What a talent."

"No, I didn't watch the Chiefs. Look, I've reached out to Bobby Ray," Jordan reported. "It'll all be over soon."

When the call ended, Jordan Browne sat at his desk, in his office, in his bank, in what he hoped would soon be his town. He needed to decide on the next steps. He pondered his decision to become an only child of parents he believed never loved him. He was about to make what was once a family of four a family of one with three members deceased, only two of natural causes. It was the right thing—the only thing.

32

Monday, December 9, 2024

At 3:30 A.M., Ronnie Steele was sound asleep. 3J was not. She had been in bed tossing for hours. Then she tried to lie on her back and stare at the ceiling. Suddenly, as if her brain was not allowing her to drift off to sleep so it could sort things out and tell her something important, she sat straight up in bed.

"Ronnie, wake up," she said as she poked him in the side.

"What's up?" he asked sleepily.

"Ronnie, I couldn't sleep. Something's not right."

"Are you okay?"

"Yeah, yeah, I'm fine. It's nothing like that."

"All right. Then what's up?" Ronnie asked, yawning.

"I've been thinking. Suppose we've been looking at the Amadi investigation all wrong."

"How so?"

"I've been thinking about all the buildings you and Moe have been casing. The first list. All Jordan Browne properties. We figured he would stash his brother in a building he owned, but you found nothing. Endless hours of you guys peeking into rooms and around dark corners and nothing. Then I pondered the sheer number of buildings over by Olive Street on the new list. It's only a few square blocks, but there are lots of buildings, and so many of them locked. No way for you guys to just waltz in. So still nothing."

"Yeah, I know, 3J. I know. And?"

"And . . . I just think everyone on the team's been looking at this the wrong way. Our focus has been too narrow. We're missing something. Not something new. Something you've already seen. Something we all already know about."

"Like what?"

"We've all assumed we needed to look into Jordan Browne and find a link, a property in which he owned an interest where he could keep his brother until after the repo expired."

"Right."

"What if all of this is more than Jordan Browne? When you told me about Robbie McFadden coming out of the bar, it started me thinking. What if Robbie McFadden is involved? Should we be looking for properties *he* owns? Something he owns in that smaller area around Olive Street? That you and Moe saw Robbie McFadden is a fact. And there are no coincidences, only unexplained facts. We need to explain that fact. Ronnie, I think he's involved. It's the only explanation."

Steele sat straight up in bed. "Shit! You're right! That's got to be it."

"I need to get Rome and Moses to find properties in which Robbie McFadden owns an interest within the Olive Street area identified by the text spoof. And we need to ask them to determine if there are any connections whatsoever between Robbie McFadden and Jordan Browne. Do you agree?"

"Absolutely."

3J got out of bed, walked from the bedroom to the kitchen, where her laptop was charging, and wrote an email to Rome and Moses requesting assistance.

Within fifteen minutes, Rome wrote back, "On it!"

Rome considered 3J's new requests. Compared to the massive reading project in which she and Bryon had been engaged for days, the latest requests had a limited scope and she was sure they would be easy to search. She was back in business and now able to help with the data. At last on this engagement, she had a task she could perform quickly. She flipped open her laptop and dove in.

As she started the new research, she quickly learned that searching for anything about Robbie McFadden's holdings wouldn't be simple. At least on the clearnet, he or his IT folks were very schooled in the art of leaving little or no digital trail that could lead to his assets. It made sense. What mob boss would publicize what he owned on the internet? The search revealed nothing, as if he owned nothing. No hits at all. Someone had done a professional job of wiping his digital breadcrumbs from the internet. If he owned an entity with real estate holdings in the four-block area, she would have to find it a different way than by Google searches on the clearnet. "Shit," she muttered to herself.

Rome spent an hour on the dark web using Tor for the search, trying to get a sense of information about Robbie McFadden and his holdings. There was a reasonable amount of encrypted but available information out there, so she needed to use a search filter. She turned to a search app she had developed with the help of GitHub Copilot, one of the many AIs available on the internet and one software developers favored. She gave it parameters: Robert McFadden; Kansas City; real estate holdings; names of each of the streets in the several block area where her SMS spoof had identified Amadi's phone was located.

Since her clearnet searches had failed to locate the names of companies in which McFadden owned an interest, she hoped that searching his name with Tor and her app would reveal any real estate he owned outright and any he owned through a company in which he held an interest. It was dinnertime. She set her search app in motion, closed her computer, curled up on her bed, and tried for the one thing she was not good at: sleep. Just a few hours was all she ever hoped for.

ᘚ

Jennifer Cuello sat in the club chair in Judge Robertson's office facing him, a yellow legal pad resting in her lap. Outside the window behind the judge's desk, the Missouri River flowed, heading east to its rendezvous with the Mighty Mississippi. She had adopted the judge's habit of gazing at the river as she tried to solve a problem. Surprisingly, it often helped.

"What did you find for us about nonprofits in Chapter 11, Jennifer?"

"As you recalled, Judge, there are a handful of cases, but fewer than I expected. I guess most nonprofits manage to stay out of financial trouble."

"Or they simply fail and need no bankruptcy protection."

"Yes, that too. What I found is consistent with your memory. They have no owners. So there is no class of owners to treat under the plan. No owners to retain stock or receive anything under the plan. Like you said, the unsecured creditors are usually protected by the notion that if they're not paid in full, the owners can't keep their stock in the debtor. But in a nonprofit Chapter 11, the unsecureds lose that protection because there are no owners."

"Exactly. Did you find any situations analogous to nonprofits?"

"I did. Farm cooperatives. I never knew this, but many of the local farm cooperatives have no owners either. They're member run, and the members are the local farmers. In the farm cooperative bankruptcies I found, same result. No owners meant the debtor could get away with paying less than one hundred cents on the dollar to unsecured creditors. And in a couple of the co-op cases, the debtor paid nothing to unsecureds."

Judge Robertson smiled, and Jennifer Cuello knew him well enough to know that meant he was pleased with her research. She'd come a long way from her first week as a law clerk when she wasn't sure she could do the job. It hadn't taken her long to realize that not only could she do it, she had talent for it. Judge Robertson valued excellence, and she valued his appreciation for her work.

"Say, did you happen to see this request to examine the owner of Commonwealth Savings and Loan filed by Ms. Jones?"

"I just scanned it before I came in to talk to you."

"Very unusual. In the filing, it represents that Ms. Jones asked Hannah Carson to agree on a date and time and Ms. Carson said no. Apparently, Carson told Jones to file a request, which is what I'm looking at here."

Cuello smiled. She could guess what was coming.

"I signed the order a few minutes ago. I ordered this gentleman, Jordan Browne, to appear at the Greene Madison offices on December twentieth at nine in the morning so Ms. Jones can examine him."

He shook his head, and Jennifer waited, knowing he had something else to say.

"Damnedest thing. This Carson lawyer seems to have started off her on-the-job bankruptcy training with some unnecessary self-inflicted wounds. We'll have to keep an eye on her strategy and look carefully at what she files. I could do without an untrained loose cannon in my court. We both have better ways to fill up our day."

Jennifer smiled and nodded her agreement.

"As you have time, let's have you draft a memo of what you've found in your research. My guess is the memo will end up being the cornerstone of my written plan confirmation ruling on this one."

Not only had Rome slept, she'd slept more deeply and longer than she expected. When she awoke, it was after midnight, London Time, and evening, Kansas City time. Her app icon flagged a notice letting her know the app had information for her. She clicked on the app as she tried to wipe the sleep from her eyes. As it opened, she ground beans and brewed a pot of coffee.

The app showed only one dark web hit, an LLC named Rabbits and Goats LLC in which Robbie McFadden owned a controlling interest. "What an odd name," she said to herself. More significantly, the app reported the LLC owned a single property at 1801 Olive Street in Kansas City. A quick look at MapQuest confirmed the property was right at the corner of Olive and Eighteenth Streets, precisely in the area identified by her SMS spoof geolocation.

She returned quickly to clearnet searches, her fingers moving at blinding speed across her keyboard. She learned it was a two-story, 1940s building with a brick façade and a subbasement. She then searched to find any connection between Jordan Browne and Robert McFadden. In due course, she discovered they had gone to high school together, and she found a picture of them in their senior yearbook clowning around.

She forwarded the information to 3J with a quick note. "Here is what I have found. The two went to high school together. McFadden has one property in the Olive Street area I identified: 1801 Olive Street. It's a two-story building with a subbasement. It's owned by a company called Rabbits and Goats LLC. Strange name. Maybe that will mean something to you or one of your team members. McFadden owns the controlling interest in the LLC. 3J, this has to be the place of Amadi Browne's incarceration. It just has to be!"

33

THE BANK HAD closed for the day but Jordan lingered in his office awaiting Bobby Ray. His encounter with Amadi had failed miserably. He knew it would. It was nothing more than the culmination of a lifetime of dispute and disagreement with family members. He was the outsider in the family, and he'd long felt they ignored, discounted, and mistreated him. His argument with Amadi confirmed it, and he believed it was his last discussion with any family member he would have. But the cold reality of what came next still weighed on his mind. He had to do what needed to be done to keep the bank and his dream alive. He was about to commission a murder.

Right before eight, Jordan moved from his office to a chair near the front door, and he caught sight of the night guard taking notice of him. At precisely eight, Bobby Ray appeared at the bank's revolving door and peered in, and Jordan went out to meet him. He and Bobby Ray exchanged no pleasantries. Jordan wasn't looking for them, and even if he was, he figured Bobby Ray wasn't the guy to hand them out.

Ordinarily, Jordan would have confirmed the person he was meeting was in fact Bobby Ray, but he needed no confirmation. As Jordan surveyed his guest, there could be no question that the creature he was now standing next to was Bobby Ray. Ray was roughly five seven and maybe a hundred fifty pounds of compact muscle, which Jordan could see showing through his well-worn sweatshirt. He saw a deeply pockmarked face from what must have been a raging case of teenage acne and a complete absence of facial hair. Ray had thin lips he seemed to press into an even thinner line, adding to his sinister look, and nondescript, unkempt brown hair.

But it was the eyes. When Jordan saw them, he knew it was Ray. McFadden had described Ray as edgy. The description didn't do Ray justice. Not when Jordan saw his close-set, dark eyes, which looked like someone had honed them sharp enough to draw blood from a jugular vein—just by their icy glare. They say the eyes are the windows into the soul, but Ray's eyes were windows into a cold abyss. While people might have an element of nothingness that showed through, Ray was only nothingness—nothing else—and it froze Jordan in his tracks.

The two of them stood under a streetlight, steam coming from their mouths in the cold December air. As Ray stared at Jordan, the temperature under the streetlight seemed to drop ten degrees and the steam seemed to turn to airborne ice. Jordan had no words. Instead, Ray initiated the brief discussion.

"You know why I'm here?" Ray asked in a sinister, raspy voice.

"Yes."

"Mr. McFadden wants to know. We're proceeding forward? Or did you get cold feet again?" Ray hissed.

"Forward. But with some rules."

"Rules? Shit. No one said nothin' to me about rules. What kind of fuckin' rules you got for me?"

"First you deal with Maximilian Cruz. Then you call me, and when I give you the go-ahead, you deal with my brother."

"Deal with?" Ray shook his head quickly as if to clear his brain of what he'd heard. "What's this 'deal with' shit? I ain't gonna *deal* with them or anyone else. I don't do deals. I'm gonna off 'em.

That's what I do. That's what you want me to do. Say it. Say it, goddamn it!"

Ray had howled at Jordan loud enough that the night guard inside the bank heard Ray's loud voice, muffled by the glass, and came to the door. "Everything okay, Mr. Browne?" he called out.

Jordan backed toward the revolving door while keeping eye contact with Ray. As his back got closer to the door, he responded over his shoulder to the guard without turning to look into the bank, "All good. Not to worry, Fred."

The guard moved away from the door and Jordan moved back toward Ray. Jordan narrowed his eyes as he looked at the short creature who had just yelled at him, compelling him to utter the words, as if invoking them were magical and would make all of Jordan's problems go away.

Ray laughed. "Banker man, Mr. McFadden warned me you might be a problem on this job. I'm a busy man. You in or you out?"

Jordan thrust both hands deep into his pant pockets, squared himself to face Ray, leaned closer, and said softly but defiantly, emphasizing each sound, "Kill them. Maximilian Cruz and Amadi Browne." As Jordan heard his voice utter the words, he realized they sounded as sinister as the words spoken by Ray.

Before Ray could say anything in response, Jordan flipped him the extra set of keys to the building and room where Cruz held Amadi, wheeled around and headed for the parking lot and his car. His hands, still in his pockets, trembled from an unholy mix of fear, anxiety, adrenaline, and a new sense of power he hadn't felt before. All unleashed from deep within him by his confrontation with the creature called Bobby Ray.

Jordan had transformed. McFadden had told him to be the boss. Now he was. He was no longer Jordan Browne, banker. He was no longer Jordan Browne, fourth member of the Browne family. He was more. He was like McFadden. He was like Ray. He was one of them. As he got into his car, he curled his lips into the sneer of a killer. It felt good.

❧

Cruz was back in his apartment at 7:45 p.m. He'd run errands for his mother that morning and then had gotten to work on watching a new mark, another project McFadden had assigned him to. But he hadn't been able to get Amadi out of his head.

He still hadn't sorted out what to do about Amadi and whatever Jordan had planned. It was a dilemma. He didn't trust Jordan to let Amadi live, but he knew he wasn't supposed to meddle. But now that he knew saving Amadi would also help save Abode, it made it difficult for him to avoid meddling. He felt an obligation to do anything he could to help Abode, even though it was definitely not a part of his job description. He was supposed to do whatever McFadden told him to do. Period. Cruz had always done that, and McFadden had been good to him.

He'd been hired to snatch Amadi and watch over him. He'd done that. But he hadn't been told to protect Amadi or free him, even if that meant helping save Abode. Helping Abode had nothing to do with his instructions.

He thumbed through his mail, dropped it back on his kitchen table, scanned his apartment to find everything in order, and then turned to head back out to the street. His other mark needed watching again.

As he got to the door, he remembered he hadn't checked for any Jordan recordings his planted bug might have captured. He shook his head, reentered his apartment, took off his hat, carefully placing it on his kitchen table near his laptop, and logged on to his computer. Once it booted up, he logged on to his wireless microphone account and found a recording it had made late the previous night. It seemed to be a brief phone conversation, and while Cruz couldn't tell who was on the other end of the line, it was clear it had to be Robbie McFadden. When he heard Jordan invoke the name of Bobby Ray, his breathing stopped for a moment and his eyes widened.

He knew Ray. Everyone in the McFadden organization did. No one in the organization got anywhere near him. He was McFadden's killer. Outsiders considered him dangerous. The people in McFadden's organization considered Ray crazy and evil. He killed for pleasure. He killed as directed. He killed for no reason. Crazy. He was used by McFadden on "special" engagements.

"Sheeeit!" he said hoarsely. Then he grabbed his hat and keys and raced out of his apartment to his car. "That crazy motherfucker has hired a stone-cold killer to get rid of Amadi," he whispered to himself as he got into his car and turned over the ignition. He shook his head in disgust, then panicked when he realized he could be too late and headed for the Olive Street building as fast as he could coax the Ford to go. He had made his decision. He would save Amadi and protect him.

3J returned to her desk from a long, late meeting unrelated to Abode to find an evening email from Rome. She read it quickly and said, "Holy shit!" under her breath before calling Ronnie, giving him the information Rome had sent her, and ending the call with, "Go!" Then she reread Rome's email and mentally agreed with Rome's assessment. This has to be the location.

She forwarded the email to Ronnie as backup to what she'd told him over the phone and sent him a text letting him know she'd sent the email and imploring him to get to the location posthaste. Only then did she call Pascale and summarize the latest news and bring him up to speed. "I've got Ronnie on the move as we speak. I still don't know if we're in time."

"Can you read me the full email, 3J?" he asked.

"Sure thing," she said as she opened the email.

"Rabbits and Goats LLC? Jesus," Pascale said as she finished reading it to him.

"You know what that is, Bill? It means nothing to me."

"I think I know what it means. In early twentieth century Kansas City, goats and rabbits referred to rival factions of the democratic party, named after the animals that lived near where each of the faction's constituents lived—West Bluff and the valley of the OK Creek, if I recall correctly. Some historians also postulate it marked the beginning of different mob groups in our fair city. Only someone with a deep interest in Kansas City's history and politics would name an LLC Rabbits and Goats."

"Damn," 3J replied. "A mobster with a deep interest in history. Well, McFadden is in this deep if he's let Jordan keep his brother locked up in a Rabbits and Goats LLC building. And even deeper if Amadi is killed. I just hope we're in time to keep that from happening."

34

As Cruz sped toward the Olive Street building, Kansas City's first significant winter weather event began: a frozen mist storm. Spring showers seemed to help wash away the city's winter, summer rain storms freshened the city's air, and fall rain hastened the color changes in the city's many oaks and maples. But Kansas City's winter freezing mist was good for absolutely nothing except perilous streets, the occasional blackout from downed power lines, and general roadway mayhem.

As the ice began to collect on the streets, Cruz had no choice but to slow down as the rear of his car yawed on the slick pavement. It seemed to him he had hit every red light between River Market and Olive Street, and Jordan's comments on the recording were still ringing in his ears. "Come on. Come on," he said under his breath as he sat at a red light.

Finally he arrived and edged into a parking spot down the block from the building, sliding to a halt inches before he would have tapped the car in front. He ran and slipped his way to the building, raced through the hallways, and went down two flights of stairs to the locked door. After fumbling with the keys, he unlocked the door, threw it open, and yelled, "Let's go!" to Amadi, who was sitting on the cot, back to the wall, reading one of the books Cruz had left for him.

"Go? What do you mean?" Amadi asked without moving.

"Up! Let's go! No time!" Cruz said grabbing Amadi's overcoat and tossing it to him.

Amadi rose off the cot slowly, and Cruz ran over to him, grabbed his arm, pulled him completely to his feet, and ran with him to the door.

"Tell me what's going on!" Amadi demanded.

"No time. Amadi, please come with me! Quickly!"

In response, Amadi began to move with a sense of urgency.

The two ran through the hallway, up the two flights of stairs, and out into the cold night. They skidded and almost fell as they traversed the remaining half of a city block to the waiting car.

"Almost there!" Cruz yelled. "Into the car!" As he yelled, he reached for his gun and readied himself just in case.

Bobby Ray was in his small Subaru Impreza speeding from the Commonwealth building north to Olive and Eighteenth as the ice storm began. His plan was simple. He would access the subbasement room, enter, shoot Amadi dead, leave the body as it bled out, and exit. He'd ditch the gun and leave no evidence for the police to link him to the shooting. In and out quickly. A plain-vanilla hit. Nothing fancy and quite pleasurable. Nothing fancy was always the better way to go in his line of work. The pleasure was his reward.

As he drove on Main Street, he had to slow down as the ice began to accumulate. "Shit," he muttered under his breath. He finally arrived on Olive Street, and as he approached the building, he saw Cruz and Amadi a half block in front of him making their way to Cruz's car, awkwardly traversing the icy sidewalk. Ray slammed on his brakes, and his car skidded sideways, hopped the curb, and landed on the sidewalk with the front wheels on a small grassy knoll in front of one of the buildings. Before the car came to a full stop, Ray popped it into neutral, slammed on the emergency brake, opened his door, and ran toward Cruz and Amadi, gun drawn. He too struggled with the ice and nearly fell twice as he tried desperately to pick up speed and close the distance.

As he approached Cruz and Amadi, he stopped and fired twice. The shots rang out loudly and echoed off of the surrounding buildings like thunder echoes off mountains. The shots took Cruz and Amadi by surprise.

The first shot went wide right of Cruz, who turned when he heard it. He instinctively put himself between Ray and Amadi as Ray squeezed off the second round, this one catching Cruz in the left shoulder. The shot passed through the muscle, exiting from Cruz's rear deltoid. Cruz cried out in pain and spun sideways but didn't fall. Amadi froze in fear. Cruz regained his balance and began to push Amadi into the passenger side of the car yelling, "Get in! Get down!"

With Amadi in the car, Cruz fired back at Ray, missing his left ear by a millimeter.

"Are you hit?" Cruz yelled out at Amadi.

"No. I'm fine! Max, you need to get in and get us out of here!"

Ray felt Cruz's shot whiz by his ear, sounding like it was sizzling as it passed. He didn't flinch and ignored it. He pointed his gun and fired a third time, again with the shot echoing, but as he squeezed the trigger, he slipped and the shot ricocheted off the sidewalk right below Cruz's feet.

Cruz slammed the passenger door shut behind Amadi, ran across the front of the car to the driver's side, shot wildly one more time in Ray's general direction, and got in. As he pulled away from the curb, he yelled "Amadi, stay down!"

Ray fired one more time. The shot glanced off Cruz's bumper, and he saw Cruz slowly pull the car away from the curb. He wheeled around and started back to his car as fast as the ice-coated sidewalk would permit. The engine had stalled while Ray was shooting at Cruz, and he pounded the steering wheel with both hands and screamed, "Start, goddamn it!" After several attempts, the engine finally turned over. He rolled his window down and transferred the gun to his left hand, in case he could get a shot off as he drove. He navigated for a few hundred feet on the sidewalk and lawn before careening back onto the icy road to begin chasing Cruz and Amadi.

❧

Ronnie and Moe were still two blocks from the Olive Street building when they heard numerous pops echoing off the buildings. "Shit! Gunfire!" Moe yelled as Ronnie clutched the wheel trying to pilot the car on the icy road. Gunfire in many neighborhoods would have brought a dozen of Kansas City's finest racing to the area with sirens blaring, but at Olive and Eighteenth, the sound of gunfire was routine. There were no police cruising the neighborhood. The locals summoned none. No squad cars were coming.

They pulled up to the building, saw nothing, and quickly surveyed the building and its surrounds. "Looks just like the one on Seventeenth and Brooklyn," Ronnie said as they entered the building on Olive Street, the front door still ajar from what appeared to be a hasty exit. They ignored the closed doors on the main floor, found the stairs to the basement, and descended two steps at a time. At the bottom, they found the stairs to the subbasement and raced down the fifteen steps to a hallway and a door with two locks.

The door was open, and they entered the room that locked from the outside. With hopes high, they looked around and found all the evidence that someone had been there—clothes, books, a paper bag in a garbage pail that appeared to have held a breakfast meal, a drying shower stall—but no one was in the room. They looked around briefly to convince themselves this was likely the room in which a captor had held Amadi.

"Ronnie, look at this," Moe said, pointing to the phone charging cable snaking from an outlet into a locked locker.

Ronnie nodded. "He was definitely here. I can see a phone inside. It must be Amadi's, but he's definitely gone now."

"Motherfucker! This guy is harder to find than a fugitive on the run."

"I'm guessing he *is* a fugitive on the run at this point. Or at least, whoever has him is the fugitive and is one step ahead of us. Now what?"

They reported to 3J that they found no one in the Olive Street building, but they were certain Amadi had been there and had left in a hurry. They apologized. Once again, they had arrived too late. Once the call was complete, they sat in the car with the heater and defroster on high, trying to figure out what to do next.

"So what do we know and what do we suspect?" Moe asked.

"I don't know that we know much at all, Moe. But I have suspicions. Top of my list—Robbie McFadden put a hit out on Amadi."

"But why would he do that?"

"No idea. Amadi owes him money? Amadi pissed him off? Who knows?"

"I don't see that here," Moe replied. "Maybe someone hired McFadden and his goons for a hit. We always knew McFadden had a hit-for-hire side hustle and that it's been a lucrative business for him. We could never make anything stick, but we've always known it."

"Okay. I'll do 'Hit For Hire' for a hundred bucks," Ronnie said, invoking a popular game show. "The winning question is going to be, 'Who hired Robbie McFadden?' What answer do you think'll be revealed behind the hundred bucks game show tile?"

"I'm of a mind the answer is 'Jordan Browne.' Why? Once again, he's the one with the most to gain and the most to lose."

"Bankers don't usually put out a hit, let alone on their own brother. But on this one, I have to agree. He's known McFadden since high school. He probably knows what McFadden does for a living. Maybe he even knows all of McFadden's lines of business. You think he could turn into a cold-blooded killer? Banker to barbarous?" He paused to think and began to consider exactly how far Jordan Browne might go for money and his dream of a crypto-centric bank. "Maybe so, Moe. Whata we do?"

"Not sure," Moe admitted. "Confront Jordan Browne? Shake things up over at his place? Confront Robbie McFadden?"

"We'd never get within a hundred yards of McFadden unless he sees it's me and wants to pick up where he left off when I was on vice: breaking my stones and loving every minute of it. And Jordan Browne? Not sure. Let's think about that one for a little while."

❧

Cruz headed north on Olive. His left shoulder was bleeding. At first, it hadn't hurt, but the more distance he put between the building and his car, the more it first ached and then hurt. The blood slowed to an ooze. The bullet had done damage, and soon he would need to attend to it. Soon but not yet.

Olive intersected Truman Road, a major east-west thoroughfare connecting Kansas City and Harry Truman's old stomping ground, Independence, Missouri. Beyond was the I-70 overpass. Cruz turned east on Truman and drove a ways before seeing a narrow, unlit alley running between a dark used tire store and an abandoned, boarded up storefront on the north side of Truman. He pulled into the alley. The concrete that formed the alley pavement was crumbling, and the car bounced as it pulled deeper into the dark. As the car bounced, Cruz grimaced, grabbing his shoulder with his right hand, momentarily leaving the steering wheel hands-free. The car came to a stop, and he killed the engine, leaving the keys hanging in the ignition.

His plan was simple. Wait in the dark alley until he deemed it safe enough to move to a different location. But after a moment, he realized that with two adults in the car, unless he started the engine again, the rear window would quickly fog up because of the cold outside and he wouldn't be able to see anything—such as Ray's car. He turned over the engine and turned on the front and rear defrosters. Then he reloaded his gun as Amadi looked on, seemingly in shock.

"Where the hell are we going and who in God's name was that back there?" Amadi demanded, staring at the gun.

As Cruz drove away from the Olive Street building, he had headed in the opposite direction from where he hoped to go after he shook Ray from pursuit. "Look, as soon as I'm sure we've lost the shooter, I'm gonna take you someplace I think will be safe for a short while." He didn't answer Amadi's question, hoping Amadi would drop it.

"And who was that back there?" Amadi asked again.

Cruz frowned as he looked out the front windshield, then he turned to Amadi, narrowed his eyes, shook his head, and said, "I didn't want to have to tell you this. I hope you can handle it, my man. That gun-toting executioner back there was someone your bro hired to kill you," Cruz said.

Amadi looked stunned and said nothing. His gaze moved from the gun to Cruz's face. Stunned changed to pained.

Cruz knew Amadi was in shock and probably needed to talk, but Cruz couldn't. He needed to direct all his attention to his rear-view mirror, trying to see out his back window to Truman Road and any sign that Ray was on their trail. He saw several drunks stagger by, heading east on Truman past the alley and into the night. He saw two homeless men, grimy and covered by tattered, threadbare blankets meander past the alley. At first, he was worried they would turn into the alley and try to find shelter from the ice storm. But they continued on. After those passersby, the street was deserted, as it should be in the middle of an ice storm. No cars. No people. No sounds except the wind and the frozen mist now turning to freezing rain.

Cruz waited and continued to watch, which was something he frequently had to do in his profession. He was a watcher. He wanted to pull out of the alley as soon as possible, but before he could, he needed to be certain that Amadi would be safe. For that, Cruz would have to be sure he had lost Ray.

~

Visibility was steadily diminishing as the freezing rain made it clear it was there to stay for a while. Ray strained as he peered through his icy windshield, frantically trying to see Cruz's Ford. He stopped at the intersection of Olive and Truman, unsure which direction to go. When Ray was about a block behind Cruz, he thought he'd seen Cruz's car come through this intersection. But now, as he sat at the intersection, he was no longer sure. He had three potential ways to proceed and no feeling for which was the correct choice.

He slammed his hands on the steering wheel and screamed, "Goddamn it to hell and back again!"

After a few moments, Ray knew he had to do something and go one way or another. He decided to roll the dice and headed west on Truman back toward downtown Kansas City. It was as good a choice as any. In minutes, he was five blocks away from the alley and getting farther away with each second he drove. While he kept looking in his rearview mirror, the ice that had formed on his back window eliminated his visibility, and he could no longer see the Olive Street intersection.

35

MAX LOOKED AT Amadi sitting in the passenger seat, eyes closed as if eliminating his sense of sight would keep everything that had transpired out of his consciousness. Without opening his eyes, Amadi finally said, "Max, the shooter seemed to be trying to kill you. Have you considered that?"

"He shot at me because I was taking care of you."

Minutes passed. Cruz wore his watch on his left wrist. As he rotated his wrist to see the watch face, he grimaced and closed his eyes for a moment. The bullet wound, which had stopped bleeding for a time, had started to seep blood again. The shoulder was still throbbing. He opened his eyes and his watch showed it was now 10:30. They had been sitting in the dark alley for more than an hour. No sign of Ray. No sign of anyone since the drunk and the homeless people passed by. Max decided it was now or never time. No time for hesitation. They had to back out and leave. He needed to get Amadi to some place safer, and he needed to take care of his shoulder. Cruz looked over at Amadi, poked his arm so he would open his eyes, and nodded at him. Amadi nodded back and closed his eyes again.

With the car lights still off, Cruz backed slowly out of the alley onto Truman Road and headed west under the Bruce R. Watkins Drive to Charlotte Street. There he turned left, past the Truman

Medical Center, and in a few blocks, he entered his mother's Abode neighborhood, checking every few seconds to make sure Ray was not on their tail.

He slowly pulled up in front of her house. Because the ice had been slowing him down, it was eleven when he arrived. He knew it was late, but he could see the lights from the television dancing on his mother's front window curtains. He hoped she was still awake and hadn't fallen asleep in her easy chair watching a late movie.

He intended to drop off Amadi and then drive back to his apartment to attend to his shoulder. His mother would see his bloodstained clothing. She had seen it before, but it would still upset her. There was nothing he could do to prevent that.

Cruz looked at Amadi and tapped him on the arm so he would open his eyes. "We're here. Let's go. Out!" he commanded.

"Where is here? Where are we now?"

"*La casa de mi madre*—my mother's house," Cruz explained.

"Your mother? Does she know we're coming?"

"Of course not." He shook his head. "You've been sitting next to me this whole time. Did you hear me call her?" Cruz asked sarcastically, showing his stress.

"I'm sorry. I shouldn't have upset you."

"Look, it's fine," Max replied, exhaling slowly to slow his heart rate. "Really. She doesn't know. Please, Amadi, get out. We need to get you inside."

They walked to the front door, and Cruz gently knocked.

"Momá. *Soy yo.* It's me," Max said through the door. "Open up, please."

He heard shuffling from within, and then the door lock turned and the door opened. Cruz's mother stepped aside and Cruz and Amadi moved past her quickly, entering the house. She peeked outside briefly, then closed and locked the door behind them.

"What Maxie? Are you running in the gangs again?" she asked him suspiciously.

"No, Momá. I told you. No more gangs for me. Momá, this is Amadi Browne. He's the president of a bank. I'm supposed to take care of him. Someone has been following us. I lost him in the bad weather. I need to leave Amadi here, and I need you to take care of him for a few hours while I get everything under control."

Cruz's mother looked dubiously from Cruz to Amadi and back to Cruz. "Banker? A few hours?"

"Yes, Momá. Only a few."

"Where will you go?"

"I've got some loose ends to tie up."

"Loose ends? In this weather, Maxie?"

"I do, Momá. Not gangs. Just business. I'll be back shortly. Please. Do this for me? Please?"

His mother folded her arms across her pink robe, silently demanding more information.

"Momá, I've tried not to involve you in my work. But I have to now. I'm sorry. I've got some trouble I need to resolve. And I need this favor from you. It won't take long. I promise."

She shook her head. "Trouble. There it is. All right, Maxie. All right." As Cruz's mother agreed, she saw the bloodstain on his jacket and shirt from the gunshot wound. "Maxie, you're hurt!"

"Nah. Not hurt Momá. It's fine. It'll be fine."

Cruz knew he hadn't convinced his mother of anything. "I need to wash this out," he said pointing to his shoulder. "I'll be right back."

He went into the bathroom to survey the damage from Ray's bullet. When he took off his shirt, he saw that the shot had gone clear through. It could have been worse, but on the other hand, it was still bleeding slowly. He washed the wound for a few minutes, put his bloody shirt back on, and returned to the living room.

He was quiet for a few moments as he watched his mother knitting in her chair, which he knew was one way she tried to stay calm. He had upset her, but there was nothing he could do about it. He had spent his life upsetting and disappointing her. And she still loved him, unconditionally. Occasionally he made her proud, but he hadn't made it easy for her to love him over the years. He had come to appreciate all the love despite what he did for a living.

He turned to Amadi. "At some point here pretty soon, I'm going to have to leave for a while. When I leave, do not—repeat *do not*—exit this house until I get back. Do you hear me? Stay here. Stay put. Stay inside. And for god's sake, call no one. No one! Not me. Not anyone."

He turned back to his mother. "Momá, when I leave, don't answer the door for anyone. Momá *entiendes*? Do you understand, Momá? No one. If anyone knocks, call the cops. Amadi, this is my *mamá*. My only *mamá*. You keep her safe, goddamn it. That's your job now."

Amadi nodded his head. He understood. Cruz's mother continued to stare at her son, and Max knew she understood too. She had excised him from the gang life, but not from the lifestyle. As she stared at him silently, shaking her head, he was sure she was wondering what he'd gotten himself into now.

"Max, what about my phone? The pacemaker. Remember?"

"No fix for that right now, bro. I'll try to bring a burner back for you."

Amadi nodded.

Momá walked over to her son, reached up, and put her hands on his cheeks. "My Maxie," she whispered, shaking her head slowly back and forth as she spoke. He bent his head so she could reach it more easily. She moved his head gently back and forth between her hands, kissed his forehead, and let him go.

Then she turned toward her kitchen and said, "Mr. Amadi, you hungry? Follow me," waving him into the kitchen like a traffic cop waving cars to proceed.

~

Ray drove farther west on Truman until he got to the Grand Boulevard intersection on the edge of downtown. By now, it was 10:30. He scanned his surroundings but not only saw no sign of Cruz, he saw no sign of any cars. Nothing but the downtown skyline lights shrouded in cloudy fog and the off-white, thin trails of descending freezing rain illuminated by the streetlights. He pulled over on Grand Boulevard, at first in front of a UMB bank branch, and then he thought better of it, not wanting it to appear he was casing the bank for a robbery job. He crept the car down the block where nearby apartment dwellers had parked their cars for the night. He was a killer, not a bank robber. There was no point having a cop stop and investigate why he sat in a parked car in front of a bank in the late evening.

He called Jordan, who answered on the second ring. "I lost them. Where does Cruz live?"

"What? Jesus. McFadden said you were the best. What the hell do you mean you lost them?"

Ray ignored Jordan's response. "Listen to me. Where the fuck does Cruz live?"

"My lord! How the hell should I know where he lives."

Before Ray could say anything else, he heard a click. Jordan had hung up on him.

"Motherfuckin' amateur," Ray muttered emphatically under his breath. He didn't know what to do next. He sat in his car for twenty minutes, avoiding doing the obvious—contacting Robbie McFadden. He had no other play. He was sure a call to the boss man in the middle of the night would be risky, but he had a job to do, and he had to find out where Cruz lived quickly.

As Ray feared, McFadden was more than unhappy when he called, but he did answer. As Ray expected, the call was quick. McFadden fumbled around for a moment when Ray asked about Cruz and then said in an irritated tone, "Apartment complex at Third and Oak in River Market. Apartment two eleven." Once again, Ray heard a click. McFadden had hung up on him.

With the information from McFadden, Bobby Ray pulled out from his parking spot and slowly drove twelve blocks north on

Grand, then over to Third and Oak. The rain had let up, but the streets were coated with a thin, black layer of ice, so the trip was treacherous and the car slipped and skidded several times. There was only one apartment complex at the intersection. The gray complex had a small off-street parking area with several empty slots.

Ray looked but didn't see Cruz's Ford parked. Cruz hadn't arrived home yet. Maybe he wasn't coming home, but staking out his apartment complex was all Ray could think of to do. It was still windy and cold as he pulled into one of the open slots and waited for Cruz to arrive. If Cruz came home, Ray would surprise him and gun him down once and for all.

If anyone ever asked Bobby Ray what he did for a living, he would have to answer that most of what he did was wait. With one steely glare, no one would dare ask him what he did when the waiting was over. But if they did, he'd have to say that when the waiting was over, the fun began. He enjoyed what he did for a living. McFadden had preached that it was important in life to be passionate about something. Ray was.

As he sat, he decided that once he took out Cruz, he'd figure out what to do about Amadi Browne. And whoever the third target McFadden had referred to was, Ray might need to take care of that one as well. A busy few days for Ray. Lots of hit inventory on his killer shelves.

36

Tuesday, December 10, 2024

A LITTLE AFTER midnight, Cruz quietly left his mother's house, locked the door behind him, got in his car, and headed for his apartment.

His shoulder throbbed. The bleeding had slowed but was still steady, and he needed to get to his special medical kit and try to quell the bleeding and kill the pain. He'd been shot before, so he wasn't panicked. When he got home, he'd pour rubbing alcohol in the wound to kill the germs. He had brown powder, hydrophilic polymer and potassium ferrate, he'd pour into the wound to seal it off and almost instantly stop the bleeding. It was miracle stuff he learned about in the gang. Someone in the gang had told him it was an old CIA trick. It would hurt like hell when he poured it into the wound, but it needed to be done. He'd done it before, and he knew what to expect.

Then he could superglue the wound shut and bandage it—another trick, this one borrowed by the gang from the surgeons of the world. The gang had been a source for all measure of life lessons for Cruz, some good and some dark. Even after he left the gang life, he looked back on it and never believed it was all bad. Now he was minutes away from repairing the damage to his arm. Then he'd have to figure out what to do with Amadi Browne.

As he drove, his thoughts turned to his mother and Amadi. He knew she'd take good care of him and do what Cruz had asked, but he wasn't so sure Amadi would do what Cruz wanted. Within minutes, Cruz became a little light-headed and even dizzy, probably from the loss of blood and the adrenaline that had been rushing through his body for the last few hours but which was now subsiding.

He stopped thinking about anything other than getting home and getting patched up and arrived at his apartment complex within fifteen minutes.

Ray sat in his Impreza, lights out and engine off, trying not to think about how cold it was in his car. His windows had fogged and he periodically wiped the driver's side window so he could peer out and watch for Cruz, but he decided not to turn on his car for fear Cruz would pull up, notice the car was on, and see him inside.

A baseball cap was pulled low across his brow and his coat collar was raised over his neck. He put his gun down on the seat between his legs, thinking only momentarily how unfortunate it would be if the gun accidentally discharged while resting so close to his crotch. He considered moving it to the passenger seat, but he didn't want it to be even that short a distance from his body as he waited for Cruz.

His breathing was causing a layer of condensation to form on the window and it was making it harder and harder for him to see with precision what was going on outside his car. For the moment, he was missing nothing because nothing was going on. The lot was quiet. River Market was quiet. Ray was certain Kansas City was quiet. For all he knew, the entire state of Missouri was quiet, at least for the time being.

As he sat, he identified the different ways he could kill Cruz.

He could kill him slowly, maybe with a shot to each kneecap, and let Cruz writhe in pain for a while before finally taking him out. Or he could put a shot in his abdomen and let him bleed out slowly on the ground. Ray imagined himself a bullfighter slowly killing the bull in front of a cheering crowd. Bullfighting was a tradition most of the world would never understand, just as Ray's chosen profession was something most of the world would not understand.

If he killed Cruz slowly, it would not be to set an example for others in the McFadden organization of what happens when a soldier goes rogue and not because McFadden wanted Cruz to suffer. McFadden never told Ray to make him suffer. No. If he killed him slowly, watching Cruz suffer would leave Ray satisfied, first by the frenzy Ray would feel just before the kill shot. Then, when he squeezed the trigger, he would have a feeling of climax and exquisite emotional release.

Ray had no boyfriends or girlfriends. No relationships with humans. He had no sex. He hadn't read *Playboy* in the bathroom as a teenager. Instead, he'd dreamed of killing while he sat on the toilet. He got off on those dreams. But now, he didn't have to dream because he had his guns and his kills. He got off on the kills. It was better than any sex could ever be.

While the slow methods would be rewarding in so many ways, the slow method sometimes had a way of going awry. If he shot Cruz and he lived, Ray was as good as dead himself. McFadden was certain to take out Ray if he failed again. Also, the longer he lingered over Cruz, the more chance someone would see him and give the police an accurate description.

No. On this job, quick, final, and fatal was the only way to go.

Killing Cruz would be one of the highlights of his career. He counted on an intense experience. He would enjoy it. His body shuddered with pleasure and he drew his thin lips into a satanic smile, the smile of an executioner about to enjoy the spoils of his craft.

As he contemplated his options, he heard a car pull up on Oak Street and slowly make its way into the lot only a few slots away from him. Ray slowly raised himself in the seat, looked out from under his cap, wiped the driver's side window with his hand, and saw it was the black Ford he had been waiting for. Cruz was home. It was showtime. Three of Ray's fingers on his right hand slowly encased the gun handle while his pointer found the trigger and caressed it gently. He slowly moved his pointer back and forth on the trigger. His hand had assumed the position, and he was ready.

From his car, Bobby Ray watched Cruz get out of the Ford. He noticed Cruz with a gun in his right hand drawn across his body and pressing against his left shoulder. Cruz looked like he was in pain. Ray figured he must have hit Cruz with one of his Olive Street bullets and smiled. His pleasure was building. He was ready to explode with delight.

Cruz kicked the car door shut with his heel, locked the doors, and slowly and deliberately trudged to the stairs that led up to the apartment building entrance. He seemed completely focused on what he was doing, and his movements were wobbly.

Ray opened his door, exited the Impreza, and stealthily moved toward Cruz like a coyote stalking its prey. Cruz turned, apparently hearing or sensing movement behind him, and as he squared his body around, he raised his gun and shot wildly at Ray twice, missing him. Then he turned back to run up the stairs and into his building.

Ray raised his weapon, smiled, aimed, and calmly squeezed off one round, hitting Cruz in the lower back of his head. Cruz buckled slowly to the steps. From the force of the bullet's impact, his hat flew off and came to rest on the top step. Ray approached the corpse and for good measure, shot Cruz again in the upper back.

"Die, motherfucker," Ray said under his breath. If he intended for Cruz to hear him, that wasn't going to be possible. What had been a handsome blue-eyed face on the front of a head sitting on a pair of broad shoulders was no longer intact. The head shot had blown off part of Cruz's lower face. His jaw and mouth were gone and with them, his signature smile. The lower portion of his face had exploded into bone, blood, and tissue splattering over the icy steps and the dormant shrubbery in front of Cruz's apartment building. But his blue eyes remained.

When Cruz fell to the ground, his left wrist hit the pavement, smashing his watch face. The watch had stopped ticking at 12:29. Ray turned and walked away from the remains of what had once been Cruz, heading back to his car. Someone in the building peeked out a window, saw Ray, saw the Impreza, and saw the body. He called 911 but hung up before answering the question, "Do you know who was shot?" The neighbor did. But the body laying on the steps was no longer Cruz. Cruz was gone.

Ray entered his car and turned the heat on high when he started it up. "Now I gotta find that son of a bitch Amadi Browne," he muttered to himself.

~

It was after midnight when Robbie McFadden gave up trying to sleep and got up. After Ray's call he'd dozed off and slept restlessly for a time, but when he awoke again, he couldn't get back to sleep. There was a time when he vowed never to bring work home with him, but he'd learned over the years it wasn't a vow he could keep. It was neither feasible nor reasonable. In his line of work, the job never ended. There was no on-off switch. Not being able to go back to sleep was simply part of the job, and another night without sleeping through until the morning was usual.

He grabbed his mobile phone, put on his gray velvet robe, slipped into his deerskin slippers, shuffled downstairs to his office, and from a crystal decanter, poured himself four fingers of Icelandic vodka. The good stuff. No ice. Not at that hour.

He needed to know what the hell was going on. He took a long sip of the vodka and dialed Bobby Ray and said immediately when Ray answered, "What the fuck is going on?"

"Mr. McFadden. Glad we're talking. I've completed the Cruz phase of my assignment. Subject has been eliminated with extreme prejudice. Now I'm gonna start looking for Amadi Browne."

"Start lookin'? What're you talking about? You're supposed to *have been lookin'* all along. Do you even know where the fuck he is?"

"Yes, yes, I've been lookin'. Cruz moved him from your building, but I don't know where he's stashed. Maybe another building? Not sure? One minute, the two of them were in Cruz's Ford together. The next, Cruz pulls up in front of his apartment building alone. I gotta hit the refresh button. But I'll find him. Not to worry. I always do."

"Not to worry? Well, shit! What a hot shit mess. This isn't how my organization runs." McFadden paused and took another sip of vodka. McFadden's expectation was that both Cruz and Amadi Browne would be dead by then. Ray had violated a cardinal rule. He hadn't met McFadden's expectations. "You listen to me, you little shithead. You find him, damn it! You find him now!"

After Ray shot and killed Cruz and reported the kill to McFadden, he drove to his Midtown apartment, a small efficiency he rented above a cannibis shop on a seedy, four-lane block of Broadway. He needed to think and sleep. He fell into a deep sleep to start, but it didn't last. Once he awoke, he lay in bed trying to organize his thoughts, but that didn't work either. He needed a change of scenery. He showered, ate, and headed for his old stomping grounds: the Columbus Park neighborhood where he had grown up, north of downtown and close to Third and Oak, where Cruz took his last breath.

Over the years, the neighborhood had been called Little Italy, Belvidere Hollow, and the North End. To those in the know, each name connoted something mob related, and in 1967, the city settled on calling it simply Columbus Park, hoping the new name would turn a page on the neighborhood's underworld roots.

It had been home to waves of immigrants, located near the Garment and Meatpacking Districts. Ray had grown up in a small brick row house near the intersection of Fifth and Troost, not far down the block from a Catholic church whose bells chimed throughout the day to summon the nearby transplanted Southeast Asian families to come and pray and thank God for their new lives.

His tiny row house was a block from where The Trap had been located, officially named the Columbus Park Social Club. It had been a storefront in a four-story brick building where mobsters of days gone by had once gathered. Raided by the FBI twice, it was a bookmaking hub until someone threw a pipe bomb through the back door.

McFadden had told Ray about the club and the Columbus Park history, as he seemed to enjoy doing for all his foot soldiers. "You need to know some of this stuff, Bobby Ray," McFadden would tell him.

Once he learned the history, Ray considered it fate he had grown up so close to such a famous mob hangout and then took employment with Kansas City's biggest modern-day mobster. Columbus Park was important to Bobby Ray, and he was comfortable retreating there to think.

As he sat on Fifth Street with his engine idling and defroster blowing to keep him warm, he struggled to come up with a plan. He knew nothing about Cruz other than McFadden wanted him taken out. He didn't need to know anything else, and Cruz had been easy to find. But now with Cruz gone, Ray realized he knew little about Amadi Browne, other than the fact that one of McFadden's clients had fingered him for extinction. For this part of the project, he needed to know more if he was going to find and kill Amadi Browne.

Ray took a deep breath. He wasn't an investigator. He was an eliminator. That was his skill set, and he wanted to avoid the pitfalls of venturing into a job for which he wasn't a seasoned pro. But McFadden had made it clear in their brief call: Find Amadi Browne and kill him now, not later. Ray had no choice. He would have to figure out this investigation line of work on the fly.

He needed to start with the simple things. He would figure out where Browne lived and visit the house. He knew Browne worked for the bank where Ray had met Jordan, Amadi's brother. He would go there next. He'd snoop around, maybe ask some questions, talk to the staff and other bankers, and see if he could get lucky. From movies he'd seen, he figured luck was the most important tool in an investigator's bag of tricks, and he needed a lot of it right now. He had gotten the McFadden message loud and clear. He needed to find Amadi Browne fast.

The last thing Ray wanted was for McFadden to drop his Ivy League university intellectual persona and fly into a rage. The rage was legendary. Ray knew McFadden often followed his rage by taking out his frustrations on the target of his outburst. That kind of rage could end up shortening Ray's life expectancy. Ray wasn't ready to move on from this earth. Some time ago, he'd learned to avoid McFadden's rage at all costs. And he planned to avoid it now.

37

RIGHT AFTER ONE in the morning, a squad car carrying two police officers assigned to River Market responded to a report of a shooting. They arrived at Third and Oak and found Maximilian Cruz crumpled and contorted on the apartment building stairs. They rolled his body over to see the face. Two wide, blue, unblinking eyes staring off into the distance met them. Below the nose, they saw the mangled remains of a jaw, and beyond the body, the fedora that had come to rest on the top step.

"Jesus, who the hell is this?" one asked as he circled the scene.

The other reached into Cruz's jacket and found his wallet containing three hundred dollars cash. "Not a robbery," he said as he placed the wallet in an evidence bag.

"I'm gonna call this in and get some crime scene folks and detectives out here to process the scene. Let's put up the tape."

Some residents of the apartment building had gathered at the building's front door in overcoats over their pajamas to watch the officers unwrap the yellow police tape from a roll and form a barrier around the immediate crime scene. Some averted their eyes when the officers rolled Cruz's body over.

As they circled the body, the second cop leaned over for a better look. He noticed the bloody left shoulder area and paused to study the remains of the face. "Looks like a head shot. But also a shoulder shot and a back shot." He stood back up. "I can't be sure, but I think I know this guy."

"No shit? How can you even tell?"

"He just looks familiar to me. I remember that hat. I think this may have been Maximilian Cruz."

"Who's that?"

"A gang guy. He graduated to being a low level mob guy, an odd-job kind of guy in the McFadden organization. Not a killer by trade. I remember collaring him once a while back for trespassing on some guy's land. He was a large man but mostly very polite. Please and thank you kind of guy. He said he was only watching—not a crime—but he was standing on the wrong side of the property line while he watched. When I told him we had received a complaint from the property owner and he'd have to move away, he declined. So I had to cuff him. At first, he resisted the cuffs. But after a few moments, he put his hands out for me to put them on, and he thanked me. Then I brought him in."

The cop continued to study the corpse, noticing a gun in Cruz's right hand. "Looks like he may have tried to fight back. Maybe a shoot-out here?"

One of the apartment dwellers called out, "I heard two shots. Maybe three."

"Two or three? Thank you, sir." The cop wrote the information down in his notepad.

"Well, if it was a shoot-out, it doesn't look like it lasted very long, and his killer shot him in the back of his head, so I'm guessing he must've tried to get out of the line of fire of whoever was shooting at him."

They moved back to their squad car and waited for the detectives to arrive.

"Any next of kin?"

"I vaguely recall his mother coming into the station and bail-ing him out after I arrested him. Short older woman leading her big son out. He had a fedora on when I collared him and he had it on when the desk sergeant processed him out." He pointed at the fedora resting on the steps. "I'm betting it was that fedora. It seemed out of place back then, considering his line of work, but he looked good in it. So if I'm right, I'm guessing he's got a mother living somewhere in the city, if she's still alive. We'll need to run that down and find her. She's gonna need to know about this."

After she fed him, Momá gave Amadi bed linens and showed him to the spare bedroom, which had been Cruz's bedroom when he was a teen. Amadi had been sleeping on a lumpy cot for more than a week, and Cruz's old bed felt like a Four Seasons Hotel luxury mattress. He fell asleep on it almost instantly without getting undressed. His sleep was black. No dreams. No nightmares. These days, most of his nightmares occurred while he was awake.

He slept through the morning and awoke at almost noon. He didn't know if Momá slept or watched TV all night. She didn't seem tired, and she cooked for him again. They ate, they talked, she knitted, they watched television. They talked about Abode. They talked about being a Latin American woman and a Black man in twenty-first century Kansas City.

But there was no call from Cruz. Neither discussed it. There was nothing to talk about. Either he would come back or he wouldn't. Either he would call or he wouldn't. But if he didn't call and if he didn't come back, Amadi would soon have to decide what to do. He couldn't stay with Momá forever. It wouldn't be safe and it wouldn't be right.

38

3J's EXPERIENCE TOLD her that all judges had multiple personas, different versions of themselves on the bench that came out at different times: cordial, warm, inquisitive, collaborative, or welcoming, and sometimes cold, quiet, demanding, dismissive, impatient, unhappy, tired, or dictatorial. She had seen many versions of Judge Robertson during her years practicing before him. She'd seen the warm, cordial version. As he tried to sort through contested facts elicited from witness testimony, she'd witnessed the quiet version. The conversational version came out as he stayed on the bench after confirming a case to talk to the lawyers and wish them well in their next matter. When he announced and explained his ruling, a thoughtful version of him was present. The patient version reigned as lawyer after lawyer presented their motions and argued their cases. And yes, the occasional crabby version showed itself as he took a particularly deserving attorney down a notch or two when they strayed over the line from zealous advocacy to inappropriate conduct.

As Judge Robertson eyed Carson and Browne from the bench, 3J saw a look that lacked warmth. It was already three, and she suspected it had been a long day for him already. When he looked over to her, she replied without walking to the podium, "Josephina Jones for the debtors." Then she immediately sat down.

3J would never take a Chapter 11 motion to dismiss lightly. She couldn't. But this one seemed to have caught the judge's attention—and not in a good way for Carson. 3J and the Franklins sat together as the hearing began, not knowing exactly what to expect.

"Your Honor, we have one witness to present today," Carson said, presuming to know the judge would hear testimony.

"Yes, well, before we get to the actual testimony, Ms. Carson, first tell me who your witness is and on what statutory elements he would offer testimony," Judge Robertson said testily.

3J caught his state of mind. Carson plowed forward, either missing the judge's state of mind or ignoring it. "The witness is Jordan Browne."

"I see. When you announced his appearance here today, you introduced him as a shareholder in the bank. Is he a bank officer as well?"

Carson looked away from the judge and toward Browne, who was sitting in the pews. He shook his head. She turned back to the judge and said, "I am advised he is not."

"I do not usually consider a shareholder of a corporation to be a corporate representative. The shareholder is an owner, not an agent like an officer, and is mostly without fiduciary duties to the company, unlike an officer. Is he on the bank board?"

Carson again looked toward Browne, who again shook his head. "I am advised he is not."

"I see. What would be the nature of his testimony?"

"Well, Your Honor, I would prefer to put him on the stand and let him tell you in his own words."

"Ms. Carson," the judge said forcefully, "you are new to my court. We are pretty simple folks here. Not a lot of rules during argument. But my number one rule is this: If I ask a question of counsel, I expect counsel to answer it. Once you do, if you want to explain something, please go right ahead. But only after you have answered my question."

"Very well, Your Honor. Apologies. Mr. Browne will testify that the Franklins caused Abode to draw on the line of credit and the bank's officers permitted it without authority."

"But if he is not a corporate officer or a board member, I am struggling with why I should permit him to testify about Commonwealth's corporate authorizations. I would expect you to want me to hear from the bank president."

"My client apprises me that will not be possible."

"Why not? Is he out of town? I can reset this for a time when he will be back in Kansas City."

"That will not work, Judge. I am told the president is missing."

"Missing? You mean, like in, no one knows his whereabouts?"

"As in, no one at the bank knows where he is."

As Carson made the statement, her eyelids fluttered—a micro expression that could reveal the spokesperson had uttered an untruth. 3J saw the flutter and wondered if Carson knew where Amadi was. Or maybe Carson was aware that Jordan knew. Or maybe she was so uncomfortable in bankruptcy court that her eyes fluttered when she spoke. She suspected that Judge Robertson had also caught the flutter.

"What about testimony from the officers who permitted the draw?"

"I am told they are not available either. Apparently, their employment has been terminated."

"Hmm. Ms. Carson, have you looked at the statute governing dismissal of Chapter 11 cases?"

Carson said nothing in response.

"The statute requires you to prove cause. There are sixteen examples of cause in the statute. I will not take up Ms. Jones' time today by reading each one to you. I will also save you the time and effort of having to refamiliarize yourself with the sixteen grounds.

Suffice it to say, even if your witness testified and told me the bank made a mistake and should not have advanced money under the line of credit before Ms. Jones filed the bankruptcy cases, none of the sixteen examples of cause would apply. In my view, none of them."

Carson stood uncomfortably at the podium, fidgeting her hands and shuffling her feet. 3J looked at her watch. It was now fifteen minutes past three. While 3J normally watched the judge when opposing counsel was speaking, she looked down at her yellow pad. She had experienced something in court when she was a brand new attorney. Another judge was very upset with one of the lawyers, and the rest of the lawyers in the courtroom looked down at their pads. 3J had whispered to one sitting next to her, "Why is everyone averting their eyes?"

"If you don't make eye contact with the judge right now, she won't hurt you," her neighbor in the pews whispered.

At that hearing, 3J immediately looked away from the judge. At this hearing, she had the same feeling. Don't look at Judge Robertson and he'll keep his ire focused on Carson. She looked over at the Franklins, whose gaze moved from Carson to the judge and back to Carson. 3J passed them a note. "Listen to the judge and Carson but watch your pad in front of you. Don't make eye contact with the judge, please."

They nodded at her.

"Ms. Carson, there is no basis to dismiss Chapter 11 cases because your bank made what I would characterize, at best, a mistake in funding a draw request. If it even was a mistake," he said narrowing his eyes. "Is that the totality of your case?"

"Your Honor, may I have a moment with my client?"

"Your client is the bank. Do you mean you want a moment to confer with Mr. Browne, since I still do not believe he is a bank representative for the purposes of today's hearing?"

"Yes."

"Go ahead," the judge said as he turned to Jennifer Cuello and motioned her to come over to the bench. When she did, the judge handed her a folded note. She returned to her seat and opened the note while Carson spoke with Browne. Her eyes got wide and she looked at the judge and nodded. Anyone in the courtroom watching her might have believed she was trying to repress the beginnings of a smile.

"Thank you for your patience, Your Honor. We will withdraw our motion at this time."

"I see," the judge said as he narrowed his eyes again. "A commendable choice. Court will be adjourned."

The judge stood to exit, paused, and added, "And Ms. Carson, I expect Mr. Browne to attend his examination on the twentieth and answer the questions Ms. Jones poses. And I expect everyone on your side to be on their best behavior." He looked momentarily at Carson, locked eyes, and then left the courtroom for his office.

3J gathered her papers and turned to talk with Carson, but as with the first hearing, Carson was already at the courtroom door, exiting. This time she wasn't alone. She had an animated Jordan Browne by her side. 3J decided it was better not to chase after her. Carson had her hands full with Judge Robertson, and it looked like her horrid day was continuing as she took an earful from Browne.

3J and the Franklins rode down in the elevator and left the courthouse through one of the revolving doors on the Oak Street side. At the top of the steps, Jordan Browne and Hannah Carson had finished arguing and were about to go their separate ways. Jordan was still visibly upset as he strode threateningly toward the Franklins and 3J and got within four feet of them.

James tried to approach Jordan, but 3J stepped between Jordan and the Franklins and pushed James back. "Turn around, sir, and walk away," she said forcefully pointing down the stairs.

"Out of my way," Jordan yelled. "I'm not done with you two," he said as he continued pointing at the Franklins.

As the altercation began, the marshals inside of the courthouse quickly came out. "Sir, walk away," one marshal commanded, pointing off to the distance.

Jordan didn't move.

"I have this, Marshal!" 3J said.

The marshal ignored her and said, "Sir, either you walk away right now or we will have you come inside in handcuffs. Do I make myself clear?"

Jordan turned and went down the stairs, avoiding an arrest.

"Are you okay, ma'am?" the marshal asked 3J.

Her heart was racing as she replied, "Yes, of course. Fine. Thank you, Marshal."

The Franklins and 3J walked back to the Greene Madison offices in silence. Losing parties take the loss in different manners. Some congratulate their opposition. Some stomp off in a huff. Jordan Browne was the first who tried to accost 3J outside the courthouse.

James looked sedate but serious and said nothing.

"Is that how bankruptcy court usually works?" Bella asked, finally breaking the silence.

"I don't know if I can say there's a usual when it comes to court hearings. Anything can happen, and often does." 3J explained.

"Did you know how our hearing would turn out?" Bella pressed.

"You never really know, but I had strong suspicions."

"It looks like the Carson lawyer is not in the judge's good graces," Bella replied.

"For today. I wouldn't expect that to carry over to every issue and every court hearing."

James finally spoke up. "Well, I would have rather been you than Carson today. You didn't have to say a word."

3J nodded. "Sometimes it happens that way."

"We live to fight another day, I guess," Bella said.

"Like I told you the first day we met," James said to 3J, "Jordan

Browne is bad news with a capital B. You should've let me handle it. You could've gotten hurt if he'd acted out."

"It all worked out. No harm . . . this time," 3J replied. "Now back to the real problem. Where the hell is Amadi?"

39

Wednesday, December 11, 2024

THE SKY WAS murky and hinted at an upcoming gray day and perhaps another round of ice. Once the winter ice started in Kansas City, sometimes it seemed it would never stop. There was just a steady frozen drizzle, as if the sky were weeping frozen pellets for hours on end. Perhaps it was the keepers of the heavens crying at the prospect they would have to drop another season of frozen mayhem on the good residents below. Either way, the frozen pellets announced the arrival of another gray, dreary Midwestern winter, and during winter's run, no sun would appear for days on end.

Through the gray, murky darkness, one fact shone through: Amadi was still missing.

For 3J, the Abode bankruptcy case had turned into a waiting game. The worst kind of case for any lawyer was one in which they felt completely helpless. With most waiting games, the players had some idea what might be in store. They had some inkling what they were waiting for. In this waiting game, 3J had no idea what to expect.

Ronnie was sleeping next to 3J, who got up quietly, showered, and made her way over to the office. After getting her cup of tea,

3J should have been preparing for her upcoming examination of Jordan Browne, but she did not do that. In court, the judge had been kind enough to lay down a little of the law of the case to guide Hannah Carson and her client, for which 3J was grateful. But focusing on an outline of the exam right then was out of the question.

After Ronnie met up with Moe later that morning, 3J and Pascale talked with them several times, but they were all completely tapped out of ideas on how to find Amadi. Ronnie and Moe conceded they had no sense where to even begin to look, but they would stand by for any information or lead they could run down.

Unstated, of course, was the fear that Amadi was dead and they were no longer looking for a banker—they were now looking for a corpse.

ᯅ

Jordan Browne phoned Robbie McFadden later in the day. "Robbie, we need to meet. Can you get to The Bottoms Bar?"

"I don't think so, Jordie. Not a good idea right now."

Jordan didn't expect McFadden to say no, and he immediately got flustered. "Then I need a report from you."

There was a pause before McFadden replied, and when he did, Jordan knew he'd pushed too far because Robbie sounded like the mobster he was.

"You need a report from me? You got some fuckin' stones asking me to report to you. Y'wanna report? Cruz is dead. No longer a member of the breathing and walking club. Like you wanted. There's your fuckin' report."

Jordan began to tremble. He was losing control of his emotions. He came on too strong but he wanted to know, needed to know, what was happening. He was a paying customer, and part of what he paid for was a report. "And Amadi?"

"And Amadi what?"

"Is he also no longer a member of that club?"

"Still working on that one. That fucker has at least twelve lives. One thing is for certain. Slowly but surely, he's using them up."

"When will you take care of him?"

"Jesus. When he's taken care of. Could be in a minute. Could be in a day. Could be never. It's that kind of business, Jordie. Unpredictable. I expected you would have known that. There's your report. Look, gotta go." Sarcastically, he added, "Good talk," and hung up.

During the day, Bobby Ray visited Amadi Browne's house and found it dark. He walked around the property peering into windows and through French doors and saw no evidence that anyone had been there in some time. The mail had piled up. In the neighborhood, he saw nothing unusual. People were walking dogs. UPS was making deliveries. It was simply a neighborhood and nothing more.

He then went to Commonwealth's bank offices on Cherry Street and asked to speak to Amadi Browne. The receptionist told him Mr. Browne had not been to the bank in almost two weeks. She looked down as her phone rang, and as she reached for the receiver, she asked Ray if she could take a message. Before she could look up again, Ray turned to leave the bank. He walked the streets around the bank and peered down several alleys. Again, there was nothing unusual, just streets and alleys near Midtown Kansas City.

He decided to drive back to his apartment. Once there, he took a shower, ate, cleaned his gun, and tried to assume the role of investigator. What was he missing? But by evening, he was still in his apartment trying desperately to morph from killer to investigator with minimal success. He had spent the day learning nothing.

"If I was Max Cruz, where would I feel most comfortable hiding Amadi Browne?" he wondered aloud. "Maybe with family?"

Ray had lost his last family member almost twenty years earlier, so the notion of family hiding someone for Cruz hadn't crossed his mind. But now that he thought of it, he liked the idea. At first he considered calling McFadden and asking about Cruz's immediate and extended families, but he quickly rejected the idea. At the moment, it was safest for him to have as little contact with McFadden as possible. Calling him could be his death knell because McFadden would know Ray had so far failed in his mission to find and kill Amadi Browne. That knowledge would likely send McFadden into another of his famous full-on rages.

While he didn't count himself as an internet guru, he decided the best course of action was to search "Maximilian Cruz" and see if he could find any familial information. It didn't take him long to find a website where, for a small fee, he could develop background information about almost anyone.

He paid twenty-five dollars with his credit card, typed in Cruz's name, put in Kansas City as the location, and waited for the website to generate a report. Minutes later, it generated a lengthy report with much of the information tracing Cruz's many brushes with the authorities. At first, he had no interest in the criminal record report. That part of the report was too long and Cruz was already dead. And Ray already knew Cruz had a record. Almost everyone who worked for McFadden did.

But there was little other information generated by the website other than Cruz's address, which Ray also already knew. It was another dead end. Lacking any other ideas, Ray read Cruz's arrest records. After twenty minutes, he stumbled on a trespassing report. As he read the record, he discovered the police had arrested Cruz for trespassing and resisting arrest some years ago. He was arraigned, the judge set bail, and Marcella Cruz posted bail. Next to her name was the word "Mother."

"Marcella Cruz?" Ray said out loud. Two more searches and he found a Marcella Cruz who lived off Charlotte Street. "Is that you?" Ray asked aloud as he absorbed the information. He figured there was only one way to find out and headed down to his car just after nine.

∽

Amadi had been at Momá's house since late Monday evening. Over thirty-six hours had passed. It was dark outside again. Inside as well.

A few hours earlier, Amadi thought he had heard a sound outside, a crunching sound like a person walking on frozen leaves. He'd looked through the windows and saw nothing, but he remained concerned that someone—maybe the person who had shot at him at the Olive Street building—had found him. He quickly went from concerned to scared and decided to violate Max's directive to stay in the house. While he had no plan for what to do if he found someone outside, he left the house to inspect the perimeter and maybe determine what had caused the noise.

He hugged the outside of the house as he carefully stepped around the perimeter, noting that his heart was pounding in his chest. It was probably just as well that he was no longer connected to his cardiology team because they might have made a remote adjustment. The good news was that the outside of the house wasn't well lit, so it would be hard for an intruder to see him. The bad news was that he couldn't see the ground in the darkness, so he tripped twice and almost fell.

As he walked to the last side of the house, he surprised two squirrels that scurried off and found nothing else. No intruder, no footprints he could see in the icy leaves. But the incident still left him spooked. As he returned to the house, he noticed that several of the lights inside the house in the front were still on, though most of the lights from the other houses in the neighborhood were off. From the front, Momá's house was too illuminated, which might invite anyone with bad intentions to investigate. If there had been someone outside, it would be obvious there was a man and a woman walking around inside the house.

"Momá, I think we should turn off the rest of the lights for a while," he said when he got back inside.

"But why?"

"Just to be safe. I think it's best. Max would want us to."

"So . . . what is this, Mr. Amadi? We sit here in the dark and wait? For how long? And what are we waiting for?"

"Yes, we sit in the dark. Maybe no television for a while. Maybe a candle or two is all we use to give us light. We wait and talk. I don't know for how long. We wait for Max to come back and tell us he's taken care of everything. Until then, we shouldn't make it easy for people outside to see in."

"There's no one outside, Mr. Amadi," Momá said sounding confident, but she looked scared. "But if you think it's best, then okay." She nodded and Amadi quickly turned all the lights off.

"Candles and a match?" he asked.

She pointed to a small kitchen drawer, found what he needed, lit two candles, and placed the candles on plates to catch the dripping wax.

She sat in a chair and Amadi sat on the floor near her with his back against a pillow pressed against the wall. They sat and they waited in the Abode house built and designed to provide shelter and comfort for marginalized Kansas Citians who wanted a part of the American dream. He hoped the dark house would keep them alive and out of the path of a paid killer. That was Amadi's only dream at the moment. That and Max's return.

They waited. They ate in the dark. They went to the bathroom in the dark. They whispered in the dark. They sat silently in the dark. They listened to the wind in the dark. They dozed on and off in the dark. And then it was time for Amadi to let his thoughts wander in the dark to ways he could take matters into his own hands. It had been too long. Max wasn't there, and Amadi was sure he wasn't coming back.

40

3J AND PASCALE had lingered in the office well after quitting time, nibbling on a pizza she had ordered, now cold. They worried that if they went home, it would signal they had moved on from Amadi. They hadn't. And they didn't want going home to signal that Abode would fail. It couldn't.

Then 3J's mobile phone rang. It was an 816 call, Kansas City's exchange, but she didn't recognize the number. Normally, she would have let it roll to voice mail, assuming it was some unwanted robocall marketing ploy she could do without. But something made her answer.

"Ms. Jones? This is Amadi Browne."

She cupped the phone, looked over to Pascale, and yelled, "Holy shit. It's Amadi."

She put her phone down on her desk and turned the speakerphone on.

"Amadi, are you all right? What's been going on? Where are you?"

"Yes, I'm fine, all things considered. Surprisingly. But I'm fine. I'm with a woman who's been kind enough to let me stay with her and feed and shelter me. But at this point, I think you need to come and get us."

3J took down the address and said, "Stay tight. Don't move. Don't let anyone in. My team will be there shortly."

"Yes, we've gotten good at not moving and staying tight, Ms. Jones. When the team gets here, they'll see that all the lights in the house are off. We've been sitting here in the dark for hours so no one on the outside can easily see inside. How will we know it's someone from your team and not someone who's been chasing and trying to kill me?"

"Kill you?" 3J exclaimed. "Jesus!"

"Yes, kill me. There's a man who shot at me and tried to kill me."

"Amadi, I'll be there with the team. That way, you'll know it's us." As 3J said the words, Pascale's eyes opened wide, and he vigorously shook his head. It was too late. 3J had uttered the words.

When the call ended, 3J called Ronnie, who was sitting in Moe's living room. The two of them had apparently been in roughly the same mental state as her and Pascale—trying not to move on from the task of finding Amadi. 3J explained the Amadi call and told them to meet her downstairs in twenty minutes. When she finished the call and looked up at Pascale's eyes, she saw both fear and fury there.

"3J, this is just downright reckless. Ronnie and Moe are trained professionals. You're not. They're armed. You're not. They've already reported to us they heard gunfire. I heard Amadi utter the word 'kill' just now. Kill as in shoot him down. Damn it, you're not going anywhere. Come up with some secret password for Ronnie and Moe to call out when they arrive at the house so Amadi will know it's them, and you stay here. Listen to me. Call Amadi back and come up with the password."

3J stared at Pascale. She'd never seen him so mad at her before. She'd never heard him be so direct with her either. She wanted to be mad at him but she couldn't be. She wanted to do what she had put in motion but slowly realized she shouldn't. He was right. She'd had this problem throughout her life—running right toward danger, often ill-prepared for the consequences.

She took a deep breath and called Ronnie back and said, "Change in plans. I'm not going with you. Don't come here to pick me up. Go directly over to the address I texted you. It's close to downtown. When you get to the house, call out this password at the front door: repo. Amadi and some woman he's with will open the door and you'll hustle them back to here where they'll be safe. We have a ton to explain to Amadi, and he has a ton to explain to us."

"Woman?" Steele asked. "What's that about?"

"Shit, don't ask. I don't know. Just retrieve both of them and bring them back here."

When the call ended, 3J looked up, but Pascale had turned to leave her office, walking deliberately, hands in his pants pockets. He looked exhausted.

She then called Amadi back and explained the change in plan. She described Moe and Steele and gave him the password. "I understand," Amadi said in response and disconnected.

3J hoped that in less than an hour, she would have protective custody of Amadi Browne and whoever the woman was with him.

Even though it was late, 3J called the Franklins to give them an update. Yes, she felt certain her team was closing in on Amadi Browne and she hoped Browne would be ready to apply for the loan to buy the Commonwealth stock back before the repo deadline expired.

No, she didn't think it was a good idea for the Franklins to come to the law firm and wait with her. Yes, she would let them know when her team secured Amadi, and then they could come over to the firm. Yes, she understood it was difficult to sit at home and wait, helplessly, when so much had to happen in such a very short time to save Abode.

No, she wasn't certain The Bank of the Heartland had enough time left to process a formal loan application and approve Amadi Browne. Yes, if the bank approved the loan, she had a plan to notify Jordan Browne that his brother had exercised his right to buy back the stock and deliver the certified check to Jordan.

"Look, folks. I can't even begin to imagine how frustrating this is for you. I know you aren't do nothing people. You take action, but right now all the action we can think of is in process and, frankly, it's very dangerous. We need to let the professionals see this through and hope Amadi gets here safely."

❧

With the information from 3J in hand, Moe and Steele raced to the address they'd been given, fighting the icy road as they drove. When they arrived, they ran to the front door, and Steele called out, "Amadi Browne? Ronnie Steele here. The password is repo!"

The door was thrown open, and before Browne could say a word, Moe asked, "Who's this?" pointing to Momá.

"This is Max Cruz's mother. She stays with us," Amadi explained. It was the first time either Moe or Ronnie had heard the name Max Cruz, and Ronnie wanted to figure out who Max Cruz was, but there was no time. They could get all the facts from Amadi later. For now, they needed to get Amadi and Momá out of the house and off to safety.

Amadi was about to speak when Steele interrupted him. "Okay, okay. Both of you are with us. No time to talk. Let's go." He took up the position of lookout at the front door while Moe waited for Amadi and Momá to move, but they remained still.

"C'mon. C'mon on, folks," Moe said, waving her hands for them to move quickly. "Both of you. Now. Gotta go."

While Moe directed Amadi and Momá, Steele kept a lookout at the front door. The streets were empty for the moment.

"Momá," Amadi said. "Come. Let's go."

With Moe in the lead, followed by Amadi, Momá, and Steele, the group began to step in unison quickly to the front door. When they reached it, they ran to the car maintaining their formation and ignoring the slickness of the ice-covered sidewalk. They piled in, pulled away from the curb, and headed toward downtown and the Greene Madison offices with Steele driving.

Right after the turn out of Momá's small neighborhood, they passed a lone vehicle going the opposite way. The fog had settled into the street, seeming to rise from the road inches above the pavement. It made it difficult for Steele to see the yellow line on the road and his car drifted close to the oncoming lane. "Shit," he yelled as he turned the wheel to the right to avoid crossing the median and hitting the oncoming car.

He took no note of the passing car, concentrating on getting as far away from Momá's house as they could. The fog, the headlights, and the speed with which both cars were moving made it impossible to see the driver of the other car. The passing car rode off into the mist and quickly disappeared from Steele's vision in the rearview mirror. His focus was the road ahead and the Greene Madison offices beyond.

Once on the road, Moe called 3J to let her know they were on their way in and heading for the firm's indoor parking garage. She said they had Amadi Browne and an older woman with them named Momá.

"Who's the woman?" 3J asked.

"Amadi was at her house. I only know a little. I'll have to try to explain when we get there," Moe replied.

3J had put the call on the speakerphone, and Pascale told them to enter the garage on the Walnut Street side and immediately to bear left. He would meet them by the security gate, swipe his key card to let them in, and direct them to a reserved parking spot nearby. Then the five of them could take the key card secure service elevator from the garage to the twenty-seventh floor, where they'd be safe.

After the call, Moe turned around to face Amadi. "We good?"

"I am now. Who are you people?" he asked as he leaned forward.

"Just two concerned citizens who save the good folks of Kansas City every night. Our superhero costumes and masks are at the cleaners right now."

41

Bobby Ray wasn't familiar with Marcella Cruz's neighborhood. He drove north on Broadway, past the predepression era Uptown Theatre, through Westport, and then northeast heading to Charlotte. Seven blocks before Charlotte, he gave the car too much gas and it skidded, heading for the curb. "Oh, shit!" he yelled out as he took his foot off the accelerator and tried to turn into the skid and right the car. What he didn't need was a crash before he got to the Cruz house. He had enough problems at the moment. Right before he would have clipped a parked car, he got the skid under control. The roads were mostly empty, which was lucky for him. Still, it was too close a call.

By the time he approached Momá's Abode neighborhood, patches of a thick fog bank had settled in, and it became more difficult for him to see very far in front of his car. He leaned forward, resting his chest on the front of the steering wheel as if getting his head inches closer to the windshield would help with visibility.

Just before the turn into the neighborhood, a lone car on the other side of the road emerged from the fog and drove past him. The other car was dangerously close to the yellow line in the middle of the road, and the cars passed each other with only inches between them. "You fucker!" Ray yelled out at the other car. "Stay on your own goddamn side of the road!" The headlights from the other car bathed the fog and the resulting glare momentarily blinded Ray. After he screamed, he took no note of the passing car or its passengers, keeping his focus on getting to his destination. He turned into the neighborhood and pulled up in front of the Cruz home. The house was dark.

Donning his baseball hat and with gun in hand, he exited his car quietly, walked up the front walk, put his ear to the front door, and listened. He heard nothing. With his shoulder, he slammed into the door, forcing it open and shattering the surrounding molding. Gun raised at the ready to shoot, he entered. The house was pitch-black.

Ray saw what might be a man sleeping on the floor and shot without waiting for confirmation, hitting his target in what could have been the chest. "Amadi! Gotcha!" he yelled. For good measure, he sprayed several more shots. Pleasure began to wash over him.

He raced to the target and bent over what he figured would be a bleeding person. "Fuckkk!" he screamed as he saw he'd only shot a pillow. Pleasure interrupted.

Ray stomped through the remaining rooms in the house and found nothing. In the kitchen he found a warm teapot and two cups in the sink. He concluded Amadi most likely had been in the house and had left not long before his own arrival. He didn't know what to make of the second teacup. He figured it might belong to Cruz's mother, Marcella.

He turned and stormed out of the house. As soon as he got outside, he heard a noise around the side of the house that sounded like someone walking quickly through the leaves. He ran and shot twice. Again, he found no human. This time, only squirrels. He took a deep breath and drawled, "Fuck me," as he exhaled.

Back in his car, he pounded his steering wheel with both hands. "This fuckin' guy. Who has this kind of luck?" He took off his hat, set it on his passenger seat, and vigorously rubbed his face from his cheeks to his forehead. Then he pushed his hair back and held it for a moment before letting it go and slamming his hands into his steering wheel again. "All my research for nothing. Now what the fuck am I gonna do?"

ঌ

After Moe's call, 3J dialed the Franklins. As she did, she contemplated how little sleep everyone on her team had accumulated over the last forty-eight hours. So many people running on adrenaline for so long. The adrenaline cycled through periods of laser focus followed by periods of exhaustion. Right now, 3J was laser focused. She would worry later about the next wave of exhaustion she knew was coming.

When the Franklins answered, she told them the team had recovered Amadi and he was close to arriving at her office.

"We're leaving now," James Franklin said, and he disconnected before 3J could say anything else to him.

3J called him back immediately and asked him to bring a casual change of clothes for Amadi. She also asked Bella Franklin to do the same for Momá. "Who's the extra set of women's clothing for?" Bella asked.

"Not entirely sure. Apparently, it's a long story. Someone will explain when you get here."

Fifteen minutes later, the Franklins arrived. Since it was after hours, 3J went down to the lobby to let them in and bring them up the elevator. Moments later, Amadi Browne, Momá, Moe, Steele, and Pascale stepped off the elevator. When the Franklins saw Amadi, it was a short but emotional reunion. 3J then took Amadi and Momá to the twenty-fourth floor where the firm had a small gym for the use of Greene Madison employees. The facilities included showers and towels. She gave them the Franklins' clothes into which they could change if they wanted, told them they could shower, and said she'd wait outside the gym for them.

Amadi showered quickly and changed, but Momá opted to remain in her dress. When they were ready, 3J took them back to the conference room on the twenty-seventh floor, and Amadi began the download of what had happened to him over the past week and a half.

As Amadi explained how Max had abducted him and held him captive in the Olive Street building's basement, Momá listened carefully. "Oh my, Maxie," she whispered quietly. "What did you do?"

When Amadi had finished, 3J told him she and Pascale had gone to The Bank of the Heartland and talked with Altair Galanos. "Do you know him?"

"Sure do. We know each other well. Why did you meet with him?"

"We had an unusual ask, but we wanted him to grease the skids for a loan we anticipated you would want to ask his bank to make to you personally for two million dollars. That would give you the cash to buy back the stock."

"What day is today?" Amadi asked.

"Wednesday the eleventh," 3J replied. "There's still time. We can get you into Heartland when the bank opens tomorrow morning. You can give Heartland whatever financial information it needs and sign the loan application. Then they can review and approve the loan. If everything goes according to plan, you can notify your brother you're exercising your right to buy the stock back and deliver to him Heartland's certified check for two million before the end of the day on the thirteenth."

"You mean the brother who hired some guy to kill me." Amadi shook his head and frowned. "When you say grease the skids, what do you mean?"

Before answering, 3J took note of the looks on the Franklins' faces. They hadn't known that Jordan Browne had planned to kill his brother, and they looked shaken by the news.

"We told Altair what's been happening, and his bank has already done its due diligence on Commonwealth. All it needs to consider the loan is a loan application from you and financial information about you."

"I don't really need and didn't expect a two million dollar liability on my personal balance sheet," Amadi replied. "But I need to get the bank back from Jordan. Then I need to fire him. Then I think I need to turn him in—have him arrested. Right? The Heartland piece will be the easy part."

Everyone was silent, but Bella Franklin reached over and put her hand on top of Amadi's hand and squeezed. Amadi looked over to her and smiled.

In the moment of silence, 3J glanced at Momá. Before everyone arrived at the office, 3J had learned of Maximilian Cruz's death from a local news post. At first, 3J wasn't sure if Cruz's mother knew, but as she looked at Momá, she was sure now.

The group took a short break, and 3J whispered to Pascale, "Momá knows her son is dead. You can see it written on her face. That's rough, Bill."

"Yeah, someone once told me things in life hurt until one day they don't anymore. I don't think that's right. Things always hurt, and all you can hope for is someday, you'll learn how to live with the pain."

42

Thursday, December 12, 2024

BACK IN HIS apartment again, Bobby Ray saw a television news report describing Cruz's death. The report said the residents of the apartment building had looked through their blinds and saw Cruz go down, the victim of an execution-style killing. They had given the police descriptions of the shooter and the car they presumed he drove. Police artists were finishing up a rough drawing and physical description of the assailant, and they had begun to canvas the city for him. The police spokesperson had described the canvas as a manhunt for an assassin.

He shook his head. "Shit. Shit." McFadden would be furious, but Ray could no longer drive around town investigating places where Amadi Browne might be. He wouldn't last more than a few hours before some cop matched him to the sketch and arrested him. It was a good thing no one had found him contemplating in his idling car on Fifth Street in Columbus Park.

The police were now an additional complication. McFadden had preached that in their line of work, complications had to be resolved. There was only one way to resolve this one: lie low. So he suspended his investigation. He realized the police could match his vehicle to his address. It was another complication he needed to resolve.

He grabbed his always packed go-bag filled with clothes, guns, and ammo, slung it across his shoulder, and immediately went back down to the street. Once he'd found a car to steal and snagged it, he headed for an out-of-the-way motel he knew of on the eastern outskirts of the city in the wasteland that separated Kansas City from Independence, Missouri. No one would ask questions there and no one would find him. It was his safe house for these types of emergencies.

The street he drove on was filled with low-rise, dilapidated motels, some still family run businesses and others somehow related to the mob and offering bed and shelter for hookers to ply their trade and pushers to sell their wares. This eastern end of Truman Road held sleazy, tattered, rundown, miserable structures just waiting to collapse during the next windstorm.

He ditched the car he'd stolen in an abandoned lot of rusting vehicles hidden from the road several blocks from the motel where he wanted to stay. There he grabbed his go-bag from the trunk, pulled his collar up and his hat down, left the trunk open, broke the driver's side window, and walked the few blocks to the motel. With cash, he rented a room at the Mercy Motel for a week, closed the door to his new room behind him, and waited.

Complication resolved.

❧

The Bank of the Heartland opened for business at nine, but 3J had arranged for Amadi to meet Altair Galanos at the bank an hour before that. She requested Galanos conduct business with Amadi in a windowless room. "Ahh," Galanos said. "Not a problem."

Moe and Steele arrived at the firm at 7:30 and picked up Amadi.

"Still no masks, eh?" Amadi asked.

Moe raised her eyebrows and winked.

Steele and Moe took him down to the law firm's parking garage. They were unsure whether someone was still looking for Amadi, but they didn't want to dismiss any possibilities. Now that they had Amadi, they didn't plan on losing him, so they gave him a Kansas City Royals baseball cap to wear low on his forehead and directed him to lie on the back seat floor and to stay down until they told him otherwise. It might have been overkill, but overkill was far better than a de facto kill.

The bank was ten minutes south of downtown on Main Street, up the hill past Union Station and the World War One Memorial, and only five blocks from Commonwealth's location. Since they were heading away from downtown, traffic in their direction was light. Once at the bank, they drove a several block perimeter before parking to survey the area for anything that looked out of the ordinary. They saw nothing and no one, whether ordinary or not. The area was devoid of people. They parked and quickly escorted Amadi to the bank entrance. Each had a hand under one of his arms, and he looked like a president in a baseball cap being hustled along by Secret Service agents. A security guard let them in.

Altair Galanos met them in the lobby and took them to an interior conference room with no windows. Once in the conference room, Amadi removed the baseball cap.

"Will you stay here or would you prefer to wait outside?" Galanos asked Moe and Steele.

"Where he goes, we go," Steele replied matter-of-factly.

"Very well," Galanos replied.

The two bankers moved quickly through the loan application, and Amadi arranged to transmit all the requested financial information to Galanos. By 9:15, the two had finished. Because there hadn't been time to retrieve Amadi's cell phone or purchase a replacement burner, 3J had given him her phone number for Galanos to call once the loan decision had been made. They shook hands, Amadi put his baseball cap back on, and he left quickly with Moe and Steele to return to the Greene Madison offices.

3J's team had ordered breakfast for Momá and Amadi, and when

Amadi arrived back at the firm, they left him to eat with Momá. While they ate, 3J, Pascale, Steele, and Moe decided to stash Amadi and Momá in the Speedway Motel, a mile north of I-70 near the Kansas Speedway. It was far from downtown and not a place they figured anyone who might be searching for Amadi would think to look, and there were so many hotels and motels in the metro area, it would be nearly impossible for them to be found in any event. Ronnie and Moe also took a room in the Speedway Motel and agreed to stagger their watch. Moe started off first and Ronnie went back to the condo. He would relieve Moe later in the day.

As he drank his morning coffee, McFadden called Ray, but the call went right to voice mail. "Shit," he muttered under his breath. He didn't leave a message. He assumed Ray would look at his phone, see the call, and call him back. Quickly. McFadden wanted a report, but he was certain the report would not make him happy. He knew if Ray had gotten to Amadi Browne and taken him out, Ray would've called to convey the news and strut his stuff to the boss. Ray hadn't called, so McFadden knew with near certainty that Ray hadn't killed Browne.

McFadden was starting his Thursday with a vodka-induced headache, and he was in a bad mood brought on by Bobby Ray. He dressed, kissed his wife goodbye, told her he might not be home for dinner, and went out the front door just like any other family man, save for the bodyguards out front and the nature of his business. He met his bodyguards standing by the SUV now pulled in front of the house, got in with them, and told them to drive around and keep the noise down. "I've got some things I need to think through," was all he said to them. After a few minutes, he added, "Oh, and drive over to The Roasterie and get me a double espresso to go. My head is killing me."

When the car pulled up in front of The Roasterie, one bodyguard went in to get McFadden his espresso. McFadden leaned his head back and rubbed his bloodshot eyes, and muttered to himself. "What a fuckin' business." When the bodyguard returned with his drink, he added, "Where the fuck are you, Bobby Ray?" The bodyguards knew better than to respond to the question.

"Let's drive around. Maybe it'll give me some inspiration."

❧

At ten that evening, the seven members of the loan committee, plus Altair Galanos, joined the Zoom meeting.

"Thanks for hopping on a call so late," Galanos said. "I wouldn't have asked if it wasn't important." He explained the proposed loan to Amadi Browne and said the collateral for the loan would be Amadi's Commonwealth stock, vacation property, and a second mortgage on his home. He told the committee that the collateral value would be approximately ten million dollars to secure a loan of two million dollars. While the committee had only a few questions about the vacation property and the mortgage, one member raised significant concerns about the stock value.

"But most of the collateral value is attributable to the bank stock, right?" Warren Levine asked.

"Correct, Warren. We've made other loans secured only by bank stock as the collateral."

"True. In the past," Levine agreed. "But in these times of rising rates, banks, at least some of them, are, shall I say, sitting on unrealized asset losses, sometimes significant ones, and some have failed over the last year because of those asset losses. If Commonwealth Savings and Loan is sitting on such assets, I'm going to have some significant heartburn approving this loan."

Levine wasn't aggressive in his comments. An economist by training, he tended to probe more deeply when called upon to approve a loan. Here he was merely calling out the obvious for discussion.

"Good observation, Warren," Galanos said. "I figured you might raise that issue. During the time we've been waiting for Amadi to surface—*hoping* he would surface—I delved into Commonwealth's investments. We list those beginning on page forty-three of the materials I sent out to the committee. As you'll see, Commonwealth has a diverse portfolio—more diverse than one might expect for a bank of its size. Commonwealth invests a good percentage of its deposits in loans it makes rather than using the deposit cash to play in the bond market.

"It has very little in the way of assets stuck with a below market interest rate like long-term treasuries. In other words, it's not SVB or Silvergate or Signature or Credit Suisse," Galanos said referring to banks that were in trouble in 2023, some of which went into receivership and others that sold their institution at a steep discount. "I don't see Commonwealth losses buried in its basement waiting to be realized in the light of day. I know the banking industry had upward of two trillion dollars of the hidden losses that came to light last year, so it's absolutely something to consider carefully. But I don't see deferred losses in Commonwealth's assets. In my estimation, the value of the Commonwealth stock is the balance sheet net value of its assets, and no depreciation factor needs to be applied."

While Galanos spoke, Levine flipped pages in the materials and stopped at one particular page. When Galanos finished, he said, "Thanks for pointing that out. You know me. I'm always thinking the worst. I'm asking myself, in the event that Amadi Browne defaults, what's Heartland's position. It looks like we would end up controlling a very valuable local bank. And one, I might add, whose business would sync up well with our portfolio here at Heartland. I think I'm satisfied."

"Okay then. Are we ready to vote?" Galanos asked.

The committee unanimously approved the loan request and the Zoom meeting ended.

❧

It was late, but 3J got a call from Altair Galanos as she was sitting on her couch with a glass of cabernet. "Just want you to know the bank has approved the loan to Amadi. Please let him know. It was a unanimous decision. I'm going to call the Franklins and let them know as well. Let Amadi know I'll get a certified check prepared as soon as possible in the morning."

As soon as she hung up with Galanos, she called Ronnie at the Speedway Motel. "Amadi got it. If he's sleeping, wake him up to tell him. We're short on time, but Galanos promised to have a check cut in the morning."

"Thank god," Ronnie murmured.

43

Friday, December 13, 2024

JORDAN ROSE ON Friday after an evening of intermittent, restless sleep. He knew something was wrong. All updates had ceased. There had been nothing from Robbie McFadden and nothing from that creature, Bobby Ray. They were both ghosting him, and he'd been angry enough the previous night that he'd texted both, but he'd received no reply.

Jordan made a mental list of things he could do. He could try to find Bobby Ray, but he dismissed the idea. He realized he would never be able to find Ray, especially if Ray didn't want to be found. And if he found Ray, there was no telling what Ray would do. Those eyes. He didn't need to see them again. There was no good reason to seek evil out, especially when it carried a gun.

He could call McFadden and demand they meet. That wouldn't work either. McFadden apparently wouldn't take his call, and an aggressive voice mail demanding that Robert McFadden immediately drive to The Bottoms Bar would not be well-received. He could drive to McFadden's house and demand an audience, but that was also a nonstarter. Apart from the fact that he didn't exactly know where McFadden lived, he worried it would be suicide to seek out McFadden for an unscheduled in-person meeting. McFadden was pissed with him. No need to confront that beast either.

Then he recalled 3J and the confrontation at the courthouse after the failed motion to dismiss hearing. He didn't like her, but he realized she might have custody of Amadi—if he wasn't already dead. Jordan decided to drive downtown and determine for himself if Amadi was anywhere to be seen at the Greene Madison offices. McFadden would have wanted him to first figure out the endgame before going downtown. But once again, Jordan ignored the McFadden advice.

He found his gun, which he hadn't shot in years, loaded it, put it in his overcoat pocket, and drove downtown, getting off at the downtown Oak Street exit and heading to Twelfth and Walnut. There was no on-street parking, so he entered the garage, took a ticket, and found a visitor's parking spot. The parking machine dispensed the ticket stamped 11:14 a.m. Gun in pocket, he left the garage and walked into the building lobby.

The lobby was empty except for the day guard. He asked the guard for the Greene Madison reception area and the guard directed him to the twenty-ninth floor. He rode the elevator to the twenty-ninth floor, the building's top floor, the only Greene Madison floor he could access without a key card, and entered the reception area at 11:21. As his right hand rested on the gun in his pocket, he scanned the area and saw nothing unusual. He observed a dramatic spiral staircase that connected the twenty-ninth and twenty-eighth floors. The twenty-ninth floor was all conference rooms. No lawyers officed there. If he was going to look around, he would have to get onto one of the lawyer floors below.

Was he there to shoot Amadi? Would he shoot 3J? How would he escape? How would he hide his identity? He had no answers. He had no plan. He had no appointment. He couldn't simply ask the receptionist to direct him to 3J. He was sure that if 3J learned he was waiting for her in the reception area, she would have security or even the police escort him out of the building, and they would find the gun. He couldn't ask if Amadi Browne was in the offices either. He was sure no one would tell him.

When the receptionist turned to sign for a package, Jordan quickly walked down the spiral staircase to the twenty-eighth floor. With his hand on his gun still in his pocket, he circled the perimeter of the floor looking into each of the glass-walled offices. His eyes were wide, but they were no longer windows to his soul. He no longer had one.

"Hey, what are you doing here?" an attorney called out. "You're not allowed on this floor, sir."

Jordan ignored the attorney and continued on the perimeter, still looking for 3J and Amadi.

"Sir, stop! I'm calling security if you don't leave immediately."

Jordan had satisfied himself that neither 3J nor Amadi were on the twenty-eighth floor. He didn't know how many floors Greene Madison occupied or how long it would take security to arrive, but he could see there were no other public staircases connecting the twenty-eighth floor to lower floors. Without a key card, he couldn't get to the twenty-seventh floor, where he had met with 3J and the Franklins and told them there would be no extensions. He didn't know if 3J even officed on the twenty-seventh floor.

He had done all he could, so he quickly plodded to the elevator banks and took the next car to the lobby, which was accessible without a key card, and his car in the garage. He had learned nothing and found nothing, but he had risked everything. He was simply no longer thinking clearly.

∽

3J had drafted a letter for Amadi to sign addressed to Jordan Browne and formally exercising the repo. The stock purchase agreement required hand delivery to Jordan of any notice exercising the repo. At 11:15, Steele brought Amadi to the firm, parked in the garage, used the extra key card 3J had given him with the firm's permission, and entered the service elevator for the direct ride to the twenty-seventh floor, bypassing the lobby and the reception area as a matter of caution.

Pascale and 3J talked to him and recommended that he not be the one to bring his brother the letter and the certified check, due to arrive at 3J's office at any moment. It was too dangerous because they all assumed Jordan was still trying to kill Amadi. Instead, they suggested Anthony Rosini deliver the notice and check.

With Amadi in the room, they called Rosini. "Hi, Anthony," 3J said before stopping abruptly. Something was wrong. Bad gris-gris. The kind New Orleans natives believed could get rid of people and the kind they could feel in their bones as if they had a sixth sense for it. She wasn't sure what it was, but she felt something ominous. Something was in the law firm that didn't belong.

After a long moment, 3J blinked, gathered herself, and explained the assignment to Rosini.

"Anything I should know about Jordan Browne?" Rosini asked.

"He's a snake," Amadi replied quickly. "He had me kidnapped, and he had someone try to murder me. There's no telling how far he's willing to go. Other than that, I can't think of anything you need to know."

"Okay. Got it," Rosini said. "While I'm on my way over to pick up the envelope, could you check with the bank and see if Jordan Browne is in today?"

"Sure thing," Pascale said. As they talked to Rosini, 3J's administrative assistant brought in the envelope with the certified check made out to Jordan Browne for two million dollars. 3J put the signed notice and the check in a new envelope addressed to Jordan Browne and sealed it.

While they continued to talk to Rosini, Pascale learned Jordan wasn't at the bank and relayed the information to Rosini. Amadi said his brother had a home office and often worked from there. He expected Jordan was probably home. But it was mere speculation. Things had changed over the last few days. Amadi said Jordan had changed and he no longer knew who his brother was or what his new habits might be.

3J told Rosini she could meet him outside the building at the corner of Twelfth and Walnut in ten minutes. Rosini explained he had one other delivery to make near where Jordan lived and then would head to Jordan's Leawood house. She went downstairs and met Rosini's car and handed the envelope containing the notice and the check to Rosini through the passenger side window.

As 3J turned to reenter the building, she suddenly stopped, and without knowing why, she turned around and looked out to Walnut Street. She saw an Audi on Walnut Street ready to turn east onto Twelfth Street and was certain the driver was Jordan Browne. "Hey," she yelled as she stormed toward the Audi, fists clenched. The car seemed to slow a bit, but when the car behind it beeped its horn, the car she was sure Jordan was in sped away, tires squealing as it made the turn onto Twelfth Street.

As she watched the vehicle disappear, she realized she'd put herself in harm's way. In the split-second before he'd sped off, she'd seen a bit of polished metal in his hand.

When 3J got back up to her floor, she immediately went to Pascale's office.

"Bill, I saw him."

"Who?"

"Jordan Browne."

"Jesus, where?"

"On Walnut Street when I handed the envelope to Anthony. He was in his Audi and drove away when he saw me." 3J failed to tell Pascale she'd approached the car and may have seen Jordan flash a gun at her before speeding away.

"What the hell was he doing near our building?"

As Pascale posed the question, 3J looked down at her mobile

phone and then said, "Holy shit, Bill. This is not real. Read your emails."

Pascale looked at his laptop and saw the following email from the firm's managing partner, Bob Swanson:

> Everyone. Earlier, an unauthorized person was seen walking the perimeter of the twenty-eighth floor, apparently looking into each office. The person is described as a middle-aged African American male, approximately five eight, wearing a white shirt and tie and a trench coat. We have confirmed he is no longer in our offices. Please remember all of our safety protocols. Only those working here with a key card are permitted unescorted on any of our floors without the firm's permission, except on the twenty-fifth floor for deliveries and in the reception area on the twenty-ninth floor, and then only if they are waiting to meet someone who works here. Let's make sure we're vigilant, folks.
>
> Bob

3J and Pascale read the email at the same time. "Bill, he was here. That son of a bitch, Jordan Browne, was here, in our offices. Looking for Amadi. That's who I saw in the Audi. My lord. This is chilling."

Pascale headed for the door. "I'll be right back. I'm going to find Swanson and talk to him. Call Rosini and explain what happened. Hopefully, Jordan Browne is on his way back to his house or Rosini won't be able to deliver the envelope to him and the repo deadline may pass. Jesus. What a shitstorm."

ꕥ

Robbie McFadden wanted to know where the hell Bobby Ray was. Ray hadn't answered his calls, and that was unacceptable. Ray also hadn't responded to his texts, which had gotten progressively more threatening. Ray hadn't provided an update in over twenty-four hours. Un-fucking acceptable. McFadden remembered a sleazy motel Ray once mentioned was his safe house where he stayed when he felt it was risky to stay at his Midtown apartment. He summoned his bodyguards and they headed off to Truman Road and the motel to see if Bobby Ray was there.

Finally, the rain had stopped.The temperature ticked up to thirty-five degrees and the ice on the road began to melt. They drove in silence as McFadden tried to finalize what he would do and say if he found Bobby Ray. He could have one of the boys kill Ray on the spot. It would be satisfying to watch and it would send a message to his troops that failure in his organization was not an option and carried with it consequences. Dire, life-ending consequences. Ray was a freak, and a dangerous one at that. There were plenty of dangerous freaks in the world, and the world would be fine without this one. But as McFadden pondered the problem, he realized he wanted Ray alive for one more job related to the whole Browne family dispute.

He looked out his window as the SUV passed crumbling strip malls housing Truman Road's wretched businesses, from peep shows and heroin dealers to every other kind of low-life activity. All of them doing business along a street named after the thirty-third president of the United States who had been a family farmer during the depression, a Jackson County judge after that even though he held no law license, and then a politician. He'd been vice president under Franklin Roosevelt and became president when Roosevelt died. In that role, he'd made one of the toughest calls any president ever had to make: to drop two atom bombs on Japan in 1945. President Harry "the buck stops here" Truman had been afforded three honors by Independence, Missouri, and Jackson County: the Truman library; the preservation of his Victorian home as a museum; and, unfortunately for him, the honor of having a decaying, neglected road named after him.

"Jesus Christ, boys," McFadden muttered, "you'd think they'd clear out this fuckin' street so old Harry has something he can be proud of in his afterlife." They drove slowly along the street to avoid sliding on the thinning ice still remaining on the road. "Would you look at all the fuckin' heroin being sold here. Maybe this is the remnants of the Purple Capsule Gang of the sixties and seventies. Y'know, the Black mafia that controlled the drugs on the east side of town back then." It was another history lesson, but unlike some others in the organization, the bodyguards didn't seem to mind.

The SUV eventually pulled up in front of the Mercy Motel. It was just as McFadden imagined it. Third-rate was probably several rates too high to describe it.

"Stay here. I'll only be a minute," McFadden said as he left the car for the motel entrance. Once inside, he found someone behind a glassed-in counter who might have been the maid, the clerk, the bookkeeper, the pimp, or the pusher. Hell, maybe even one of the junkies. Or all of the above. He was balding and had pasty, white skin that seemed so thin it was almost translucent. His glasses were wire-rimmed like those worn by John Lennon and his attire included a rumpled white shirt with sleeves an inch too long and a tattered western style wool vest.

McFadden figured the glass was bulletproof—the only luxury appointment this motel had to offer and the only improvement the owners had made in decades. McFadden wasn't sure what to make of the vest.

"I'm looking for a short guy, five seven, hundred and fifty pounds, brown hair. He wouldn't be one of your rent-by-the-hour guests. More of a long-term type guest," McFadden said as he leaned close to the glass barrier, leaving a small round haze from his breath as he spoke.

"Sorry, mister. We can't give out information like that. We got rules. Privacy to protect. It's our policy here at the Mercy Motel," the clerk said in a mousy voice.

McFadden smiled. It was the same dance every time. He reached into his pocket, pulled out a hundred-dollar bill, slid it through the narrow space between the glass and the counter, and said, "My friend Ben Franklin here says it's okay to tell me. He was a great American. Why don't you be one too and just this once make an exception to your policy. Understand?"

The man grabbed the bill, slid it into his shirt pocket, and said, "Room 101. Around back. We don't want no trouble here, mister."

"There won't be any, friend. This gentleman in Room 101 works for me, and I'm here to give him a new assignment." McFadden smiled, turned, and left. He got into the SUV and said, "Drive around back, boys. Park near Room 101." When they found Room 101, McFadden said, "Let's go, boys. Get the cannons out, will ya?"

The bodyguards retrieved automatic weapons from the SUV's spare tire well and all three approached the door, the bodyguards standing on either side of McFadden, who knocked loudly. There was no answer. McFadden yelled, "Bobby fuckin' Ray. Open up this damn door or the next thing that happens is the boys are going to open fire and you'll probably get hit by a stray bullet or ten. Be smart. Open the fuckin'—"

Before McFadden could say "door," he heard the lock turn. Ray opened the door and moved back into his room, allowing McFadden and his bodyguards entry.

As they entered, McFadden saw that Ray held his gun by his side, pointer finger stroking the trigger. "You won't be needing that, Bobby Ray," he said, pointing to the gun but not taking his eyes off of Bobby Ray's eyes.

Bobby Ray said nothing and made no move to put the gun down. Instead, he stood there in cowboy pose with his left thumb hooked behind his belt, the remaining fingers pointing toward his crotch, and his gun at the ready.

McFadden's face slowly turned to a glower. "Look, Bobby Ray, I'm here to talk to you. If you don't put the gun down, the boys here will have to use their artillery, and that'll be the end of you and our little chat before we even get started. Not a great way to start your afternoon. Not a great way for me to have a chat. So I'm only gonna say this one more time. Put it down."

Bobby Ray's nostrils flared and his upper lip curled into a look of disdain, but he slowly complied, first grabbing the gun with his thumb, pointer, and middle finger by the barrel, holding it up for McFadden and his bodyguards to see he didn't intend to use it, and then setting it down on the bed.

"There. That wasn't so hard," McFadden said, narrowing one eye.

McFadden and his bodyguards looked around the small room. "Nice digs you got here, Bobby Ray," McFadden said sarcastically. The room could test McFadden's theory that the only difference between a shack and a mansion was scale. Even scale couldn't help explain the squalor and stale odor of Ray's room. He shook his head and rubbed his eyes. "Okay, on to business. I need you to take out Jordan Browne."

"*Jordan* Browne? When?"

"ASAP."

"What about Amadi Browne?"

"What about him?"

"Am I still looking for him?"

McFadden shook his head and smiled. "Bobby Ray." He paused before saying more softly, "Bobby fuckin' Ray. Y'know, it doesn't look much like you're out and about trying to find Amadi Browne. Not from what I'm seeing here. So I'm not following why you're wondering if you're *still* looking for him."

"Mr. McFadden, I'm laying low 'cause the cops got a description of me and my car from some of the other apartment dwellers where Cruz lived."

"How the fuck did they get a look at you? Jesus. They only got a look at you 'cause you showed them your face and your car." He shook his head again slowly. "Lord, give me strength. Well, good to know, but I don't give a flying fuck about it."

Ray said nothing.

"Look, Bobby Ray, that's all your problem. Buy a car or steal one. I don't care. Cover your face this time or wear a disguise. Whatever. But you drive over to Jordan Browne's house in Leawood. Find him. Take him the fuck out. Leave quickly. Make sure no one sees you. Report to me when Jordan Browne is dead. Understood?"

"And then?"

"And then what? Jesus. Can you believe this guy, boys? Bobby Ray, let's just take care of Jordan Browne for me and then we'll figure the rest out. Sound like a plan?"

44

WITH THE ENVELOPE on the passenger seat, Rosini set out for the thirty-minute drive to Leawood. On the drive, Pascale called and reported Jordan Browne's appearance downtown. "Jeez. Everyone okay?"

"Yes."

"Hmm. I hope he headed back to his home, Bill. I can't leave the envelope at his house. I have to hand it to him personally."

After serving his first court papers on an elderly couple who lived a couple of miles from Jordan, Rosini headed to Old Leawood and arrived at 12:50. The Audi Pascale had described was in the driveway, and across the street he saw a parked red Nissan Altima. It looked like any car parked in front of a house in an upscale neighborhood, and he took no note of it. Rosini grabbed the envelope sitting on the passenger seat, paced up the front walk, and noted the brass plate at the front door that read "J. Browne." He not only rang the doorbell, he banged on the door for good measure.

"Coming, coming!" he heard a voice inside yell. "Who's there?"

As the door opened, Rosini asked, "Jordan Browne?"

"Yes?" Browne answered tentatively.

"This is for you."

"What is it?"

"It's all in the envelope, my friend."

"Who are you?"

"It's not important."

"But what the hell is this?" Jordan asked, becoming agitated. As he asked, he reached for his gun in his pocket but didn't remove it.

"I believe it's the end of your reign as head of Commonwealth S and L. Quite a run as I understand it. Short as it may have been, I'm told it was memorable." Rosini smiled and took a phone photo of Jordan holding the envelope to prove delivery, making sure the shot was date and time stamped. Leaving Jordan at the front door with the envelope in his hand, he then turned and headed to his car and the trip back downtown.

After McFadden departed, Bobby Ray dressed, made sure his gun was loaded, and peered out of his motel room window. He wanted to take out Jordan Browne quickly to try to get back in McFadden's good graces. No delays and no mistakes on this new assignment.

Right outside his room, he saw a parked, upscale looking, red Nissan Altima. It likely belonged to one of the johns who rented a Mercy Motel room by the hour and paid for pleasure by the orgasm. Ray figured he'd borrow the car for an hour or so. The owner hadn't locked the driver's side door. He got in, hot-wired the car quickly, and headed off to Leawood and Jordan Browne's last meeting of the day, month, year, and life.

He arrived moments after 12:45, parked, exited the car quickly, and walked up the front path. It was a quiet neighborhood, but right before he got to the front door, he heard a car come around the corner. He jumped behind a row of hedges in front of Jordan's house to wait for the car to pass, but instead, it parked in front of the house. A man with an envelope exited the car and approached the front door. When Jordan Browne answered the door, the man handed him the envelope and took a picture.

As the man went back to his car, Browne remained at the front door, opened the envelope, and saw what was in it. "You win again, Mom and Pop," Ray heard Browne say to himself with a look of anguish and defeat, sounding like a child about to cry after being disciplined. Browne took out his phone and appeared to start writing a text.

This was the best time for Ray to complete the job. The envelope delivery man had returned to his car, and no one else was around the quiet neighborhood. He jumped out from behind the bushes and squeezed off two shots. The first hit Jordan between the eyes and he was dead instantly. The second was just for good measure. Ray giggled, turned, and ran to the red car he had parked across the street.

He'd completed his assignment and got a bit of pleasure in the kill while he was at it. Now all he had to do was ditch the car and call McFadden. He had no idea what would happen next. He'd deal with that when it came.

Back at his car, Rosini heard two shots ring out and turned to see a crumpled Jordan Browne still clutching the envelope in his right hand and a man running to a car. The man fired up the car engine and peeled out before Rosini could respond. Not knowing if Browne was dead, Rosini made a split-second decision to run to Browne to administer first aid while calling 911. He had to let the fleeing man go.

A quick check of Browne's wrist revealed no pulse. He was dead, and the scene was a mess with blood splattered everywhere and more still running from his head. In short order, the EMTs arrived, followed by the Leawood police. The cops found Jordan Browne dead on the front porch, phone nearby, envelope in hand, and a gun in one of his pockets. Rosini had been unaware of the gun. Rosini showed the cops his ID, told them what he had seen, and explained the reason he was at Jordan Browne's house. He told them what was in the envelope, and they checked to confirm its contents. But they had a dead body with a gun in his pocket, shot to death right there in broad daylight in cloistered Leawood, Kansas, and there was only one man left alive at the scene.

As they consulted, Rosini called his lawyer and asked him to come to the Leawood Police Station. He knew what was coming and he had a criminal lawyer on retainer. Long ago, after he left the Jackson County Sheriff's office, he learned that if he was going to be a process server and investigator, he would have brushes with law enforcement that would require the services of a solid, well-respected criminal lawyer to keep him out of jail.

The cops returned, told Rosini they would have to bring him in, cuffed him, read him his rights, and walked him to their patrol car. He was a suspected killer, at least for the time being, and the only suspect the cops had.

At the Leawood Police Station, the desk sergeant processed Rosini, and an officer took him for a swab of his hands testing for gunshot residue. His attorney arrived as the police completed the swab. "I need a moment with my client and a private room where we can talk," Nathan Smith said in a booming, authoritative, baritone voice.

A police officer led Smith and Rosini to a conference room, and as they walked, a police captain came out of her office, saw Rosini and the cuffs on his hands, and asked, "Anthony, what the hell brings you here?"

Rosini smiled. "Gotta talk to my counsel here, Cap. See you in a few."

After ten minutes, Rosini and Smith emerged to find the captain sitting on the edge of a desk waiting for them.

"Are you charging him, Captain?" Smith asked.

"Only a person of interest at this point."

This status didn't require Rosini's presence in the station or the jail, and since he wasn't being charged, there would be no court arraignment hearing before a Johnson County, Kansas, judge to take his plea and set bail.

"Then we're free to go," Smith said as a statement rather than a question.

"You are free to go," the captain agreed. "Catch up with you another time, Anthony. Don't leave town just yet. You know the routine."

"You bet, Cap," Rosini replied.

On his drive back from the police station, Rosini called 3J, who let him know she was putting Pascale on speakerphone.

"I served Jordan Browne and took a picture to prove delivery. The photo is date and time stamped. I'm texting it to you as we talk. Then I had a slight complication."

"Complication? Jesus. Like what? Are you okay?" Pascale asked.

Rosini explained what had happened. "Folks. Jordan Browne is as dead as a doornail."

3J reported that the photo had just arrived on her mobile phone and she was showing it to Pascale.

"My Lord, Anthony. That's awful," Pascale said. "But your photo shows you served him with the envelope before he died?"

"Yep. He had opened the envelope and was looking at the contents when some guy jumped out from behind the shrubs and shot him between the eyes, point-blank. They found a gun in Jordan's pocket. Not sure what he intended to do with it."

"Do you think whoever shot him confused him for Amadi?" Pascale asked.

"Kinda doubt it, Bill. This guy was lying in wait. And there was a brass plate on Jordan's door that said 'J. Browne' not 'A. Browne.' I gotta assume it was a hit on Jordan Browne."

3J wished Rosini good luck with the Leawood police.

"I think it'll be fine, folks. They'll figure out the gun used to kill Jordan Browne wasn't mine. My lawyer also told them to check for a video doorbell. If you look closely at the picture I took, you'll see a Ring doorbell. When the cops review the video footage, they'll see that someone else pulled the trigger, not me."

"Bill, I can't believe any of this," 3J said when the call ended. "A killer looking for Amadi. Jordan coming here to kill Amadi. A killer taking out Jordan. What the hell is going on?"

"I'm speechless, 3J." Pascale admitted.

"We need to call Jordan's lawyer and run the whole notice process by him."

The pair phoned Bryce Donaldson and explained what had happened.

"Dead? Jesus," Donaldson said when he learned of what had transpired. "How?"

3J explained what they had learned. "Bryce, we have a date and time stamped photo of Jordan Browne receiving the envelope containing the repo notice letter and the certified check for two million dollars. Our process server hand delivered both before the repo expiration deadline, which is later today. Jordan obviously didn't have time to deposit the check and maybe not even read the whole notice. Both are now with the police, held as evidence in their murder investigation. I'm sure we won't see either for a very long time. The agreement is your handiwork. Do you agree the notice was effective?"

"Since Jordan received the written notice and the certified check, there's nothing more you need to do," Donaldson replied. "The notice was self-executing like so many contractual notices. The contract required only delivery of the check. Cashing or failing to cash the check is irrelevant. In my opinion, the bank stock is now owned by Amadi Browne."

Once that call was completed, 3J and Pascale talked with Moe and Steele. It was clear they couldn't keep Amadi and Momá in an out-of-the-way motel forever. With the death of Jordan Browne, 3J and Pascale decided it was time to release Amadi and Momá back into the world. But Moe and Steele advised that both have bodyguards.

Just before quitting time, Amadi Browne was on his way to Commonwealth and Momá was headed to her house. Amadi had agreed with Moe and Steele to hire a bodyguard for some period of days, length to be determined, and he sat next to his new best friend as the bodyguard drove him to the bank. Moe and Steele offered the same protection for Momá. She declined. "Don't want no one with guns near my home," she explained.

At the bank, Amadi and his bodyguard walked to the office of the bank president, formerly occupied by Amadi, then by Jordan, even though the board never actually made him president, and now by Amadi again.

"Welcome back, Mr. Browne," the receptionist called out.

At the office door, he removed the brass strip with Jordan's name on it. That accomplished, he entered, surveyed it, and sat down in his desk chair. The bodyguard entered behind him, also surveyed it, and drew the blinds. He expressed concern that the office windows looked out onto Cherry Street. In his opinion, the corner office wasn't safe enough. Amadi assured him things would be fine for a few minutes and promised to set up shop for a while in one of the interior, windowless conference rooms. The bodyguard didn't argue, moved a chair outside the office, and sat.

45

Saturday, December 14, 2024

Another Saturday. Another weekend day at her desk. But while 3J had walked over to the office as she usually did on a Saturday, this time she really had nothing planned to work on. She was there at work because that's what she did on Saturdays.

Pascale came around to her office at 11:30 with his cup of coffee and a cup of Earl Grey tea for her. He knew from long experience she would be there at her desk.

"Bill, this is going to sound a little macabre, but before the last couple of days, I planned on being here to block everything out and prepare for Jordan Browne's examination next week. I figured it would be a contentious one with an obstreperous Ms. Carson leading the charge. Well, I'm here, but I guess I don't need to prepare that outline anymore."

Pascale nodded. "You know the proverb about dead men telling no tales and revealing no secrets, 3J. Remind me how long you've had these cases."

"Jeez. Seems like this nightmare has been going on for months and months. But the bankruptcy cases are only ten days old."

"Ten intense days, to say the least. In my concerted and expert opinion, you, my friend, need to get the hell outta here. For once, spend a weekend doing anything but the law dance."

"I will. Pretty soon. I'm not staying all day."

Pascale frowned, and she knew that was a reaction to her not abiding by his opinion, even though he didn't push back. Instead, he asked, "What comes next in the bankruptcy cases?"

"I suppose we can go forward with a plan, but now that Amadi Browne is in charge of the bank, we ought to schedule a time to talk with him and see about an agreed upon compromise."

"Yeah. That would be way more preferable than a bankruptcy plan."

"I'll try to set something up for next week." She sighed. "I guess we'll have to go through Hannah Carson for the time being since she's still the bank's attorney of record. I don't look forward to that call or a meeting where she's speaking for the bank."

"Carson," Pascale said slowly. "Yeah, she's still the one we have to contact I'm afraid. You think Amadi has ever met her before?"

"I doubt it. She was completely a Jordan selection."

They sat there sipping their morning beverages. "Well, I'm not contacting her today and not even this weekend," 3J finally said. "I could do without her attitude right now, and for me, there's lots of dust that has to settle on this one." She gazed out her windows. "Bill, it's Saturday, not Friday, but how about we hit O'Brien's tonight for a little while?"

"How about Bryant's first?" He smiled. "And how about now?"

She smiled widely, grabbed her backpack, and replied, "Let's blow this joint."

Bryant's was Arthur Bryant's Barbeque, self-dubbed the "king of ribs" and self-described as "the most renowned barbequer in history." The restaurant rose to fame when it was only a few blocks away from all things sports in Kansas City: Municipal Stadium, home to the Negro Leagues' Kansas City Monarchs; the Kansas City Blues; the Kansas City Athletics; and the first home of the NFL team, the Kansas City Chiefs. All sports had long ago abandoned the immediate area, but the Bryant's legend lived on because the small restaurant smoked its proteins to tender perfection every day.

When they arrived, they lined up outside in the cold along with the usual Kansas City weekend crowd who waited patiently for the line to move to enter the restaurant. Like every barbeque joint in Kansas City, the complex aroma brought on by the cloud of hickory smoke lingering on meats cooked at two hundred degrees for twelve hours or more hung in the air around the restaurant. It made the line worthwhile. The line moved, and eventually, they arrived inside at the glassed-in counter behind which skilled smoke masters stoked the hickory fire where they produced Kansas City's most famous barbeque.

Pascale and 3J arrived at the glass, leaned down to speak through the opening, and each ordered a smoked brisket sandwich and fries platter. By the time they paid the cashier, the food was ready. They loaded up a healthy pile of pickle chips, found a table in the second dining room, slathered on their favorite Bryant's sauce, Sweet Heat for him and Original for her, and began by eating in silence. Talking interfered with the appreciation of the aroma and taste, so silence at the table was the norm. The sauces had attracted presidents Truman, Carter, Clinton, and Obama over the years. 3J knew that the rich Sweet Heat sauce with a tinge of sweetness was Pascale's favorite sauce in the city.

After making a sizable dent in the food, 3J said, "I wanted to thank you, Bill."

"For what?"

"For everything and anything."

"Well, that's pretty unspecific, but I'm always happy to say you're welcome," Pascale said playfully.

"What I mean is, for stepping in and insisting I not go with Moe and Ronnie to get Amadi and for always being there for me. We've worked with each other for almost twenty years. That's almost as long as Papa and Momma were there for me."

"Thanks for making me feel real old. But seriously, of course, and always."

"You help me fit in."

"Fit in? You mean at the firm? 3J, you *are* in. You're a star. This is your world now. The real question is how the rest of the folks at the firm fit into *your* world, not how you fit into theirs."

"Maybe. It's always so complicated. You know, Bill, I've always had a problem with learning and applying the lesson of not running toward danger. Papa told me not to. But I did back then, and I still do. I guess the rush I get from taking chances has always hypnotized me."

Pascale nodded knowingly. "Oh, I think it worked out okay this time. I think you're probably trainable. You just gotta work at it."

"Maybe. Hope you're right."

They returned to their meal as 3J picked at her fries.

"On another topic, I'm going to perform with my friends at an open mic night in a few days," Pascale said. "Wanna come?"

Pascale had never before invited 3J to hear him play guitar with his band. "Sure. I'd love it."

"We're gonna be showcasing a new tune I wrote."

"Oh? Name?"

"'Someday, Someday Soon.'"

"Sounds upbeat and hopeful. Genre?"

"Actually, it's a bluesy number. The entire name is 'Someday, Someday Soon (You Won't Love Me Like You Used to Do.)'"

"Ahh, well that sounds a little different than I was thinking."

"It's not heavy. More of a playful novelty song."

"I'm so proud of your music, Bill."

"Well, hold that thought. I haven't subjected you to an entire set of it yet."

3J grinned. She was looking forward to finally hearing Pascale play his tunes. "I don't think you've ever told me about you and music."

"Not much to tell. My mother had an old upright piano in the living room. She made me take piano lessons. I hated it. The notion of having to practice somewhere everyone could hear me was horrid. The piano was her instrument, not mine. At some point, I said no more and took a year off from music. A neighbor let me borrow an old guitar. I could take it to my room and close the door. No one could hear me. No YouTube in those days, so I mostly taught myself. As an adult, it's kept me grounded. It's like the calm after the storm. The hurricane of my life comes with its wind and rain, then the music clears it, and my beat goes on."

3J nodded and smiled as Pascale explained the music.

"When I write a new song, it's like I built another world that lasts for a few minutes. I guess it's like writing a book, except with books, the other world lasts for fifteen hours. Or through an entire series. That's building a whole galaxy. Whew! But the point is, it's mine to create. It's a place that's totally mine. A place to escape."

"That's a depth—or height, considering you're talking galaxies—you've never talked about before when it comes to music. Thank you. But I'm going to have to be stuck in the real world for a while. Galaxies created in someone's imagination will have to wait."

Now it was Pascale's turn to smile. "Y'know, I wouldn't have needed this law gig if I could have harmonized on cue, written songs like Paul McCartney, and danced like Mick Jagger and Michael Jackson. God, I wish I could dance."

"Well, none of them can cross-examine a witness like you."

"I suppose," Pascale agreed. "But maybe, for a day, it would be nice . . ."

She knew what he meant. Lawyers thinking of other ways their life could have gone was nothing new. "I'm intrigued. Thanks for asking me to come. Text me where and when, and I'll be there."

46

Robert McFadden recalls Saturday, December 14, 2024

I REMEMBER THINKING to myself, what a project this turned out to be. I'd decided to call off the hit on Amadi Browne. No point fulfilling Jordan Browne's wishes. I had rules and I had my code. No one gets killed unless there's a good reason. It's a prerequisite. The only one who wanted him dead was his brother, and on the balance sheet of life, Jordan Browne had now moved from paying client to dearly departed. So there was no longer a reason to kill Amadi Browne.

Just business. Nothing personal.

Amadi Browne wasn't a loose end. He didn't know about me and I didn't need to know about him. I was sure I'd read about his do-good efforts from time to time in the *Star*. A new piece of Kansas City history in the making that I might pay attention to. Who knew? I even wondered about making an anonymous donation to one of his pet causes. But reading about him and his good deeds was as close to knowing him as I figured I'd need to get.

Amadi Browne? Nah. Not a loose end.

I only had one of those left. Bobby Ray. I wondered how it had come to this. He was a crazy fuckup and too damn unpredictable. And he knew too much. He knew everything. I could send him away, but I had no way of knowing whether he'd go and if he did, whether he'd stay away or return. Eventually, the cops would figure out that Ray killed Cruz and Jordan Browne. Hell, I figured Browne had a video doorbell that recorded Ray pulling the trigger for all the world to see. What a moron. No attention to detail. I told him to cover his face, but I thought he'd probably shot the guy on his own front steps with a live camera recording it. Jesus.

Once the cops saw the video, it wouldn't take much for them to find Ray. They'd talk to him, and once they did, who knew what he'd say. As I chewed on my Ray problems and the complications he could cause, I could feel my blood pressure rising. All of it made me very unsettled, and unsettled was not the way I wanted to go through my day.

I brought him into the organization when he was a teenager. I'd have to take him out as a young adult.

I liked to think I wasn't a violent man. After all, they nicknamed my alma mater the Quakers—the pacifists in the city of brotherly love. No, I wasn't a violent man at heart, but for certain, the business I was in could be violent. Spot killings. Hits. Contract killings. Hits for hire. Call it what you will. Some people in this world wanted other people in this world dead, sometimes deservedly and sometimes not. Simple as that. If they were willing to pay a fee, I asked no questions. It was a good fee. Supply and demand. A good profit margin. There was a need to be filled, and I was in the business of filling it from time to time.

Somebody had to do it. Might as well be me.

Most of the spot killings were for tactical reasons, or, as with Maximilian Cruz, to send a message to everyone else in my outfit. The "don't fuck with me" message. The "do what I say" message. Occasionally I bumped into the potential client who had personal reasons for a hit. Emotional. I tried to steer clear of them. Too volatile.

At first, I believed Jordie's problems were all business. I wouldn't have taken him on as a client and helped him out otherwise. I wasted a lot of breath talking to him about business and businessmen. He said it was good business to get rid of his brother, and it made sense to me. He sold me on it. He was convincing.

But after a while, I wasn't so sure it was all business with Jordie. It didn't really matter anymore, but I was starting to believe that for old Jordie, it was personal. Very personal. In his mind, he had been taking shit from his family and his bro since the day he was born, and he'd decided it was time to pay it forward. Jordie had a plan, and if his bro wouldn't play the ballgame Jordie had in mind, Jordie would go ahead and cram his plan down his brother's throat . . . with prejudice.

That kind of cram down is nasty business. Nasty business, indeed.

But Jordie wasn't my problem anymore. Just Bobby Ray. Yeah, I figured I needed to take care of Bobby Ray once and for all. It wasn't personal. I had Bobby Ray, a white guy, kill a Black banker and a Cuban soldier of mine. Now I figured to balance the ledger, so to speak, I'd have one of my Black soldiers take out Bobby Ray.

But Bobby Ray was dangerous, so I needed to be careful about it and plan it all out. It was the last remaining complication on the project. I needed to be smart. No emotion.

Speaking of planning, I remember hearing about a saloon some years ago—the Last Chance Saloon near State Line Road and Southwest Boulevard. Some mobster named Goulding ran it in the fifties. Half the club was in Missouri and the other half was in Kansas. The damn building was in both states. Can you imagine? Genius idea. Whenever the cops from one state showed up, everyone would move to the other side of the saloon and sit in the other state, beyond the reach of the coppers. Was that some kind of careful planning or what? Inspiring. Fuckin' inspiring.

That's the kind of careful planning I needed. Then quick implementation. And I figured that would do it for my remaining loose end. I knew just the guy to help me out on it, and I figured it wouldn't take much. An in-and-out quickie, then on to new endeavors.

47

Monday, December 16 through Tuesday, December 17, 2024

When 3J's phone rang first thing Monday morning, it was Amadi, and in a matter of moments, they set a meeting for the following day at Greene Madison. Carson could yell at her for talking to Amadi, but at that moment, 3J didn't care. Technically, Hannah Carson was still the bank's counsel, and the communication to set up the meeting should have gone through her, but Amadi had simply been proceeding as bank president with no lawyer.

She had no interest in speaking with Hannah Carson live and didn't know if Amadi had informed her of the meeting. So 3J waited until very late on Monday evening to leave Carson a courtesy voice mail on her office phone advising her of the meeting date and time.

As the meeting was about to begin on Tuesday, Hannah Carson arrived at the reception area looking perturbed and apparently thinking she was still counsel for the bank. 3J's assistant brought Carson to the conference room, and as soon as she entered, Carson challenged 3J for having talked directly with her client. Amadi rose, introduced himself, and asked Carson to step outside for a moment.

3J and the Franklins watched as the two appeared to have a terse discussion. After a few moments, Carson grabbed her backpack, turned for the elevators, and left. Her face appeared to be flushed, but there was no way for 3J to know if it was the flush of anger or embarrassment.

Amadi came back into the room, sat, looked at 3J and the Franklins, and smiled as he said, "The bank no longer will need Ms. Carson's services. She told me you weren't permitted to talk with me, Ms. Jones, since she was still counsel for the bank. So I terminated her engagement, effective this past Friday. Thus, when we talked on Monday, the bank had no attorney of record and our discussion was perfectly appropriate."

"Do you want to wait to have this meeting until the bank hires new counsel, Amadi?" 3J asked.

"Not necessary. I think I can handle these discussions."

"Very well. We're here to talk about how we should proceed with the bankruptcy cases. There are only two choices now. Abode can file a Chapter 11 plan, in which case we'll need to work out the terms of the bank's treatment. Or we can dismiss the case if the bank first rescinds the decision to let the loan mature and retroactively renews it for another year."

As Amadi listened and took notes, 3J continued. "We don't like the plan option, to be honest. It's expensive, and depending on the bank's decision, it could still entail cram down issues and a court fight. And we'd run the risk that another creditor could object to plan confirmation. What Abode needs is a working line of credit, not bankruptcy court time battling with creditors. Without the line, we're going to have to get court buy-in to pay the bank less than it's owed to extend Abode's life while it looks for a new lender and a new line. We assume that will make the bank board peevish and perhaps even litigious. We would have to be prepared then to cram down such a plan over the bank's objections. Very expensive process. High stakes. We think the bank will come out the loser."

"Yes, I've had experience with bankruptcy cram down," Amadi conceded. "Messy process. Powerful tool. It makes the bank's board members unhappy, to be sure. For the debtor, it's usually a bet-the-company process. For the bank, it's just dollars and cents. Cram down is exactly like the phrase implies: unpleasant all around. You know, before I fired her just now, Ms. Carson told me she could successfully beat back any attempt in bankruptcy court to cram down the bank. She was a little edgy as she spoke. She'll need to work on that as her career progresses." Amadi paused and closed his eyes as he continued. "Before he died, Jordan told me he would take any cram down plan and cram it *up* the Franklins' asses. Pardon my Greek."

3J didn't respond. She waited for Amadi's decision. The Franklins said nothing.

"That was Jordan's way. He was always involved in some form of cram down. With me, to try to force me to bend to his banking vision. With you, to fight your attempts to use the bankruptcy code to protect Abode. And I guess with Ms. Carson, who had him convinced they could fight Abode and beat back a bankruptcy cram down plan."

Amadi shook his head slowly. "He was such a damn fool. Weeks ago, I had no interest in the stock buyback. All he had to do was renew the Abode loan one more time. The repo deadline would have passed, and the bank would be his for good, albeit he'd suffer a slight delay in his plans to conquer the local banking world. But delay wasn't his thing. Nor was common sense. Kidnapping, attempted murder, and mayhem apparently were. Who knew?"

He sighed and looked at the Franklins. "You should know I bought back the shares because I wanted Commonwealth back in my hands, in my control, and doing the work I think is important. Part of that work is Abode, but it's not the only bank customer that benefits. There are many. For your purposes, I want Abode as a customer like my parents did. I want Commonwealth to be Abode's bank, and I want Abode to continue to succeed. I see no reason to have a cram down plan and no reason to have papers shoved anywhere the sun doesn't shine, notwithstanding my departed brother's views.

"I will say this. Ms. Carson and my brother shared two not so endearing qualities. Both seemed to be 'my way or the highway' folks. And they lacked a good sense of when to hold and when to fold. I'm truly sorry we've put you through the ringer, but it's behind us, and if you will still have Commonwealth as your lender, we would still like Abode as our customer."

"Of course we do, Amadi," Bella said immediately. She added softly, "Are you going to want the recent draw money back?"

"Why would I? I approved it. The draw was proper. The project is important." Amadi smiled. "Later on, we can talk about whether Abode should bank at KCBT or Commonwealth. You moved to KCBT because you didn't trust us. We need to earn that trust back."

"Thank you," James said.

"I'll need to talk with my board, but my strong recommendation will be to reinstate the line, renew the loan, and support dismissal of the bankruptcy cases. I'll need a few days to get the board to approve all this."

"Excellent," 3J said.

Amadi nodded. "I would like to discuss one other matter with you if you will indulge me."

"Of course," James said.

"My brother made mention that you and he discussed the possibility of loan sales and securitizations to raise cash for Abode to build more houses. At the time, you made the offer to appease him, seeking as the quid pro quo renewal of the line. There's no longer a need for the quid pro quo discussion. Shortly, I expect the board to approve the reinstatement and renewal without conditions.

"But the mortgage sales and securitizations present an intriguing new strategy for Abode and the bank to consider seriously in our revived partnership. Both options would generate cash: cash in addition to the bank's line of credit and your fundraising efforts. There isn't any real urgency at this point, but after we get through this next chapter, I'd like to sit down with all of you and explore these options. It's a very creative way to turn long-term assets—thirty year mortgages—into current cash. I know lots of banks in town who desperately need mortgages in neighborhoods populated by members of marginalized groups so they can stay out of the regulators' crosshairs. I see the prospect of mortgage sales and securitizations as a win-win."

"Happy to discuss that with you whenever you're ready," James said. "More cash in our coffers is always a good thing. You know how we put it to work."

"I should add that I expect we'll be able to arrive at a formula where some of this new cash goes to the bank to pay down the line so you can borrow more and some would go straight into Abode's pockets. We'd need to get our arms around the collateral to make sure it still supports the line. It should, but I haven't gotten quite that far in my thinking." He tilted his head to one side and shrugged. "I've been a little preoccupied the last couple of weeks."

3J was ecstatic. What had started out as an unformulated idea to make the bank happy had turned into a potential way to expand Abode's mission in the city. She tried to rein in her excitement. Lots could go wrong before the parties could agree on new ways for Abode to raise money, but even the *chance* to expand Abode's mission was a dramatic development. In a very short period of time, Abode had gone from fighting for its life to the potential for expanding its mission.

Interlude

September 14, 1999

"MR. JONES, PLEASE COME in and sit down," Doctor Imelda Jefferson said as she gestured to a chair in her office. 3J's father took a seat and waited.

"Thanks for taking time off work to stop by and talk about Josephina."

3J was a sophomore in high school. Weeks before, after getting into a fight when she came to the aid of a boy involved in a tussle in the schoolyard, 3J's father had become concerned she was exhibiting risky conduct. She seemed to always be running toward trouble. "This is exactly the opposite of what we taught her, May," her father had said to her mother as he suggested 3J should see a counselor or psychologist.

May agreed, and to his relief, 3J was agreeable to the process. Dr. Jefferson gave 3J a series of tests and talked with her to determine her level of risk-taking.

"Mr. Jones, let's start with a little background. Risk-taking is acting in ways that take chances with one's well-being. We pursue something with possible harmful consequences. Adolescents take risks for a host of reasons: curiosity, experimentation, excitement, rebellion, growth, courage, conformity, freedom, impulsivity, and substance abuse among them."

3J's father looked alarmed. "Substances? Are you saying Jo is taking drugs?"

"I am not. She has her sports. I'm not saying athletes are drug free, but I think with Josephina, the competition outlet itself helps fulfill some of her risk-taking inclinations. I mentioned substances only because I want to be complete and I want to make sure we lay the general groundwork for our specific discussion about Josephina. Please know that some amount of risk-taking is a normal part of growing up. During adolescence, our kids go through enormous physical, cognitive, emotional, and social changes. They learn what is dangerous, and most eventually decide to steer clear of it. Do you have questions so far?"

3J's father shook his head.

"Good. Based on my discussions with Josephina and the tests I gave her, I believe she is in a higher bracket of potential risk-taking than the average adolescent. Meaning simply, at this point in her development, she is more willing to take chances, either without considering the potential consequences or by dismissing them."

"Would that explain the fights she's been getting into at school?"

"It could."

"And if May and I are correct, her recent sexual activities?"

"Again, it could."

"Does this go away on its own?"

"Yes and no. Sometimes things happen that help the teen make better decisions. They jump their skateboard off a ramp, fall, and break their collarbone. The pain can help them learn that skateboard jumping can be dangerous. They get pulled over for speeding and lose their license. Losing their driving freedom helps them learn that reckless driving can have negative consequences."

"I honestly thought we had taught her to *not* run toward trouble."

"Wise advice, but teens who are risk-takers find pleasure in the hunt and tend not to think as much about consequences—like bad things that could happen. You find this same tendency among skydivers and extreme mountain climbers and some backcountry skiers. And yes, kids who turn to drugs. Their executive function has not yet developed sufficiently for the little voice in their head to tell them to avoid doing something. Or that voice is there but it isn't loud enough or forceful enough to stop them. So they make the risky choice."

"So what should we do, Doctor?" 3J's father asked, shaking his head.

"The good news is that along with risk-taking comes grit and determination. We don't want to dissuade the development of those personality traits."

"Very complicated stuff, Doc."

"Yes. We humans are a conundrum wrapped in a mystery. My advice is for you to keep talking to her. Keep piling on the love. You and your ex-wife have great relationships with Josephina. Use them. Keep setting good examples. I know you're not married anymore, but be a team for your daughter. My feeling is that Josephina will mostly grow out of this, but perhaps not completely. She may carry some risk-taking into her early adult years. And perhaps beyond that. Oh, and unless you have religious opposition, make sure she takes the pill."

"Lots to think about, Doctor. Thank you."

After his meeting, 3J's father called his ex-wife and reported what the psychologist had said. Once he had given her the details and answered her questions, he added. "May, I'll tell you what. Jo's teenage years may be the death of me. I guess when she grows up and I'm gone, all of this will be on someone else's watch. Whoever that is, I hope they have her back."

48

Friday, December 20, 2024

The previous day, Amadi Browne had let 3J know his board voted to approve the reinstatement and renewal of the line of credit. She drafted a motion to dismiss the bankruptcy cases and filed it first thing Friday morning, and she told the Franklins that approval of the motion, while likely, was not automatic.

Judge Robertson had decided to close his office at two o'clock and send everyone home for an early start on the upcoming holiday. There would be no further hearings until after Christmas. Before he headed out, he saw 3J's motion to dismiss and called Jennifer into his office.

"What do you make of this?" he asked.

"Kind of ironic. Only a couple of weeks ago, the debtors fought off the bank's request to dismiss the cases."

"True enough, although 'fought off' might be a bit of an overstatement. Ms. Jones didn't need to utter a word other than her name and the names of the clients. Probably the easiest hearing she's handled and won in quite some time."

Jennifer smiled. "Yes, that wasn't much of a hearing and not much of a fight after all."

"Well, whatever's happened, I'm sure it's good news for Abode, and Ms. Jones will explain it all to us at the hearing. Before we head out for the holiday, can we set a hearing on the motion for the second week of January and we'll see what's up?"

"Sure thing, Judge."

"It'll be interesting to see if Ms. Carson is still representing the bank and if so, what she has to say." The judge smiled and nodded. "Yes, I expect that part could be quite interesting."

Over several days ending on the Friday before Christmas, the *Kansas City Star* ran an investigatory series titled, "Mobsters Among Us?" Of course, the *Star* concluded mobsters had always been "among us" in Kansas City, had never gone away, and would be around for some time to come. The article interviewed a history professor at the University of Missouri - Kansas City who opined that like jazz, Civil War battles, and barbeque, mobsters were simply part of the Kansas City fiber and, he expected, would always be.

The stories discussed a series of very recent murders and gun violence around the metropolitan area. The reporters talked to residents of the Olive Street building area and the Third and Oak apartment building. The former discussed recent gunfire and the latter discussed the execution of Maximilian Cruz as he ran for his life. They also talked to neighborhood residents about a reported shooting in a house where no one was home near Charlotte and Twenty-Eighth. They wrote of a doorbell video somehow leaked to the press showing an apparent hit man walking up to Jordan Browne, Kansas City banker, and killing him at point-blank range in cold blood right on his Leawood front porch.

In the final piece, the *Star* concluded with a report of the mysterious death of a known, low-level gangster whose body the police found in a dumpster behind the Mercy Motel on Truman Road, a bullet through his chest. And the article quoted an anonymous source willing to talk about a bank president who'd been kidnapped and almost killed, but the story did not mention Amadi Browne by name.

The articles didn't tie it all together in a neat package, but they set out the recent crime spree, suggested it was all the work of the mob, and let the reader draw their own conclusions.

Things had slowed in the Greene Madison office as everyone moved into the weekend leading up to Christmas. 3J and Pascale had agreed to meet at O'Brien's a little earlier than their usual quitting time. They deemed it a good time to get back into their routine. Since the attack by the White nationalists they'd foiled some months ago, they had become less regular about their Friday afternoon get-togethers at the bar. They wanted to get into the habit of meeting there again to put a period after another week in the legal trenches.

Pascale drove them to the bar, and 3J planned on taking an Uber home. As they entered, they waved to the bouncer, Eugene Martin—Bitty to his friends—sitting on his stool near the entrance. Ronnie Steele was manning the busy bar, and he smiled and nodded when he saw them enter. He knew what they drank and turned to fill the unstated order.

Near the rear of the bar, they saw a table where Anthony Rosini, Moe Sterling, and bankruptcy lawyer Jacob Steinert sat. Rather than sit in their usual booth at the very back of the bar, they walked to the table. "Room for two more?" Pascale asked.

As they sat, Steele brought over their drinks—Kansas wheat beer for Pascale and Irish whiskey for 3J. "Happy holidays, all," 3J said as she lifted her glass and toasted her friends. "Will Papa Noël treat you good this year?"

"Mr. Rosini here was just telling us about his brush with the Leawood police department and the death of Jordan Browne," Steinert said. "He had quite the noteworthy afternoon."

Rosini nodded. "I don't know who the killer was, but it had

professional hit written all over it. Except for the doorbell video. Modern tech conspires to bring down the hitman."

"I bet the hitman wishes he'd considered the doorbell video before squeezing the trigger right there in broad daylight," 3J said.

"I don't think he's doing much wishing these days. Did you see the series in the *Star*?" Moe asked.

"Did not. I'm kind of in a front section news time-out these days. If it's not on the sports page, I probably didn't see it," 3J admitted.

Rosini raised his eyebrows. "You should read it. Fascinating stuff. The *Star* did a series on the rash of shootings and killings around town lately. The last part of the series reported on a guy who may've been the Jordan Browne hitman, although since they found him in a dumpster a week or so after someone put a bullet in his chest, the rats had done quite a number on his face, and he was hard to identify. Not really recognizable. But from the description, it sounded like the guy I saw in Leawood. They even found a torn up baseball cap next to him in the dumpster like the one worn by the guy I saw. This guy was apparently hiding out in the Mercy Motel on Truman Road near Independence."

"The only time I ride down Truman is when I need to be at the Jackson County Courthouse in Independence," Pascale confessed. "Usually a foreclosure. I can't say I remember the Mercy Motel, but if it's like everything else on that road, it's instantly forgettable."

"I gotta say, all of this smacks of Robbie McFadden's organization," Moe said. "It's no coincidence we saw him as we followed that Cruz guy from the Olive Street area to a bar in the Bottoms where McFadden apparently conducts what he calls his business. No coincidence the description of the guy who offed Cruz in River Market matched the description of the guy who offed Jordan Browne and the description of the guy, or what was left of him, in the dumpster. I feel it in my bones: Dumpster boy had to have been working for McFadden."

"But why?" Steinert asked. "Why would Robbie McFadden

care about Amadi Browne and Commonwealth? And why kill a guy working for him?"

"I bumped into McFadden more than once in my years with the sheriff's department," Rosini said. "Always impeccably dressed. Always smiling. Always with an army of top-shelf criminal lawyers at the ready. Always walking into our offices with counsel and out of our offices shortly thereafter. Never taking up residence in our jail facility. Just never availed himself of the more permanent accommodations and three squares a day we offer to certain members of the public."

Moe looked over at Rosini. "So why would McFadden care?"

"My guess? Probably didn't care. Probably never heard of the Brownes or Commonwealth before. Probably took on a job to snatch Amadi Browne. He used to call his operations business 'transactions' when we interviewed him. Probably nothing more than a business transaction for a client."

"My gut tells me most likely, McFadden's client was Jordan Browne," Moe replied. Looking at 3J, she added, "You said they went to high school together, didn't you?"

3J nodded.

"At some point, McFadden probably decided the entire operation was spinning a little too close to his universe," Moe continued. "Probably thought Jordan Browne was a little too shilly-shally for his taste. Before McFadden got sucked into the KCPD and Leawood PD investigations, he cleaned house. He's reputed to do that from time to time. In this case, cleaning house was probably Jordan Browne and dumpster boy . . . and Maximilian Cruz."

Rosini sighed audibly. "The problem with McFadden is that there are lots of probablys tied to him but no definitelys and no arrests that stick. The man's good."

"So the prevailing theory is that Jordan hired McFadden to take out his brother, and then McFadden took out Jordan?" Steinert asked.

"Yep. You lie with dogs and you get fleas," Moe replied.

Everyone nodded.

"The title of the article was a little naïve, don't you think?" Moe said. "'Mobsters Among Us?' They wrote it as if they'd never heard of Robbie McFadden and his crew. My lord. I guess it sells newspapers, but get with the times, folks. Right? Surely someone on the paper's crime beat knows about Robbie McFadden and his KC organization. That UMKC professor got it right. It's all part of what makes Kansas City, Kansas City."

Everyone nodded again.

Rosini shook his head. "How do you write a Kansas City mob piece and not mention Robbie fuckin' McFadden?"

"You knew McFadden before all the recent events, right Moe?" Pascale asked.

"Oh, yes. A thorn in Steele's and my side for years while we were on the force. Can't tell you how many times Ronnie interrogated that son of a bitch with me watching through the one-way mirror and grimacing. Often suspected; occasionally charged. Always smiling; never convicted. Slicker than Teflon. A true non-stick gangster if there ever was one."

3J jumped in. "Maybe we ought to get the band back together and come up with a plan to take down McFadden. The city would be better off, right?"

Everyone at the table put their drinks down and looked at her in disbelief. "Negative," Rosini said emphatically. "It's Robbie McFadden you're talking about. I'm gonna pretend I never heard you say that."

Pascale shook his head. "Jesus, 3J. I remember you telling me your father taught you to never run toward trouble. What is this thing lately with you?"

3J smiled. "Chill, people. Just kidding."

Steele came over to the table. "Refills for everyone?" They all nodded. "So what're we talking about?"

"Well, besides mobsters in Kansas City and the *Star* piece, 3J here wants to put our little band back together and go after Robbie McFadden," Pascale explained.

"No fuckin' way, woman," Steele blurted out. "You help people with their debts. Let's stay in our lane and keep with that program. That should give you more than enough to do to be fully engaged." He turned back to the bar shaking his head.

"Chill, people," 3J repeated.

They all returned to drinking in silence.

"This has been quite the last several weeks in bankruptcy court, folks," she finally said, trying to draw everyone back into a discussion.

Steinert nodded. "You don't see this kind of thing too often in bankruptcy."

"Jacob, lately, my cases seem to bring out the underworld, or split personalities, or the dark web, or Swiss assets, or who knows what. I guess it keeps things interesting. And I guess it's just another day at the bankruptcy rodeo. Or at least my version of it."

Pascale wondered if 3J self-identified as a rodeo spectator or a bull rider. He figured bull rider, and it worried him.

ᯣ

Robbie McFadden was in his SUV on his way to his new favorite place to conduct business, The Bottoms Bar. The car drove past the Country Club Plaza strung with three hundred miles of holiday lights that lit the shopping district from dusk to dawn. He had been there with his family on Thanksgiving night for the annual Plaza lights event. Hundreds of thousands of Kansas Citians gathered each year to watch a dignitary flip the switch, turning on the lights and officially ushering in another holiday season. He and his family always went, but he mused from time to time that no one in the city ever asked him to pull the switch.

"Hey boys," he called out to the front seat as they drove. "That

Bobby Ray must've been the only human alive who never heard of a video doorbell. Jesus!"

The bodyguards joined him in a laugh.

The *Star* series had made him think of Bobby Ray. McFadden had read the series each morning at breakfast in his home office. He noted two things. First, he had been successful in tying up loose ends. There was no specific mention of him or his organization. Second, he found the title of the article amusing.

Calling out to the front seat again, he said, "What say we stop at Browne's for some sustenance?"

Browne's Irish Marketplace at Thirty-Third and Pennsylvania, opened in 1887, claimed to be the oldest Irish business outside Ireland. That claim had been verified by an agency of the Ireland government. It was home to Irish food and drink, including a large selection of Irish whiskeys and grocery and imported items. The lunch crowd usually flooded in for sandwiches made on traditional soda bread and for those who could get away with it over their lunch hour, a dark Irish beer. McFadden's father would take him to Browne's when he was a kid each St. Patrick's Day, and as an adult, he regularly stopped by to grab lunch.

"Sure thing, Mr. McFadden."

As they headed to Browne's, McFadden returned to the series in the *Star*. "Mobsters?" he asked his bodyguards as they passed by the Plaza heading toward Westport, Browne's, and then the Bottoms beyond. "Right here in Kansas City?" He laughed, feigning shock over the statement. "Are they fuckin' kidding me?"

The bodyguards chuckled at McFadden's contrived surprise.

The articles made him think about his depleted army. He was down two soldiers. "Boys, I gotta find two new men for the organization. It's not like I can hang out a help wanted sign, right? Y'know anyone?"

Both bodyguards said they'd be on the lookout.

His thoughts returned to the newspaper exposé. After he'd

finished the articles, he whimsically considered seeking out the reporters and offering them an interview with a real mobster for a follow-up story. It would be his chance to come out of the shadows. After all, he was a businessman. Why shouldn't he get a little press in the spotlight like the other businessmen living on Ward Parkway? "Maybe I should give the *Star* an interview," he said to the bodyguards.

This time, they were silent.

He laughed, half expecting one of them to turn around for a sanity check. "Chill out, boys. Just kidding."

It was the life he had chosen. He lived the life he wanted to live, and that was what mattered to him. No one told him what to do. People who owed him money paid him back. No one crammed anything down on him over his objection. Society's rules were suggestions. Laws were mere propositions. Mores were for patsies.

He knew the lay of the land. His land. He lived in the shadows, and he was comfortable there. He conducted his affairs in the shadows and would continue to do so.

It was just business. His way to conduct his kind of business.

༄

Later that night, 3J and Steele sat on her couch listening to KANU in Lawrence play new release jazz music. For years, Steele had listened to Dick Wright play jazz tunes and offer jazz history lessons on his Saturday morning KANU show, *The Jazz Scene*. If he had no particular music in mind, he always went to 91.5 FM on the dial to listen to the jazz playlists. He knew 3J loved KANU's music, and she seemed more relaxed than he'd seen her lately as she drank a glass of red wine while he sipped on a wheat beer.

"Nickel for your thoughts, Ronnie," she said, and as she spoke, she took a nickel from her pocket and placed it on the coffee table in front of them.

Steele leaned forward, reached for the coin, and shook his head slowly. "Robbie McFadden is bad news, 3J. The worst. Promise me you really were kidding at the bar today."

"Just kidding. Promise." She put her head on his shoulder. "I'm sure we could pull it off, but just kidding," she added in a voice barely above a whisper.

Steele shook his head again. She had put herself in harm's way when she insisted on accompanying him to serve a potentially dangerous witness with a court order and ignored his demand that she stay in the car. She almost got herself killed running after and then fighting with a gun-toting assailant outside O'Brien's. She had ignored his instruction to stay inside the storeroom at O'Brien's while Moe, Steele, Biddy, and Rosini disabled the White nationalist. In her latest risky behavior, she had planned on going with him to pick up Amadi at Momá's house, ignoring the danger posed by a killer who was on the loose. Fortunately, she had backed off from that one. And now she suggested that she and her crew of friends go after Robbie McFadden.

He recognized she was one stubborn human being but hoped she would back away from her risk-taking tendencies. She sometimes failed to think things through, and that scared him. It perplexed him that someone so trained in detail-oriented planning, someone who, in her professional career, considered any and all possibilities, could so readily ignore all training and logic. She wasn't a firefighter trained to run toward the fire. She was a lawyer. And she was a human, not a superhero. He couldn't figure out why she took such chances with her well-being.

All he could do was talk with her. And love her.

49

Thursday, January 9, 2025

"I'LL TAKE APPEARANCES, counsel," Judge Robertson announced when he took the bench and surveyed the attendees in his courtroom.

"Thank you, Your Honor. Josephina Jones representing the debtors, Abode LLC, and its officers, Bella and James Franklin, who appear in person."

"Mr. Steinert, welcome. What brings you by my courtroom this afternoon?"

"Your Honor, Jacob Steinert representing Commonwealth Savings and Loan Bank. Mr. Amadi Browne, its president, also appears here today in person."

The judge glanced around the courtroom again and found one other person in his courtroom, Amadi's bodyguard. "I see. It looks like the bank has an entirely new team here today. Was it free agency time in the Kansas City banking world this past month?" he asked, tongue in cheek.

"Your Honor, the bank has decided to change counsel," Steinert explained. "I expect, however, I will be a one-hearing wonder in these cases, assuming Your Honor grants the debtors' unopposed motion to dismiss them."

"And Mr. Amadi Browne? Welcome, sir. I do not believe you were at the last hearing."

Amadi stood and addressed the court. "You are correct, Your Honor. I would have very much liked to have been here. But . . . certain events in my life made it . . . well, impossible for me to attend."

"Yes, yes. I think I recently read something in the *Star* about the kidnapping of a bank officer. Was that you?" the judge asked.

"Yes, sir. But the newspaper did not actually know or report on the half of it."

"No doubt. I am sure it was harrowing. Well, I am glad to see you are back in the saddle and looking okay."

"Thank you, Your Honor. It is good to be back. I am not one hundred percent quite yet, but I expect I will get there."

The judge turned his attention to 3J, who was now standing at the podium. "Ms. Jones, it is your motion. There is no opposition I find in the record, and the United States Trustee advises it has no objection to dismissal as well. But I believe under the bankruptcy code, you still have to convince me this is the right thing to do. So we will need to make a record of why this is a good idea. A bit ironic, is it not? At the last hearing, you opposed the bank's motion to dismiss, and now you are asking for dismissal."

"Yes, Your Honor. Events have moved quickly in this case. The irony is not lost on us. Our world changes, so our strategies do, as well, to keep up. The debtors filed their bankruptcy petitions to protect themselves from Commonwealth's decision to let the twelve-million-dollar line of credit mature. The bank's decision left Abode without a source of funding. At the time, the bank was under the control of Amadi Browne's brother, Jordan Browne, who you met at the last hearing."

Judge Robertson nodded.

"The last six weeks have been, to say the least, very complicated and fluid. And I am happy to go into greater detail for Your Honor if you would like me to. But suffice it to say that Amadi Browne is now in control again. He is the bank president, he has the full support of his board, and he is again the majority shareholder of the bank. And under his control, the bank has rescinded its prior decision and has renewed Abode's line of credit for another year. With that, the debtors no longer need or want bankruptcy protection. We can do just fine outside of bankruptcy, and we no longer need to try to cram down a plan over the bank's objection. For these reasons, we seek dismissal of these cases."

"Is Mr. Amadi Browne's position as president permanent or is there a chance for more uncertainty?"

"Your Honor, Jordan Browne will not displace Amadi Browne again."

The judge raised his eyebrows.

"You may remember that the *Star* reported the death of a banker in the same articles you read. That banker was Jordan Browne. So Amadi Browne is now the only living bank shareholder."

"I see. Quite a case you have here, Ms. Jones. Well . . . thank you. It is always a quandary for a judge to decide how much he or she *needs* versus *wants* to know. It certainly sounds like there is quite the backstory here. So purely from the standpoint of curiosity, I might like to know the backstory . . . someday. But for today's purposes, I do not think it is necessary for me to know all of that to make my decision. I am glad the bank and the debtors are once again on the same page and cram down will not be necessary. It is always a dangerous process for a bank to go through the rigors of cram down, especially with a nonprofit that has no owners and therefore, no risk of violating the absolute priority rule."

3J and Steinert nodded.

"I hereby grant the motion. Good work by all involved. Thank you. Submit an order for me to sign, and then the Franklins can go back to business as usual. Anything further?"

"No, Your Honor," 3J replied.

"Excellent. Then court is adjourned. We will be off the record."

As the judge stood and collected his papers, he beamed broadly. "Ms. Jones, it is not part of my ruling here today, but find me for a drink at the next continuing legal education conference and regale me with the backstory."

Back in the judge's chambers, Jennifer asked, "What do you think the backstory is, Judge?" as he stretched by his window and watched the Mighty Mo roll along.

"Did you read the *Star* articles?" he asked, turning to face her.

"I have not, Judge."

"You should. Interesting stuff. Someone kidnapped Mr. Amadi Browne. Someone murdered Mr. Jordan Browne. Figure out who committed those crimes and you'll have gone a long way to learning the backstory."

Jennifer raised her eyebrows.

Bankruptcy law clerk appointments were often two-year stints working for a bankruptcy judge after graduating from law school. As the new year began, Judge Robertson had on his mind to find out if his law clerk had plans for when her clerkship ended in August. As Jennifer rose from her chair and gathered her papers to return to her desk, the judge addressed the issue. "Jennifer, this will be your two-year anniversary with me. Have you given any thought to what comes next for you?"

She smiled and returned to her chair. "I've given it some thought. This has been the most wonderful experience for me. I'm pretty sure that when I'm sixty-five, I'll look back on my clerkship and say it was the pinnacle of my career."

The judge smiled. "I'm not so sure about that."

"Right now, I'm thinking a few things. I'd like to stay in Kansas City. I like it here. I like the bankruptcy lawyers who practice before you. And I'm thinking of applying to work as a bankruptcy associate at some firms in town that have a bankruptcy department and see if any of them will interview me and make me an offer."

"So you've deliberated about this quite a bit. Good for you. Any firms in particular?"

"Greene Madison," Jennifer replied quickly and definitively.

"Aha. Excellent. You couldn't go wrong working for Ms. Jones and Mr. Pascale. Do they know yet?"

"Not yet."

"You and they should grab a coffee and talk. They don't really know you, and you don't really know them. Might be a good ice-breaker. Even if they don't have an opening, they know everyone in town and might help with some leads."

He liked the idea of his law clerk working at Greene Madison, and he wondered what Josephina Jones and William Pascale would think of it.

50

Saturday, January 11, 2025

THEY SAT ON the couch snuggling as the January skies darkened. It was bitter cold outside. Spring was too far away to even think about. Mother Nature's winter division was in full swing. The Kansas City winters didn't last as long as those in Wisconsin, but they tended to hang around for longer than most lower Midwest natives wished.

The couch and the company were warm. Everything was where it should be. Everything was in its proper place. Abode survived to continue to build homes for the legions of forgotten, left behind minorities in Kansas City. It would continue to save a little corner of the world, every day, one nail, one board, one house, and one family at a time. At 3J's and Pascale's behest, the firm's banking lawyers were hard at work completing a plan to sell and securitize Abode mortgages to raise new cash.

Amadi was back in his corner office looking out over Cherry Street, sitting in his old office chair, surveying the city for new projects to help the forgotten and left-behind communities. No more bodyguard.

Jordan was dead. No arrest, no bail needed, no arraignment,

and no trial on the docket. He had found a more permanent sentence than a state court judge and jury could dole out.

Over lunch, Amadi had confided in 3J that the sudden loss of his brother still shocked him. He needed to allow himself the space to feel bad for his brother and for himself, and he needed time for the stain on the Browne family legacy to fade. When 3J asked about the stain, he said he regretted Jordan's legacy was that Kansas Citians would remember his family for all the evil things his brother did and wanted to do. Amadi feared the legacy was now spreading slowly across the city like blood disperses and pools as it flows from a fatal gunshot wound.

Amadi mentioned that Maximilian Cruz's mother had showed up unannounced in the bank lobby asking to speak to Mr. Amadi, the bank president. Amadi had greeted her and ushered her into his office. Once there, she had hugged him. Then she had put his face between her hands, squeezed gently, moved his head slowly back and forth, kissed him, and hugged him again. No words. Just her deeds of love and gratitude.

"She's quite a woman, 3J," Amadi reported. "Her boy, Maximilian, was quite a man, as well. I hope he's okay, wherever he is."

Pascale was . . . well, consulting. And doing just fine at it in 3J's estimation.

And tonight, 3J was on the couch with Ronnie. He had been on her mind lately. Truth be told, Ronnie was always on her mind. Things were comfortable. Comfortable was good. But she wondered if comfortable was all he wanted? Was it all she wanted? Was it all there was?

She cued Kansas City's own Bobby Watson on her Sonos. Watson played his rendition of Duke Ellington's "I Got It Bad (And That Ain't Good)," from his definitive hard bop release, *Present Tense.* Watson had been the musician in residence at the local university for years. When he traveled, his music brought all things Kansas City to the far corners of the world. She had met Watson several times, and he and Pat Metheny were her two favorite contemporary hometown jazz icons, touring and bringing Kansas City's influence to the world to enjoy.

She particularly loved the songs on Watson's album *The Gates BBQ Suite* paying homage to one of the city's hometown barbeque legends, Ollie Gates. People knew his chain of restaurants for the fare and the staff, who loudly greeted every patron who entered with the question, "Hi. May I help you?" Another favorite was *Back Home in Kansas City*, which let all the jazz world know where Watson had planted his roots. His music was his tribute and his songs his love letters to Kansas City. His albums were his audio promotional materials for the city, there to review by everyone who had never visited the City of Fountains. She thought there was nothing better than being serenaded on a Sunday night by Bobby.

As "I Got It Bad" played, she turned to Ronnie. "Ronnie, are we going anywhere or are we just where we are?"

"Where is that, 3J?" Ronnie softly replied.

"Mmm. Y'know. The sex is amazing. The companionship is warm. We're comfortable. You're always on my mind. All so needed in my life."

He smiled. "Amazing, huh? For a second I worried you might go all big firm lawyer on me and give me a double negative. Something like, 'Ronnie, the sex is not unpleasant.'"

3J grinned. "No. Amazing was the right word," she said softly.

"Well, it feels like there's a 'but' or an 'on the other hand' coming."

"No buts. No other hands." She bit her upper lip. "I'm so bad at this, Ronnie. Look, we enjoy each other's company. I'm just asking, is that where we are in this relationship? Enjoyment. And are we at a fork in the road?"

"Oh, I get it. No, I don't think that's where we are."

"Okay then, where do you think we are?"

He paused. "I think we love each other. I know I love you.

I'm pretty sure you love me. I think that's where we are, and if you agree, we have some choices for where we're going. Love has a way of lighting the way. All we need to do is to follow the light. And no fork in the road ahead of us. We passed that fork a while ago."

3J smiled but shook her head slightly. "I don't know. My whole adult life I've had this juxtaposition. I have a complicated professional life, and it's sometimes messy. But I know what I'm doing. I'm rarely confused and almost never scared. I know where the case needs to go. I usually know how to get there. Sometimes I lose, but more often, I win. This time, I saved Abode. I helped right the wrongs, and I helped folks get back on their feet and on their way."

She swirled her Columbia Valley, Washington, red meritage wine in her glass and watched it form legs on the glass wall. Then she took a sip, tucked her legs under her on the couch, and continued. "But in my personal life, I don't know, it's just . . . well . . . personal. I don't always see the light. I don't always know what I'm doing. Relationships almost always confuse me and sometimes even scare me. I don't know where I'm heading, so I certainly don't know how to get there. I don't know that I'm doing things right. Usually, I'm cautious—cloistered behind my wall of protection to save me from who knows what. More bewildered than calculating."

She leaned back on the couch and looked at him as he smiled again. It was another moment of 3J self-analysis with its own winding, sometimes lengthy, road she traveled down from time to time. Confidence in court didn't translate into self-confidence in love and life.

She opened her dazzling, hazel eyes wide. "And then you arrived in my life. No caution. The wall of protection came tumbling down. Nothing cloistered. Heck, something must've been up from the start because *I* even asked *you* out on our first date. First time in my life I'd ever done that. Meanwhile, I've waited for the fear of commitment to arrive, as it always has in the past. But this time it hasn't. And it doesn't appear to be scheduled for delivery.

I'm not scared. Even so, relationships, this one included . . . well, they can leave me confused."

"3J, I think we're meant to be. Just chill, turn off your brain, at least for tonight, and ride the wave. You'll see. It's meant to be, kiddo."

"Do you think anyone really believes that what's meant to be will be?"

3J was the psychology major. It was in her blood and it would stay there. Add the lawyer gig on top of that and she was as over-analytical as a human could be.

"Hey, come here, will ya?" he whispered. She turned on the couch to face him and they embraced again. They both closed their eyes, forehead resting on forehead, and she let the Bobby Watson saxophone experience sweep her away. The music was in them, where it belonged. Where music was supposed to be. As Bobby took his turn to improvise, it was clear to her that she—they—had it bad, but unlike Duke's song, that didn't mean it wasn't good. A lawyer double negative, but apropos.

Later, 3J fell asleep next to Ronnie on the couch. Somewhere in her mostly asleep state, she heard him cue *Back Home in Kansas City* and drifted up from sleep as he whispered, "You and me against the world, kiddo. Not to worry. We got this."

She opened one eye and said, "Papa used to say that to me." Then she squeezed both eyes shut, put her head on his shoulder, and smiled a smile of contentment.

Maybe it was true. Maybe I got this, she thought as she drifted back down to sleep.

51

Sunday, January 12, 2025

AMADI BROWNE STOOD in his gray winter coat at the edge of a deep hole in the ground. The hole would be the next grave, one of over thirty thousand whose occupants called the Elmwood Cemetery their eternal home at the corner of Truman Road and Van Brunt Boulevard.

Families had buried many Kansas City dignitaries there: Bill Davis, the first Black Kansas City policeman; William Gregory, Kansas City's first mayor; Jacob Loose, owner of the Sunshine Biscuits Company; and Morris Helzberg, jeweler and philanthropist, to name a few. Blacks, Jews, Whites, and dignitaries all resting side by side, no redlining, and finally learning to coexist. The occupant of this grave would be buried there along with his sister-in-law, Meg, his niece, Alice, and generations of banking Brownes. Over forty-three acres of Kansas City history.

Now it was Jordan Browne's turn. The medical examiner's office had finally finished its autopsy and had released the body to Amadi. He'd arranged for the funeral to bury his brother next to his ancestors. The only living attendees were the pastor, Amadi Browne, two cemetery workers, and four people Amadi didn't know, one of whom was a tall, redheaded, blue-eyed, fifty-something man in a stylish suit and tie and a black trench coat. The nonliving attendees were the ghosts of many former residents of the city, Jordan Browne in his casket, and the cold winter wind, howling as if alive and administering its own version of the last rites.

As the pastor finished his prayer and comments, he asked Amadi if he wanted to say a few words. Amadi shook his head. He was unemotional. He'd already had his last discussion with his brother. There was nothing left to say. Not to Jordan. Not to the living. Not to the dead.

Amadi was aware of the redhead eying him carefully as he declined to speak.

As the workers lowered the casket into the ground, the pastor said the obligatory, non-biblical "ashes to ashes, dust to dust," and then added, from Genesis, "For dust thou art, and unto dust shalt thou return."

As the pastor spoke, Amadi remembered a particularly grim discussion he had with his brother years before about death. "Death doesn't scare me," Jordan had said. "It pisses me off. And it fascinates me. When it's my time, I look forward to whatever comes and wherever I'll go next."

Amadi grabbed a shovel and deposited dirt on top of the casket. "You won't be going anywhere, Jordan," he whispered as the dirt fell from his shovel to the casket. "You are where you will be and no place else. Adios, amigo." Amadi would have said, "Rest in peace," but he doubted Jordan would find rest or lasting peace in his afterlife. Only lasting death.

Others present also deposited dirt on top of the casket. The redhead did not. The pastor made the sign of the cross in the air and closed his worn Bible. The service was over. Jordan was officially gone, although anyone who knew him knew he had been for some time.

Amadi turned and headed back to his car. The redhead slowly walked to his black SUV.

❧

"My pops always told me to pay my respects, boys."

The bodyguards nodded their heads as the SUV pulled onto Van Brunt.

"Rest in peace, Jordie. What a messy fuckin' life you had and what a messy fuckin' way to go."

Acknowledgments

Thanks and gratitude to: Cathy Ann Bixby for backstopping me on my use of Spanish; Ruben Jimenez for guiding us through risk-taking; Megan McWilliams, the real Megan Ricci, for keeping an old man in better shape; Bob Monroe for helping guide me on bank regulatory issues;

Melanie Mulhall for another great editing job; John Wilcockson for his professional proofreading; Michaela Reid for the New Orleans history lessons of Tremé and the Lower Ninth;

Jason DeWitt Photography, JasonDeWittPhoto.com, for the great back cover portrait.

Zac Shaiken for helping me understand SMS Spoofing; and Celina Tio for being the best chef I've known—visit *The Belfry*, people.

And to Emily and Loren for letting me run out of the room whenever and wherever to write and edit and to live out my little version of a galaxy I seem to have created.

Resources

Let Us Put Our Money Together, The Founding of America's First Black Banks, by Tim Todd.

Racism in Kansas City: A Short History, by G. S. Griffin.

The Negro as Capitalist, by Abram Harris.

Storied & Scandalous Kansas City: A History of Corruption, Mischief and a Whole Lot of Booze, by Karla Deel.

Forgotten Tales of Kansas City, by Paul Kirkman and Kristen Solecki.

Wide-Open Town: Kansas City in the Pendergast Era, edited by Diane Mutti Burke, Jason Roe, and John Herron.

The Story of the Negro, by William Loren Katz.

Take Up the Black Man's Burden: Kansas City's African American Communities 1865–1939 (Volume 1), by Charles E. Coulter.

Kansas City Jazz: A Little Evil Will Do You Good, by Con Chapman.

Tom's Town: Kansas City and the Pendergast Legend (Volume 1), by William M. Reddig.

Kansas City Crime Central: 150 Years of Outlaws, Kidnappers, Mobsters and Their Victims, by Monroe Dodd.

Five Little Known Historic Mob Locations in Kansas City, by Gina Kaufmann, Sylvia Maria Gross, and Matthew Long-Middleton, *https://www.kcur.org/show/central-standard/2015-04-22/5-little-known-historic-mob-locations-in-kansas-city*

The History of the Kansas City Family, by Alan May, *http://crime-magazine.com/history-kansas-city-family*

All Music for all its content-rich history of jazz.

About the Author

Mark Shaiken lives with his wife, Loren, and their dog, Emily, in Denver, Colorado. He schooled at Haverford College and Washburn University and practiced commercial bankruptcy law for several decades before moving on in 2019 to write, volunteer, travel, and play music.

In addition to his award-winning memoir (of a not famous lawyer) *And . . . Just Like That: Essays on a Life Before, During, and After the Law,* he is the author of four books in his award-winning 3J legal thriller series: *Fresh Start*, *Automatic Stay*, *Unfair Discrimination,* and this latest, *Cram Down*.

Connect with Mark at *http://markshaikenauthor.com.*

Review Request

You would make an author happy if you would please leave a short review of *Cram Down* on Amazon, Goodreads, or wherever else you fill your reading pleasure.

My Library

Cram Down, *https://tinyurl.com/3svm9f3x*

Unfair Discrimination, *https://tinyurl.com/5n8c4jtn*

Automatic Stay, *https://tinyurl.com/4pmvt44y*

Fresh Start, *https://tinyurl.com/49dkfs7w*

And . . . Just Like That: Essays on a Life Before, During and After the Law, *http://aws.org/HNT9GF*

Automatic Stay Litigation in Bankruptcy (coauthored with Cindi Woolery), *https://tinyurl.com/9hh9bdz3*

Made in United States
North Haven, CT
26 July 2024